To Tracey, Nicole and Ashley, without their
encouragement this story never would have been
written or told.
To Zalso, Keith, Eri, Elizabeth and Richard whose
input was greatly appreciated and needed!
And most of all, my thanks to God who makes all things
possible!

Hatch

The old woman peered towards the heavens as a streak of light flashed past the crescent moon and continued south across the night sky. Such an event a few days before a dragon hatch was a powerful omen to those who believed in such things. There was a time when she herself would have announced it to the kingdom as a sign of things to come. But now, she had all but forsaken those beliefs and lost her trust in the stars and her faith in the prophecies. Too much had changed and too many had died to allow hope to remain in her ancient heart.

She slowly walked back inside her dilapidated house and removed the teakettle from its place above the fire. Her withered hands trembled slightly as she poured the steaming liquid into an earthen mug. The sweet aroma of herbs and spice reminded her of her youth and days surrounded by gleaming palace walls in the royal court. The most powerful kingdom in the world had shattered as easily as the fluted glasses that had held their wine

She gasped as the tea leaves floating in her cup formed the perfect shape of a dragon. What purpose were these omens after everything had been destroyed? She closed her eyes and let the image of light replay in her mind. Something extraordinary was about to happen. Or something terrible. Only time would tell.

***

Chapter 1
The Nest

Sweat beaded heavily across Ammon's brow. The heat from the furnaces was nearly stifling and cleaning out the ash from the bins meant being uncomfortably close the roaring inferno behind the iron door. The thick hinges glowed dull red and shimmered in his vision as he drew the long metal rake out of the small hole beneath the door that allowed for removal of the ash. With a sigh he scooped the ashes into two tin lined wooden pails, then leaned the rake against the wall. Stepping back, Ammon kicked the latch on the side of the furnace and the heavy door swung open to reveal a bed of white-hot coals. Squinting against the blistering heat, he quickly shoveled in fresh coal past the showers of sparks and smoke. Satisfied that the firebox was full he used the handle of the shovel to slam the door shut and a resounding clang echoed through the chamber. He once again wiped the sweat from his face and leaned against the wall to catch his breath.

It was a routine he had done a dozen times a day and soon it would be over. He'd kept the four furnaces in the Nest going for nearly a year and now the late summer's new moon marked the end of Incubation, which meant his job was almost finished. He hadn't decided where he'd go next, but he wasn't worried. Not yet anyway. With a grunt, he grabbed the handles of the heavy ash pails and carried them to where an ash chute was carved into the stone near the stairs. The chute was simply a steep, narrow tunnel leading down to the street where a wooden oxcart waited to catch the ash. Standing on his toes, he hefted each pail up and dumped it down the chute, listening to the skittering sounds as the unburned coals tumbled down.

At seventeen Ammon was short for his age, but his muscles were strong and hard from the strenuous work in the Nest. As an orphan, he knew how lucky he was to work for a wage; anything was better than starving. When Keeper Calis came to the marketplace looking for cheap laborers, Ammon practically begged for the job as a tender working the furnaces in the Nest. Certainly the work was difficult and the conditions less than pleasant, but food was provided, and in the dead of winter, the furnaces kept the entire Nest warm.

The inside of the Nest was a marvel few people had ever seen. Cleverly carved inside of a small mountain was a large room with a towering ceiling twenty feet high and more than double that in length and width. One wall was dominated by a set of thick wooden doors mounted on massive hinges that opened out to a sheer cliff overlooking the city of Gaul below. Once a year those doors were open for the dragons to come and lay their eggs, then they were sealed shut for the Incubation. Four iron and stone furnaces placed in each corner of the large room provided a constant, steady heat throughout the Nest. Ammon's job as the tender was to keep those fires going.

Now that the furnaces were done, Ammon filled a small pail with water from the rain barrel and turned to his next task. In the center of the Nest floor was a bowl shaped depression nearly four yards wide. It was as deep as a man was tall and its steeply sloped sides were polished smooth as glass. A year ago, a large black dragon had laid six eggs there. Five of them were nearly half the size of Ammon, but the sixth was no bigger than his head. At the edge Ammon used his foot to push a coiled rope ladder over the side and, with the handle of the water pail in the crook of his arm, he climbed down to where the eggs lay. Carefully, he inspected the bone white leathery shells for any sign of weakening or discoloration that might indicate it had gone bad.

It was rumored that less than half of all dragon eggs hatch, which made them highly prized by the king's knights. Ammon suspected that rumor was true when Calis offered to pay one gold talon for each egg that hatched. Ammon grinned hopefully. Perhaps he might see four hatch! Four gold talons was a lot of money, enough to support him for quite a while. To give the eggs their best chances of hatching, each day he moistened the shells with a damp cloth and turned them gently. He held little hope for the small egg, though. While the others swelled in size, their shells stretching taut, the little one remained unchanged. Had the shell changed color, he probably would have thrown it down the ash chute as trash.

Just as Ammon had finished turning and wiping down the last egg, he heard the footsteps of the keeper coming up the stairs. Quickly, he threw the cloth into the pail and started climbing the rope ladder. His head just cleared the top of the Nest in time to see the keeper's velvet boot swing forward. Gripping the rope tightly, he braced against the impact as the blow glanced off the side of his head. He barely managed to keep from toppling over backwards and landing on the eggs. Dazed, he looked up, unsure if he should continue climbing out or descend to the relative safety of the eggs. It was unlikely that Calis would come down after him, or even could for that matter. The man's oversized stomach and stubby legs could never navigate the flimsy rope ladder. Ammon stepped back down into the Nest and waited.

The keeper snorted and his jowls swung as he scowled down at Ammon with a thick tongue. "Slacking, eh? I oughta come down there and drag you out by yer ears! If anything happens to them eggs, it'll be yer hide, and you'll wish ya'd never been born!"

The fat keeper removed a dainty lace handkerchief from his sleeve and dabbed at the sweat glistening above his close-set eyes. "Make sure this place is spotless come mornin' or I'll beat ya like a thug! Them knights will be here t'morrow evening for hatch and I don't want no bad impression on 'em!"

Ammon stared at his feet, trying to look respectful. "Yes, sir, spotless."

Calis tucked the kerchief back in his sleeve and grunted. "And I'd best not see any sign of youse either, so be sure yer in the tender's chambers with the door shut before evening meal or ya won't get a single talon!"

With a sniff, he waddled off out of Ammon's sight. The footsteps faded as they went down the stairs and at the bottom the door slammed with a loud crash that echoed through the chamber. Sighing in relief, Ammon leaned against the polished side of the Nest and slid down beside the eggs. Idly he reached over and gently stroked the side of the small one. Calis didn't come into the Nest often, but when he did, he was increasingly abusive. Ammon knew he just had to tolerate it a few more days, and then he could collect his money and move on. Just a few more days and he'd be free.

Standing once again, he brushed a stray strand of blonde hair out of his eyes and again climbed the ladder. The rest of the afternoon he spent sweeping the already spotless floors and daydreaming about gold. Wisely spent, a few gold talons could get him through until next winter, but then what? He frowned in thought. If he stayed on another year as a tender, he might have enough to buy a small farm in the Outerlands. He had no desire to live in the city, and most of the useable land nearby would be much too expensive anyway. The outland areas were sparsely populated since the war with the barbarians, but he'd grown used to isolation since he started working as a tender. In fact, he liked the peaceful solitude he'd had in the Nest, with the exception of the occasional visit from Calis. The simple daily routine was the only consistency he'd ever had in his life besides hunger.

The creaking sound of the stair door opening marked the evening mealtime, and he heard the solid clunk and scrape of a wooden bowl being slid across the floor. He checked the furnaces once more before descending the stairs to collect his bowl and retreated to his chambers for the night. The thin, tasteless mush barely filled his belly, but at least it kept the hunger pangs away. He dropped the empty bowl on the table beside his bed and sighed. Tomorrow was the final day, the hatching. Stretching out on the tiny cot, he stared at the ceiling and watched the shadows dance from the flickering tallow candle. His mind drifted as he thought of his gold and the next week of celebration when the entire city celebrated the hatching with pies and cakes shaped like eggs. He licked his lips and wondered how many of the fruit filled pastries he could buy. Sleep crept up and settled on him slowly.

A searing white light shot through his brain as a voice thundered. "AMMON?"

He leapt to the side of the bed, his heart beating wildly in his chest. The candle had burned down to nothing in its small holder and blackness surrounded him. Forcing himself to calm down, he listened intently but could only hear his own heartbeat. Minutes passed and he still heard nothing. Was it a dream? It sounded so real! Shaking his head, he rose from the cot and fumbled his way through to the doorway. He peered into the dark and could just make out the glow from the furnace doors. Barefoot, he carefully made his way around the Nest. Reflections from cracks around the furnace doors threw fingers of light across the darkened room, but nothing moved.

Shrugging his shoulders, Ammon chuckled at himself for jumping at voices heard in his dreams and stumbled back to his bed. Tossing the thin blankets aside, he flopped down on the cot and yawned. Strange how the voice had sounded so real, so clear, like the blast of a trumpet echoing over the hills. He closed his eyes and tried to get comfortable. This time sleep did not come easily, and he lay there for hours unable to think of anything else. When he did finally doze off, fitful dreams of the voice haunted him the rest of the night.

Sunrise came with the dull ringing of the morning church bells, and Ammon gratefully arose. His morning breakfast waited at the bottom of the stairs, and it consisted of the same cold gruel he'd had for supper. He spooned the thin mixture into his mouth with one hand while he stoked the coals of the furnaces with the other. Soon he had the fires roaring in two of the four furnaces. No need to fire the other two, it was already promising to be a hot and humid day. He couldn't help but think it was possibly the last time he would clean the ashbins unless he signed up again. After dumping the ashes down the chute, he refilled the water pail with clean water and clambered down the rope ladder to moisten the eggs. After tonight he would have one last duty to perform before he was discharged and paid. He would have to clean out the discarded shells and dead eggs after the hatchlings had left. Once he'd collected his pay, he'd have to find lodging in town and then decide what he would do next. The laying season was still a month away, so he had time to decide on whether to stay or not.

After the last egg had been carefully cleaned and turned and his chores were done, he returned to his chambers to pack his belongings. From beneath his cot he retrieved a small bag and dumped its contents onto the bed. A handful of copper talons and a metal fishhook tumbled out, and he studied them ruefully before pushing the coins deep into his pocket. Tomorrow his pouch would be heavy with gold, but for now he was painfully broke. Flipping open the flap of his shoulder sack, he dumped a few pots and pans in beside his tinderbox. Then he folded a faded brown cloak and a spare shirt over the top. He was going to need clothes soon. The thick leather shirt and breeches he wore had been very effective for stopping the sparks and embers that shot from the furnace, but they were seriously worn. Perhaps that should be his first investment.

He dropped the sack to the floor and reached under the cot. His hand slid along the edge of the wooden frame until his fingers found the small knothole that had fallen out. It was there he hid the one thing he had of value, a thin golden ring that he wore on a string around his neck as he slept. He'd had it for as long as he could remember, although he couldn't quite recall how it came into his possession. Slipping it onto his finger, he held it up to catch the candlelight. The intricately carved dragon design that completely encircled the ring glittered as it moved, revealing the astonishingly tiny detail. He smiled slightly before taking it off and slipping it inside a hidden pocket sewn in the sack. He could have sold it many times but could never bring himself to do it. It was the only connection he had to a past he could barely remember. He'd kept it with him, always carefully hidden, especially since he'd come to the Nest. If Calis had ever found it Ammon was sure the fat man would accuse him of theft and take it away before throwing him out on the street, or worse, have him brought before the King's Guard for punishment.

Ammon tied the sack closed and stretched. For the first time in almost a year he had nothing to do. It was barely past noon and hours before Calis and the knights would arrive. Normally he'd be hauling coal up to the bins at this time, but there would be no need of fires tonight. He descended the stairs and pushed the door open just wide enough to peer through before stepping outside. Blinking in the bright sunshine, he stood in the doorway and waited for his eyes to adjust. A rickety old ox cart stood haphazardly to the left of the door beneath the ash chute. A thick mound of black and gray ash piled unevenly against the high wooden sides and it listed precariously into the otherwise empty street. The noise of people shouting and the clanging of horseshoes against the cobblestones drifted up the hill.

With a quick look around, Ammon reached down and jammed a small stone into the door so it wouldn't latch shut. It wouldn't do to be locked out of the Nest today of all days. Calis would very likely have a fit worthy of a pig in a poke if he knew Ammon was outside. Hooking his thumbs onto his belt he tried to look innocent as he casually made his way down the street. He didn't plan to be gone very long, just enough to stretch his legs.

Rounding the corner at the end of the street, Ammon found himself shoulder to shoulder with a river of people streaming in and out of the little shops surrounding the Nest. Dust swirled heavily as farmers with heavy carts goaded tired looking oxen to the warehouses down by the riverside. Ammon breathed deep as a hundred different aromas flooded his nostrils. The smell of breads and smoking meats from the foodware shops mixed oddly with the heavy stench of burning metal and coal of the blacksmiths and the pungent refuse of animals. Ammon eyed one woman carrying a basket of pastries, and his mouth watered as he considered spending some of the few coins he had brought with him.

A murmur arose above the din of the crowd and suddenly people started pushing to the sides of the street. Caught in the human tide, Ammon was carried further down the street and into an alleyway beside a small shop. He could hear shouting growing closer, but he wasn't tall enough to see over the shoulders in front of him. Backing up, he bumped against a low bench about a foot tall. Stepping gingerly so as not to tip it over, he climbed up and looked towards the commotion coming towards him.

A large man with a thick staff walked down the center of the street, poking and pushing anyone not able to get out of the way fast enough. Behind him pranced a huge black stallion trimmed with black armor and tiny bells on the reins. Its hooves were polished and glinted in the sunlight as brightly as the fine silver chains dangling from the sides of the saddle. Astride the great steed sat a man suited completely in black armor like a great ebony statue. On one arm he carried a plain black shield, while large gauntlet covered hands gripped the reins confidently. The visor of his black plumed helmet was up, exposing pale flesh and cold, cruel eyes.

Ammon whistled softly to himself in admiration. A knight! A real, live Dragon Knight! Ammon could barely keep his knees from buckling as the thrill ran through his spine. He'd heard of the knights of course and even seen dragons flying high overhead, but had never been this close before. As the figure drew near, the helmeted head turned towards him and in a mixture of awe and fear, Ammon stumbled off the bench and pushed his way back up the street.

The low rumble of voices from the crowd picked up again after the knight passed. Shopkeepers again shouted their wares and Ammon idly browsed among them, but little seemed interesting after seeing a real knight pass by. At least nothing seemed interesting until he walked past the blacksmith and saw a small sword placed among the tools and implements for sale. Curious, he removed it from its worn leather scabbard and inspected it closely. Despite the plain grip and an unadorned pommel, the strange gray metal blade was flawless as if newly honed. It was smaller than the long two handed swords the knights carried, and very different from any other sword he'd seen. Holding it out in front of him, Ammon smiled. With his small size, it fit him perfectly.

The blacksmith briefly paused from his work and growled. "Iffin you ain't buyin, ya ought not be touchin the merchandise!" As if to punctuate his statement, he hefted a large hammer and pounded it against glowing iron fresh from the forge.

Ammon jumped back from the shower of flying sparks and raised his voice above the clanging. "How much?"

The blacksmith turned and raised an eyebrow at him before shoving the iron back into the flames and scowling. "I dinna suppose it were much good anyways. Couldn't even melt it down fer making a right usable tool. But maybe a young lad yer size might make some use of it I s'pose. Ten coppers and it's yours."

Ammon shook his head and jingled the coins in his purse. "Three. I'll give you three."

"Hah!" The big man crossed his hairy arms and glared. "Couldn't let it go fer less than seven!"

Pulling the purse from his belt, Ammon peered inside it and frowned. "Five and not a talon more."

The blacksmith smiled through crooked teeth and held out his hand. "Done."

Elated, Ammon hurried back to the Nest with the sword and scabbard wrapped in an old oilcloth and an empty coin purse in his pocket. He'd spent much more time outside than he'd planned and the sun was slowly creeping towards the horizon. The rock still held the door ajar and it fell to the ground as he pulled it open. Kicking it aside, he quickly stepped in and leaped up the long stairs, carrying the sword vertically in front of him so it wouldn't drag against the narrow walls.

Once inside his room, he lit a candle and set it beside the bed. Unrolling the oilcloth across the mattress, he excitedly inspected the sword once again. Surely something like this would come in handy. He would, after all, need to protect himself with all the gold he'd earn tomorrow! With a wry smile he rolled it back up and leaned it next to his sack. He'd practice with it later, for now he had to prepare for the Hatch.

He lit all the candles in each of the small hollows carved into the stone walls and placed a tiny mirror behind each to direct the light towards the center of the Nest. With the room glowing brightly, he once more checked the eggs and stoked the remaining coals in the furnace for the last time. There was no need to heat the Nest now, the eggs would hatch at midnight and the dragons would be gone by sunrise.

Somewhere in the city a church bell tolled, marking the evening mealtime and Ammon quickly surveyed the Nest to make sure it was clean before racing to the bottom of the staircase to pick up his meal. Sprinting back up the uneven stairs with bowl in hand he closed himself in his bedchamber. Tonight the gruel seemed even more tasteless, but he ate it quickly anyway. The excitement from his jaunt through the city had worked up his appetite and the wooden spoon hit the bottom of the bowl much sooner than he expected. No matter, tomorrow he would feast like a king!

He heard the stairway door open and voices echoed up the dark passageway. He recognized the thick, nasally voice of the keeper and heard the heavy footsteps and clink of armor as, one by one, the knights passed by his door. As quietly as he could, Ammon leaned near the thin wooden door of his chamber, and listened. He could hear the nervousness in Keeper Calis' voice as he assured the knights of the Hatching.

"Oh sires, I'm quite sure this'll be a grand Hatch! I do b'lieve all six will probably hatch! I m'self took great pains ta make sure the eggs are well cared for! Why I even check 'em myself twice a day!"

Ammon smirked. Aside from his first week of training, he had only seen the keeper maybe a dozen times in the past eleven months and no one else was ever allowed into the Nest. The footsteps and voices grew fainter as they went further into the Nest. Ammon could still hear them, but words were too muffled to understand. He blew out his candle and very carefully pressed his face to a crack in the door. He could see six armored knights without their plumed helmets standing in a circle around the Nest. Strapped to their backs were the two handed hilts of their long swords. In the candlelight their pale faces made a stark contrast against the dark armor.

Ammon leaned back a bit where he could sit more comfortably and watched. He knew the Hatch wouldn't occur until about midnight, and if he was lucky he might get to see the young dragons as they crawled out of the Nest. No one was permitted to attend a Hatch except the knights and the keeper. If he were caught watching, the penalty from Calis would likely be severe, but the temptation was too much. As the hours passed, the only thing that changed was the increasing nervous chatter of Calis. Ammon yawned. The lack of sleep from the night before was catching up to him and his eyelids were growing heavy. The Keeper's voice droned on like a buzzing in the background.

"AMMON?"

Ammon sat bolt upright with his heart pounding and his eyes wide open in the darkness. It was the same clear voice he'd heard the night before, but this time it seemed louder and closer. He shook his head. It must have been another dream, but it sounded so real! He pressed his face to the crack in the door. A thin stream of light came into his chambers from the small gap. Perhaps they had called for him? No. None of those men could possibly have had a voice like that, it was too clear…too perfect. It was almost musical. No, it had to be a dream.

Keeper Calis was in the far corner, wringing his hands nervously while the knights stood on the very edge of the Nest, intently watching something. From where he was, Ammon couldn't see the eggs, but he guessed the hatching must have begun. A few minutes later a noise like the tearing of cloth echoed through the chambers, followed by several quieter ripping sounds. Something large, black, and damply glistening suddenly leapt up onto the edge of the Nest in front of one of the knights. It was about the size of a large dog, with a tail as long as its body. Small leathery wings unfolded and folded rhythmically against its thin body. In awe, Ammon watched as the knight and dragon silently stared at each other for a full minute. Then the knight reached down and tied a loose cord around the long neck before moving away from the Nest towards the wall. The dragon followed obediently, taking his place beside the knight.

More tearing sounds and again the scene was repeated for the next knight. A long silent stare, and then they also retreated to the wall. The third and fourth dragons were gray in color and the fifth was black, but each time the sequence didn't change. The dragons climbed from the Nest, selected a knight and joined their fellow knights against the wall. Finally, the last remaining knight stood impatiently staring into the Nest. He shifted from one foot to another, his agitation beginning to show.

Calis timidly approached from his corner. "Lord Tirate…I'm sorry, but it's now well past the midnight hour, and if it hasn't hatched…."

Tirate spun on his heel and shook his fist at the keeper. "I'm WELL aware of it, keeper! This is the ninth Hatch I've attended!"

The keeper backed up a step and the pitch of his voice raised so high he sounded like a pig squealing. "I'm sorry sire! Truly I am! But if an egg doesn't hatch within the first hour of midnight, it's dead."

Tirate trembled visibly with rage and for a moment Ammon thought he might draw his sword and attack the keeper. He couldn't help but wonder what would have happened if the other knights hadn't been there.

Barely restraining himself, the knight turned back towards the Nest. "I will remain here until it hatches or the sun rises! And so shall you Keeper Calis! I must have…I WILL have my dragon!"

One by one, the other knights led their newly hatched beasts away from the Nest and towards the stairs. Ammon softly backed away from his door and climbed onto his cot. Ammon could hear the low mumbling of voices and a few chuckles as the knights passed by his door followed by the clicking of dragon claws on the stone stairs. Suddenly he felt giddy. Five Dragons, that meant five gold talons! He'd never seen that much money in his life, and knowing that the purse was soon to be his filled him with excitement. He closed his eyes and tried to will himself to sleep. Tomorrow was the beginning of a new life. Five talons! That little farm he fantasized about was so close he could feel the dirt beneath his feet. Hours passed before he finally dozed into a dreamless sleep.

When the morning church bells tolled, Ammon groggily rolled out of the bed. Today was his last day! Standing up, he slipped on his thick leather shirt, breeches, and boots. With a yawn, he rolled up the blankets and stuffed them into his sack with the rest of his belongings. Then he tied the sword and scabbard wrapped in the oilcloth tightly to the side of the sack with a long piece of rawhide rope. Dropping the bundle beside the door, he stepped out of his chambers and tried rubbing the sleep from his eyes. After he cleaned the eggshells from the Nest he could collect his pay and would be free to join the festivities in the streets.

He was so preoccupied thinking of meat pies and his plans for the day he didn't notice the candles were still burning. A slight movement caught his eye and startled, he looked up and froze. The knight was still standing beside the Nest and a miserable looking Calis was cowering in the corner. Confused, Ammon looked from Calis to the knight and back again before remembering the knight had vowed to stay until morning.

Calis seemed to suddenly realize this was a potential chance for him to escape. He puffed himself up and strode towards Ammon. Grabbing him by the ear, he dragged him to the side and pointed at the Nest. "It's about time, ya sloth!" Turning towards the knight he lowered his tone. "Sire, this is the whelp whose charge it was ta tend those eggs. Any loss is his responsibility and I'll happily punish him severely for ya!"

Stunned, Ammon turned his eyes toward Tirate, but the knight didn't move. For several long moments they held that pose. Ammon's head was held back by the keepers grip while Tirate stood unmoving, glaring silently into the Nest. Finally, the he turned away and walked towards the back and stared at the great wooden dragon doors. Calis breathed a sigh of relief, realizing the knight had finally accepted there were no more dragons to be hatched.

Looking at Ammon, he sneered under his breath. "Git in there and clean that mess, and don't break that rotten egg! I don't want no stench filling my Nest!" With a cruel push, he shoved Ammon over the side of the Nest.

Without the rope ladder, Ammon had nothing to slow his decent and he half tumbled, half slid on his stomach down the polished sides of the Nest until he skidded to a halt, his face inches away from the small egg that remained. Looking up at the egg, he slowly exhaled. Had he hit the rotten egg with his head it would certainly have burst, and the smell never would have come out of his hair and clothes. Pushing himself up onto his knees, Ammon made the decision not to come back as a tender again. He would start looking for that small farm as soon as the festival was over.

He wrapped his arms carefully around the egg and lifted it very slowly. It felt swollen and ready to burst and he tried not to think about how bad it would smell if it broke. Turning carefully, he started towards the rope ladder and realized it still lay coiled at the top out of reach. From inside the Nest, he was unable to see either Tirate or Calis.

Reluctantly, he was about to call out for help when the sound of ripping froze the words on his tongue. In horror he looked down as the top of the eggshell began to split apart. He held his breath. Legend said that nothing was more putrid than a rotted dragon egg, and he resisted the urge to drop it. Instead, he slipped one hand underneath to support the bottom and fervently hoped he could carry it like a bucket without spilling the contents. Again, he started to call out for help when the sound of ripping started again. This time he felt something move inside the leathery shell. The tear opened wide and a small golden claw half the size of his hand pushed out and ripped off the top half of the shell.

Ammon froze in shock. Inside was a tiny, glistening golden dragon curled up in a ball. Its long tail was wrapped tightly around itself and he could clearly see the razor sharp claws on each of its four feet. It wasn't nearly as big as the other hatchlings he had seen the night before, but other than its small size, it was absolutely perfect. The little head moved and its tiny mouth opened silently, taking in the fresh air for the first time. Slowly and deliberately, it turned its face to look Ammon in the eyes. Ammon was about to shout to the men above. It seemed that the knight would get his dragon after all!

Something made him stop. He wanted to call out, but he couldn't…those eyes…he gasped. It was like looking into two pools of liquid sunlight. For a long minute neither blinked as they gazed at each other. There was something familiar that seemed to draw Ammon in. His eyes burned and he blinked but still he couldn't look away, he didn't want to look away. For the first time in his life he felt a kinship, a belonging. The look in those eyes staring back at him pulled on his very soul. Silently they gazed at each other until his head began to ache. How could this be possible?

Drawn by the tearing sounds, both Calis and Tirate returned to the edge of the Nest to investigate. A deep moan escaped from the knight's lips as he stared down in disbelief while Calis' head swiveled back and forth from

Tirate to the dragon and back again. Dazed, Ammon looked up and somewhat distantly noticed the very red face of the knight.

"Lord Tirate?" Calis squeaked as the knight shoved him aside.

"That's MY dragon, boy!" He kicked the rope ladder down and turned to climb down.

Calis pleaded to him, "But sire Tirate…they already linked! Ya can see it in his face!"

The knight growled a curse so fiercely that Calis squeaked and twisted the kerchief in his hand so tightly it nearly shredded. Mumbling incoherently, the keeper began to slowly walk backwards towards the door. Dazed, Ammon just stood still in the middle of the Nest and waited for the knight to take the dragon. The pain in his head was throbbing. Maybe after he finished cleaning the Nest he'd try to find some willow bark tea.

The rope ladder creaked under the weight of the knight and his armor and he fumbled awkwardly for each rung as he descended. Two steps from the bottom, he turned to Ammon and growled. "The dragon is young, perhaps he can still link to me if the first link is severed!" He reached behind his back and drew out his long sword.

"W…wait!" Through the foggy ache in his brain, Ammon suddenly realized Tirate wasn't going to simply take the dragon from him. Holding the tiny dragon close to his chest, Ammon stumbled backwards. Desperately he looked around. He could never climb the polished sides of the Nest, and wasn't tall enough to reach the lip and pull himself out. The only way out was the ladder, and the knight still stood on its last rungs.

Cursing, Tirate heaved himself towards Ammon, slashing downward with his sword. The rope ladder that had stretched so much under his weight suddenly sprang back, entangling his foot. The big knight jerked to a stop in mid-leap and with a loud crash of armor against stone, he fell heavily on his side.

The sudden crash frightened the baby dragon so badly that it quickly scrambled from its shell, over

Ammon's shoulder and onto his back where it clung, shivering. Dropping the empty shell, Ammon turned in a circle trying to shake the creature off, but it gripped his leather shirt tightly. The knight, now enraged, slashed madly at the rope with his sword. Finally he cut himself free and stood up. He was easily a foot taller than Ammon and he grinned wickedly as he raised his long sword again. Trapped, Ammon had no place to run. Swallowing hard, he closed his eyes and covered his head with his arms, waiting for the blow to come.

Instead, Ammon felt the weight of the small dragon on his back disappear, and he opened his eyes just in time to see a streak of gold flash between himself and the knight. A bloodcurdling scream erupted from Tirate as he fell to his knees, shock on his face. His sword clattered and slid a pace away across the polished floor. Three neat gashes peeled back the black metal armor on his gauntlet and a trickle of blood dripped down his fingertips. The small dragon faced him with its head lowered, back arched like a cat. The golden eyes now glowed as white as burning coals and a tiny drop of crimson oozed off one of its front claws.

Ammon looked at the rope ladder that now hung lopsided behind Tirate. Realizing this may be his only chance, he lunged past the kneeling knight and leapt over the two broken rungs, climbing as quickly as he could. Before he cleared the last rung of the ladder, he felt something grab the back of his shirt. Expecting to be yanked back, he threw himself over the top with all his might. He tumbled forward and skidded across the floor on his hands and knees without resistance. Confused, he looked over his shoulder and saw a small dragon claw gripping his thick leather shirt.

In a panic he reached back and tried to pull it free, but its grip was like iron. He grabbed the shirt and tried to pull it over his head, but the dragon tightened its grip and pulled the leather tight against his chest. The claws pierced through and pricked his skin underneath. Ammon let go of his shirt and the dragon eased its grip.

Rattling armor and cursing rose from the Nest and the rope ladder creaked. Tirate had recovered his sword, and as he was climbing out he was screaming to Calis. "Dead! I want that boy DEAD! DO YOU HEAR ME, CALIS?"

Hoping to escape unnoticed, the fat keeper had nearly made it to the bottom of the stairs and out the door. Now that Tirate was calling him, he abandoned that hope and reluctantly started back up the long staircase.

"Yes, Lord Tirate! He won't get away!"

Ammon groaned. He didn't know why Tirate wouldn't simply take the dragon from his back and be on his way, and he didn't have time to figure it out. He certainly had no intentions of letting the clumsy fat keeper stab him with a sword. Ammon sprinted towards the stairs.

If he had to fight either man, he knew he had a much better chance of getting past Calis. He remembered his belongings as he ran past his chambers and reaching in the doorway he grabbed his sack and turned towards the stairs.

Calis was half way up the long passageway and panting heavily as he hurried up the steps. Seeing Ammon standing at the top, he paused for a second to draw his sword, but because of his large girth and narrow walls of the staircase he had difficulty pulling it from its scabbard. Turning sideways he gave it a great yank and it finally came free, nearly cutting his hand off with the effort. Feeling braver with a sword in his hand and facing an unarmed boy, the keeper lurched forward up the stairs again.

Trapped, Ammon spun looking for an escape. The knight had just climbed out of the Nest and had his long sword in his hand. With Calis blocking the stairway there was no other way out. Ammon leaned against the wall and felt a light breeze against the back of his neck. He spun to face the ash chute and without a second thought, hefted the sack in front of him and dove headfirst through the tiny door. He plunged through the darkness banging against the walls at breakneck speed, his shoulders scraping painfully against the walls on both sides. Great clouds of ash swirled around, into his eyes, nose and mouth as he slid downward until, with a loud crash, he landed in a heap in the ash cart at the bottom.

Coughing and sputtering, he scrambled out of the cart and ran down the street, turned a corner, then followed the road until he came to the bottom of the hill where the inner city walls rose up. Panting, he slipped into a narrow alley between two buildings and stumbled his way to the back. With his heart pounding, he listened for the sound of pursuing footsteps, but none followed. He sat down on an old wooden barrel that lay on its side and gasped for breath as he tried to think. What just happened?

Calis said he was linked to the dragon, but what did that mean? All he'd done was to pick up the egg and it wasn't his fault it hatched in his hands! He was just cleaning out the nest, he certainly didn't plan this! All he wanted was to finish his job and collect his gold! This couldn't be happening! His headache was throbbing even worse now and his mouth tasted of bitter ash. He tried to spit but his mouth was too dry.

He buried his face in his hands and leaned back against the building. The sudden feel of a lump on his back made him jerk forward again. He felt the blood drain from his face and his stomach turned. He had almost forgotten he still had the dragon on his back! Turning his head, he could just see a claw over each of his shoulders, but now the golden color was blackened with soot. Warily he reached up and tried unsuccessfully to pry the claw from his shirt. The beast had gripped his thick leather shirt so hard there were holes poked through. Despite that, at least the claws had missed his skin and for that he was grateful.

He shook the back of his shirt vigorously but it didn't fall off. Maybe if he could remove the shirt and wrap the thing up with it, he could leave the dragon there in the alley. Someone would surely find it and then it would be their problem, let them bring it back. Gingerly, he tried to slide the shirt over his head, but as soon as he started to pull the dragon again gripped it hard, drawing tight against his chest. Frustrated, he let go and the dragon relaxed. He sighed, taking the shirt off was not an option. For a brief moment he thought about returning to the Nest. Perhaps if he explained to Calis that he didn't want it he'd have mercy on him. Maybe he'd just take the dragon and let him go. But what if he bumped into Tirate? The man had said he would kill him, and Ammon doubted anything was going to change his mind. Calis certainly wouldn't interfere, not when he could save himself the six gold talons he owed Ammon.

He knew he would never get paid the gold talons he had earned. At this point he didn't really care either, all Ammon wanted was to be rid of the thing on his back and to get away with his life. There had to be a way somehow. His thoughts were interrupted by the sound of shouting a few streets away. They were probably already gathering men for a search.

Quickly he decided his best chance was to leave the city. If he stayed, it was just a matter of time before he'd be caught. He figured Calis and Tirate had already alerted the city guards. So it wouldn't be long before word reached the gates, then they would stop and search everyone trying to leave. Escaping with a bright golden dragon hanging on his back was obviously out of the question. If he couldn't remove it, then he had to hide it somehow.

He dumped the contents of his sack on the ground and using his belt knife, he cut a flap between the shoulder straps of the sack. Then he unwrapped the oilcloth around the sword and stretched it out in front of him. He placed everything but his blanket in the middle of the cloth, rolled it back up, pushed it to the bottom of the sack, and closed the top. Then he tied the blanket between the shoulder straps and carefully slid it over his back. The dragon was now completely covered by the sack with its body snugly in the hole and out of sight. He buckled his sword to his belt and looked over his shoulder one more time. With a deep breath, he strode down the alley, turned, and walked quickly towards the gates. Just another dusty traveler passing through.

Chapter 2
Escape

With his hands shoved deep in his pockets to hide the shaking, Ammon slowed his pace to a casual walk. The closer he got to the entrance to the city the more he realized how difficult it would be to escape if the guards were looking for him. The double gates were made of thick timber and large enough to drive three wagons through at once. Two guard towers rose high above the walls on each side while half a dozen disinterested soldiers stood lounging about watching the people come and go. Ammon lowered his head and joined the steady line of people waiting to pass through the gate.

Shouts rose near the base of one of the towers and Ammon resisted the urge to run. Through the crowd he could see several rough looking men with long curved swords arguing with one of the guards. Instinctively Ammon moved to the opposite side of the crowd. The last thing he wanted was to get involved in a dispute and draw attention to himself. With a hard thud, he bumped into something and when he turned he nearly choked. The leather breastplate identified him as one of the guards, but what made Ammon gasp was the sheer size of the man. Towering over everyone in the crowd by several feet, the guard was easily the largest man Ammon had ever seen. His shaved head revealed a strangely pale scalp and beneath his heavy brow glared a set of blood colored eyes. From his jaw hung a thick silver beard that reached half way down his chest. Massive arms as big as tree trunks easily swept Ammon aside as he pushed his way towards the growing argument.

When he realized everyone's attention was directed towards the scuffle, Ammon hurried past the onlookers. Holding his breath, he slipped past the gates and out of the city. Once outside he avoided the busy bridge to the south and turned north towards the rarely traveled wooded hills.

He didn't look back, even when the shouting suddenly got louder and a trumpet blasted, signaling more men to the gate.

It wasn't until he reached the edge of the woods almost a quarter mile away before he turned around to look back. Even from a distance he could see the gates were now shut and he felt his stomach tighten. The gates were only shut once darkness fell, so either the guards had locked them down to quell a riot, or word finally got through and they were searching for him. Quickly he stepped off the road and into the thick woods. It would be wise to stay off the roads for awhile until he decided where he was going to go, just in case search parties were sent. As valuable as dragons were, he doubted Tirate would give up trying to get it back so easily.

Pushing through the woods became more difficult as the day went on. Brambles tore at his leather breeches and the low brush made walking a challenge. As the sun climbed, so did the temperatures until even the horseflies remained hidden. The few berries he found still in season did little to quench his thirst or quiet his growling stomach. His tongue was parched and his head still throbbed but he kept moving. He only hoped he might find a stream or a pond along the way.

A branch caught on his shoulder strap and he pulled it free with a jerk and felt the dragon on his back move slightly. Idly he thought it couldn't weigh much more than a cat, which was a blessing. If it had been the size of the other hatchlings he'd never had been able to carry it this far. He topped a small rise filled with cedar trees and from there he could see a swamp on the other side. There the grasses grew chest high and on the far end of the swamp a thick population of cattails waved slightly in a faint breeze. Smiling, he trudged through the soft turf and grabbed a dozen of the long stalks and pulled them up one at a time. He twisted off the tops and shoved the roots into his pocket. Then he followed the edge of the swamp until he came to the source of its water, a small spring bubbling up out of the ground from the side of a bank.

Dropping to his knees he shoved his face into the tiny pool and drank greedily, pausing only to gasp for air between gulps. After he had drank his fill and completely drenched his head, he slid back and sat down on the bank. Slipping the straps off his shoulders, he let the sack drop to the ground. Once more the dragon on his back stirred slightly and he wondered how he could remove it without losing his own hide. If he used his knife to slice open the front of his shirt would the dragon stay with the shirt or would it climb onto his bare back? The thought of those razor claws raking his bare skin turned his stomach.

Still, the dragon had done nothing except cling tightly to his back. The only reaction he'd seen was when it had attacked Tirate. Ammon chuckled to himself. He could hardly find fault for that reaction. After all, Tirate had charged at both of them with a sword. He looked over his shoulder and gently tugged at his shirt. The tiny claws tightened their grip, then relaxed again. Ammon sighed. For now he would leave it where it was until he could think of a way to safely remove it. He certainly had no intentions of spending the rest of his life with the beast on his back.

Not far from the spring he found a dry spot on a large flat boulder surrounded by a small pile of rocks. He cleared away the smaller stones, leaves and sticks and dropped his sword next to the sack beside one of the larger stones. Using his belt knife, he shaved splinters off a cedar branch, then with a few quick strikes of his flint he soon had a roaring fire. If there was one thing Ammon had learned working as a tender, was how to build a fire quickly. He pulled the dented pot from his sack, filled it with water and set about boiling the roots. He had to refill the pot several times before the fibrous roots were soft enough to chew, but at least they were filling and his headache seemed to lessen somewhat.

As he sat by the fire staring into the flames, he suddenly felt the dragon release his shirt and drop to the ground. Not daring to move, he watched and waited. Very slowly, the little dragon crawled past him and towards the fire. Still covered mostly in soot, a few glittering gold scales showed through the dirt as it curled so close to the fire Ammon thought it might burn. It stared through the flames at him with unblinking amber colored eyes and they sat that way for some time before the dragon's lids drooped sleepily, the warmth of the fire apparently making it drowsy. Ammon leaned back against the boulder and studied his unusual traveling companion. Somehow the tiny creature didn't seem quite so threatening now that he could see it clearly and he marveled at its long tail and sleek lines. He yawned and rubbed his eyes. His own lack of sleep was finally catching up as the afternoon sun beat down and soon Ammon's head nodded to his chest as he drifted off.

He awoke just as the evening stars began to appear and he groaned. It was too dark to travel now and although he'd put some distance behind him, he knew his best chances were to get as far away from the city as possible. Something moved against his leg and he looked down in surprise. The dragon was no longer near the fire, instead it was stretched out on his lap exposing the gold scales on its stomach. The tiny head hung down from Ammon's lap and the sound of soft snoring filled the air. Ammon almost laughed it was such an odd sight. Unable to resist the urge, he very carefully reached out and gently stroked its belly. The dragon grunted softly before opening one eye and looking at him. Then with an indignant snort, the eye closed and the snoring resumed.

He chuckled lightly to himself. "It appears I have a baby dragon for a pet!"

He pulled the blanket from his sack and carefully stretched it out to cover them both. Tomorrow they'd have to make up for the lost time, but tonight they'd rest. He leaned back and closed his eyes.

Something brushed against Ammon's face and he turned his head. It tickled him again and he opened his eyes slowly, blinking at the bright light. The first rays of the morning sun streamed through the tree branches overhead. Droplets of dew clung to the blanket in little beads and the distant chirping of birds filled the air. He groggily lifted his head to look at the dragon sitting impatiently on his lap. The golden scales were clean now, and nearly blinding to look at as the sunlight danced across its sides. Its inquisitive face peered up at Ammon with its head cocked to one side and its ears perked forward. Sad amber eyes looked back expectantly as if searching for something. It looked lost.

Overwhelmed with pity, Ammon gently stroked the tiny dragon behind its ears. He honestly felt sorry for the magnificent little creature. Having hatched only yesterday it probably had no idea how to survive on its own and he certainly had no idea how to care for it. Like most commoners, he knew little about dragons other than they were the mysterious and fierce beasts ridden by the knights that protected the city. He'd never seen one up close before, only from a distance as they flew high overhead. Remembering the size of the eggs in the Nest, it suddenly dawned on him how large they must be when full-grown. Most of the eggs had been big enough that he could have fit inside one himself, which meant the adult dragon that laid those eggs must have been massive!

The dragon hopped off his lap and he felt something roll across the blanket. When he pulled back the folds there were three speckled pheasant eggs. Surprised, he gingerly picked them up. "By the dragons teeth!"

It wasn't long before he had them boiled over small fire. His stomach growled noisily as he eagerly broke the shells and tossed the hot eggs from hand to hand waiting for them to cool. Popping the first one in his mouth, he offered the second one to the dragon. Its golden neck stretched out and the tiny nose sniffed the egg. With a snort it turned away and curled up beside the fire like it had the night before.

Ammon sniffed. "Well, I'm not be the best cook, but one could hardly mess up boiled eggs. You need to eat something too!" Again, the dragon snorted but otherwise showed no interest, so Ammon gratefully ate all three.

Getting up to refill his cup from the spring, Ammon heard something move in the leaves a few feet away.

Before he could even turn his head, a gold streak shot across the grass in front of him. He nearly dropped his cup in surprise when the dragon lifted his head up with a mouse in its jaws. In one quick swallow, it was gone, and the dragon slipped silently back through the tall grass to reclaim its spot by the fire.

Ammon filled his cup and sat down to look at the dragon. "Well, I guess I shouldn't have to worry too much about feeding you, eh?"

The dragon stretched and yawned.

Ammon shook his head, "As long as you don't mistake me as your next meal!"

Lifting its head slightly and pinning its ears, the dragon glared at Ammon. They stared at each other for a moment before Ammon shifted uncomfortably. "Okay, I'm sorry!" With an indignant grunt the dragon put its head back down and closed its eyes.

Ammon studied the little golden body curled around the fire. The flames danced across its mirror-like scales making it appear to be a part of the flames. He could easily carry the dragon in one hand which made it difficult to imagine it growing to the size of a small house. How fast did they grow? And more importantly, how much would it eat? Hiding in the woods would be difficult as it was, but once the dragon reached its full size it would be impossible not to be noticed. Although it was unfamiliar to him, he had chosen to go north because it was largely unpopulated. But he knew hunters sometimes would trek deep into the woods for months at a time, and sooner or later the dragon would be seen. He would have to get even further away from the city than he had originally thought. Perhaps he could escape into the snow-covered mountains he could see in the distance.

He picked up the sword and buckled it around his waist as he looked around. A few small hardwood saplings grew sparsely between the scattering of rocks. He picked out an ash tree about three fingers thick that had no branches near the bottom and drew the sword. Holding it awkwardly in front of him he swung it like an axe and to his surprise, the sapling fell easily as the blade slashed through with little resistance. He measured out two sword lengths and cut the top off with another swipe. He slid the sword back into its scabbard and brought the sapling back to camp and began stripping the bark off with his knife.

The fire had died down to coals and the dragon sat very close to the glowing embers with its long tail curled around its feet watching him curiously. Small ears flickered at each sound the knife made as it scraped along the surface of the wood. A piece of bark broke off and landed in front of the dragon. Cautiously, it sniffed the bark curiously before dragging it closer with a clawed foot and playfully shredded it with its teeth.

Ammon grinned. "I suppose I should at least give you a name if we're going to be traveling together."

The dragon, satisfied the bark was thoroughly chewed was again silently watching him. Ammon picked up a strip of bark and tossed it, laughing as the dragon leapt several feet to snatch it in mid air. The golden scales flashed brightly in the sun and Ammon rubbed his chin thoughtfully. He suspected the dragon was male, although he wasn't sure why.

"How about Fulgid? That would certainly fit you."

The only answer he got was the crunching of bark.

"That settles it. Fulgid it is."

Ammon whittled away at the sapling, making the thickness equal the entire length. It would work nicely as a walking staff as well as a spear for fishing if he found a stream or pond. He was nearly finished when the little dragon suddenly stood up on his hind legs, ears pointing forward and eyes focused intently on something in the treetops. Ammon turned, expecting to see a bird or a squirrel, but what he saw instead made his blood run cold. Between the trees a patch of blue sky opened towards the east, and there he could see the distant shape of a dragon perhaps a mile away. It flew in a sweeping pattern, first north, then south. Ammon swallowed hard, they were searching for someone or something, and it had to be him.

Before he could stand up, Fulgid scrambled onto his back. Ammon looked over his shoulder and saw the claws gripping his leather shirt tightly as the dragon settled himself into place. Jumping to his feet, he kicked the shavings under a rock, then stamped on the remaining glowing coals, scattering the ashes. Then he grabbed the sack and quickly slipped it over his back and scrambled over the rocks to where he'd cut down the sapling. He dragged the discarded branches under a large cedar that had boughs reaching almost to the ground. He unrolled the gray oilcloth and lay down on his side and covered up. The small cloth wasn't big enough to cover all of him, so he curled into a ball and pulled the cut branches over him. Luckily the cloth was almost the same color as the surrounding rocks, and if he hadn't already cut the branches he doubted he would have had time to camouflage himself before the dragon flew over.

He lay there for several minutes not daring to breathe for fear of being heard. He stayed motionless and silently cursed himself for not watching longer to estimate how long before the dragon flew overhead. He could see the ground just beyond the cedar boughs, but not up. Impatiently he waited a few more minutes, then slowly reached for the corner of the cloth to push it back. A shadow suddenly passed overhead and he heard the beat of huge wings as it flew directly above him. Fulgid gripped hard on his shoulder, but neither one moved. A minute went by, then another, then the sound of beating wings passed again, but not as close. Half an hour passed before he would again dare to look out from under the cloth.

Once he was sure it was safe, he emerged, drank as much as he could from the spring, and started making his way north as fast as he could. Pushing his way through the thick brush with the oilcloth draped over his shoulders in case he needed it, his eyes moved constantly between the sky and the ground for a place nearby to hide. By the time the sun had reached its climax, they had traveled several more miles into the increasingly harsh terrain. Several times he had to stop and backtrack because of a steep ravine too difficult to cross. Twice he came across small streams that offered a cool drink of water and a brief relief from the heat. Fulgid came off his back only once for a sip of water and immediately climbed back beneath the sack again.

Ammon was actually glad the dragon decided to ride on his back. Despite how fast Fulgid could move, he was still a baby and he doubted the little dragon had the stamina to keep going on foot. Besides, it was less likely that his glittering scales could be seen from the air beneath the sack.

They kept moving at a steady pace the rest of the afternoon, picking more cattail roots when the passed through another marsh. There were berries in some of the low bush, which he grabbed by the handful and ate as they went. They didn't fill his belly, but it helped keep his mouth moist.

They slowed to skirt around a large grassy plain because there were no places for cover if the dragon flew overhead. For half a mile they walked just inside the woods on the edge of the field before finally reaching the other side. Ruefully Ammon thought about how much time they could have saved by walking straight across, but the risk of being seen outweighed the benefits. Just beyond the field in the hollow of a dead tree, Ammon found a large bees nest, and he paused for a few minutes and tried to think of a way to extract some of the honey without getting stung. He decided not to and moved on. Running through the woods from an angry swarm of bees wasn't going to help his situation at all.

As evening turned to twilight, it became increasingly difficult to travel. Long shadows blended with branches and roots that stung his face and tripped his feet. In the fading light he made his way towards a large tumble of rocks on a small hill. He would have to make camp for the night and would need a fire to cook the roots he had gathered. A fire out in the open, even under the trees would be a beacon in the night for anyone looking for him. He had no idea how well a dragon's eyesight was, but he suspected they could see better in the dark than he could. With luck he would find a sheltered place under those rocks that would be fairly hidden from all directions.

The dark outlines of the boulders loomed overhead, and as he got closer he could see a stone twice as tall as he was that leaning against a couple even large stones. Where they came together was a hollow that looked just big enough for him to crawl through. He strained his eyes as he hurried around the smaller, crumbled rocks, small trees, and thick brush that surrounded it.

He was almost there when he stumbled in the darkness. Slipping on the loose gravel, his right foot slid into a hole, and he fell to his side hard. A wrenching pain shot up his leg and he cried out as he clawed at the rocks with his fingers. In agony, he rolled to his stomach and used the staff to push himself upright. Gritting his teeth, he reached down with his right hand and wrenched his foot free. He stood still for several minutes gasping in agony as his foot hung limp. Was it broken? He couldn't tell in the low light, but he could already feel it starting to swell and tighten against his thick leather boots. Now he needed that shelter more than ever. Using the staff, he gingerly placed his foot on the ground and immediately brought it back up as tears ran down his face. It was now too dark for him to see much further than a few feet in front of him; it would be hours before the sliver of moon would rise. Starting a fire out in the open to see his injuries was out of the question.

Silently he stood leaning heavily on the shaft and wondered if he could guess the direction of the rock opening. Suddenly the dragon shifted on his back, and he felt Fulgid jump to the ground. Even in the darkness, his golden scales shimmered faintly. He walked around in front of Ammon, his eyes glinting and then disappeared into the blackness to Ammon's left.

"Oh great, now you decide to leave me?"

The dragon returned and gently gripped the staff in his teeth and pulled.

"Hey! Stop that! I'm barely standing as it is."

Ammon had no choice but to hop on his good foot or risk falling again. As soon as he started moving, the dragon let go and walked a pace away before turning and looking at him.

Irritated, Ammon snapped. "What are you doing?"

Again, Fulgid came back and gripped the shaft in his teeth and pulled Ammon off balance until he hopped a few steps.

"Okay, okay, I'm coming!" Ammon winced. "I hope you don't expect me to help you catch mice."

Putting as much of the weight on the staff as he could, Ammon followed after the dragon. Each time he got close, the dragon moved forward until he was almost out of sight. Again and again, until finally Ammon found himself standing in front of the large rock formation he had seen in the distance. Fulgid slipped inside the opening between the rocks then reappeared a minute later, waiting for him to follow. Ammon ducked his head and limped in.

Feeling around, Ammon found the space inside was mostly clear of cobwebs and he discovered he could stand up straight holding onto the shaft. Dropping slowly to the ground, he felt around and found a pile of twigs and small branches that lined the edges, but the center was layered in sand and leaves. It was likely used by some animal as a den once, but not for some time. He cleared a place in the center and used the twigs for kindling to start a small fire as far from the entrance as possible. Searching the cave interior, he found enough larger branches to keep the fire going for awhile, so he unlaced his boot with a grimace and set about getting it off his foot. As soon as he pulled the boot free, a stab of pain raced up his leg. After a few minutes he sat, panting and sweating with the effort not to scream. In the firelight he could see the swollen ankle but still couldn't tell if it was broken; at the very least it was sprained badly and any hope of travel in the morning was dashed. Frustrated, he threw his boot against the stone and it nearly bounced back into the fire.

"Now what am I gonna do?"

Carefully stretching his leg out onto the soft sand he leaned back. "Fulgid, I think we're…" Ammon looked around the cave as he suddenly realized he was alone. "Fulgid? Awww…Dragon spit!"

The occasional pop of the small fire was all that broke the stillness of the night, and its tiny flames did little to warm Ammon's bones. He'd grown accustomed to the constant heat of the furnaces and his leather shirt and breeches did little to ward off the night chill. He pulled the blanket tighter around his shoulders and laid the sword beside him within easy reach. Cold and miserable, he sat shivering until the growling of his stomach forced him to think more about food than his throbbing ankle. Pushing one of the cattail roots onto the tip of his knife, he slowly roasted it above the flames. When he thought it sufficiently cooked, he blew on the steaming root before cutting it into small pieces. As he lifted one to his lips, the smell of damp earth filled his nostrils and he hesitantly bit into it. The fibrous wad refused to yield to his teeth, and after trying unsuccessfully to chew it for several minutes he finally spit it into the fire. Listening to it hiss, he buried his head into his hands and groaned as the low rumble of thunder echoed in the distance.

As midnight approached the storm grew closer. Brilliant flashes of light burst across the night sky and the wind swirled leaves and dust into the cave, threatening to extinguish the tiny flames. Stoking the embers, Ammon built up the fire then crawled to the opening and placed his tin pot outside to catch the large fat droplets that were beginning to fall. The rain was coming down in heavy sheets when Fulgid returned as suddenly as he'd left. Relieved, Ammon was about to scold him for wandering off when the dragon dropped something from his mouth beside the fire. Three fish glistened wetly in the firelight. Ammon stared back at the little dragon in amazement.

"You're just full of surprises aren't you?"

With a flick of his tail, Fulgid curled up close to the fire, and soon steam began to rise off his scales.

Ammon placed the pot over the fire then cleaned one of the larger fish, dropped it into the pot and filled it the rest of the way with the cattail roots. The other fish he placed on a forked stick over the fire to smoke. They would keep for awhile wrapped in the oilcloth when done. He hoped his ankle would look better by morning, and perhaps they'd be on their way again in a few days. For now, a warm fire and a full belly would have to do.

Later that night after the fire had died down, he felt Fulgid slip under the blanket next to him. He reached down and pulled the little dragon closer, and soon the sounds of tiny muffled snores drifted out from under the blanket. The miserable feelings that had overwhelmed him earlier began to slip away as he dozed off. He was unsure of what tomorrow would bring, but at least he wasn't alone anymore.

Chapter 3
The Search Begins

Tirate's mood was as black as the armor that lined his chambers. It was nearly a full day since that impudent little runt had run from the Nest with the dragon. Somehow the boy escaped the city and a search of the surrounding area had turned up nothing. In frustration he slammed his fist into the polished surface of his desk and winced as fresh blood oozed through the bandages of his sword arm. The wicked little beast had ripped through the steel gauntlet as easily as if it were paper. He was lucky he still had his hand. Flexing his fingers, he felt the bandages pull against the scabs that formed over the gashes. That boy would pay dearly for this.

He took pride that unlike most knights, he had no scars on his body. It was a testament to his prowess with a sword. Looking up from his desk, he stared at the paintings on the walls depicting his ancestors astride massive black or gray dragons. In each pose their long swords pointed towards an unseen enemy. He grated his teeth. All of them had been linked to a dragon by their twentieth year without exception, a fact he was painfully aware of. Tirate was twenty-seven and had attended every hatch since he was nineteen. He would have been removed from the service as a knight years ago if he hadn't been the only heir to his uncle's throne.

He turned his attention back to the maps spread across his desk and studied them. The boy couldn't have gotten very far on foot. Patrols had been sent to the most likely escape routes to the south, east and west. Anyone matching the description were being held and questioned. He had not sent anyone north towards the mountains yet, it was an unlikely route through treacherous country that offered little chance for escape. Still, that would soon be taken care of. The boy and dragon must be found, or at least the dragon must be found. The boy was of little consequence to his plans.

It didn't matter that the tender had already linked with the dragon. He knew enough about dragons to know what was going to happen the moment he'd seen its unusual gold color. That dragon would fit his needs perfectly. Years of planning and scheming within the circles of the royal court were finally coming to fruition. All he had to do was to get the beast into his possession.

He rose from his desk and gazed out the window. In the courtyard below he could hear the clack of wooden practice swords and the booming voice of the captain knight bellowing instructions to a new recruit. The captain was a great ox of a man named Boris who moved with surprising speed and agility for his age. He was also unquestionably, the greatest swordsman in the history of Gaul. Tirate watched as Boris pushed the recruit aside, picked up the practice sword and squared off with his opponent. With a quick step he lunged, spun, and deftly knocked the sword away from the other man's hand. Tirate snorted in disgust.

Most of the Kings Guard worked secretly for Tirate, bought with a little silver and a few promises. A few of the older Guards like Boris were King Erik's men to the bone and could never be swayed. Their numbers were dwindling steadily as he reassigned them or forced them into retirement. Boris however had become a major stumbling block to getting his men promoted to the higher ranks. Those positions were necessary if he was going to assume the throne from his dear uncle Erik once the man died of his unfortunate illness. When Tirate got the dragon, that would happen quickly.

Turning his back to the window, he rang a small silver bell kept on the end of the desk to summon a servant. Within minutes a page was leaving his quarters with orders to bring Boris to his chambers. The page returned quickly with the older man following behind him. Broad shoulders nearly filled the doorway as Boris entered with his simple cloth shirt pulled tight across his muscular arms and chest. A few strands of gray hair hung around his balding head like a halo, and he stood tall and erect. Clear blue eyes missed nothing as he entered the room, including the bandages on Tirate's hand, yet he said nothing.

Tirate motioned Boris to sit and turned the maps to face him. "I have a job for you captain, if you and your dragon are up to it?"

Boris grunted. "Ellis and I are as fit for duty as we were twenty years ago sire."

Tirate sat on the edge of the desk and looked down at the man. "Of that I have no doubt," he said with obvious disdain. "I need someone well versed in tracking by air and ground, and you are the most experienced in that area."

Boris rubbed at the white mustache that flowed across his face, the sharp blue eyes never wavered. "If you don't mind me asking, exactly who are you tracking that is so important that you need to take me from my duties? A kidnapper? Murderer? Why send the captain of the King's Guard, why not one of your own men?"

Tirate leaned down and hissed. "Worse than a murderer, a thief! He has stolen a hatchling dragon from the east Nest."

Boris sat back with raised eyebrows. "He stole a hatchling? Who in their right mind...? How?"

Standing up, Tirate continued, "One of the tenders took it, a miscreant not even old enough to shave yet. He's hatched the beast and somehow escaped the city on foot. I have my men searching the surrounding areas but I want you to look in the northern forest. I want that dragon back."

Boris nearly burst out of his chair, his face red. "WHAT? You want me to fly north to find a boy that has already linked a dragon and bring him back just because you want the dragon? And what do you expect to do with it? Once linked it cannot be undone!"

Tirate smiled and slid the map towards Boris. "An untrained link is a liability to the kingdom. I want you to bring the dragon back to me. Kill the boy if necessary, but a rogue link must not be allowed to continue. That is the law."

Boris reached out with a large callused hand and ripped the map off the desk and stalked to the door.

"Oh and Boris? You are to leave immediately. Don't come back without him, I want that dragon back. Take as many men as you feel necessary, but I think you can handle this alone."

Boris hesitated slightly before giving a curt nod. "Yes, sire."

Tirate watched him storm out the door with satisfaction. It was unlikely the boy went north, but if he were headed into those mountains, Boris would find him, though it would likely take weeks if the boy had any skills at all. By the time Boris returned Tirate would have the entire King's Guard under his control and Boris would come back as powerless figurehead until he could be dealt with. Perhaps an accident could be arranged for Boris and they could hold a double funeral for the King as well. Tirate's mood suddenly improved for the first time in days. To celebrate, he rang the tiny bell again and ordered tea to be brought.

***

Boris could feel his pulse throbbing in his temples as he marched towards his chambers. For some time he'd been blocking Tirate's attempts to control the Guard. Until now he'd managed to keep his position of captain only because he was also King Erik's personal advisor and friend. Sadly, with Erik's declining health and Tirate the only heir, it was just a matter of time before his position was eliminated. He had hoped he could at least serve until Erik's death, but as Tirate gradually took power, it was becoming more obvious that was unlikely.

So now he was being sent north on a wild goose chase to catch a tender that ran off with a hatchling. Although it was a large area, it was surrounded by immense mountains and bordered by the raging Olog River. Only a fool would try escaping into that wasteland. It was much more likely that the boy had gone over the bridge and escaped to the south and they simply hadn't found him yet. Still, it bothered Boris how a tender had managed to link with a dragon. The protocols of a hatch were strictly enforced and, except for the knights and the keeper, no one was allowed in the Nest until dawn. It was unthinkable that the boy could come close enough to actually link.

There would be repercussions for the boy without a doubt. By law, only royalty and appointed knights were allowed to link. In all the recorded history of Gaul, such a thing had never happened before and was, at the very least, a royal offense. The most likely scenario was that the boy would be pressed into knighthood for training. Despite what Tirate ordered, there was no way to take the dragon away. When a hatchling emerges from its shell, it seeks out a kindred heart and forms a link that can only be broken by death. Even just separating the boy from the dragon would not be easy, as young dragons are notoriously protective of their links. He hoped the boy, when found, would return peacefully and quickly before Tirate took the crown.

Boris sighed and shook his head sadly. The chances of that were slim. Everything had changed three years ago after the strange death of the Erik's dragon Laud. It was rare that a dragon died before its link and the toll it took on the old king was profound. As time passed, he became increasingly recluse, gradually assigning all of his duties to others and appointed Tirate to oversee them. An audience with the king was all but impossible now without first petitioning Tirate. For most, trying to sidestep around him would be fruitless anyway. Everyone knew Erik's reign was about to end, and Tirate stood in line for the throne. Once Erik died, Tirate could take the crown the moment he was linked to a dragon.

Boris planned to retire before that day came. Perhaps after he'd finished this mission was as good a time as any. Years ago he'd inherited his family estate in the country. He rarely visited but always kept it staffed with servants. It was a comfortable place of moderate size, certainly big enough for him and Ellis to live out the rest of their days in peace. He stopped one of the pages in the hallway and made the necessary arrangements to have all his belongings brought there.

By the time he'd eaten his midday meal, Ellis was waiting in the courtyard, saddled, and loaded with several weeks provisions. Two thick leather belts encircled the dragon's massive girth between his front and rear legs. Behind his wings on each side were large oilcloth bags filled with the supplies. Nestled between his shoulders at the base of his neck was the great leather saddle, polished and gleaming in the sun. Ellis put his head close to the ground and let out a great snort as Boris strode towards him.

Boris rubbed the big black nose affectionately, the only part of his body that wasn't covered in scales the size of a man's fist. A deep rumble of appreciation echoed from inside the huge chest. Boris slowly walked around the dragon, methodically checking the harness and girths, and rubbing his hands down the sides looking for loose scales. Most were still black as ebony, but a few gray ones appeared here and there, scattered across the large body like stars in a midnight sky. A larger dragon than most, Ellis was just beginning to show his age. Even so, he was an impressive sight to behold and Boris took great pride in being his rider.

Stepping into the stirrup, Boris swung into the saddle and buckled himself in.

"Well, Ellis old friend, shall we fly together as we did in the old days?"

As if to answer, Ellis unfolded his great wings, leaned back on his haunches and leapt into the air. With each powerful stroke, whirlwinds of dust rose across the courtyard. Slowly circling upward, they climbed higher and higher until the city was far below them. Looking around, Boris noticed a line of dark clouds forming on the horizon.

"We'd best get as much searching done now and decide where we'll be taking shelter before that storm comes in!"

Even from high up, Boris could still hear the low rumble of the river Olog as it wound past Gaul. Rushing out of the northeast mountains, it was nearly fifty yards wide before it made a sharp turn around the city and headed northwest towards the mountains again. The ancient builders of Gaul had chosen this location well. Using the impassible mountains to the north as the base of a giant triangle, the river's drastic change of direction neatly closed the other two sides. Except for an easily defendable bridge leading south there was little chance of a successful invasion.

Boris turned his eyes north. If that's where the boy headed, then the river and the mountains have him boxed him in. How long it would take to find him was another matter. The land between the city and the mountains was rugged and stretched for miles. Only one small road led into the wilderness and it didn't lead far. Previous efforts to farm and log the area had failed. Strewn with large boulders, the rocky soil made it nearly impossible for plowing or twitching lumber with horse or oxen. So it was left as a hunting ground for the dragons to find wild boar which heavily populated the area.

As the forest became denser, they began to fly closer to the ground. It would be too easy to hide beneath the branches of some of the thicker trees and not be seen. Besides, it would be easier for Ellis to pick up a scent or see movement. A dragon's sight, hearing, and sense of smell were legendary, and that was one many reasons why they were so highly prized by the Kings Guard. Even without those senses, an opposing army stood little chance against a dragon. Their scales were harder than good steel and their strength immeasurable. Combined with the obvious advantages of flying, their mere presence had kept peace in the land for two decades after the war.

Boris' memories of that distant war were far away now, replaced by pure exhilaration as the wind whipped his thinning hair and blew his moustache back. He felt the pull of the earth as Ellis climbed in altitude before banking a turn to the left, heading back for the next sweep. Smiling, Boris patted Ellis gently. It was more than just duty that had kept him in the Guard this long.

Half way through the next pass, Ellis cocked his head to one side, his nostrils flaring as he breathed in deeply. He'd caught the scent.

"Ahhh, so the lad did pass this way, eh?" Boris chuckled. Perhaps this wasn't going to be a wild goose chase after all.

Below them was a good-sized swamp littered with boulders, dense trees, and brush with no good place for Ellis to land. Mentally, he marked the position in his mind and urged Ellis onward to look for a clearing of some sort. There was no telling how long ago the boy had passed through, and he wanted to try to narrow the gap before the oncoming storm. Some distance away, they found a large open meadow where they could easily land. Ellis swooped in, back-beating his tremendous wings to slow his landing.

Once on the ground, Boris climbed down and began to search for signs of the boy. The grass was almost waist high, and the only tracks he found were from deer passing through. At the edge of the woods he found a large bee's nest in a dead tree but nothing else. He walked back to the meadow where Ellis patiently waited. Overhead the sky was filling with darkening clouds.

"No sign of the boy yet and that storm looks like it'll be here soon. I think we'd be better off on the other side of the field away from those bees. My hide isn't as thick as your scales."

Boris mounted back up and Ellis lumbered across the field. Even with his large strides, it took several minutes to cross the meadow to the opposite side near the edge of the woods. Experience and the ache in his bones told Boris that the storm was building quickly as he made camp. He set up a low tent beneath two evergreen trees, then gathered several armloads of firewood and tied a canvas over it to keep dry. Ellis backed himself under the thick boughs of some tall pines that would shelter him from the worst of the coming rain.

As Boris began cooking himself a meal over a small fire of dry, smokeless wood, Ellis suddenly picked up his head and peered intently towards the other side of the meadow. Boris yawned and waved his hand at the dragon.

"Oh relax, it's just that big bees nest I found. Probably getting ready for the storm too."

Snorting softly, the large head sank slowly to the ground, but the black eyes remained suspiciously fixed towards the woods on the far side.

That night the storm came in with a fury. Torrential rain whipped across the open field and threatened to lift the tent off its poles. Boris slept soundly through it all, his snoring carried away by the wind. Only Ellis was close enough to hear, and with his massive wings wrapped tightly around him, neither the snoring nor the storm interrupted his sleep.

***

By morning the storm had eased to a light rain. Ellis flew off in search of a meal while Boris started a fire and prepared his own. He was finishing his second cup of coffee when Ellis returned. The woods were full of wild boar and deer, and finding a meal big enough for a dragon wasn't too difficult. By midmorning they were packed up and Boris once again scouted the area. Rain had washed away most of the tracks but a few traces still remained.

He nearly burst out laughing when he realized the boy had passed within five hundred yards of his camp. He'd had enough sense to skirt around the open field and away from sight, so he must have known he was being pursued. Yet he took no care in hiding his tracks, or at perhaps didn't know how. Boris hurried back to Ellis. With any luck, he'd have them in custody by noon.

Flying low, they swept the area looking for fresh signs of the boy and dragon. Stopping wherever there was a place big enough to land, Boris would scout the woods on foot and look for tracks. The ground eventually gave way to more rocky terrain and scraggly brush, with fewer trees for cover. They flew on for what Boris decided was a reasonable distance for someone on foot to cover and landed again, searching the ground for any traces.

Boris grumbled under his breath. "We should have seen him by now. We'll have to backtrack, he couldn't have gone any further than this on foot."

Boris continued on foot while Ellis flew in circles overhead watching for movements. It was early afternoon when Boris finally signaled the big dragon to land for a break. Years ago they would have gone from dawn to dusk, but Boris was mindful of his aging dragon spending too much effort staying aloft. He was frequently reminded of his own age limitations as he scrambled over the rough terrain of boulders and scrub brush. His knees ached from the effort and a bruise on his hip throbbed after slipping on a damp rock slick with algae. Ellis landed in the only open area he could find, atop a small hill littered with stones and loose shale. Scrambling up the steep slope, Boris made his way up to meet him.

The rain had stopped and a few light fingers of a misty fog draped across the mountains in the distance. From the hilltop Boris could see a fair distance around him and he studied the terrain. Large chunks of granite thrust up between thick blankets of brush and scraggly trees. The ground twisted and turned unpredictably with shallow ravines and short boulder covered hills. Shaking his head, he realized there was a million places in this tortured land someone could hide. Either the boy was incredibly smart, or incredibly lucky. Reaching into one of the saddlebags, he retrieved a water skin and some dried meat and sat down.

Chewing thoughtfully, he considered his situation. He knew his quarry was somewhere in this area. The problem was that even if he could see him, there was no way to get to him easily. There were very few places a dragon could land here. If the boy exposed himself, Ellis might be able to swoop down and snatch him, but Boris doubted anyone would be fool enough to allow that to happen. Pursuit on foot was certainly out of the question. His best option was to continue to track him from the air and wait for him to emerge into a more hospitable terrain. If the boy decided to stay hidden, it could take weeks, maybe months to extract him. There was nothing left to do but watch and wait and hope he made a mistake.

Boris smiled and took another swig from the water skin. He didn't have to wait long. In the distance he could see a thin line of smoke rising.

***

Fulgid was gone again when Ammon awoke and the fire had died out. The rain had slowed to a steady drizzle, but inside the cave was dry. Shivering slightly, he rummaging through his sack for his hooded cloak and slipped it on. His stomach was unwilling to wait for him to build another fire, so he ate the cold congealed stew of fish and roots. It still tasted better than the gruel he was used to eating everyday at the Nest and it was certainly more filling.

He dropped the wooden spoon back into the pot and slid towards the light at the opening of the cave and pulled up his pant leg. An angry purple bruise surrounded his swollen ankle and any movement of his foot nearly brought tears to his eyes. There was no possible way he could walk, but he didn't think it was broken. He pulled his spare shirt from his sack and cut the sleeves off with his knife. Wrapping them tightly around his ankle, he then bound two sticks on either side of his leg with the leather ties from the oilcloth. Pushing himself to his feet, he took a couple clumsy steps before the pain became too unbearable.

Shuffling outside the cave, he leaned back against the stone. It had been dark when Fulgid led him here, and as he looked around, he was amazed he'd gotten to the cave at all. Thick brush grew so close together that there was hardly any space between them. Ammon couldn't see where he'd come through in the night, and the rain had washed away the tracks. How the little dragon managed to find this in the dark, he wasn't sure, but he certainly was grateful.

A glitter caught the corner of his eye, and he turned his head in time to see Fulgid coming out from under a nearby bush with a pheasant in his jaws. Walking up to the cave entrance, he laid the bird at Ammon's feet, sat down and looked up questioningly with his head tilted to one side.

Ammon grinned and picked up the bird. "Looks like I owe you another meal, eh?" The dragon stared at him unblinking. "Well, we'll save it for dinner. We still have fish left over from last night."

Ammon eased himself down onto a rock and talked as he plucked and cleaned the bird. Fulgid watched and listened with keen interest, occasionally playfully chasing at a feather that drifted too close. At first Ammon talked about working in the Nest and caring for the eggs. He talked about his plans for the gold he would have earned and working as a farmer. He even talked a little about being an orphan and about the few memories he had of his early youth like the image of his mother's face. All the while, the little dragon sat quietly as if understanding each word.

Finally he held up the prepared bird and looked at Fulgid. "Ready for the fire!"

He used the sword to cut down some branches and made a crude spit inside the cave. Then, using the staff like a crutch, he gathered small armloads of branches from the surrounding brush until he had a good-sized pile of firewood stacked in the back of the cave. The effort of walking back and forth caused his ankle to throb, and he winced as he slid to the floor. He made a small pile of twigs and leaves under the spit and reached into his sack for his flint box. As rummaged around inside the bag, his fingers found the hidden pouch containing his ring. He pulled it out and slipped it off the cord before placing it on his finger like he had a million times before.

Finely crafted of gold, the ring was engraved with the image of a dragon with its mouth open and its teeth exposed. A finely contoured head connected to a serpentine body with wings folded back. Its long tail wrapped all the way around the ring until it reconnected at the head to make a complete circle. The fine detail even showed tiny scales covering the body. Holding it up, he compared the artwork to Fulgid, who sat still as a stone in the cave entrance, facing outside. The artist had come very, very close to imitating Fulgid.

Looking closer at the golden dragon, Ammon realized how much he'd grown in just a few days. When Fulgid hatched, he was about the same size as a weasel but with a tail as long as his body. Now his body was about the size of a cat, and his tail had grown at least another foot! Ammon whistled softly, and Fulgid's ears swiveled towards him. How long before he was full-grown?

As if listening to his thoughts, the dragon left the entrance to sit beside him. Stretching his golden nose out, he sniffed at the ring on Ammon's finger then rubbed his head against his hand. Ammon scratched the dragon behind the ears and watched as Fulgid closed his eyes and slowly laid his head on Ammon's lap.

Even in the darkened cave, the polished scales glittered like faceted sundrops. The scales down his sides were the largest and Ammon could see a hundred reflections of his own face looking back at him. They grew steadily smaller as they descended down the legs before stopping abruptly half way down each of the four toes on each foot. Three toes faced forward and the forth faced back like a thumb. Each toe ended with a curved talon almost half as long as Ammon's finger. Fulgid pushed his head under Ammon's hand again when he stopped scratching. With a smile, Ammon stoked the dragon's head. He found it comforting to have the dragon close.

Fulgid never lifted his head off Ammon's lap when he pulled the flint box out and started the fire under the spit. They stayed in that position all afternoon while Ammon slowly turned the pheasant. The only sound in the cave was the hissing of fat dripping into the flames. When the bird was done, he let the flames die down to coals. It was still early, and he wasn't hungry yet, so he left the bird hanging on the spit and leaned back using the rolled blanket as a pillow and listened to Fulgid's soft snores.

Ammon closed his eyes. It would be days before his ankle would be strong enough to walk on, and perhaps even longer before he could try to weave through the boulders and brush. For now the cave provided good shelter and Fulgid seemed quite capable of providing food, but still he was concerned he might be found. He was only a few days walk from the city, and he wanted to be much further away than he was, but that couldn't be helped. For now it would probably be best to keep Fulgid inside the cave during the day. His gleaming scales would catch the sunlight, and any dragons flying nearby would easily see him. Could he teach the dragon to stay in the cave though? He'd never had a pet before and had no idea where to even begin.

As he lay there thinking, his head began to ache, and he wished he'd thought to take bark off a few willows when he was in the swamp. The tea he could've made would have helped with the pain in his ankle too. Closing his eyes, he decided to make it a point to start collecting things like that as they traveled. You never know when you might…

"AMMON"

Stunned, he opened his eyes and found himself looking into Fulgid's deep unblinking, amber eyes. That was the same voice he'd heard in his dreams twice before, but this time he was awake! He sat up, and his head pounded in rhythm with his heart. Fulgid watched him as he awkwardly scrambled to his feet and limped to the entrance to look outside. The clouds had broken up, and thin shafts of sunlight streamed down. A few birds chattered in the bushes. Shaking his head, he turned to see Fulgid had followed and was sitting beside him, curiously watching.

"That dream is so real, I'd swear someone was out there calling me!"

Rubbing his temples, he looked around one more time before hobbling back inside and kneeling down by the ashes. "Maybe I'm just going crazy."

He restarted the fire from the few live coals that lay smoldering in the ashes, and put on the pot filled with the last roots and some rainwater he collected that morning. Fulgid stayed at the entrance still as a statue. Ammon was busy stirring the mixture when the cave suddenly grew dark. He banged the wooden spoon against the sides of the pot and turned to see a large figure filling the doorway and he nearly screamed. Tirate had found him!

Chapter 4
Found!

Boris mopped his face with a clean handkerchief and studied the tumble of boulders scattered before him. He had nearly walked past the boy's hiding spot, and probably would have if he didn't see the smoke rising up from between the chunks of granite again. Ellis had flown in as close as possible but he still had to pick his way through a quarter mile of thick brambles and rocks. Finding the entrance of the cave had been a challenge in itself and then it was all he could do to squeeze through the narrow opening. Once inside however, he found he had room to stand up, and as his eyes adjusted to the light, he could see the boy clearly.

Boris chuckled silently at the sight sprawled out in front of him on the cave floor. Gaping up at him was a short, but muscular lad with unruly blond hair and shocking blue eyes that peered out from a soot covered face. Obviously stunned, the boy didn't try to move from his position beside a small pot bubbling over a tiny cook fire. A spit with a freshly cooked bird stood off to one side near a tattered blanket and a sheathed sword. Boris sighed. Finding the boy was only half the mission, there was no sign of the dragon anywhere.

Spreading his hands, he broke the silence.

"Well, aren't you going to invite me in for dinner?"

A long silence filled the cave before the boy nodded. Easing himself to the ground, Boris leaned over and inspected the contents of the boiling pot.

"I'm not sure what you're making there, but I think it's starting to burn."

Wordlessly, Ammon removed the pot from the fire and pushed the wooden spoon into it furiously. As he did Boris noticed the bandages around his leg.

"Now what happened here, lad?"

Ammon pulled his leg away, eyeing him suspiciously. Boris smoothed his moustache with a large callused hand and frowned.

"I'm not gonna hurt you son. Now here, let me take a look at that leg."

This time Ammon held still, but his blue eyes watched intently.

Boris carefully untied the splints and slowly unwrapped the ankle before letting out a long, low whistle. He'd seen enough injuries to know it was badly sprained, and possibly fractured. It was no wonder the boy had stopped running; it was a miracle he'd made it into the cave. He gently moved the foot back and forth and the boy soundlessly gritted his teeth. He at least had to give the boy some credit, an injury like this would have most men screaming.

He leaned back against the stones and rubbed his forehead in thought. There was no way for the young man to hike out to where Ellis waited, and he was too big to be carried across the rough terrain. There was no easy way to get him out, and even if he could, there was still the problem of the missing hatchling.

"Well, you aren't going anywhere until that ankle heals a bit. I've got a few things back in my saddlebag that'll help some with the pain and swelling. It's horrid tasting, but it works."

The boy stared at him silently as he stood up and dusted himself off.

"I'll be back before sunset with what we need so don't try to go anywhere. Not that I think you could anyway." He crawled out the opening and pushed his way into the brush. Perhaps the hatchling would be there when he got back. It puzzled him that it was not in the cave with the boy. Dragons didn't like being separated from their link, especially young ones. This didn't bode well.

***

It was almost dark before he returned with a large pack slung over his shoulder. He dropped it on the cave floor then eased himself down next to it and wiped the sweat from his brow. The boy was still sitting in the same place as when he'd left and there was still no sign of the dragon. Could this tender really have linked somehow? It certainly seemed unlikely. He couldn't ignore the possibility that this was just another one of Tirate's schemes to draw him away from the palace, and the boy was paid to run off with some wild story of taking a dragon.

Boris removed a small teapot and two small tin containers from his sack, then filled the pot with his water skin. From one container he carefully measured out a few spoonfuls of black powder into the teapot and placed it over the fire to boil. He opened the other tin and with two fingers removed a glob of dark green paste, which he smeared liberally over Ammon's ankle. He rewrapped it loosely and placed it gently on the ground. When the tea was ready he poured it into a cup and handed it to Ammon.

"Here, drink this."

Reluctantly, Ammon took the cup as a strong putrid smell filled the cave. Wrinkling his nose, he looked doubtfully at Boris.

The older man grinned. "Yeah, it doesn't taste any better than it smells, but it'll help with the pain."

Ammon held his breath, took a big mouthful and gagged.

Boris roared with laughter. "Small sips! Small sips!"

Still chuckling, Boris pulled a piece of meat from the side of the cooked pheasant and leaned back.

"Suppose you tell me a story, boy." Testing a bite of meat he nodded approvingly as he chewed. "Tell me what happened at the Nest."

Finally, Ammon spoke. "My name isn't boy, it's Ammon."

A dangerous glint shone in Boris' eyes as he looked up from the meat in his hand.

"Alright, Ammon. I am Captain Boris Dejias, knight of the King's Royal Guard and quite possibly the only friend you have in the world right now. So, now that we have our introductions aside, shall we continue? What happened at the Nest?"

Ammon watched as Boris tore off another piece of meat. As a child living on the streets he'd learned to distrust strangers. On the other hand, this man could have killed him easily several times and no one would have ever known. Why did he want to know what happened at the Nest? If it was Fulgid he was after there was no way Ammon could stop him. He sighed. He had nothing to lose, except the meal the man was devouring.

With a deep breath, he described the events starting with the night of the hatch and how he'd watched through the crack in the door. When he told how Tirate and Calis were still there in the morning and that the egg had hatched in his hands, the expression on Boris' face was disbelief. But when he described how Fulgid had attacked Tirate he suddenly burst out laughing.

Slapping his knee Boris grinned. "So that's what happened to his hand!" Shaking his head, he chuckled. "The fool should've known better than to try to interfere with a link!" Boris looked up to see the confusion in Ammon's face. "You don't know much about dragons do you?"

Ammon shook his head.

"Well, you've got a lot to learn, that I can see."

Boris reached over and refilled Ammon's cup with more of the foul tea, then poured himself a cup of water from the water skin. He gestured towards Ammon's foot.

"We're not going anywhere anytime soon, so I'll give you a few quick lessons. Dragons form a link moments after they hatch. Mind you, they won't link to just anyone either. They seem to like men with certain qualities." Tapping his temple with a thick finger he looked at Ammon. "How's your headache?"

Ammon's jaw dropped. "How did you…?"

Boris smiled again. "It's part of the process and no medicine in the world will help alleviate it. I remember mine like it was yesterday. Thought my head was going to explode. It goes away after awhile." Rubbing his chin Boris frowned. "What puzzles me is that the egg hatched at all. I've never heard of an egg hatching any later than maybe an hour or so after midnight. I've read all the dragon books of Gaul and such a thing has never been mentioned." He was silent for a moment.

"The dragon is healthy I assume?"

Staring into the fire, Ammon nodded. "Yes. He's smaller than the other hatchlings I saw but seems perfectly healthy. His gold scales shine so bright in the sun I'm surprised you didn't see him from the air." The sound of a tin cup hitting the ground made Ammon look up.

Boris was staring at him hard. "Listen boy, I was just beginning to believe you were telling me the truth! I don't like liars, and if you want to get out of this situation

I'd suggest you start being honest with me!" The force Boris put in his words nearly knocked Ammon over.

"But…I am telling the truth! Why would I lie?"

Standing up, Boris towered over Ammon. "So be it." He growled. "But remember this, I don't play games. I hoped you might be better than that, but maybe I was wrong."

Leaning over Ammon, he put his face close. "I have been around dragons for longer than you've been alive boy. If you think you can lie to me and get away with it, you'd better think again. Now let's try this one more time and this time I want the…"

A golden flash streaked into the cave striking Boris in the ribs and sending him sprawling face down in the dirt. Growling, Fulgid pounced onto his back and wrapped his jaws around Boris' neck.

"NO Fulgid! NO!" Ammon screamed.

The snarling dragon hesitated and looked at Ammon. "Let him go, Fulgid…Please, let him go."

Reluctantly Fulgid released his grip and, keeping a wary eye on Boris, hopped onto Ammon's lap and lay down.

Boris pushed himself up onto his knees with a grunt. "So you do have a dragon after all, eh?"

Clapping the dust off his hands he looked up and his eyes widened in shock. The light of the fire reflected off Fulgid's glittering scales, casting a thousand tiny gold dots that sparkled and shimmered along the walls and ceiling of the cave in a dazzling display. Boris knelt there with his mouth open for several long minutes before he visibly shook himself from his daze. Finally, he jerkily moved back to where he'd been sitting before and eased himself down to the floor, staring at Fulgid.

Faintly he whispered "Gold? Is this truly possible?" He looked at Ammon questioningly. Shaking his head he absently poured himself a cup of the tea he'd given to Ammon. He took a large gulp before realizing what he'd done and started gagging and coughing before he tossed the rest on the ground near the fire.

"My apologies young man. It appears I'm woefully in the wrong, you did indeed tell the truth!"

Several minutes of silence passed before Ammon decided to ask a question.

"Why did you think I lied? About what? I don't understand…"

Boris looked down and rubbed his palms against his pant legs.

"No, no I don't suppose you would…it's just that…well…"

He looked up at Fulgid again, then at Ammon and back at Fulgid. "It's unheard of! I've been teaching Dragonhood for almost twenty years! I've read every book ever written on the subject. I know the histories since the building of the Nests over eight hundred years ago and even some of before that…but this? This is…" He trailed off without finishing and stared at Fulgid.

The little dragon stretched out on Ammon's lap and closed his eyes as if nothing unusual had happened.

Boris leaned forward and whispered. "May I touch him?"

Surprised that he would ask, Ammon nodded and Boris crawled forward to sit beside Ammon. Very slowly he reached out and gingerly touched Fulgid's back. Smiling, he gently ran his hand down the side of the dragon, feeling the hard smooth scales. Wonder lit up his face.

Softly, Fulgid began to snore and Ammon grinned. "I still don't understand? What is unheard of?"

Never taking his eyes from the dragon, Boris began to explain. "I don't understand what has happened here myself. Perhaps it has something to do with his late hatching, which is a definite oddity in itself. All I can tell you is that there are no gold dragons. Never were, either. Dragons are either black or gray and there are no variations in those colors. The blacks are stubborn, but are favored because they usually grow larger and stronger. Grays are more submissive than blacks, but are quick, like lightning. Only once in all the history records we've kept since the founding of Gaul was there an exception. A dragon hatched that was both black and gray, split right down the middle. It was also stunted, which is a mutation that is not so uncommon. It died very young, not long after hatching as is typical of that mutation. But that is nothing compared to this! How is his appetite? Is he eating okay?"

Ammon nodded. "As far as I can tell. He goes hunting and brings me back food. I saw him eating field mice once."

Boris raised an eyebrow. "He brings you food? Interesting. Well, he certainly doesn't look thin, but he is quite small. You'd know if he was hungry anyway, you'd feel it."

Ammon blinked. "I would feel it?"

The older man's eyes squinted. "Yes, it's hard to explain but hopefully you'll understand soon enough. Dragons are empaths."

At the blank expression on Ammon's face Boris explained. "Empaths…he senses your emotions, and you will eventually sense his. That's what the link does, and if he's hungry, you'll know it."

Ammon bit his lip. "You mean he'll tell me when he wants to eat?"

Boris shook his head. "No, it's not like that. They don't talk, they just feel. How do you know when you're hungry? Your stomach tells you. Same thing with the dragon, you just…know."

Fulgid snored softly, oblivious to their conversation and Ammon idly scratched him behind his ears. "Tirate said that because Fulgid is young, the link could be broken and a new one formed to him?"

Boris snorted in disgust. "Tirate is a fool. No, the link cannot be broken like that and he knows it. He's desperate for a dragon and will do anything to get one. The king's health is failing and Tirate is next in line for the throne. By law he has to have a dragon before he can ascend to the throne. Whether the dragon lives or not doesn't matter I guess, as long as he has been linked. He has been attending hatches for years trying to link, but it's the dragons that make the decision. I'd imagine at this point he'd settle for anything, including one that has already linked or one that may not live to adulthood. If he can give the appearance of having linked, once it dies, no one can prove it otherwise."

Ammon's blood ran cold. Licking his lips, he tried to speak and his voice croaked. "So you want to take us back...back to Tirate so he can become king?"

Boris turned and looked him in the eye, his gaze hard and unblinking. "I want nothing of the sort. Tirate is the last man I ever want to see on the throne." His eyes shifted back to the dragon. "He has men looking for you. A lot of men. You won't be able to hide in these woods forever, it's a favorite hunting ground for both men and dragons. Eventually you'll be seen. I found you in just a couple days."

Ammon's mind raced. "I'll keep going, as soon as I can walk! I'll head north over the mountains!"

Boris shook his head. "Not that easy. There is no passage through those mountains. They're too high to fly over even if your dragon could carry you. The only way in or out of here is through the city." He picked up a stick and drew a triangle in the dirt. "The woods are shaped like this with the mountains blocking one whole side." Gesturing to the other lines he dragged the stick across them. "The river takes up these two sides, it's too wide and too fast to swim across."

Drawing a half circle around it, he continued. "Tirate has his men already deployed watching for you all along the river. If you manage to get to the other side, he's got you." The stick crunched in his hand. "I have an idea, however. The law states that only someone of royal blood or a knight may be allowed to link to a dragon. If I can get you an audience with King Erik, he'd likely just enter you into knighthood. Once you're link has been formally recognized, you and your dragon would be worthless to Tirate." He sighed. "The biggest obstacle will be getting you there before Erik dies. He's not been well for some time, not since his own dragon died."

Ammon groaned. He wanted to be as far from Tirate as possible, but Boris had made his point. Shrugging his shoulders with resignation he leaned back against the stone with his arms folded.

Boris nodded reassuringly. "I'll do my best to keep you from his clutches. There are still a few of us in the palace that remember what honor is."

Picking up the pot of stew that Ammon had made, Boris sniffed it suspiciously. Dipping the spoon in, he touched it too his tongue and spat.

"How about I do the cooking from now on, eh? I don't know what this is, but a man could eat dirt as easily as this!"

He threw the whole thing out the door with a loud splat and put another pot of water on to boil. Removing a few of the packages from his sack, he dumped them into the water and soon the smell of stewed beef filled the cave. They shared their supper in silence, and Boris made Ammon eat three helpings and drink another cup of the horrid tea before they settled in for the night. Fulgid stayed close to Ammon, climbing underneath the blankets and curling up against his chest with only the tip of his golden nose poking out. Later that night, when the sound of Boris' loud snoring filled the cave, Ammon stared into the darkness. There was no way out it seemed and no escape.

Chapter 5
The Master Swordsman

When Ammon awoke, Fulgid was still lying on his stomach, but Boris' bedroll was rolled and neatly put away. He pushed the blankets aside, and with a yawn, Fulgid reluctantly slid off. Carefully Ammon struggled to his feet and hobbled out into the bright morning sunlight. Just outside the entrance was Boris, standing on a flat rock where he had cleared away some of the brush.

Stripped to the waist and glistening with sweat, he held his large sword in front of him. With arms slightly bent, he slowly and deliberately moved as if dancing. The tip of the blade whistled softly as the sword dipped and arced gracefully. Unfazed by the obvious effort, he flowed from one stance to another, the steel in his hands a natural extension of his arms.

Curious, Ammon watched until Boris finished the exercise and sat beside him on a boulder. Laying the long sword across his lap he lifted his water skin to his lips and took a long drink.

Ammon couldn't help but stare at the long sword. The slightly curved blade was oiled and polished to a mirror like finish. The well-worn silver hilt was inlaid with ebony dragons, and a small golden crown was stamped deep into the pommel.

Boris lowered the water skin and wiped the sweat from his eyes.

"You have no idea how to use one of these do you?"

Ammon straightened defiantly. "I own a sword!"

Boris burst out laughing. "You own a cook pot too, but you can't cook! Son, owning a sword doesn't mean you know how to use one."

Squirming, Ammon lowered his eyes. "I do okay."

Boris grunted. "A sword is a tool that requires skill to be useful. Unless you know how to use it, you're more likely to hurt yourself than anything else. You could just as easily defend yourself with a kitchen knife without the proper...oh ho! What do we have here?"

Fulgid appeared at the mouth of the cave dragging Ammon's sword in his teeth and he dropped it in front of Ammon.

Boris looked at Ammon. "Did you teach him to do that?"

Ammon picked up the sword and shook his head. "No, I haven't taught him anything."

Leaning forward, Boris studied the little dragon.

"He seems very attuned to you already. More than I'd expect for a hatchling his age. He paused for a moment and his voice softened. "Are you sure you don't sense him yet?"

Ammon shook his head.

A small furrow formed across Boris' forehead. "Strange. The link works both ways so it should happen soon I'd say, no cause for concern yet."

Boris plucked the sword from Ammon's hands and drew it from its scabbard. Holding it in one thick-fingered hand, he tested the weight and balance before handing it back, pommel first.

"Time to learn boy. If you're to stand before King Erik as a future knight, you should know what you're about."

***

Tirate swaggered down the hallway and watched with mild amusement as the servants dodged from his path. As he rounded the corner to the king's chambers he nodded to the two guards standing on each side of the entrance. Both of them had started under his pay less than a year ago and neither questioned him as he walked past.

King Erik sat in his chair facing the window. Now in his late sixties, Erik appeared much older than he was. The large man's body was now thin and frail. His skin drawn tight around pale sunken eyes with his chin drooped down on his chest as if the silver crown were too heavy for his head to hold. Long bony hands stretched out from the sleeves of his fine robes like withered branches of a dead tree. He didn't look up when Tirate approached.

With barely a hint of a bow, Tirate stopped in front of him. "My King…Uncle, how are you today?"

Although his body was withered, his voice was still clear and strong. "What is it you want, Tirate?"

Tirate sneered slightly. "Sire, as always, I come to inquire on your well being."

A guttural sound that might have been a laugh came from the king's throat.

"Pah! You know as well as I that my time is near. The same accursed illness that wastes my body and confounds my physicians will hand you the throne as surely as the sun rises each day. Don't waste my time with polite frivolities, state what you want and be done with it."

Tirate turned to the table against the wall where a pitcher of wine sat. With his back to the king, he filled a goblet, and from a hidden pocket on his belt, discreetly produced a small vial. Pouring it into the wine, he swirled the contents until it dissolved, then brought it to the king and pressed it into his hand.

"Uncle, the physicians are doing their best. In turn you must also try to keep your strength, now drink. Have you eaten today?"

With a sudden fury, the king threw the goblet against the wall splashing the wine onto the carpets. "Eat? Drink? What for?" He shouted. "Every day is the same! Weaker and weaker I get while all those around me look on in pity! Just go away! Leave me in peace!"

With an irritated bow, Tirate turned on his heel and stalked out the door. The scowl on his face as he strode down the hall was enough to make everyone step aside. Grumbling under his breath as he rounded a corner, he nearly knocked a maid off her feet, but he didn't stop to apologize. Perhaps he should just kill Erik now and get it over with. It was unlikely anyone would be surprised by the death. The small amounts of powder he'd slipped into his food and drink over the years wasn't enough to kill the man in one dose, but over time it accumulated, taking effect as if it were a disease.

Only three years ago, the king's dragon Laud had been the first to fall victim to the same poison. Buying a single dose large enough to kill a dragon had been expensive and difficult to hide, but wonderfully successful. After that, it was easy to convince everyone that the king's grief over the death of his dragon had caused him to fall ill.

The problem was that as he grew sicker, he ate less, and it was becoming increasingly difficult to administer the poison. Soon he'd have to take more drastic actions, and he was cautious of doing that until he'd removed everyone in the palace still faithful to the king. He knew he could not rule effectively as king if the people knew or suspected him of treason. An uprising could certainly be quelled, but the cost to maintain it would be heavy. Commerce would suffer, and that would affect taxes. Those taxes paid for his militia among other things, and eventually money would run out if he had to keep paying hired men to stop a revolt. He had to keep anyone close to the king from learning the truth, which is why he had started by slowly weeding out the guards loyal to Erik.

Removing Boris however had proved more difficult than he anticipated. Not only was he well known and respected throughout the court, Boris had served in the war with Erik. They had trained for knighthood together and their dragons had even come from the same Hatch. After the war, Boris rose in the ranks to become an advisor to the king as well as captain of the Guard. A position that he was well suited for. Very little ever happened in Gaul that escaped his notice.

His presence made eliminating the loyal guards difficult. Sending him out to recover the boy and his mutant dragon was a streak of luck. In the few days he'd been gone, all but one or two of the remaining loyal guards had been relieved of duty, the rest would be discharged sometime today. By the time Boris finally gave up his fruitless search and returned, Tirate's men would already have found the dragon. A tragic accident would be arranged for Boris, and the resulting shock would, of course, kill Erik. A very convenient answer to several annoying problems. The mutant dragon would die soon enough. He just had to make sure it lived long enough for a few people to see him with it, to give the appearance of a link. The timing had to be perfect.

Once he arrived at his quarters, he sent a page for his secretary, and a short time later, there was a soft knock at the door. Diam was a thin man of middle years and stooped slightly at the shoulders. There was nothing particularly remarkable about his appearance, which made him perfectly suited to his chosen profession.

"Diam, I have some loose ends I need you to take care of."

The secretary's face split open into a grin, showing several wide gaps where his teeth were missing. "Certainly, my lord! I'd be happy to assist you in any way I can…"

Tirate waved his hand and looked down at the papers on his desk.

"There is a keeper at the East Nest named Calis that witnessed an event that could prove to be problematic if exposed. I'd like that situation addressed."

Diam stood, rubbing his hands and nodding his head. Tirate shuffled the papers irritably.

"That is all for now."

Diam bowed and shuffled back towards the door a few steps before turning and leaving quickly. Tirate hated the man. His pose and posture made his skin crawl. But despite the unpleasantness, Diam was quite adept and efficient at his work, as he had proven several times in the past. Calis couldn't be allowed to live. He had been at the Hatch and knew the mutant dragon was linked to the boy tender. That information could never be revealed, there could be no witnesses. By tomorrow there would be news about the robbing and killing of a fat keeper; just another unpleasant and unsolved crime in these troubled times. Tirate rang the bell for the page and ordered tea.

***

Boris inspected Ammon's ankle and nodded in approval. After just a few days of treatment it appeared to be healing well, but it would be best to wait a few days more before attempting to walk through the rough terrain.

"Well, I'm going back to Gaul this morning for supplies. We're running low on food," Boris grinned. "I wasn't expecting to have to feed that bottomless pit stomach of yours."

Ammon smiled sheepishly and shoved another biscuit into his mouth.

Boris chuckled as he folded his now empty sack over his shoulder. "It'll take me a full day to pickup the supplies and get back. You should be alright until tomorrow morning I expect."

Boris had no doubt the young man could handle himself for one day. After spending the past few days with him, he had learned much about Ammon. He was quiet and independent. Despite the obvious pain he was in, he never complained and insisted on doing things himself, although Boris made it a point to do the cooking. He worked honestly at the sword lessons Boris had given him and was quick to learn. He was exactly the kind of man Boris would have tried recruiting into the Guard.

Ammon watched Boris finish packing before he finally blurted out. "You forgot your bedroll."

Boris shook his head smiled. "No, I left that for you. I'll bring another back with me."

He reached out and clasped Ammon's hand firmly. "Keep practicing with that sword." Without another word he turned and strode into the bushes.

Picking his way through the rocks was easier now that the saddlebags were empty, and he made good time getting back to the clearing. Ellis was waiting patiently when he got there, and as Boris wiped the sweat from his forehead, the big dragon cocked his head and looked at him with concern. Boris patted his side reassuringly.

"Don't worry old fella, it was just a long hike."

The saddle was still beneath a tree at the edge of the clearing where he'd left it, and with a grunt he slipped it over Ellis's shoulders and tightened the cinches. After one last look around, he stepped into the stirrup and swung himself into position.

"Alright, my friend, lets fly!"

With a tremendous heave, the black dragon leapt into the air, his huge wings beating rapidly. They circled around once before flying over the cave where Ammon and Fulgid stood watching.

The air felt cooler as it blew against his face and Boris watched as the ground slipped away beneath them. It was against his nature to disobey orders, but then Tirate had only ordered him to find Ammon and Fulgid and bring them back, there was no mention of whom he should notify or how quickly.

He reached Gaul not long after noon and as he circled above he immediately noticed there were changes in the battlements atop the protective walls around the city. Puzzled, Boris urged Ellis to fly lower so he could get a better look. Dozens of workmen were installing large crossbows mounted on pedestals. Judging by their size, they would be able to shoot a spear sized projectile quite a distance. Hand cranks located on each side suggested that it required at least two men to operate each one.

Something strange was happening, but what? There had been peace with the Boer barbarians for twenty years under King Erik's rule; was there a new war brewing? Certainly he could understand maintaining and improving the military; it seemed rather odd to have implemented these changes in the few days he'd been gone! Besides, those bows couldn't possibly be as effective as dragons.

Ellis slowed as he approached the landing area of the courtyard beside the palace and Boris felt his temper rising. The landing area had been designed to allow room for several dragons to land or take off simultaneously without the danger of hitting anything, but as they got closer, he could see the entire yard was littered with wagons, carts and men loitering about. Never in all his years of service was anything like this allowed to happen, and it would never happen again if he had anything to say about it.

Picking the least congested area, he skillfully guided Ellis down. The moment the dragons giant claws touched the earth they dug deep into the ground, showering everything nearby with dirt and small stones. Panicked horses and men ran in all directions, knocking over a wagon of ale and splintering dozens of the wooden kegs. Boris' temples throbbed in fury as he watched the contents of the barrels spread over the landing area. No alcohol of any kind was ever permitted within the walls of the guard's quarters! What could have happened to his Guards?

He jumped from the saddle and stormed across the yard towards the supply warehouse. Stretched out in a chair tipped against the wall lounged a man in a guard uniform that Boris didn't recognize. Disgusted, he hooked his foot under the chair and kicked it out, sending the surprised man crashing to the ground.

Scrambling clumsily to his feet with a loud curse, the guard snarled at him.

"See here old man, who do ya think ya are? I could skewer you right now and none would be the wiser…" His hand fell to his sword hilt.

Squaring his feet Boris crossed his arms and leaned forward, his eyes glinting.

"If you think you can, do it."

The guard's eyes narrowed and he grinned as he grabbed the sword at his side. Boris took two steps back and waited, calmly assessing the man's skill. With a roar, the guard charged forward, leveling his blade at Boris throat. Boris' hands moved so quickly that all the guard saw was a blur. In one quick, fluid move, Boris drew his long sword and brought the flat of the blade down squarely on the man's sword hand, breaking his wrist. Screaming, the guard dropped his sword and fell to his knees holding his hand tightly against his chest.

Boris re-sheathed his sword, reached over, and grabbed the man by his collar with one hand and lifted him until his feet came off the ground. He put his face so close they almost touched and growled.

"This old man is the captain of the Guard, and you are poor excuse for a pig. You are relieved of duty. Gather your things and get out. Now. Before I lose my patience."

Wide-eyed, the man stared back in disbelief and shook his head. Boris shoved him aside and walked into the supply warehouse. A thin, bespectacled old man sat at a small desk just inside the doorway where he was watching the whole event with a sly grin. Winking merrily at Boris he leaned back in his chair.

"Ah Boris! I see you haven't changed much have you? Still good at making friends with the new recruits!"

Shaking his head, Boris looked back out the door at the man stumbling across the yard to retrieve his sword from the dirt. "Shane, if this is the way of the new Guard, it is definitely time I retire."

The older man looked up at Boris, his voice now sober. "My friend, we've both been doing this longer than any of these whelps have been alive. Until recently, that riffraff never would have made it past the gates. Now they are in charge of them."

Shane sighed and lowered his voice so only Boris could hear. "Times have changed, and not for the better I'm afraid. Tirate forced the rest of the Guard with dragons into retirement two days ago, and he's slowly weeded out anyone else worth their salt. These new guards have replaced them all. Any of the men they suspected you were training were ushered out as fast as possible. Not even knights with the newly hatched remain in service; tossed out the door like so much trash to make room for more of Tirate's mercenaries. I can't even imagine where he's found them all. Today is my last day too. It's time for this old man to leave gracefully before they throw me out."

Boris was speechless. "The Dragon Knights are gone? Even the recruits? That's insane!"

He nodded. "That's not all. Tirate claims he's linked with a mutant dragon. Supposedly he's nursing it in private, trying to keep it alive. He also sent notice throughout the city that King Erik is near death from his long illness, and he will take succession of the throne when it happens. I don't doubt that the king is ill and dying, but no dragon would ever link to a black heart like Tirate's. You know as well as I do that if they sense bad intentions they'd rather die in their shells. That was taught to us the moment we entered into knighthood! If he really has linked then the rules of dragons have changed, and not for the better."

Boris studied the old man in front of him. Shane had lost his dragon twenty years ago near the end of the war with the Boer. The loss had left him devastated and he resigned from the service a broken man. Like most knights, he had never married and had no close family. Eventually he had come to work in the supply warehouse just to be nearer to the dragons coming in and out of the landing yard. He took his job seriously and somehow had a knack for knowing what supplies would be needed and how much to pack.

Shane's attention turned to Ellis out in the yard. "How is the old boy? Still turning left instead of right?"

Boris chuckled. "Oh he's long gotten over that little quirk. He's doing well, but like us, he's getting older and his joints don't like the cold weather."

Shane cackled. "Show me a dragon that does like cold weather! So, what brings you down here? You shouldn't need supplies again for another week at least."

Boris lowered his voice. "The traits of dragons may be changing, but not as you think!"

By the time he finished telling Ammon's story, Shane's eyebrows had lifted nearly to the top of his head. "Ah! Now things are starting to make sense! If the mutant dies in Tirate's possession, he can claim to have been linked and nobody will be the wiser!"

Boris nodded. "The Houses of the Court require the future king to have linked before taking the throne, but nothing says the dragon has to live past coronation. And because other dragons sense when a person has been linked…"

Shane lifted his hand to his forehead. "…the dragons would pass their suspicions on to their riders, and the knights would eventually figure it out! No wonder he's run them all out of the palace!" Silence fell between them. Shane leaned back at his desk, and with a gleam in his eye looked up at Boris. "How long will you be here?"

Rubbing a thick hand across his jaw, Boris glanced out the door at the shadows and estimated the time. "After what I've seen here today, I'm like to leave before dark, although if the king is really that sick, I may try to see him one last time."

"Good." Shane smiled and leapt to his feet. "I'll ready your supplies. Meet me back here in a few hours. If I'm not here, wait for me as long as you can. Now go!"

Boris stepped out of the warehouse and strode across the yard to check on Ellis before he headed into the palace. As he turned to go down the hallway, he bumped into a page heading the other way. Bowing low, the page apologized and Boris recognized the young boy as one he used frequently in his own quarters.

"What are you doing here in the palace instead of the guards' quarters?"

The boy looked nervously around. "I…I'm sorry sire! After you left the new guards ordered the headmistress to close the knights' apartments! They said the knights weren't coming back, so I was not needed there anymore! I removed your belongings and sent them to your estate like you asked before they could take them."

Boris snickered. It was a good thing he'd made arrangements before he'd left. He patted the boy on the shoulder and pressed a gold talon into his hand. He had been a good worker, and Boris hoped that moving into the palace meant he would receive better pay and living conditions than what the Guard was able to provide. He left the smiling boy behind and climbed the stairs to the royal chambers.

It had been many weeks since he'd last seen Erik and he wanted to at least pay his respects one last time. As he approached the chamber door two unfamiliar guards leaned lazily against the wall. One put out a hand on Boris' chest and stopped him. The man needed a shave and his hair was oily and unclean, obviously one of Tirate's men.

Shoving the dirty hand aside, Boris narrowed his eyes. "I'm here to see the king; I'm his adviser Captain Knight Boris."

The guard sniffed and rubbed his grubby nose with the back of his hand. "I don't care who ya are, nobody gets to see the king 'cept Lord Tirate."

Boris raised an eyebrow. So the dispersing of the Dragon Knights was not the only thing that changed. Only Tirate was allowed to see the king?

Boris thumped the man in the chest with a finger. "You go announce to his Highness the King that his adviser is here. Now. If he refuses to see me, I'll leave."

The two guards looked at each other for a moment and the oily-haired man squinted at him, sizing him up. "Boris is it? Lord Tirate sent word that ya might come, he wants to see ya. I'll show you to his quarters."

Boris crossed his arms menacingly. "I will see the king first, then talk to Tirate when I'm done."

The two men exchanged glances once more, and one went sprinting down the hall. Before the other man could move Boris pushed past him, slipped through the door and slammed it shut behind him, twisting the lock with a satisfying click. It wouldn't hold the man out for long, but it would at least delay him for a bit. He hurried across the chambers knowing if he wanted to speak with Erik, he had to make it fast. Already he could hear the man's fists pounding against the door.

From across the room he could see the pale face of the king as he lay in a large canopy bed against the wall. He approached from the side and stopped to kneel with his fist against his chest.

"My king. It is your adviser, Boris."

The king opened his eyes slowly, barely turning his head. "Ah, Boris, my friend! I am glad to see you. Few come to my bedside these past few months. I thought I might pass on without seeing your face again!"

Boris raised his head and looked at his friend. His face was ashen and his eyes sunken and dull. The once-strong body was now reduced to skin and bones.

"My king, your nephew Tirate has refused anyone audience with you. He even posted guards at your door to try to prevent me from entering. I...forced my way past."

The king's thin gray eyebrows rose and he chuckled weakly. "Yes, I wouldn't think a few guards would ever stop you from doing anything you had a mind to do. So, he refused my own adviser? Boris, that man has no honor. Even as a child he was wicked, and I prayed he would change. But now, I suppose it doesn't matter. He is the only heir to the throne, and now that he has a dragon, once I'm gone, the kingdom belongs to him."

Boris touched the king's hand. "Sire, that is why I've come to speak to you. He has not linked to a dragon! He sent me off to chase after a boy tender that accidentally linked to a mutant dragon. He plans to sever that link and claim the mutant as his own until it dies so he can take the throne."

The king's eyes widened. "Sever a link? How? By killing the boy? And how is it possible this tender became linked?"

A loud crash signaled the entrance of the guard as he finally broke through the door. Rising, Boris turned to face the oily-haired guard as he burst into the room. A sneer spread across the guard's face as he drew his sword.

"Lord Tirate will be pleased to have you delivered to him, dead or alive!"

Boris pulled his own sword from its scabbard on his back. The two men squared off, each waiting for the other to move.

King Erik called out from his bed. "Guard! Withdraw immediately!"

The guard spat on the rug towards the king. "Go to sleep old man, your time has come and gone. It's Tirate's game now."

Boris relaxed into his fighting stance. Years of wielding a sword had taught him that it was skill, not strength that determined the outcome in a sword fight. The man was younger than Boris was and nearly as big. Confident, the guard lunged forward, his sword swinging in an arc. Boris dropped the tip of his long sword and neatly blocked the strike. As the man stepped back, Boris brought his sword across and sliced open the man's shirt. Another lunge opened the guard's sleeve, and yet another opened the pant leg of his breeches.

Boris calmly stepped back. "You wish to continue? You're running out of clothes."

Furious, the man charged, swinging his blade wildly. Boris sidestepped and brought the hilt of his sword down on the man's head, knocking him flat. He lay there unconscious.

Erik was desperately trying to get out of the bed but could do no more than sit weakly on the edge, his eyes dark with anger. "You should have killed him Boris."

Boris re-sheathed his sword and ran quickly to help the king to his feet. "Perhaps, but that was like fighting an unarmed man, hardly what I'd call fair play."

Erik shook his head and smiled. "You are too honorable for your own good."

Boris pulled a cloak from the wardrobe and wrapped it around the frail man's shoulders. "You can demote me later, right now I think it would be best to leave this place while we still can. More of Tirate's men will be arriving soon."

Erik leaned heavily on his shoulder and Boris half carried the man to the doorway and down the hall. As he rounded a corner he found the young page running another errand. This time the boy's jaw dropped at the sight of the king standing in front of him.

Boris snapped at him. "Don't just stand there! Help me get the king to the landing yard!"

Without a word, the boy slipped beneath the king's arm and the three of them hurried down the stairway. When they reached the doorway leading out to the yard, Boris stopped and peered out. Ellis was lying near the middle of the yard a hundred yards away while half a dozen of Tirate's men armed with long spears stood nearby obviously waiting for Boris.

Boris stepped back from the door and whispered to the page. "Lad, you are loyal to your king, are you not?"

The boy nodded enthusiastically.

"Good! I have a job for you, more important than you could ever imagine. When we leave here, I want you to spread the word among the loyal servants, staff, and dragon knights that King Erik is alive. Make sure everyone knows and don't get caught or Tirate will have your hide. Do you understand?"

Again, the boy nodded. Boris pulled from his finger a thick ring inscribed with a black dragon and handed it to him. "Show this to anyone who doubts you, and be careful whom you trust. Tirate is a ruthless criminal and will have many spies helping him to steal the throne. We will return soon with proof of his guilt."

Erik watched the boy run down the hallway. Turning to Boris he whispered. "Do you know what you are doing here?"

Boris just grinned and let out a sharp whistle. Ellis leapt to his feet, his sharp ears pointing towards the door. Boris whistled again and Ellis thundered across the yard. Men shouted as they scrambled out of the way. Carts and wagons overturned as Ellis crashed through, oblivious to everything in his path. He skidded to a stop in front of the door and Boris lifted Erik over his shoulder like a sack and ran towards the dragon. With his free arm he grabbed the saddle as he thrust his foot into the stirrup and heaved Erik into the seat.

"LET'S FLY!" He barely had time to swing his leg over the saddle before Ellis leaped into the air, knocking over more carts and sending the guards diving for cover. They circled as they gained altitude and Boris looked sadly down at the rooftop of the warehouse.

"Sorry Shane, looks like I won't be meeting up with you after all."

Ellis suddenly lurched to the left as a black streak shot past. Surprised, Boris peered down to see men atop the battlements, arming the large crossbows. Another shaft flew past as Ellis jerked to the right.

"So that's what those are for! To defend against the dragons!"

Ellis quickly gained speed and was soon out of range. Erik sat unsteadily in the saddle and let the wind dry the tears from his cheeks as the city of Gaul disappeared behind them.

***

Tirate, followed by six of his best soldiers, stepped through the shattered door and into the king's chambers. One of the guards he had posted at Erik's door now sat dazed, in the middle of the room. A thin trickle of blood ran through matted hair and down one temple onto his torn clothes. He grabbed the man by the collar and roughly lifted him to his feet.

"Where are they? Where is the king, and where is Boris?"

Groaning, the man squeezed his eyes shut. "I...don't know sire, he...I...don't know!"

Tirate heaved the man backwards, causing him to collapse in a heap. Growling, he turned to his armed men.

"Find them and find them NOW! I don't care what you have to do! I want them back!"

As the men scattered, Tirate charged down the hallway fuming. He hadn't expected Boris to come back for provisions for at least another week and he certainly didn't anticipate an escape from the palace with Erik. Boris had to be stopped.

A grinning young pageboy running up the hallway skidded to a stop at the sight of Tirate, his smile melting.

"You!" He bellowed. "What have you seen boy? Anything unusual?"

The color drained from the boy's face as he shook his head. "No Sire!"

Tirate snarled. "Then be on your way before I have you whipped."

"Yes sire!"

The boy broke into a run and flew down the hallway at an impressive pace.

Chapter 6
To The North

Ammon practiced with the sword as the last rays of the sun disappeared over the horizon. The repetitive motions were nowhere near as graceful as Boris' fluid-like movements, but the blade felt more comfortable in his hands each time he picked it up.

He moved from one stance to the next, careful to keep the majority of his weight on his good leg, and began the slow dance again. He held the sword at arms length until a slight movement on the horizon caught his eye. Shielding his eyes from the glare, he focused on the tiny black dot rapidly approaching.

"A dragon?" He murmured.

Hastily he thrust the sword back into its scabbard and hobbled towards the cave. Boris wasn't due to return until morning and from what Boris had told him he didn't think it could be one of Tirate's men, but why take the chance?

"Fulgid get inside before he sees you!"

Sprawled across a rock just outside the entrance, Fulgid yawned and lifted his head at the approaching dragon and then lay back down.

"Fulgid!"

Ammon fumed. It would be impossible to hide with those bright golden scales lying out in the open! The dragon was getting closer, making a straight line for the cave.

Ammon begged. "Fulgid will you PLEASE come inside?"

Lazy amber eyes glared up briefly at Ammon, and with a disgruntled sigh, Fulgid rolled to his feet and ambled inside. Exasperated, Ammon moved deeper into the cave and tried not to make any noise. Minutes passed before a shadow darkened the cave entrance and Boris' booming voice shouted his name. Confused, Ammon looked at Fulgid.

"You knew it was him didn't you?"

He limped outside and looked up. Boris rode Ellis so low over the cave, the dragon's belly was almost touching the boulders as they passed overhead.

"Ammon, can you hear me?"

Cupping his hands to his mouth Ammon shouted, "Yes!"

The dragon turned and passed over again. "I need your help! There is a clearing to the north about a quarter mile, can you make it there?"

Ammon frowned. Boris needed his help? He looked doubtfully at his foot. The poultice had helped considerably in just a few days and the swelling was down. As long as he had it splinted with branches, walking around the campsite wasn't too bad. Making his way through the brush however would be a different story. He could probably do it, but it would be slow going at best. The big dragon circled as Boris waited for his answer.

"Yes, but it will take me awhile to get there!"

Boris had been kind and had treated him fairly. If Boris needed help, the least he could do was try. Besides, he suspected the man wouldn't ask for help unless he really needed it.

Boris' voice echoed against the rocks as they passed over again. "Meet me at the clearing as soon as you can!"

Without waiting for an answer, the dragon turned north and disappeared behind the trees.

Ammon hurried into the cave wondering what Boris could possibly need his help for. Had he been injured? If so, he'd need the medications he'd left behind. Ammon stuffed what he could into a sack, but there was no way he could carry it all with his bad ankle. Fulgid nosed one of the smaller sacks of food and Ammon chuckled.

"I don't suppose you'd carry some of this would you?"

To his surprise, the little dragon slipped his head through the strap of the sack and looked up at him expectantly. Ammon gazed down in wonder.

"Sometimes I think you really do understand what I'm saying!"

He used a few leather straps to tie the sack securely on Fulgid's back and smiled. "You aren't exactly a pack mule, but it'll do!"

***

It was well past midnight by the time he reached the edge of the campsite where Boris had a large fire going. The crescent moon gave just enough light for Ammon to see the dark outline of Ellis in the center of the clearing. He shook his head in awe. How something that large could fly was beyond comprehension!

Fulgid nudged him from behind and Ammon paused to scratch the little dragon behind the ears. "Will you get that large? How will I ever feed you?"

Fulgid bounded past him towards the fire and Ammon followed. Two figures sat on a log beside the fire, one bundled tightly in blankets and hunched over. As they approached he could hear Boris' baritone voice.

"Ah, here they are now!"

A shock of gray hair framing a drawn face and sunken eyes peered out from under the blankets. The stooped figure suddenly bolted upright as Fulgid stepped into the light of the fire. Boris chuckled as he threw a thick branch into the flames, sending up a shower of sparks.

"This is Ammon, the tender I told you about, and this…this is Fulgid. From your expression, I'd say he speaks for himself, eh?"

The old man sat with pale blue eyes staring in disbelief. Boris turned to Ammon and grinned.

"Ammon you should kneel, you are presenting yourself before King Erik himself!"

The King? Gaping, Ammon managed to drop to one knee and lowered his head. King Erik? Boris brought the king here?

Despite his fragile appearance, King Erik's voice was clear and strong.

"Boris, you know how I hate that! Arise Ammon, come sit and tell me about this wondrous gilded dragon of yours!"

Nervously, Ammon sat beside the king and retold the events of the past week, careful not to leave out a single detail. Erik listened carefully, occasionally nodding or raising an eyebrow in wonder. Fulgid curled around the fire reflecting the light off his mirror like scales, sending thousands of tiny bright dots dancing across the ground.

***

Boris hammered the last tent stake into the soft moss-covered ground beneath a twisted pine and peered up at the star-studded sky. Although the tent was certainly big enough for the three of them, he had no intentions of sleeping in it. During the war he'd shared a tent with Erik many a-time and the experience had been painful. The man had a nasty habit of kicking and yelling all night, so tonight, Boris would sleep out in the open.

He unloaded his bulging saddlebags and noticed with satisfaction that Shane had restocked them with enough supplies to last them for a month or more. He pulled out a package of the dried meat and biscuits and carried them to the fire where Erik and Ammon sat talking. Before dropping the meat into the boiling pot over the fire, he tossed a piece to Fulgid and watched as it bounced off his nose and landed in the dirt. The little dragon sniffed halfheartedly before putting his head back down, leaving it untouched.

Raising an eyebrow Boris crouched down and whispered softly. "You feeling okay little fella?"

With one finger he gently scratched behind Fulgid's ear, but the dragon didn't move. He sighed and turned his head to watch Ammon talking with Erik. The boy hadn't noticed. Mentally he counted off the number of days since the hatch occurred and shook his head sadly before going back to work setting up the camp.

***

Erik calmly observed the young man beside him as they talked. There was something familiar about him that he couldn't quite put his finger on. Although shy at first, with a little prodding, he spoke freely, and the story he told was shocking. The fact that Fulgid had hatched at all was incredible. Dragon eggs always hatched about midnight of the last new moon of summer. No one really knew why, but it was theorized that they needed to avoid the distraction of light and sound to establish their links. If they miss that brief window of opportunity to link after hatching, they soon die.

He closed his eyes as he remembered attending a hatch in his youth; watching a nervous knight stumble back and distracting a young dragon as it crawled from the Nest. The horror he felt as it cried out in anguish, desperately searching for the link that would never be. The hours it took for the pitiful creature to die. It was for that very reason only a few were allowed to attend a hatch.

Softly he sighed. Not once in the young man's description of the past few days had he mentioned being able to feel his link with the odd-colored dragon. By now Ammon should have been able to sense Fulgid as easily as he could feel his own hand. Sadly, it was probably for the best. Mutated and stunted, it was amazing the dragon had lived this long. If the link had completely formed before it died, as all stunted dragons do, the boy would have been devastated. The severing of that link was like having your soul ripped out and thrashed, a feeling Erik knew all too well. It had been three long years since Laud had died. Those three years had seemed like an eternity. He hadn't rode on a dragon since. His grief and his disease didn't allow him to get any closer than his chamber windows. The ride here with Boris had brought it all back again with painful clarity.

Boris pushed a bowl of stew into his hands and they ate in silence. He forced himself to eat as much as he could, but his appetite was as weak as he was. Placing the bowl beside the fire, he announced he was going to bed. He'd had more activity in this one day then he'd had in a year and he was exhausted. One look at Ammon was enough to see he wasn't in much better shape. The long hike on his bad foot had worn on him and he looked tired.

Erik placed a hand on the young man's shoulder and whispered. "Come to the tent and sleep. As I recall, Boris snores like a raging dragon! Last time he and I shared a tent I spent the whole night kicking him to make him stop!"

Ammon grinned and nodded in acceptance before followed him into the tent.

***

Boris stayed up well into the night watching the flames die down. Fulgid still lay curled up very close to the fire.

"You're going to break that boy's heart, you know that?"

Fulgid didn't move and Boris grunted. He stood and stretched, listening to his joints as they popped. Once more he tried offering the remaining stew to the little dragon, but Fulgid just turned his head away. Boris shook his head sadly before giving it to Ellis who was more than happy to finish it off. After cleaning the bowls, he slid into his bedroll and stared into the night sky. The stars shone down brightly and a partial moon had risen half way up the sky. He drifted off to sleep wondering if he should tell Ammon what to expect or let him learn on his own. He decided he'd have to tell him. Ammon wouldn't have recognized the signs, he was too new to Dragonhood. He would tell him in the morning. After all, a man should know when his dragon is dying.

***

Ammon slept fitfully that night. Dreams of suffocation, squeezed by his own skin haunted him. Desperately he tried to call out into the darkness but found he had no voice. He awoke in a cold sweat, gasping for air, only to fall asleep and dream it again. By morning he wondered if he'd have been better off staying awake and listening to Boris' snores. As the early sunlight brightened

the entrance to the tent, He slipped out, careful not to
disturb Erik. Boris already had a fire going, and the smell
of bacon and eggs drifted through the camp. Fulgid still lay
curled around the fire in the same spot he'd been the night
before. At the edge of the clearing, the looming shape of
Ellis lay stretched out, his giant wings opened to catch the
first warming rays of sunlight.

Fascinated, Ammon stood marveling at the creature
until Boris came and handed him a steaming cup of dark
black liquid. Accepting it gratefully, he took a large sip and
gagged as the bitter fluid scalded his tongue.

Boris chuckled and slapped him on the back.
"That's made from the finest beans in Southern Gaul!
Nothing better for getting the blood moving in the
morning."

Gesturing at Ellis with his own cup, Boris smiled.
"You can go see him if you like, he won't hurt you."

Ammon nodded politely and waited until Boris
returned to the fire before discretely dumping the contents
of the cup on the ground. He wasn't sure he wanted his
blood to move if it required drinking that vile fluid. As he
cautiously walked towards Ellis he realized the dragon was
even bigger than he imagined. In the darkness of last night
he had thought Ellis was big, but now in the daylight he
was downright intimidating. His jaw dropped as he stared
in stunned silence.

Just ten paces away rested a massive foot armed
with long talons easily big enough to carry a full-grown
horse. Ebony scales the size of dinner plates covered the
entire beast like armor, and sharp fangs protruded from the
mouth. Eyes as dark as coal and as big as Ammon's head
watched him approach, leaving nothing unnoticed. As its
gaze swept over him, Ammon's stomach turned with the
sudden realization he was little more than a morsel if the
dragon decided to make a meal of him.

His knees suddenly felt weak and he decided to
return and see if breakfast was ready. It was definitely
daunting to be so close to a dragon and he doubted few men

stood against one in battle without becoming unnerved. It was no wonder Tirate wanted a dragon!

Fulgid was different though. He felt no fear around the little dragon, at least, not anymore. It wasn't because of his small size, or that he'd hatched in his arms. Despite the fact that those little claws and teeth could inflict serious injuries, he didn't just didn't feel any fear. He knew, without knowing why, Fulgid would never harm him.

Erik was up and sitting with Boris beside the fire slurping cups of that foul black liquid and talking in low voices. The thin old man actually looked better than he had last night but Ammon couldn't decide why. The talking stopped as he got closer and both men suddenly seemed interested in the contents of their cups. Ammon picked up a plate that Boris had set aside for him and began to shovel food into his mouth. Between bites he decided to break the silence.

"Ellis is amazing! I've never seen a creature so large before!"

Boris dropped his cup next to the fire and exchanged a brief glance with the king.

"Ammon, we need to talk." The serious tone of his voice was unmistakable. "You don't know much about dragons…which isn't your fault. So you wouldn't know what to expect because you've never been educated…not that it would make things any easier I suppose." Boris fidgeted uncomfortably.

Erik mumbled under his breath. "Get on with it!"

Boris looked sideways at the king, then stared at Fulgid who still lay curled up close to the fire.

"Yes, yes of course. I uh, I will, it's just…" Clearing his throat, he turned and looked Ammon straight in the eye. "Fulgid is dying."

Ammon let the plate slip out of his hands.

"Dying? What do you mean? He's fine!"

Boris shook his head slowly. "I'm sorry, son, but he's not. When was the last time he ate? Dragons have a bottomless pit for a stomach. He should be begging for food and he isn't. He hasn't left that fire since you got here and that means he's cold. He shouldn't need a fire this time of year to keep warm. He's sick, Ammon, real sick. I had hoped this wouldn't happen but it has, and I'm afraid there isn't anything we can do about it."

Ammon stood up. "No! I know him better than you do. He's NOT sick!"

Just because he hadn't eaten all day didn't mean anything. Angrily he picked up one of the sausages that had fallen from his plate and waved it in front of the golden nose. "Here, Fulgid, show Boris he's wrong! You just weren't hungry right?"

The little dragon didn't move, his amber eyes reflected the flickering light of the fire as he stared into the embers. Kneeling beside him, Ammon whispered softly.

"Fulgid? You aren't really sick are you?" He dropped the sausage and began to scratch him gently behind the ear. "What…what's wrong with him?"

Boris rested his hand on Ammon's shoulder. "There are several things I'm afraid, the worst being that he is stunted and that color mutation doesn't help. Mutated dragons don't live long. Besides that, I don't think he ever shed his first skin. A dragon has to shed their scales to make room for their growing body. If they don't shed, it will crush them. Normally it happens in the first few days after they've hatched. It's not an easy process, and you have to use the link to coax them through it. I don't know if it's because of his mutation or because Tirate interfered, but your link was never fully formed. Without that link, the dragon becomes lost and loses its will to live.

This isn't your fault Ammon, and there is nothing you could have done to change it. I'm sorry, son. I wish it were different."

Ammon felt a tightening around his chest as he looked down at the little dragon lying motionless beside the fire. It wasn't fair! Fulgid was just a baby, barely a week old, and he was dying? No this wasn't Fulgid's fault, it was his. If someone else had formed the link the dragon would have lived. Nothing in Ammon's life had ever turned out right, why should this have been any different?

He slowly got to his feet. "I'm not your son."

Stiffly he limped to the tent and closed the flap behind him before throwing himself down on his bedroll. He clenched his teeth as hot tears built up behind his eyes. "I was better off alone!"

Boris started after Ammon, but Erik stopped him.

"Let the boy go. He has to deal with this on his own terms. When the time comes, I'll talk with him. I think only someone who has lost a dragon can know how it feels."

Boris winced. "Yes, sire. I was only trying to look out for the lad, I can't help but feel…"

He was interrupted by a dark shadow passing overhead. They both looked up to see a dragon wheeling in the sky and several more in the distance. Swooping low, the rider of the first dragon yelled down to them.

"Captain Boris! Permission to land sir?"

Puzzled, Boris leaned to Erik. "That is my Second of the Guard, Theo. What is he doing here?"

Boris turned and surveyed the clearing. With Ellis crouched in the end, there was room for one dragon to land, but only just barely. He signaled back to the rider and watched as the dragon swooped down from the sky and skidded to a halt. The rider dismounted and approached them at a trot.

Placing his fist to his chest, he dropped to one knee before Erik and bowed his head. "Sire, Second of the Guard, Theo reporting. I bring with me knights loyal to your crown!"

Erik raised an eyebrow at Boris. "Tell me, Theo, how many knights are with you?"

Raising his head, Theo smiled. "One hundred and fifty-seven knights, twenty three trainees and eighteen newly hatched."

Boris coughed. "One hundred and ninety-eight dragons and riders? And what do you expect to do with them?"

The kneeling knight frowned. A slim, handsome man of middle years, gray had not yet touched his hair, and his eyes were bright as he looked at Boris.

"As you know, Tirate had removed most of the loyal guardsmen from duty, forcing them into retirement or discharging them to be replaced with his own men. The very day you were sent north, the rest of the knights were removed from service and sent out of the armory with their dragons, even the newly hatched! Many of us stayed in the city trying to decide where to go while our dragons remained outside in the hills. Yesterday, Shane, the warehouse supervisor came and told us you'd been sent north to find a boy and hatchling."

Glancing at Erik, Theo continued. "Early this morning word came from the palace that King Erik had died during the night, and now that Tirate was linked, he would be crowned after a brief mourning period. Shane had told us that his claim of having a mutant dragon was false, but we'd been disbanded, so what could we do? Then a young pageboy from the palace came out to the tavern spreading the word that you'd taken the king from the palace. We didn't believe him until he showed us this ring!"

Smiling, he handed the ring back to Boris. Turning back to Erik, the knight lowered his head. "Sire, the Knights of Gaul are at your disposal. Say the word and we will besiege the palace and take back your throne from Tirate!"

The King of Gaul sat silent for a moment. "Not yet, sir knight. A king must think of his subjects as well as his enemies. The people of Gaul do not deserve to be in a war and my time as their king is drawing to a close. In my seclusion I have neglected too many of my duties as king and allowed Tirate's corruption. It is as much my fault as it is his. An evil allowed to grow as long as this has will take time to root out, and a single siege may not do it. The hearts of the people must be won back too."

Boris nodded in agreement. "This will take time and planning. Tell me Theo, where is Shane and the rest of your dragons?"

Theo's face turned grim. "The young page said Shane was arrested and imprisoned before we left. The rest of our group is gathering at a large clearing near the base of the mountains in the north where the Olog River passes through. I was on my way there with a hatchling and his link when I saw your camp. We've been searching for you, but expected you to be further north than this."

Boris turned to look at Theo's black dragon and could see a rider still astride the dragon with a small gray hatchling clinging to the larger dragon's back. "I think it would be wise for us to join them there, and plan our strategy."

Erik nodded his head. "Yes, Boris, I agree. Unfortunately we have some unfinished business here that must be taken care of as well."

Boris looked at the still form of the small golden dragon next to the fire and sighed. "Yes, sire, we do. I'm afraid that with the two of us and all our gear, there won't be room on Ellis for Ammon and his dragon, if it lives long enough to travel that is. I'll have to make two trips."

Theo looked around in confusion before his eyes settled on Fulgid. His eyebrows rose in surprise. "So this is the dragon Tirate wants? Is it alive?"

Boris shook his head. "If it is, it won't be for long, I'm afraid."

Theo's shoulders dropped a bit and his voice softened. "My condolences to his link."

Boris looked at the tent at the edge of the clearing. "I'll tell him that I'm bringing you north and that I'll come back for him. I have a shovel in one of my packs that I'll leave by the fire. I suspect he'll need it soon."

***

It was a long time after Boris and the others had left before Ammon finally left the tent. The fire had died down to a few smoldering coals and beside it, plainly visible in the sunlight lay Fulgid. A hard lump formed in his throat as he forced himself to look at his dragon. He collapsed to his knees and ran his hand across the cool snout. The amber

86

colored eyes were closed and bits of ash dust from the fire had drifted over his body like snowflakes. Dusting them off with his hands, Ammon lifted the limp form and held him close to his chest, cradling the small head in the crook of his arm. The golden scales seemed paler than they had before. He put his face down against the dragon's chest and closed his eyes. If only there were something he could do…

Ammon never heard the hollow sound of the shovel hitting the back of his head or the echo of laughter as the world went black.

***

He awoke with a splitting headache that threatened to burst from his skull and his hands wouldn't move. A wave of nausea rippled through his stomach and he forced his eyes to open. Blinking in confusion, his eyes slowly came into focus. His hands and feet were bound together tightly with rawhide rope and he hung upside down from a pole carried on the shoulders of two men. Swinging back and forth with each step, he tried to orient himself. What happened? Who where these men and why were they doing this? Where was Fulgid?

He could only see the back of one man clearly, but he could hear them talking. A gruff sounding voice belonged to the man in the front.

"A tidy little reward these two will make! Enough I say to keep me in wine for a month!"

From behind, a high pitched, nasally voice snidely remarked. "Olms, ya never could save a copper! Not me! I plan on investing it!"

The laugh of the man named Olms sounded like two rocks rubbing together. "Investing, aye Pock? Not likely! If I know you, it'll all be in a card game before dinner, and tonight you'll be crying in your bed as broke as ever!"

Pock's shrill voice sneered. "At least I got a chance to make my money back instead of spilling that rotgut down my throat!" Olms roared with laughter.

Ammon tried to speak but his tongue felt like a piece of leather. Working moisture into his mouth he finally rasped. "Where are you taking me?"

Pock gave him a sharp kick in the small of his back that sent him swinging wildly on the pole and he grunted in pain.

"Nothin' you need worry 'bout little piggy! Just Tirate himself wants to see ya!"

Ammon gritted his teeth. "Where's my dragon?" He demanded.

Pock snickered, "Oh? Your dragon ya say? I've seen no such thing! Right Olms? Nothin' at all! Course I do have a lovely lump of gold in this sack, would ya like a look-see?"

Something hit Ammon in the ribs so hard it knocked the wind out of him.

Olms growled. "See here Pock! You be careful with that carcass or Tirate will have both our heads swinging from the city gates!"

Pock cackled with glee. "Ya can't damage a dragon! Them scales is harder than steel! Drop 'em on the ground and ya as likely to break a rock than give 'em a scratch!"

Ammon squeezed his eyes shut in anger. Fulgid's body had been just tossed in a sack and would probably be sold in a market. The little dragon deserved better than this, and he was helpless to do anything about it.

It was late afternoon when the men carried him into a small clearing where three horses were tied. Ammon was thrown over a saddle and strapped down like a bag of grain, and the sack containing Fulgid was tied to the side. The men pushed the horses at a hard run through the thick woods and Ammon bounced painfully the whole way. It was nighttime when they arrived at the gates of the palace with the exhausted horses blowing and sweating. Olms cut the ropes from Ammon's feet and the two men half dragged him down the halls as he tried to force his wooden legs to move.

They stopped at a large iron strapped door with a barred window and Olms rapped on it with his knuckles. After exchanging a few muffled words through the opening, the door swung open, and he was dragged down a hallway and shoved into a small windowless room. The heavy door to the room slammed shut, cutting off all but a thin trickle of light through a narrow opening at the bottom of the door. It was just enough for Ammon to see the ropes on his wrists, and he tore at them with his teeth until they worked loose. He rubbed circulation back into his hands and looked over the tiny room. Widthwise, if he spread his arms he could touch both walls and lengthwise there was just enough room to stretch out on the bare floor.

Tired and in pain, he lay down on the cool stones and closed his eyes. It didn't matter anymore. Fulgid was gone. He had no place to go and no place to live. His sword and all his belongings were gone, even his gold ring. He'd taken that off and left it in the tent so he wouldn't lose it digging Fulgid's grave. The two men had probably searched the camp and taken everything of any value anyway. He wanted to howl in fury, but he had nothing left.

***

Boris returned to the camp to pick up Ammon just before dark. The dragon was gone and the shovel had been moved from where he had left it. He sighed. So the dragon finally died and Ammon buried it. He lifted the flap of the tent and saw Ammon's belongings still inside but no sign of Ammon. He probably needed the time alone. He wouldn't have been able to go far with that ankle though.

Boris began packing up the rest of the camp while he waited for Ammon to return. As he rolled up the bedroll he saw something flash as it fell from the blanket. He picked it up and looked carefully at the finely crafted gold ring engraved with a dragon. He knew it belonged to Ammon; he remembered seeing the boy wearing it the first day they met. An odd thing for a penniless tender to own and he had intended to ask about it, but after seeing Fulgid he'd forgotten. He slipped it into his pocket and finished packing everything else and pulled down the tent. As he placed everything neatly into the bags on Ellis's sides, he remembered the shovel. He went back to get it and as he picked it up he saw a dark wet stain on the blade. Peering closer he realized it was dried blood and cursed.

In the fast-fading light, he found the footprints of two men leading away from the camp heading south. Tracking them in the dark would be difficult, and they had a good head start on him already. If they had horses waiting where the terrain was better, they'd be within the city long before he could catch them. Cursing again, he quickly headed back to Ellis and took to the sky.

They flew as far south towards the city as he dared. He didn't want to get any closer to those crossbows than he had to. Getting shot and killed wasn't going to help Ammon or anyone else for that matter. He peered into the fast growing darkness and grated his teeth. If Tirate had time to install those crossbows inside the city, he may have more scattered throughout the nearby woods. Circling low, Ellis picked up a scent and snorted. Boris' knuckles cracked as he gripped the hilt of his sword. As he feared, he was too late. Whoever had taken Ammon had already made it to the city and was out of his reach. Frustrated, he turned Ellis back north. That boy had the worst luck in history.

***

It was well after dark when Boris reached the camp next to The Wall. The faint light of the rising moon illuminated the sheer face of a line of mountains that had been thrust violently up from the ground by some ancient cataclysmic event. From the air he could see campfires evenly spaced in neat rows near the bank of the Olog River. Even from a distance he could hear the water roar as it rushed past the camp and disappeared through a massive split in the mountainside.

Theo had chosen this site for good reason. The Wall and the Olog secured the camp on two sides. Any attacking force would be slow getting across the rugged wasteland, and then would then have to penetrate nearly two hundred dragons and knights to reach the king. Attack from the air was impossible considering all of the dragons were following Erik.

He let Ellis glide in to land on his own. Dragon eyes could see much better in the dark than his eyes ever could and Ellis had no problem choosing a spot. When Ellis came to a stop, Boris slid down and gave the black dragon an affectionate scratch behind the ear. It had been a long day for both of them, and it wasn't over yet. A young trainee followed by a gray hatchling came running and offered to lead Ellis to his evening feed of several large wild boar carcasses. Nodding thankfully, Boris watched until Ellis began to eat before he headed to Erik's tent.

The king's camp was nestled in a small hollow carved into the cliff wall by centuries of wind and weather. A tent the size of a small house glowed warmly from the lights within. Lifting up the flap, Boris ducked and entered. The king sat with Theo at a makeshift table in the center. Several maps were scattered across the length of it and bright lanterns hung from the ceiling on short ropes, illuminating everything. Their heads rose in unison as he entered and Erik's face broke into a sad smile.

"Well, Boris my old friend, it seems we're at a crossroads. Theo seems to think Tirate's declaration to claim the throne is not just treasonous, but an act of war. Although I agree it is certainly dishonorable, he could hardly do worse than I have these past few years." A frown crossed his face and he continued. "Anyway, he won't get the support of the Royal Court without a dragon. The kingdom won't follow a leader without proof that he linked a dragon and he hasn't got one."

Boris stood silent for a moment, then nodded. "It is an act of war, and he has a dragon now. A golden one."

Surprised, Theo stood up. "What? How?"

Boris threw his gauntlets onto the table in disgust. "By the time I got back to Ammon, he was gone. Taken by force. The dragon too. I don't know if either of them is alive or dead. The dragon is more than likely dead but that won't matter to Tirate. If he already spread the rumor that he'd linked to a sickly dragon then a dead one would be easier for him to handle I suppose. He'll put on a show of mourning just as he's doing right now for your supposed death, Erik, and nobody will be the wiser. The Court already thinks you are dead and if Tirate has a…had a dragon, and the law was fulfilled."

Bowing his head towards Erik, Boris continued. "We could have proved him a liar just by bringing you back except…pardon me for saying this, sire…I hardly recognize you myself in your condition. We'd be hard-pressed to prove your identity to the Court before Tirate interfered."

Theo sank back into his chair and cursed under his breath, and Erik tapped his chin with his forefinger thoughtfully. With a deep sigh, he looked at the two knights.

"As much as I like the boy, even if he still is alive, I must put the needs of Gaul above all else. Our first priority is to get that dragon back before Tirate can use it. Without it, he cannot claim the throne easily. Once we have the dragon, then we can free Ammon.

Traditionally a week of mourning is observed throughout the city after the death of a king. On the seventh day the new king has his coronation. Tirate has that much time to convince the Court he is linked. During the mourning period, he must allow all twelve of the Court members to view his dragon and satisfy them before they'll offer their support. Today is the second day, we have very little time."

Both Boris and Theo nodded in agreement.

***

When the sun rose, Boris found Theo dressed in a simple dirty cotton shirt, woven breeches, and a worn pair of work boots. It had taken him all morning to scour the camp finding worn out clothes that fit him. Boris walked around him, inspecting the disguise. He chuckled as they walked towards Ellis and he mumbled under his breath, barely audible, "Never thought I'd willingly have one of Tirate's men in the King's Guard."

Theo's eyebrows rose in mocked indignation. "Now see here! I'm a fine upstanding thug, and a good looking one too I may add!"

Boris missed a step and nearly choked. "Good looking? So you're ugly and conceited too? It's a wonder you don't have brides awaiting in line for a chance to tie you to a farmers plow!"

Theo's mouth gaped and Boris patted him gently on the shoulder. "Gifted with a silver tongue too? My you are quite the catch aren't you?"

Theo felt his face turning red and Boris suddenly roared with laughter. Shrugging his shoulders Theo grinned. Very few knights ever married. Not many women could accept spending their life with a knight who shared his emotions through a link with a fierce-some beast. It was the price the knights paid to ride these venerable animals while their homes lay empty and their hearths remained cold.

After he'd said goodbye to his own dragon Theo helped Boris saddle Ellis, and the two rode south. A few hours later, Theo watched as Ellis flew into the distance. He heaved a tattered sack over his shoulder and pulled an old weathered hat down over his eyes, then strode off towards the city of Gaul. He estimated he would reach the City gates by noon. After that, he'd find a tavern where he could rent a room. There was a lot of work to be done in only three days.

**

Ammon walked in small circles in the confines of his dark cell. It was difficult to know how long he'd been there. The only measure of time passing was when a bowl of thin gruel was passed through a slot in the door. His head ached almost constantly since he'd arrived and his skin felt so tight against his body he thought it might burst with each breath. The desire to dig at it with his fingernails was overwhelming, so he walked to keep his mind occupied. There was little else he could do.

The bang of the hallway door and the muffled sound of voices meant feeding time again and Ammon knelt down beside the hole in the bottom of the door. It hadn't take long for him to realize the rats would devour it quickly if he didn't take it the moment it slid through the slot. He grabbed the bowl and sat with his back against the door, spooning the foul mixture into his mouth. It wasn't much different than the stuff at the Nest.

Outside his door he could hear the guards talking and he lowered his head to listen. The rasp of an old man's voice shouted with indignation. "Slop? You throw me in prison without a trial, and feed me slop? After all the years I served the throne! In my day…"

A deeper, gravelly voice interrupted. "Oh shut up, old man, you won't be eating slop for long anyway. You and that whelp of a boy will be facing the headsman soon enough, I wager!"

A third, higher pitched voice chimed in. "Yeah, lucky for you we ain't allowed to execute while the city is in mourning!"

The voice cackled as it grew nearer and Ammon heard a sudden banging on his door. "Ya hear that, youngun? Tirate won't need you much longer to keep that little mutant lizard of yours alive! And then it's pop, off with your head!" Raucous laughter rolled down the hall as they left and suddenly it was silent again.

Fulgid was still alive? Shocked, Ammon's felt his heart leap. How was it possible? He got to his feet and threw himself against the heavy door and met with a solid thunk. Wincing as he rubbed his shoulder, he backed up and threw every ounce of strength he had against the door, stirring up dust that sent him coughing and choking.

A tired old man's voice drifted across the corridor. "Son, you'll do nothing but hurt yourself that way. It'll take more than the muscle you got to bust down an iron strapped door."

Lying down on his stomach, Ammon pressed his face to the slot under the door. "Who are you? Why are we here?"

The old man laughed with something that sounded more like a wheeze. "I'm supposedly here for treason to the throne. Treason against King Tirate! Ha! I'd rather be fed to the ravens than submit to that scoundrel!" A fit of coughing overtook the old man and it was a few minutes before he could talk again. "My name is Shane. You must be Ammon, am I correct?"

Surprised, Ammon answered. "Yes! But how did you…?"

The old man cackled again. "I thought as much. I figured it had to be you when those two sluggards mentioned your dragon. Tirate is charging you with the murder of a keeper, but the real reason you're here is because he needed your dragon to take the crown."

Ammon shook his head in disbelief. "I don't understand? I didn't kill anyone!"

Shane was silent for a moment. "Boy, you aren't old enough to understand everything that's going on here, but I'll try to explain it the best I can. Whether or not you murdered Keeper Calis doesn't matter. He may have been a bloated scoundrel, but he didn't deserve what he got. Tirate would have found something to charge you with anyway to get your mutant dragon. Those men said it's barely alive and if he kills you it will surely die, so for now he wants you alive, at least until he can convince the Houses of the Court that he's the one linked to it, and it's too weak to do more than just lay there and suffer. So who can argue? In that condition it would be nearly impossible for anyone to dispute whose dragon it really is. I know once he has the crown he intends to kill both of us and the dragon."

He continued talking, but Ammon didn't really hear anything after he said Tirate would kill the dragon. Poor Fulgid was so sick yet still clung to life. Somehow, he had to save him! He had to!

Ammon suddenly interrupted him. "Do you know Boris?"

The old man half giggled. "I've known Boris since he was a boy and taught him his first dragon lesson, why?"

He took a deep breath. "Boris told me the link between my dragon and I wasn't complete. That's why he was dying. Tell me everything about the link? Please?"

Shane coughed. "It's true. If the link is incomplete, the dragon will die and there isn't anything you can do about it. But if he has a mutation…well, I'll tell you what is known anyway if you like."

Ammon listened intently as the man began to lecture, only stopping him occasionally to ask questions. Later, long after the old man had gone to sleep, Ammon sat in the middle of the floor and concentrated. He had to find a way to complete the link. It was Fulgid's only chance. He couldn't feel Fulgid, but Boris had said Fulgid could feel him. Perhaps he could force it, and then the dragon would live and escape from Tirate.

He closed his eyes and focused on the memory of the golden voice he'd heard in his dreams. He tried to clear his mind completely except the memories he had of Fulgid. Over and over he repeated the same thought in his mind. "Escape! Get away! Live!"

Long into the night he concentrated until finally, his head pounding and his body exhausted, he fell asleep. As he slept he dreamed of wandering down the endless empty paths of a giant maze, trying to find Fulgid. He called out, but only heard his own empty voice and felt his skin grow increasingly tighter across his chest until he could barely breathe.

Chapter 7
A New King

From the window of the palace throne room, Tirate watched as dozens of workmen assembled various versions of the dragon-killer crossbows. Smaller machines mounted on carts filled a good portion of the courtyard, and all along the ramparts, more of the large ones were visible. Although his plans were moving along satisfactorily, they were far from perfect. He'd been waiting for the capture of the mutant dragon before setting things in motion, but when Erik escaped, he was forced to move ahead prematurely. Within hours he had announced that the king was dead from his long illness, marking the beginning of a weeklong period of mourning. He intended to use that week to double his efforts to find the mutant. It was pure luck that a mere day later, two of the men sent north to keep an eye on Boris had found the dragon and brought it back. It was now safely hidden in a small room down the hall and chained securely to a wall with a large lock.

He carried the only key around his neck as a precaution. That dragon was essential to his crowning and he wasn't about to let it slip so easily from his fingertips. It escaped his grasp once, it wouldn't happen again. Fortunately, the horrid little beast hadn't moved since it was thrown in there a few days ago, and he had four armed and experienced guards posted in front of the door and making hourly checks to make sure it was secured.

Still, he was uneasy. He wouldn't relax until the crown was firmly placed on his head and the beast was dead. The fact that the mutant was still alive at all was a testament to how tough the miserable creatures were. Idly he fingered the vial of dragonsbane in his pocket. It didn't contain enough to kill an adult dragon, but it should be plenty for a weakened mutant.

Soon the heads of each of twelve Houses would come to view the dragon. He had to convince each one that he had fulfilled the requirement of linking to a dragon and was therefore eligible for the crown. It was important to gain their trust before the coronation. He needed their financial support to run the kingdom. The Houses helped supply the necessary funds for maintaining the protection of the city and could override his decisions and withdraw their funds if they voted unanimously, a right that hadn't been used in known memory. It was one of the first laws he intended to quietly rewrite once he took power.

For now, he would bring the unconscious beast into his chambers and wait for each member of the Houses to arrive. While they watched he would fuss and pet it like a favorite dog, then send them away with a tear in his eye. It was unlikely they would doubt his sincerity, the members of the Houses were educated enough to know it was almost impossible to touch another man's dragon without permission.

Tirate pushed open the door of his chambers and handed his personal guard the key with instructions to bring the dragon to his quarters immediately. After the man trotted down the hall, he walked around his chambers placing the room in disarray. Tirate was practiced in the art of deception and knew grieving men do not keep a neat house. Eyeing his work with satisfaction he nodded to himself with approval.

A knock on the door signaled the return of his men and he hurried to the door. Flinging it open, he stepped aside as two men carried in the mutant wrapped in a blanket. He motioned to a spot on the floor beside the bed where a few pillows had been arraigned. The men heaved the dragon roughly out of the blanket and let it bounce on the polished stone before it slid, belly up against the pillows.

Tirate scoffed. "Go easy! I don't want it dead yet. At least not until after our guests have left. Now go. Let me know when they arrive."

He waited until after the guards left to prepare for his performance. He looked in the mirror, unbuttoned his silk shirt, and ruffled his hair. Moments later the guard announced the Houses were ready to see him and with a deep breath he nodded to let them in.

The twelve men and women that filed in solemnly shook his hand as they expressed their sympathies. Shuffling like a man wracked with grief, he led them to where Fulgid lay and sat on the floor beside him. They all stared for several minutes watching its shallow breathing as

Tirate smiled sadly and stroked the exposed belly of the unmoving dragon. One by one each member gave eloquent condolences to which Tirate gracefully accepted. As they talked he reached past the dragon's head for another pillow. No sooner had his hand slipped near Fulgid's mouth when a set of sharp fangs sank deep into his wrist. Barely able to keep from screaming, he felt blood trickling down his fingertips. He gritted his teeth and looked up, none of the twelve had noticed.

Clearing his throat, a stream of real tears began to slip down his cheeks. "Please…excuse me…I think I'm feeling a little…overwhelmed. Can we continue this…discussion later at the coronation? If you don't mind?…I'd really like to be alone for a bit with my…dragon."

Bowing quickly and apologizing, the twelve heads of the Houses exited, exclaiming how brave and composed he was in the midst of this tragedy. Before the door had even closed he yanked his wrist from the dragons mouth and jumped to his feet. Blood poured from the large gash onto the carpet, staining it crimson.

Furious, he ran to the wall where his newly polished armor hung. Choosing his best sword, he approached the dragon and snarled. "That was the last time you'll bite me you filthy little beast!"

Raising his sword over his head, he struck the tiny dragons' belly with all his might and watched with glee as the scaled skin split apart.

***

Ammon sat cross-legged in the middle of the cell. In the darkness he pushed away his thoughts and concentrated on the voice he thought of as Fulgid's. It didn't matter that Shane said it was hopeless. If the link must be completed for the dragon to survive, he had to at least try! Clearing his mind he sat and listened to the sound of his own breathing.

"AMMON?"

Shocked, Ammon's eyes popped open. The golden voice flowed into his brain like sunlight through a window, but it sounded much weaker than before.

Hesitantly, he called out. "Fulgid? Is that you?"

The old man across the corridor rasped. "Who you talking to boy? Nobody here but you and me…"

Ignoring Shane, Ammon again closed his eyes and listened.

"Ammon? Ammon! AMMON!"

He gasped. There was no doubt this time that he had actually heard it! Forming words in his mind, he reached out to Fulgid.

"Fulgid run! Escape!"

He waited, listening.

A sudden searing pain drove deep into his chest and knocked the breath out of him. Clutching his shirt, he rolled over on the floor groaning in intense pain. It felt as if his very skin was being stripped from his body layer by layer. It spread across his arms and legs and across every part of his body until he howled in agony. Then, just as suddenly as it started, it stopped. He lay on the cold stone sobbing and gasping for breath.

Dimly he was aware of Shane shouting to him from his cell but he couldn't answer. Every ounce of strength he had left he used just to breathe. Tears streamed down his face, and his stomach roiled as he slowly pushed himself to a sitting position and leaned against the wall.

Shane's voice was near frantic now, and Ammon summoned enough strength to answer.

"I…I'm here. I'm okay…I think."

Impatiently the old man yelled back. "By my dragons teeth, what is going on over there?"

Ammon shook his head. His brain seemed foggy and a deep ache throbbed in his temples. He took a deep breath and slowly explained what he'd tried to do and what he'd felt. When he was finished the old man snorted.

"Foolish boy, I told you that you can't force a link! It either is, or it isn't. As for what just happened, I'd rather not try to guess."

Ammon rubbed his forehead with his fingers. Whatever happened, it wasn't something he wanted to try again. "I heard him call my name."

There was a long pause before Shane spoke.

"Ammon, dragons can't call you by name. They can share feelings and emotions through the link, and sometimes they may do what you want or sense what you need, but they cannot talk."

Irritated, Ammon looked around the tiny confines of his cell. He didn't care what Shane said, he knew he had heard that voice! Arguing was pointless; how could you prove what happened inside your head? Anyway, it was about time he looked for a way out of there somehow. In the faint light he could see the windowless walls were made of heavy stone, and the door was constructed of thick timbers strapped with iron. He got to his feet and started to pace, his agitation growing. He needed…something! Something that was outside his cell. It was close, he could feel it. He paced the length of the cell as the feeling turned to desperation. He had to get to it, he had to!

An earsplitting crash and a bloodcurdling scream echoed down the corridor, and still he paced. Need! In mid-stride he suddenly stopped and turned toward the cell door. That desperate need and desire, what he had to have was there! The door blew into splinters sending shards of wood and twisted iron into the cell. In the middle of the maelstrom was Fulgid.

Even in the dim light the brilliant gold scales glittered like the noonday sun, and his glowing eyes flashed white like molten steel. Razor sharp fangs glistened from his open mouth as he stalked into the room like a lion hunting its prey. Ammon had never seen Fulgid look so horribly terrifying before, and yet he was unafraid. It was Fulgid, and he was alive! He rushed forward to him and was immediately thrown to the floor. Snarling, Fulgid stood on his chest, pinning back his shoulders with sharp claws.

Stunned Ammon stammered. "Fulgid…It's me! Ammon!"

His heart beat against his chest and he scarcely dared to breathe as Fulgid lowered his head until his nose touched Ammon's cheek. With a faint snort, the dragon lay down on top of Ammon and pushed his head close to Ammon's face and...sighed. The fierce white glow in his eyes faded to amber.

Ammon threw his arms around Fulgid and hugged him. Loose scales moved beneath his hands and rattled when he touched them. Shane shouted from his cell across the hall.

"Ammon? Are you all right? What is going on over there?"

Ammon smiled down at the dragon clinging to the front of his leather shirt and got to his feet. Carefully he stepped over the broken door and crossed the corridor. A thick iron lock hung from Shane's door and he pulled on it uselessly.

"I'll have you out in a moment Shane!"

He hurried up the hall and cautiously peered around the corner and saw a pair of boots lying beside the guards' station. Swallowing hard, he walked towards them to see the man they were attached too. Unmoving, the guard lay face down as a dark crimson pool gathering beneath him.

He looked away. He didn't want to know if the man were alive or dead; the very thought sickened his stomach. He reached over the desk and pulled a large set of keys from the hook and rushed back to Shane's cell. Fumbling, he tried each key in the lock until it popped open. He dropped it to the floor and pulled the heavy door open.

Blinking, the old man gingerly stepped into the hallway and looked at the remains of Ammon's cell door, then at Ammon, and then at the dragon clinging to Ammon's chest. Rubbing his eyes he bent over to look closer at Fulgid and whistled through his teeth.

"Incredible! I never would believe this if I wasn't seeing it with my own eyes!"

The sound of distant shouts and a horn blowing snapped him from his stare. "Quickly, lad, we need to get out of here now if we're to escape!"

They hurried down the hall past the guard station, and through the remains of the door to the main hallway. Wordlessly, Shane directed Ammon through the hall and down a stairway. As they rounded a corner into a wide corridor, the old man pointed towards a set of wide doors.

"Hurry, in there!"

They burst through the doors into a large kitchen. Fireplaces lined the walls on both sides, and pots and kettles bubbled and boiled over the fires. Four women wearing wide greasy aprons looked up in surprise. One of the cooks, a short, stout woman with gray hair and a round face placed her plump hands on each hip and eyed each of them suspiciously.

"Well, Knight Shane, I declare it's been a number of years since I had the pleasure of throwing you out of my kitchen!"

Shoving Ammon ahead, the old man spoke quickly. "No time to chat, Maise, if you were ever loyal to King Erik you'll let us pass!"

The cook raised an eyebrow. "You know I'm a loyal subject of the king, or was until he died! Now if you've caused Tirate grief and he's set his men after you, then you're an even better man than I thought! That scoundrel deserves the worst! Isn't that right girls?" The other three cooks nodded enthusiastically.

"Now if you need to get out of the palace, follow me." Spinning on her heel, the large woman moved with surprising speed.

She opened a small door in the rear of the kitchen and motioned them inside. "This is where the workmen haul the firewood for the ovens. It leads down to the street below the palace. Go to the inn at the bottom of the hill called The Silver Dragon and ask to see Kyle the innkeeper. Tell him I sent you. He'll help you out of the city. Now wait a minute."

She disappeared into the kitchen and came back a minute later with two warm sacks filled with food and a large empty sackcloth. "You won't get far with that shiny thing sticking out of your belly!" She wrapped the cloth around Ammon and Fulgid and tied it into place, then stood back to look at her handiwork. "Well, I'd say you look like a rather plump little fellow this way!"

Ammon grinned. Being plump wasn't something he'd ever been accused of. One of the younger cooks peeked around the corner, smiled and winked at him. Ammon felt his face redden. Maise threw back her head, laughed, and pinched his cheek with a fat thumb and forefinger, then turned to Shane.

"You best take care of this one, with a face like that he'll get himself into trouble right quick. Reminds me of someone else I knew at his age." Grabbing Shane by his collar, she gave him a peck on the cheek. "Now off with you. Go, go!"

They fumbled down the dark stairway and pushed open the heavy door that lead into the street below. As they stepped into the sunshine, Shane mumbled under his breath. "Blasted interfering women never let you forget anything!"

Ammon followed Shane to the Silver Dragon Inn and stood hidden in the alleyway while Shane went in to talk to the innkeeper. A moment later he leaned around the corner and motioned him to go to the back of the building. Ammon nodded and hurried down the alley and waited until Shane opened the back door.

Kyle, the innkeeper stuck his head out behind Shane and looked around nervously. "Quickly! Upstairs!"

Ammon climbed the narrow stairwell as fast as his ankle would allow. Kyle unlocked a door on the top floor and led them inside. A balding middle-aged man, the innkeeper was shorter than Ammon, but with wide shoulders and a broad back.

Mopping the sweat from his face, he sat down on a stool in the corner. "Maise sent you to see me? You must be trying to escape Lord Tirate?" he whispered hoarsely.

Ammon nodded. "Yes we are."

Shane shot him a fierce warning look and turned to the innkeeper. "We need to get out of the city, quickly and discreetly."

Kyle tapped his pudgy nose with a thick finger. "It can be done, but you'll have to wait until after the change of the guard around midnight. Tonight the guard in charge of the East Gate is my nephew Derek. You might have seen him; he used work here at the tavern. Real handy to have around when the drunks get out of hand. He's nearly the size of a house and bright as a dark cellar." He chuckled. "He's a right ugly boy with a face only a dragon could love, but he's a good-hearted soul. Tirate thought he was one of the mercenaries and hired him as a guard, and Derek took the job for the extra money. Puts on a good act as a toughie but he wouldn't hurt a fly."

Shane nodded impatiently. "As long as he can get us out of the city. We don't want to cause a commotion."

"I also have a man for you to meet." Kyle continued. "You'll want to talk to him, I'll wager. I'm sure he'll be willing to help. In the meantime make yourself at home; you'll be safe here."

After the innkeeper left, Ammon unwrapped the sackcloth from around his stomach. Fulgid still clung tightly to his shirt with his eyes closed. Shane leaned closer to have a better look.

Reaching out his hand, he looked up at Ammon. "May I?"

Ammon nodded, and Shane gently stroked the little dragon's neck as he studied him carefully. "Ammon, how many times has he shed since Hatch?"

Ammon shrugged. "I don't think he has, why?"

Shane pinched the loose skin on his neck and several scales clinked as they fell to the floor. "See how loose this is? It's his old skin peeling off. This should've shed two or three days after he hatched, and it doesn't usually happen again until they're about six months of age. If this is his first shed, it's a wonder he lived this long. His body would have continued to grow beneath these hard scales. He must have been nearly crushed by his own flesh!"

Ammon scratched Fulgid behind the ear and a few more tiny scales fell to the floor, rattling like coins. "So is that why I felt my own skin was squeezing me? Because of the link?"

Shane nodded. "If a dragon can't shed, it dies. I've known knights that tried cutting the first skin off when this happened to their hatchling, but a simple knife won't cut through dragon scales. Something must've started it for him, something hard!"

Ammon gently pulled Fulgid off the front of his leather shirt and cradled him in his arms belly up. Shiny new scales glistened and sparkled across his belly and a few more old ones fell to the floor. One by one he began peeling them off and placing them in a small pile.

Shane shook his head and smiled. "It's always good to see a dragon survive its first shed." He stood up and walked to the window and stared out into the street.

Ammon leaned back in the chair with Fulgid still laying on his lap. It suddenly struck him that his throbbing headache had dulled, and in its place was something different nestled in the back of his mind. Like a tiny transparent bubble, he could feel the fierce determination coming from the little dragon, and he wondered why he hadn't felt it before. He closed his eyes and gently stroked behind Fulgid's ear. The bubble rippled as a gentle golden voice whispered from within. "Ammon!"

***

Theo sat quietly in the rear of a tavern sipping water from an ale mug. Since he had arrived the previous day, he had spent most of his time trying to find a set of rooms before he finally settled at The Silver Dragon Inn. Once a favorite gathering place for the King's Guard, it was now mostly empty but for the occasional traveler. Kyle the innkeeper was a friendly man with an impressive girth and a ready smile who kept the inn clean and neat despite the lack of patrons.

Theo drained the mug and placed it gently on the table. So far, the first part of his plan had gone well. He had already made contact with the palace page that had informed him of King Erik's escape. The boy would be an invaluable resource and could be his key to getting inside the palace. The page knew who was loyal, and Theo had instructed him to send every one of them to the inn to meet with him. Now he just waited as they trickled in one by one.

Kyle collected the empty mug and wiped the polished table with a rag. "Would you like a tankard of ale?"

Theo shook his head. "No, thank you."

Kyle shrugged. "I never had much use for it either, but my patrons demand it." He jerked a fat thumb at the door. "Those louts out there that call themselves the new Guard drink it by the bucket! In my day we were never allowed to touch the stuff or our captain would have broken us down to a street sweeper!"

Theo raised his eyebrows. "You were in the Guard?"

"Aye, I was. A foot soldier in the barbarian war. Caught an arrow in my knee in the Battle of Coulee. Almost killed me and worse, ended my career."

Theo let out a low whistle. "I've read about that one. Why didn't you stay on? Certainly you could have worked elsewhere for the king?"

The big man sat down heavily beside Theo. "I wanted to be a Dragon Knight. After the injury I was only suitable to sit behind a desk." He spread his hands and gestured around the room. "This is the closest I'll ever get to a dragon, so I make the best of it." A sudden sadness swept over the innkeepers face and he shook his head. "I suppose it's time to sell this place and move on. Gaul will be no place for an honest man with Tirate as the new king."

Theo smiled. This was exactly the kind of connections he needed to make. A retired Guard still loyal to Erik would be a valuable ally. He pulled his knight's ring from his pocket and slid it across the table. The man's jaw dropped and he gaped in astonishment. "How did you come by this?"

Theo leaned forward. "How would you like to once again serve King Erik?"

Kyle sadly slid the ring back across the table. "Good King Erik is dead."

"What if I told you he wasn't? Would you be interested?"

Kyle gasped. "Alive? The King is still alive?"

Theo nodded. "Are you interested?"

Kyle studied Theo's face a moment then extended a large hand. "I'd be honored if you'd let me sire!"

***

By the next day Theo had added a fair number of supporters to his list, some were friends of Kyle but most were servants from the palace. One of them was a large, boisterous cook who insisted her entire staff wanted to see Tirate thrown to the dragons. He couldn't help but smile as he sat in the back of the tavern sipping water and waiting for the next meeting. It seemed Tirate wasn't very popular with most of the palace staff and was apparently unaware that he needed them for things to run smoothly. Without staff, life in a palace that size could be quite uncomfortable.

Kyle came out of the kitchen and smiled. "I just brought two more visitors upstairs to the room adjacent to yours. They were sent from the cook."

Theo nodded and headed up the stairs. As a precautionary measure everyone was sent to the room next to his where he could listen to their conversation through the walls. It was far too dangerous now to take a chance on being caught when he was so close to finding the dragon.

He slipped into his room and pressed an ear against the wall. As the voices drifted through he could tell one was an older man, the other a boy or perhaps a young man. The older man was talking, something about shedding and, dragons? He continued to listen but the two men had gone quiet. He waited a few more minutes and decided to take a chance. He tucked a knife in his belt behind his back as a precaution. There was no way to be absolutely sure which side they were on, so it was better to be prepared.

Silently he slipped into the hallway and threw open the door of their room. With one quick step he entered and slammed the door shut behind him. He barely had time to recognize Shane's startled face before a golden bolt struck him hard in the chest and sent him reeling. He dropped to his knees and gasped as he tried to force air back into his lungs. Within moments Shane was helping him to his feet and laughing in near hysterics.

Theo collapsed into a chair still wheezing and gasping and found himself staring face to face with the dragon he'd thought dead and the two men he'd come to rescue. Between gasps he started to chuckle.

Shane pulled a chair up beside him and heartily pounded his back.

"He may be small, but he's fast! Unlike anything I've ever seen before."

Theo nodded in agreement. "Me neither." He rubbed his chest with one hand and grimaced. There would be quite a bruise there. "I came back to steal it from Tirate and, if possible, free you and the boy. This however, is not what I expected!"

Shane grinned and winked at Ammon. "Well, we're certainly grateful for all your efforts, but as you can see, we already have things well in hand."

***

Tirate awoke with a screaming headache. He forced his swollen eyes open and brought his hand to his temples to find his head tightly wrapped in bandages. Several attendants hovered over him and protested when he tried to sit up. Searing pain enveloped him from head to toe, and he gingerly lay back down again with a muffled groan.

He snarled. "What happened? Tell me now, or I'll have you flogged! I'll have all of you flogged!"

The attendants backed up meekly, and Tirate's personal guard stepped forward.

"Sire, you were alone in the room when we heard you scream. By the time we entered, we found you lying on the floor with most of your clothes in tatters. Beside you was your sword…what was left of your sword that is. We found only a few shards of metal and the pommel. The dragon…uh, your dragon, was still in the room after it attacked you. Sire, it…shredded…all of your armor and everything in the room! We tried catching the beast, but I'm afraid it got past us. It put five men in the infirmary; at least one isn't likely to pull through. I have doubts the others will be returning to service…ever."

Tirate's bloodshot eyes nearly bulged out of his head. "Where is it now? Where is my dragon?"

The guard lowered his eyes. "It broke through the prison doors and attacked the guards there. It appears to have released the boy and one other prisoner escaped with him. We've secured the gates and are searching the city now. Sire, how are we to stop such a creature?"

Tirate started to grit his teeth only to find several missing, had the dragon spared any part of him? "Give me a mirror!"

An attendant handed him a small mirror and he grabbed it impatiently. He looked at his reflection and gasped. His nose was broken and both eyes were swollen and black. Most of his hair was gone, and his ears were bandaged. He threw the mirror violently, and it crashed against the wall sending splinters of glass everywhere. In anger, he slammed his fist into the bed and a flurry of feathers shot into the air. As the feathers drifted down like snowflakes, he suddenly realized the condition of his quarters. The mattress was shredded, as were the pillows. Every curtain, rug, and piece of furniture he could see lay tattered or in pieces. The dragon had completely destroyed his entire chambers; every stitch of clothing and every personal object he owned!

***

It wasn't going to be easy getting to the city gate with Tirate's men looking for them, and neither Theo nor Shane could agree on the best plan. Ammon quietly contented himself by plucking loose scales from Fulgid while the two men talked. Suddenly the little dragon's head popped up and focused his attention on the door. Theo motioned for them to be silent as he slipped the knife out from his belt and moved beside the door. There was a soft tap at the door, and it opened just wide enough for the bald head of the innkeeper to cautiously peer into the room.

"I'm sorry to bother you, but you didn't come down for your meal."

Relieved, Theo sheathed his knife and invited the man in with a wave of his hand. The innkeeper quickly waddled in, carrying a large wicker basket and froze, mouth gaping at the sight of the golden dragon sprawled across Ammon's lap. His jowls swung back and forth as his head turned, looking at Shane and Theo, then back at the dragon.

"A dragon! A real live dragon! In my inn! I never thought I'd see the day! And such an unusual color too!"

Visibly excited, he bent down in front of Ammon. "Could I...touch him?"

Ammon nodded, and the man's chubby hand gently stroked Fulgid's neck. Several loose scales dropped to the floor, clinking like coins. Kyle picked one up with his thick fingers and eyed it with awe.

"Sire, if you would be so inclined, please, I would be greatly honored if you would bestow one of these on me?"

Ammon shrugged his shoulders. There was already a fairly good-sized pile of them next to him and he hadn't really thought about what he'd do with them. "Yes, of course you can."

Theo buried his forehead in his hands and groaned softly while Shane rolled his eyes and turned to the window shaking his head.

Kyle's broad face broke into the largest smile Ammon had ever seen on a man. "Thank you, sire! Oh thank you! You won't regret it, I promise!"

Jumping to his feet, he stuffed the little scale into his shirt pocket and handed the basket to Shane. "I thought you might want some food for traveling tonight. I noticed when you came you had not much more than the clothes on your back." Looking back at the dragon he beamed. "However, it seems you had much more than I ever imagined!"

Kyle bowed slightly to Ammon and patted the scale in his pocket. "Thank you, sire!"

Ammon stared after the man. That was the third time Kyle had called him sire. Certainly no one could mistaken him for a person of rank or status, especially when he was still wearing the worn clothes of a tender. Theo left the room and came back a moment later with a small empty sack and tossed it at Ammon's feet. He looked up quizzically.

"That is for the rest of those scales. Collect every one of them that you can and try not to give any more of them away!" He looked at Shane and mumbled something under his breath.

The old man just chuckled. "Easy Theo, the boy has no idea; remember that."

Out of the basket Kyle brought, Ammon pulled a piece of broiled chicken and held it in front of Fulgid's snout and watched as he devoured it, bones and all.

"Did I do something wrong?"

Theo knelt to the floor and picked a golden scale from the small pile and turned it over in his hands. "Ammon, you need to save these for several reasons. When you have enough of them, it is tradition to have them sewn together into a suit of armor. They're harder than steel and much lighter. But more importantly, a knight, as a symbol of contract, only gives the first scales of a hatchling to his servants. By giving one to Kyle, you have agreed to accept him as your employee. From now on you must be more careful what you do with these. Fortunately for you, Kyle is a good man and loyal to the king."

"What…wait!" Ammon stammered. "He can't be my servant! That's impossible! I'm not knight! I'm just a tender!"

Shane chuckled and Theo rubbed his forehead. "Ammon, it appears that dragon of yours is going to live, and that means you're much more than a tender. With King Erik's blessings you will become a Dragon Knight and be sworn to uphold the laws of the crown. You will begin your education and training as soon as possible. Of course, you will have some catching up to do. Normally it's three years of service in the Guard before you would be allowed to attend a hatch."

Overwhelmed, Ammon could only sit and stare. Things were happening so fast that it felt like his head was spinning, and it all seemed so complicated. In less than a fortnight he'd gone from cleaning the ashes of a furnace to having servants? With a deep sigh he pulled another loose scale from Fulgid. His days of peaceful seclusion were long gone, of that he was sure.

***

It was near midnight when Kyle came to their room with four mugs and a large steaming pot of the same vile black mixture that Boris had given him. Kyle passed out the mugs and poured Ammon's first and stood waiting for him to drink.

"I hope it's satisfactory, sire? I ground the beans myself just for this occasion!"

Ammon nodded politely and tried to swallow without gagging. He wasn't sure which was worse, the drink or being called sire. Under Kyle's watchful eye, he reluctantly drained the cup, and despite his protests, Kyle gleefully refilled it. With a sigh, Ammon resigned himself that, unless he wanted to insult Kyle, he was destined to drink it. Sipping very, very slowly he hoped the other men would drain the pot before he emptied his cup.

Theo placed his mug down and stretched. "It's time to move while Kyle's nephew is guarding the gate. The sooner we leave the city the better our chances will be. I'm supposed to meet Boris first thing in the morning at a clearing outside the city to give him an update. I never expected we would have achieved so much this quickly though!"

Kyle patted the gold scale in his pocket. "I'm coming with you. It's my duty now."

Theo raised his eyebrows. "Kyle you can't do that, it's too dangerous! If we're caught…"

The innkeeper's face saddened. "I have no reason to stay anymore. Since Tirate took control of the city an honest man like me can't make a living. Besides, I've already made arrangements for anyone still loyal to King Erik to meet elsewhere."

Theo sighed. "Alright. Perhaps it's best this way. You can introduce us to your nephew at the gates."

Kyle's face beamed as he followed them out the door and into the shadows on the street.

     ***

The gate was brightly lit with lanterns, and Ammon nervously tightened the sackcloth around his stomach that covered Fulgid. The little dragon's shiny new scales would reflect the slightest bit of light like a mirror and that would be sure to attract unwanted attention.

As they neared the gate a loud voice shouted "Hold! Who comes?"

There were three guards at the gate, one of them the large man Ammon had bumped into the first time he sneaked out of the city.

Theo's hand slipped cautiously to the knife at his belt, and Kyle hissed. "Wait! It's okay, he's my nephew!"

The big guard held his hand up to the others, his deep voice was gruff. "I'll handle 'em." As he got closer, his red eyes seemed to glow in the dim light. He placed a large hand on each hip, leaned down, and smiled, showing two rows of uneven teeth through his thick silver beard. He spoke softly so only they could hear. "What are you doing here, Uncle Kyle?"

Kyle had to tilt his head all the way back to look up at the man. "Derek, we need to leave the city tonight. Right now!"

Derek shook his head. "Tirate ordered us locked down, nobody in or out. He even tripled the guard as you can see." He jerked his thumb at the two men behind him. "I'm sorry uncle, you'll have to wait until they find whoever they're looking for."

Kyle shook his head. "You don't understand, Derek! We are the ones they're looking for!"

A voice behind Derek made Ammon's back stiffen. "What do they want, Derek? Send 'em home, we got our orders! The gates are closed until Tirate says so!"

Both guards were standing directly behind Derek, trying to peer around his bulk into the shadows where Ammon and the rest stood.

One of the guards held a lantern up, illuminating Ammon's face. "Say, you kinda look like the one they described! Blond hair, blue eyes, 'cept you ain't skinny enough."

Now suspicious, the other guard held his lantern up to Shane. "Hey! Ain't you the old man from the warehouse! We got a warrant for your arrest!"

Both men drew their swords and positioned themselves in front of Derek. One leveled his sword at Ammon's belly and sneered. "Give it up boy or I'll stick you with this! Tirate won't care if you is dead or alive!"

Ammon stepped back and the guard followed, stabbing his sword into Ammon's abdomen. The blade barely pierced the sackcloth before it suddenly stopped with the tip almost touching Ammon's skin.

The man pulled back on the sword and frowned when it stuck. With a grunt, he grabbed the handle with both hands and yanked hard. The sword came free with a loud crunch, and he stumbled back, his eyes wide as he stared at the missing tip of the sword. Stunned, he looked down at Ammon's belly as several shards of steel were suddenly spit out the hole in the cloth.

The color drained from his face as he stammered, "Demon…! Ghost!"

The guard turned and ran face first into Derek who very calmly thumped him over the head with a massive fist. The broken sword clattered to the ground as the man crumpled in a heap. With surprising speed, Derek lunged at the other guard and plucked the sword from his hand before rendering him unconscious too.

Kyle picked up one of the lanterns. "Derek, I'm sorry to get you involved in this but we have to leave the city before they find us! Can you get us out?"

Derek shrugged as he walked to the gate. "Sure."

Effortlessly, he reached up, slid the large beam off of its braces and opened the gate wide enough for them to slip through. Derek came through last, carrying the beam on his shoulder. With one huge hand, he pushed the door closed and wedged it shut with the beam.

Kyle lowered the flame in the lantern until it barely emitted any light. None of them said a word until they were well into the woods.

Kyle spoke quietly. "Derek, you don't need to come with us. If you do you'll be a hunted man too!"

Derek's laugh sounded like rolling thunder. "I don't mind. Besides, I didn't like those men."

Kyle chuckled. "Derek, you're a gem! Don't let anyone tell you otherwise!"

Derek frowned at Ammon as they walked. His deep voice rumbled. "I saw you get stabbed, are you okay?"

Ammon patted the sack covering Fulgid and nodded as Kyle burst out laughing.

    ***

The road dwindled to little more than a rough path, and the worsening terrain made traveling in the dark slow and tedious. Ammon's ankle was throbbing painfully by the time Theo led them to the edge of a small clearing. The stars were still faintly visible as the sky gradually lightened from black to lavender. Grateful for a chance to rest, Ammon leaned back against the trunk of a fallen tree while Kyle rummaged through the basket and passed out portions of food.

Ammon ate half and set the rest aside for when Fulgid awoke. The little dragon had slept most of the trip beneath the sackcloth with only an occasional snore that caused confused looks from Derek. The big man sat on the ground away from everyone and Ammon watched him uneasily. Despite Kyle's assurances and his assistance escaping from the city, Ammon still wasn't ready to trust him.

Fulgid stirred against his belly and a sensation of hunger suddenly oozed from the bubble in his mind. He looked down at the hole in the sackcloth and saw a single golden eye peering up expectantly. He dropped a bit of food into the hole and felt the dragon move as he wolfed it down. Smiling, he looked up to see Derek's astonished eyes staring at him in amazement. Desperately trying to hide their amusement, the others watched as Derek's thick fingers twisted into his beard in confusion.

Once the scraps were gone, Fulgid decided to crawl out of the sackcloth and investigate his surroundings. With a yawn, the little dragon slowly emerged and stretched. The first few rays of the rising sun reflected off his scales and bathed them all in shower of light.

Derek whistled softly, his face awash in wonder. "So that's why you didn't get hurt!"

The three men broke into hysterical laughter and even Ammon chuckled. Wiping a tear from his eye, Kyle patted the big man on his shoulder.

"I'm sorry nephew, I guess I should have told you, but it was much more fun to watch you tie your brain in a knot!"

Still awestruck, Derek shrugged and held out a bit of sausage. Without hesitation Fulgid leapt from Ammon's lap and jumped into the palm of the massive hand before happily gobbling the morsel down.

Derek's face broke into a childish grin as the dragon licked the grease from his fingers.

"He likes me!"

Amused, Ammon watched as Fulgid removed all traces of food from Derek's hand, then wandered off to explore. At the far edge of the clearing he was enthusiastically digging up a small bush when he suddenly became alert, swiveling his ears wildly. With speed almost too quick for the eye to follow, he raced towards them. In the back of Ammon's mind the tiny bubble sprang to life with its clear golden voice ringing like chimes.

"Ammon! Ammon! Ammon!"

With a graceful leap, he jumped into Ammon's arms and stretched his neck towards the northern sky. Moments later the shadow of a black dragon appeared over them, followed by two more. They each circled once before landing roughly in the meadow, their talons ripping the ground in large gashes as they struggled to slow themselves.

Boris shouted from his saddle. "Hurry! Tirate's men are coming just beyond the next rise! Ammon, you come with me!"

Ammon limped across the field with Fulgid clinging tightly to his shirt and climbed up behind Boris. He had no sooner settled himself into the saddle when Boris signaled Ellis to fly. Ammon gripped the edge of the saddle so tight his knuckles turned white, and one by one, they leaped into the sky. He looked over his shoulder and saw a group of men pulling a small wagon loaded with some sort of mechanism. One man was frantically turning a crank on the side, but they quickly faded from sight as Ellis gained altitude and headed north.

A few minutes later Boris turned in the saddle to look at Fulgid, then at Ammon.

"Welcome back! I thought we'd lost you for good! I'm sorry, I shouldn't have left you behind, but I hadn't expected them to be looking for us so soon."

Ammon smiled. That was the second apology he'd gotten from Boris. "I guess I need more practice with that sword."

Boris laughed so loud that Ellis twisted his head to look back at him. "Boy, it helps to have your sword in your hand, not in your tent if you expect to make use of it!" He looked back at Fulgid and raised an eyebrow. "How is he?"

Ammon scratched the little dragon behind the ear and Fulgid arched his neck. "He's fine! He's eating, moving around and even …shedding!" Reaching into the bag Theo had given him, he pulled out a handful of the golden scales.

Boris raised both eyebrows this time. "By my dragons teeth…!" Looking back at Ammon he frowned slightly, "and the link? Has it finally formed?"

With a broad smile Ammon pointed towards his head. "I can hear him in my head now!"

Boris tilted his head. "You can sense him now? Good! Then the link is complete!" He turned to face forward again. "Times are changing Ammon. We'll need every dragon and every man if we are to survive."

***

Ammon helped Boris strip the saddle off Ellis after they landed, and the big dragon joined his brethren sunning themselves at the edge of the makeshift landing field. Fulgid eyed them curiously, but seemed content to remain attached firmly to Ammon's shirt.

Boris put his hand on Ammon's shoulder and directed him towards the encampment. "Come with me, Ammon. You need to tell King Erik everything that has happened. He'll be glad to know you're still alive."

Theo and the others followed as they neared a large tent, and Boris spoke loud enough for them all to hear.

"Kyle and Derek, please remain outside unless called upon. Ammon, you must also wait outside with Theo and Shane until I bid you to enter. You must be respectful and don't speak until spoken to. Most importantly, tell everything exactly as it happened. Remember that he is your king and is to be treated as such."

Boris entered the tent and returned a moment later. "You may go in."

With a deep breath, Ammon ducked through the door with the others and stood awkwardly, unsure what to do next. The others dropped to one knee and he followed their example.

King Erik stood up and gestured with one hand. "Please stand my friends. There is no need for the formalities."

As Ammon stood, Fulgid dropped to the ground and sat by his feet. Erik smiled genuinely and embraced Ammon with a strong hug.

"Ammon, I feared I'd never see you again! And your dragon too! He looks magnificent!"

Stunned by the unexpected show of affection, Ammon stammered. "Yes, uh…thank you…sire!"

Erik greeted both Shane and Theo warmly. "It is good to have you all back!"

Theo stood slack jawed, staring at Erik in disbelief. "Sire, I mean no disrespect but I must say you look much, much healthier since I saw you last!"

Shane nodded slowly. "He should, now that Tirate isn't able to poison him anymore."

Boris suddenly stepped forward from the back of the tent. "WHAT?"

King Erik raised his hand towards Boris. "Easy my friend. Tell me Knight Shane, what do you mean?"

Shane rubbed his withered face with a wiry hand. "After you escaped with Boris, I started shipping wagonloads of supplies out to all the knights I knew were still in the area and instructed them to head north with their dragons to find you. I knew a battle with Tirate was likely, so I emptied the storeroom of all the herbs and medicines I could. In the back I found an empty barrel of dragonsbane."

Confused, Boris shook his head. "Dragonsbane?"

Shane nodded. "Yes. There was a breakout of River Fever about nine years ago and we discovered it was an effective treatment. When it was over Tirate insisted we keeping a large enough supply to treat the entire city if necessary."

Erik frowned. "Tirate has never done anything charitable unless he stood to benefit from it somehow."

"Exactly my thoughts sire," Shane continued, "but regardless of his motive, at the time it seemed a very reasonable request. It took two years for the local mistresses of herbs to obtain enough to fill one small barrel. She gave me strict warnings on its usage, for any more than an occasional small amount would cause the body to waste away. She also told me a great secret, one that I had not thought about in fifteen years. Dragonsbane is odorless, tasteless, and extremely poisonous to dragons. For that reason, I kept it in a locked storeroom. Only myself and Tirate had a key."

Boris' face darkened and his knuckles cracked as he clenched his fists. "Sire, if Shane's suspicions are true, that was what killed your dragon Laud! Tirate poisoned him just the same as he poisoned you!"

Erik suddenly looked old as he turned and sat heavily in his chair. His eyes glistened wetly and he buried his head in his hands.

"Leave me for awhile my friends. I need to be alone with my thoughts."

Wordlessly, they each bowed before leaving. Ammon walked to the door but Fulgid stayed behind, refusing to come.

Boris pushed Ammon out the door and whispered gently. "Don't worry. He may be of more comfort to him than anything we can do."

King Erik sat quietly with his head in his hands unaware of Fulgid's presence until the little dragon crawled into his lap. Staring down in surprise, he stroked the golden head, then pulled him close and wept until the tears wouldn't come anymore.

***

In the center of the open meadow the sun beat down unmercifully on Ammon's bare back. The muscles in his arms throbbed and his palms were sweating, making it difficult to keep his grip on the sword. For days now, Boris and Theo had been training him hard. He had learned quickly that his biggest advantage was in his ability to move and strike rather than match blow for blow. Still, Boris insisted he learn to stand his ground, in case a time came when he could not dodge in and out.

With the tip of his sword, Boris pointed at Ammon's mostly healed ankle. "Imagine an injury like that during a fight. If you can't stand and fight, you're in serious trouble."

So now Ammon stood in one spot as Boris approached from different directions with his leather-wrapped sword.

"You will never win a fight by just deflecting your opponents blows. You have to find an opening and attack! Always think at least one or two moves ahead. Use the momentum of your swing to power the next move, whether it's a strike or defense."

Ammon only nodded. After two hours of nonstop sword work, his arms felt limp and he was breathing hard. Boris however, had hardly begun to sweat, and once more, he began his relentless barrage against Ammon's defense.

A strong, distinctive voice behind them made Boris pause in mid-strike. "Teaching the young lad the finer points of diplomacy I see?"

Boris glanced over his shoulder and Ammon, seeing his chance, gently poked Boris in the stomach with the rounded tip of his leather-wrapped sword. Boris jumped back in surprise and the voice suddenly roared with laughter.

"Aye, you've taught him well too! Distraction can be as effective as the sharpest sword!"

Boris shook his head and chuckled good-naturedly. "Skewered by a boy! I must be getting too old for this!"

Ammon smiled as Erik walked towards them. As the poison gradually left the king's body, his health once more returned with vigor. His eyes were now bright and his back ramrod straight as his lean frame moved through the tall grass. Fulgid loped beside him, a bright beam of living sunshine. Every time Ammon started sword practice, the little dragon ran off to find Erik and pester him into walking about the huge camp. The two were becoming a common sight as they strolled together inspecting the dragon regiment just as Erik used to before the death of Laud. Boris privately commented to Ammon that Fulgid's sudden friendship with Erik had done more to restore his health than anything else had. Soon after, Boris insisted that Ammon's tent be placed beside Erik's.

Erik paused to take a long sip from a steaming cup of black brew he carried with him. "Has Theo returned from his rendezvous this morning?"

Boris nodded and pushed a few loose strands of gray hair from his eyes. "Yes, but he'll make another trip later today with more dragons. We underestimated how many loyal subjects were left in the palace and couldn't bring them all back at once. Yesterday he brought back the entire kitchen staff! Everyone from the head cook to the spit dogs, not to mention all the supplies they could carry to the meeting place. By the end of today we'll have every one of the palace pages, the seamstress, laundry maids, blacksmiths, fletchers, just about the entire staff!" He smiled broadly. "Tirate may call himself king, but he'll have to wash and sew his own undergarments!"

Erik drained the last few drops from his mug and said wryly, "It would be too much to hope he'd succumb to his own cooking as I almost did." He passed the empty cup to Ammon. "Would you bring this back to Kyle please? It looks as if you'll have the afternoon free if Theo is heading back to Gaul. Boris and I have to start planning how to get past those crossbow defenses."

Ammon slipped on his shirt and headed back to the tent with Fulgid bouncing along beside him chasing grasshoppers from the tall grass. Since his arrival a week ago, he'd had very little free time between his sword lessons and dragon training. It would be nice to walk around and maybe see the other dragons or sit by the river and relax. He walked past the tents until he was in the sliver of shade cast by the sheer vertical face of the mountain called The Wall. Small rocks and boulders that had broken off from high above littered the ground and he picked his way through.

He was just within sight of his tent when Fulgid charged past in pursuit of a horsefly. He suddenly leapt behind a flat boulder leaning against the wall and disappeared. Ammon stopped and could hear the scraping sound of Fulgid's claws against stone. He peered around the boulder and saw a hole in the wall formed by a crack. Pushing the boulder away he stuck his head into the hole and yelled.

"Fulgid! Get back here! FULGID!"

The sound of claws against stone grew fainter as the dragon moved deeper into the dark crevice. Ammon placed the mug on top of the boulder and bent over to inspect the opening. The hole was big enough that he could crouch down on his hands and knees and crawl in, so he went in a short way and called again. He could only just barely hear the scraping sound now.

He clenched his teeth and scowled. Why wouldn't Fulgid listen to him? Exasperated, he crawled in a little further and called again and waited. The sounds continued to fade and finally he decided Fulgid would come back down when he got hungry. He shuffled backward a few inches and felt the sword at his waist jam against the sides of the crevice. He tried to twist it free, but the hole was so narrow he couldn't turn or reach behind him to pull the sword free. As he moved forward it came loose but each time he backed up it would only wedge itself again. Over and over he tried but only managed to work himself further up into the hole. Panting with the effort he stopped to think. Calling for help was useless. Only Boris, Kyle, the king, and himself frequented this part of the camp. Boris and the king were discussing plans, and Kyle would be at the tent cooking the next meal.

The faintest gust of cool air lightly brushed his face and he peered up into the darkness ahead. Air movement coming down the crevice meant there must be an opening somewhere! As long as it didn't become any narrower he should be able to continue and either turn around or find another way out.

For what seemed like hours, he crawled on his elbows, pushing himself forward and up. The hole didn't get any narrower, but it didn't get wider either. It just continued to rise steadily before him until finally he came to a steep incline. Dim light shone at the top and he climbed upwards until he scrambled out of the opening. He found himself standing inside a large cavern filled with a dazzling display of white and yellow crystals that seemed to sprout from the floor and walls like flowers. High above him a thin beam of sunlight streamed down from a small hole in the ceiling.

Ammon looked up just in time to see Fulgid bounding up a large pile of rocks where a portion of the cavern ceiling had collapsed and scampering out through the hole.

"Fulgid!"

The echoes of his voice inside the cavern were nearly deafening. Grumbling, he climbed up the mound of rocks and squeezed through the hole. He sputtered as he wiped dirt away from his face and paused as his eyes adjusted to the bright sunlight.

It was cold, and as he gazed upon his surroundings, his jaw dropped. There was no grass or trees anywhere on the steep rocky surface he stood on, and patches of ice glistened in the sun further up the slope. Fulgid stood just a few strides away, staring at three large shapes in the distance half-buried in the snow. Ammon gasped, even from a quarter mile away he was pretty sure he knew what they were, but he had to be positive.

He picked up Fulgid and the little dragon climbed onto his shoulder and held tight to his leather shirt. It took longer than he expected to climb the hill and he seemed unable to catch his breath. The ice-coated rocks made it difficult to get good footing, and as he picked his way up the slope, his stomach started to tighten with nausea. Finally he stopped a few paces away, disbelief pulling at every fiber of his body. This was so…wrong!

Shivering with cold, he skidded and slid back down the hill as fast as he possibly could go. He had to get back and tell Boris and Erik what he'd seen! He had to tell them he'd found something horrible!

In The Ice
Chapter 8

Boris sat quietly and frowned while Erik rubbed his temples and stared at the papers strewn across the table. The population of the camp had exploded as more refugees from Gaul were flown in and their limited amount of supplies was diminishing quickly. The dragons were providing some food by hunting the wild boar common to the area, but that too would be quickly depleted, and then food for everyone would become a major issue. They were running out of time and hadn't yet gathered enough information about Tirate's defenses to attempt to retake Gaul.

They both looked up in surprise when Ammon barged in and almost collapsed in front of them. Alarmed, Boris jumped to his feet. "Ammon? What happened to you? You're covered in filth!"

Ammon gasped, his sides ached and his chest heaved as he tried to catch his breath. "I…I found…I found DRAGONS!"

Boris exchanged confused looks with Erik. "Uh, yes well, there are nearly two hundred dragons here, Ammon…"

Ammon shook his head furiously. "No! You don't understand! Three of them! On the mountain! They're dead!"

This time it was Erik that came to his feet in alarm. "Boris? You'd better find out what he's talking about!"

Boris was already pushing Ammon towards the door of the tent. "I'm on my way! Show me where Ammon!"

Ammon explained everything as he led the way back to the crevice. Boris took one look at the hole and shook his head. There was no way his wide shoulders would fit into that narrow space. He pushed a few stands of white hair out of his eyes as he looked back over the camp.

"Come with me."

With surprising speed, he took off at a run to the landing field to where Theo was unloading more refugees. Halfway across the field Boris shouted. "Theo, I need you NOW!"

Theo dropped the sack he was carrying and ran towards them. Boris' voice boomed with authority. "I need you to follow Ammon. He's found something, and we need to know if we're facing a possible threat."

Hurrying back to the crevice, Ammon again explained what he'd found. Fulgid jumped down and scurried into the hole. Ammon removed his sword and leaned it against the boulder, and Theo reluctantly did the same. On their hands and knees, the two entered the blackness with Ammon in the lead.

Theo gasped in surprise when they finally crawled out into the cavern with its dazzling crystals blossoming from everywhere. Fulgid waited impatiently for them up above until they came out into the cold sunlight, and he immediately latched onto Ammon's back the moment he climbed through the hole.

Slipping and sliding, they scaled up the steep slope until they reached the first of the dragons. The great black beast was sprawled out on its belly, one wing folded and the other partially extended. Theo walked around, and Ammon followed. A strange looking ornate saddle was attached above its shoulders, and Theo let out a low whistle as he studied it.

"See the rigging on the side of the saddle? That's for carrying weapons like extra swords and lances. These two leather pouches below the stirrups are for carrying rocks. A rope was attached to a flap on the bottom so you could drop them on your enemy as you flew over. It was a primitive, but useful weapon. This style of fighting saddle hasn't been used in a hundred years or more and I've only seen drawings of them in books. If I had to guess I'd say these dragons have been laying here frozen for ages!"

Shaking his head in amazement, he looked back down the hill. "It's in incredibly good shape all things considered, probably because it's so cold. We could certainly use it against Tirate if we can remove it without breaking it and haul it back through that narrow passage."

He gazed up the hill at the next shape lying in the snow and took a deep breath of the thin air. "I want to check out the others, they may be similarly outfitted. Are you coming?"

Sadly, Ammon looked at the large dragon and nodded. He didn't really want to see another dead dragon, but he didn't want to be left alone next to one either. "Yes, I'll come."

The second dragon was also a black and similarly outfitted, but the third dragon was gray, and Ammon gasped when he walked around to see the saddle. An armored figure still hung from one stirrup. Face down he lay half-buried in the ice.

Theo studied the man soberly as he knelt beside him. "He's been shot with an arrow, the fletching still shows through the ice. I think I understand what has happened here."

He rose to his feet and led Ammon back down the mountainside. As they walked back he explained. "A dragon needs their link to survive. A knight can live if his dragon dies, such as what happened to both King Erik and Shane. It's a horrible experience, but they live. However, if the knight dies before his dragon, the dragon becomes lost. Their connection to this world is cut. They usually just fly away and are never seen again. I would guess that there must've been a terrible battle and these dragons came here to die in the cold."

Ammon swallowed hard and he felt Fulgid tighten his grip on his shirt.

When they got back to the first dragon, Theo studied the saddle once more. "I wonder if we could disassemble it once it's removed? Then we could bring it back through the hole in smaller pieces and reassemble it at the camp."

The saddle was facing downhill, so Theo climbed above the dragon and found the buckles of one of the girths. Warming it briefly between his hands, Theo then pulled on it gently. The frozen leather creaked beneath his fingers but didn't break. Carefully he unbuckled the straps, then using a sharp rock, he chipped at the ice beneath the dragon.

"You'll have to help me with this Ammon. I know it's unpleasant, but this might be a significant help to us against Tirate."

Reluctantly Ammon grabbed hold of the saddle and the two dug their heels into the snow. After several hard yanks on the straps beneath the dragon, it finally let go, and they pulled the saddle behind them as they half slid down to the entrance of the cavern.

Theo immediately began disassembling it into smaller pieces.

"Tomorrow we can come back and salvage what we can of the others."

Shivering, Ammon looked up the hill and shook his head. "Not the gray one."

Theo paused and raised an eyebrow.

Ammon's voice was soft but stern. "They rode together in life, they should be able to ride together in death as well."

Theo followed Ammon's gaze, and after a moment agreed. "Yes, you're right. We will leave that one alone. Ammon, perhaps you are already more of a knight than any of us realized."

Ammon looked down in surprise, but said no more. Theo finished taking the saddle apart then passed the pieces through to Ammon in the cavern where they tied everything into bundles. Using some of the leather straps, Ammon made a small harness for Fulgid and tied some of the pieces to his back. With Fulgid in the lead, the three of them slipped headfirst into the crevice with their bundles dragging behind them for the long crawl back.

***

The sun dipped below the horizon, reluctantly giving up the last few rays of daylight shining on the small group gathered at the base of the Wall. Boris was striding back and forth impatiently while Erik studied the stones in front of the crevice. Fulgid suddenly popped out of the hole and scampered over to Erik, dragging his little bundle behind him. Boris stopped pacing but didn't breathe easy until both Ammon and Theo were standing in front of him and had explained what they'd found.

Boris let out a great sigh of relief. "I was afraid someone was killing dragons up there and we had no way to help!"

Clapping Ammon on the back, the king looked at the bundles thoughtfully. "Bring it all to my tent. Perhaps we may learn something about how long it's been up there."

Boris untied the bundle from Fulgid and turned the thick leather over in his hands as they walked back to Erik's tent. "A dragon graveyard, who would have guessed?" He shook his head sadly.

After they lit the lanterns, they spread the pieces across the table where they could examine the saddle.

"Fascinating!" Leaning close, King Erik pointed to a small faded yellow insignia stamped deep into the leather of the seat and he traced it with his finger.

"That is the crest of the House of Les, an old family line that died out about fifteen years ago. If their line had continued, The House of Les would have been next in line to the throne after mine, provided they had an heir linked to a dragon. I had no idea there were ever any knights within their House that had died in battle, but I suppose they may have at some point. They were a close ally to my own House and were powerful in their own right, owning large portions of land and businesses throughout the kingdom. Unfortunately, bandits killed the last members and ended the line."

Erik smiled at Ammon. "You would have liked their House crest Ammon, it looked very much like Fulgid."

Ammon peered down at the insignia and felt a shock of recognition run through him. Not only did look like Fulgid, but it was the exact same design as the ring he'd lost! Boris leaned past him to look at the design, and then suddenly stood up straight with his jaw open.

Erik looked back and forth at the two of them. "Now what's the matter with you two? You look like know something I don't!"

Boris fumbled through his belt pouch and mumbled to himself while Ammon slowly sank into a chair in confusion. Suddenly Boris shouted, "Got it!" and he held the ring up in front of him. Smiling, he handed it to Ammon.

"You left this back in the tent when you were captured. I'd completely forgotten about it until just now!"

Ammon sat with his mouth open, holding the ring in the palm of his hand.

Erik folded his arms across his chest. "Would somebody mind telling me what is going on?"

Boris pulled up a chair and sat down. "I think Ammon will have to tell this one, because I don't yet know the story either, but I believe you should take a close look at his ring."

Ammon handed the ring to Erik and sat wordlessly while he studied the engraving of the gold dragon. Turning it over in his hands, he looked at Ammon with a raised eyebrow.

"Well, son, where did you find this ring?"

"I didn't find it!" Ammon lowered his eyes. "It was given to me by my mother."

Erik's blue eyes peered at him intently. "Your mother gave this to you? Tell me about her, how did she get this ring?"

"I…I don't know where she got it. I was little when she put it on a string around my neck. She died right after that."

Erik was quiet for a minute. "Ammon, do you remember what your mother looked like?"

He nodded. "I remember some. She had long blonde hair and blue eyes, and she had a little mark on her cheek that deepened when she smiled."

"Do you know how she died?"

Ammon's voice grew tight. "No. She put the ring around my neck and died. I stayed with her for a long time but…she didn't move. Then I started walking. That's how Ms. Garret found me and she took me in. That's all I remember!"

Boris nodded slightly. "Ms. Garret has been taking in orphans for years, that doesn't surprise me."

Erik studied the ring once more before he handed it back to Ammon. "A very interesting story. A story I wouldn't believe if it were told by anyone else. However, several things lead me to believe you are indeed telling me the truth.

First, was the perfect description of your mother, Eleanor. She was a woman of remarkable beauty despite the small scar on her cheek she received as a child when picking wild thornberries. Second, you are not only the right age, but you have many of the same characteristics of your father Hale. Like you, he was also slight of build but strong as an ox and twice as stubborn. Were you to grow a beard, I suspect you'd look just like him."

Looking at Boris and Theo, Erik leaned back in his chair and gestured with his hands. "I knew there was something familiar about Ammon, but I couldn't quite place it. Now I know why. What is your opinion, knights?"

Boris cleared his throat. "Sire, I honestly would not know. I spent as little time as possible in the political arena surrounding the throne. My career, indeed, my entire life, has been devoted to the Kings Guard and as your military adviser."

Theo sat quietly for a moment. "My career has been much the same, but not nearly as long as Captain Boris'. My knowledge of the Houses is probably even less than his. I'm sorry I cannot be of much help."

Ammon listened carefully to every word. Was Erik actually saying that he knew his parents? Hale and Eleanor? Until now, he had never even known their names. That they were actually members of the Royal Court mattered little to Ammon. He had no idea what it even meant.

Suddenly, Erik jumped to his feet and shouted irritably. "Well, I am still the king am I not? Therefore I declare it to be true!" He pounded his fist on the table so hard that pieces of the saddle fell to the ground.

Startled, Ammon stared at the king in awe. The man standing in front of him was not the frail old man he'd first met. Instead, there stood a wizened man, full of vigor and strength and certainly not someone who could be easily dismissed, or trifled with. His voice boomed with authority.

"Knights, it is time for a celebration and a House recognition! Something the kingdom hasn't seen in many years." Erik smiled down at Ammon. "Back at the palace, it would take weeks of preparations, but out here we have only simple accommodations. I think tomorrow afternoon will be more than enough time to gather and feast."

Turning his head to Boris and Theo, the king smiled even wider. "I think you'd best start informing everyone tonight! The cooks Theo brought in will want an early start." He chuckled softly for a moment. "Have Knight Shane himself inform the head cook of tomorrows festivities!" Erik placed a hand on Ammon's shoulder. "And find Kyle! Ammon will need help preparing for tomorrow and we'll need a good breakfast to get started."

Erik sat down across from Ammon and smiled. "Ammon, tonight you will stay here with me. I'm sure you have many questions that deserve to be answered."

With all the excitement, no one noticed Fulgid move to the back of the tent to stare at the back wall suspiciously. A few minutes later, a figure slipped silently from the shadows, and no one heard or saw the release of a messenger pigeon into the night.

***

Ammon pulled the covers over his head but it did nothing to stop Kyle's voice or his persistent shaking of the bed.

"Ammon? It's time to rise sire! A busy day ahead!"

There was no point ignoring him, no more sleep was to be had this day. Reluctantly, Ammon swung his legs over the edge of the cot and rubbed his eyes until Kyle shoved a cup of the dreaded steaming liquid into his hands.

With an inaudible groan, he forced a sip past his lips and Kyle beamed in satisfaction. If nothing else, the foul black drink did seem to help wake him, so he continued to drink it. Erik had kept him up most of the night with unfathomable discussions about politics, the Houses of the Court, and other topics that were all far beyond anything he understood. Erik was convinced he was the only descendant from the House of Les and needed to know the intricacies of the palace, but Ammon had serious doubts. The more he heard of the politics of Gaul, the more he wanted just a small farm in the country somewhere.

Kyle refilled the nearly empty mug and the moment he turned, Ammon dumped most of it behind the bag of Fulgid's old scales beside the bed. He had learned quickly that emptying the cup completely only seemed to encourage Kyle to give him more. So he cradled the cup in his hands until Boris entered the tent.

He nodded to Ammon and gratefully accepted a steaming cup from Kyle. He took a long sip and sat on the corner of the cot next to Ammon.

"Where's Fulgid this morning?"

Ammon reached over and lifted the pillow to expose the sleeping dragon curled underneath. Fulgid had decided the space beneath the pillow was reserved for him and had made himself quite comfortable there. Ammon didn't mind it too much except for the snoring.

Boris peered at the sleeping dragon and chuckled. "Well, I'll be!" He shook his head. "He's definitely different, isn't he? So tell me, are you ready for today?"

One look from Ammon's bloodshot eyes and Boris nearly spit his drink across the tent. "Try to curb your enthusiasm just a bit eh?"

Ammon stared down at his hands. "Boris, I don't even know what I'm supposed to do! King Erik talked all night about the House of Les and politics and all these responsibilities! I don't understand any of it! All this because he thinks that I'm the son of Hale and Eleanor Les! To be truthful I'm not sure I fully believe that. Anyway, what difference does it make? Even if I am their son, the House is dead and anything of value was probably given away. What good is it to announce it to everyone that I might be an heir?"

Boris sat for a minute. "You really don't understand do you?"

Ammon shook his head. "Not at all."

"Well," Boris began. "I'm probably not the best one to explain it, but I'll tell you what I know. The king is convinced you are from the House of Les. That means the House is not dead, and it means you are the rightful heir to all the lands and properties of that House that were forfeited to the throne. You have just become a wealthy young man; very wealthy and a powerful figure in the political arena as well. Controlling that much currency in the kingdom makes any of your decisions carry a lot of weight in the Royal Court. That's not all though."

Boris' crystal clear blue eyes focused intently on Ammon's face. "Tirate was next in line for the throne as the only heir of Erik's house. Because he has attempted to assassinate Erik and declare himself king, he is a traitor and will be dealt with as such. His right to the throne has been cast out, which means the throne would be passed on to the next most powerful house. You, Ammon, are to be the next king of Gaul."

Ammon almost didn't notice Kyle refilling his cup.

***

Kyle had a seamstress waiting outside the tent when Ammon went out for his breakfast. He felt his face redden as she measured him from head to toe and wrinkled her nose at his leather shirt and breeches. Wordlessly she scrawled numbers across a small sheet of paper and hurried away, leaving him standing there, feeling like a fool.

Erik had already left by the time Ammon arrived for breakfast, so he mounded as much food as he could fit on a plate and sat outside with Fulgid to eat. Everyone in the camp seemed to be bustling about on some errand or task, and he watched with mild interest until he and Fulgid had picked the plate clean.

With their bellies full, Ammon nestled Fulgid into the crook of his arm and strolled towards the riverbank. Perhaps there he could do something useful like catch fish while he thought more about becoming a farmer. All the talk of being part of a big House would be forgotten once Erik was back on the throne and Ammon would be free to do as he pleased. After everything that had happened, he was certain the king would loan him enough money to buy a small lot of land. Perhaps he could raise animals or vegetables to pay off the debt.

He was almost halfway to the river when Theo caught sight of him.

"Ammon, wait up!"

Ammon sighed. So much for a relaxing day of fishing.

"I need to borrow your sword!"

Puzzled, Ammon looked up at Theo's face. "I left it next to my cot back at my tent. Are you going to give me lessons?"

Theo smiled. "No, not today. What about your collection of Fulgid's scales, is that there too?"

Ammon nodded. "I know I'm supposed to keep those safe, but I have no place to put them and I can't carry them around all the time!"

Theo chuckled. "No, I don't suppose you could in this camp. Don't worry, I'll take care of that for you right now. Anyway, I'll see you in a little while!"

Ammon scratched Fulgid's ears and watched as Theo trotted back to camp. "I guess we'll get to fish after all!"

Near the bank of the river, he stopped and selected one of several fishing poles leaning against a tree. Almost everyone took turns fishing to help provide the camp with food, but today the banks were deserted. He sat on a flat rock at the water's edge while Fulgid stretched out in a sunny spot and watched. The Olog River ran fast and deep, but it held a plentiful supply of fish. He leaned back, closed his eyes, and listened to the roar of the water as it passed by.

By noon he'd caught half a dozen good-sized fish and a few small ones that Fulgid ate before Ammon could even get them off the line. He was about to cast the line upstream again when a dark shadow fell over him and a voice rumbled like distant thunder.

"What are you doing?"

Startled, Ammon paused in mid-cast to look at Derek. "I'm fishing!"

"Oh." The big man bent down and gently scratched Fulgid behind the ears with a thick finger.

Ammon smiled. Kyle had explained that during the war, he'd found Derek as a baby beside the river and brought him home to his sister to raise as her own. Despite his fearsome appearance, the man was as gentle and as simple as a lamb. For some reason he had developed an amusing fascination towards Fulgid. No matter what he was doing, Derek always stopped to admire Fulgid and the little dragon seemed content to accept his doting.

"Oh!" The bald head jerked up, as if suddenly remembering. "They are looking for you."

Ammon sighed. He knew people would start looking for him eventually, but it was nice to get away for awhile. Reluctantly, he leaned the pole against a tree and handed the string of fish over to Derek's big hands.

"Would you bring these fish to the cooks? I'd better go to my tent and find out what I'm supposed to do."

Derek looked down at the fish and nodded. "Okay."

Ammon found Boris, Theo, and Kyle waiting impatiently by his tent. Boris' voice boomed across the yard at him.

"C'mon, boy! Where've you been?"

Ammon simply shrugged his shoulders. "Fishing."

Boris shook his head. "Probably the most important day of his life and he goes fishing! Unbelievable!" He motioned Ammon to the tent entrance where Kyle waited with a new set of breeches and a silk shirt. "You'll need to change into those. There is a set of boots in there too. We'll wait here for you."

He reluctantly took the clothes and ducked into the tent. After wearing thick leather for so long, the new clothes felt thin and uncomfortable, and he felt foolish as he stepped outside.

"Well, look at that!" Boris let out a low whistle. "He almost looks presentable!" He fingered Ammon's long hair and frowned. "Now if we could just get rid of most of this...but we don't have time for that now." He bent over and picked up the old clothes and handed them to Kyle. "Please take these out to the edge of camp...and burn them! Oh, and make sure we're not downwind!"

"Burn my clothes?" Ammon protested, but after one look from Boris his mouth snapped shut.

Theo laughed and placed a sympathetic arm over his shoulder. "You'd best get used to changes Ammon, there will be plenty more ahead for you!"

Ammon twisted his mouth silently. Once he started his own farm he could wear whatever he wanted. Perhaps he'd raise cows. There was always a demand for milk in the city.

"Come!" Boris turned and started walking towards the landing field. "It's time to go." Fulgid trotted beside Ammon as they walked towards the center of the camp, and as they got closer, Ammon could see what appeared to be a large gathering around King Erik. Every knight, cook, and smithy was standing there and Ammon felt his stomach tighten.

"What is going on?" He whispered to Boris.

Boris turned and looked at him in surprise.

"Don't you know? I thought Erik explained this to you? This is a recognition ceremony of The House of Les being raised anew. The king has decided that you'd receive his official blessing for acceptance into knighthood at the same time."

Ammon felt his nerves quiver as he looked out at the sea of faces. "What do I have to do?"

"Sinply do what he tells you to do." Boris patted him on the back reassuringly. "Don't worry, it'll be short. Erik hates long winded speeches."

Ammon followed Boris through the crowd until they stopped in front of Erik. Every eye seemed to stare down at him and his hands felt cold and sweaty. Fulgid nudged his leg gently and he realized Boris had knelt down in front of the king. Quickly, he dropped beside him and waited. The murmur of two hundred knights and countless other loyal subjects that had been brought into the camp suddenly ceased.

Erik's clear voice echoed over the field. "My people! Today we gather to recognize a lost member of the House of Les from the Royal Court of Gaul! For many years the House of Les has laid empty and silent until this moment, when its lone son and rightful heir retuned to resurrect it from the grave!"

Ammon kept perfectly still, his heart beat wildly in his chest.

"Ammon, son of Hale and Eleanor, rise!"

He stood and faced Erik. His knees felt weak and he was nauseous.

"To you I present your first armor and bestow upon you the honor and duty of the Dragon Knights of Gaul!"

Erik held up a glittering vest covered in the gold scales Ammon had saved from Fulgid, and he heard the crowd behind him gasp. Each scale was sewed on carefully and polished until it shined so bright it almost hurt to look at it. He slid the vest on and ran his hand down the front in awe. It was stunningly beautiful!

Erik picked Ammon's sword up from a table beside him. With the dull gray blade exposed, he raised it over his head. Slowly he brought it down and kissed the blade before deftly putting it into a scabbard covered completely in the dazzling golden scales. His voice rose again. "Knight Ammon of the House of Les, the Throne of Gaul recognizes you and welcomes you home!"

Erik handed the sword to Ammon and smiled as he fumbled to tie it to his belt. The crowd behind him roared in applause, and over the whistles and shouts, Erik spoke just loud enough for Ammon to hear.

"Welcome home son, welcome home!"

Fulgid suddenly leapt up on Ammon's shoulder and rose up on his hind legs to look down over the crowd. Ammon's thoughts turned to chicken farming. No, maybe not that. He hated chickens.

***

Tirate painfully hobbled across his chambers and slowly eased into the chair behind his desk. Never in his life had he ever been so miserable, but at least now he could walk without the assistance of a crutch. That infernal beast had sliced him up like a cabbage from head to toe leaving scarcely an inch of skin unscathed. Every movement was an excruciating reminder of how his carefully laid plans almost came crashing down. There was no way to hide his wounds from the Court, so he conveniently blamed it on a failed assassination attempt by his personal guards and had all four men executed. They had, after all, allowed both the dragon and the boy to escape.

For several days he refused audience with anyone and claimed his dragon had died, and he was in mourning. That gave him precious time to heal and reconsider his plans. At least he had the dragon long enough for all the members of the Court to see it. He was certain some of them may have had doubts, but none would dare question him now. Everything was in place and it was just a matter of days before he could officially claim the throne.

Erik's funeral was held after he'd located a suitably sized body to fit the coffin. It was a lucky coincidence that one of the executed guards had been about the right size. Traditionally when a king died his casket was left open for public viewing for at least a day, but he had no time for such nonsense and had it buried quickly in the courtyard beside the tombstone of the dragon Laud. Had anyone managed to look into the casket, the result would have been disastrous.

He shuffled through the papers stacked neatly in the middle of his desk. It had been difficult to stop the flow of rumors of Erik and the knights gathering in the north. Replacing all the palace pages with his own men eliminated most of the talk and allowed him to monitor and alter communications between the Houses. As an ever-growing number of palace staff abandoned the palace to join Erik, it had been easy to slip a spy in among them. Messenger pigeons arrived at regular intervals revealing exactly where they were camped, and how many were there.

Two hundred dragons had followed Erik into that wasteland, a formidable army under normal circumstances. But Tirate's craftsmen were working night and day to make a slew of the more portable versions of the large crossbows. It wouldn't be much longer before he had these moveable units hidden throughout the woodland surrounding the city and up and down a good portion of the riverbanks too. Several barges were being constructed with crossbows mounted on the decks. All would be stationed upstream and could be floated down with the current at a moment's notice.

Heavy recruiting of mercenaries and ruffians had increased the ranks of his army considerably. The majority of them were rough and uneducated, but he was preparing for a war and didn't have time to be choosy. As long as they could fight, he didn't care. As far as the public was concerned, it was a simple matter of spreading a few rumors about the western barbarian tribes stirring up trouble to explain the sudden disappearance of the dragons and the buildup of the army.

A soft knock at the door disturbed his thoughts.

"Yes, what is it?"

A guard reluctantly opened the door and entered. "I'm sorry to disturb you my lord, but a new message has arrived by pigeon."

"Give it to me and return to your post."

He waited until after the guard had left before he broke open the seal on the tiny letter. His eyebrows raised and he barked a laugh. So Erik has raised the boy up to lead the deceased House of Les? Surely the man had lost his mind! Of what use would that be out in the wilderness? That House was dead and its last remaining members disposed of fifteen years ago when he first began his plans to take the throne. As a young boy Tirate learned quickly that the best way to deal with opposition was elimination. He knew the House of Les would be a major obstacle to his ascension, so he'd paid a small fortune to have Hale and his wife killed. Closing his eyes, he could remember the last day he saw the man alive. Before leaving for the countryside, Hale was discussing his properties with King Erik and...

Tirate's eyes popped open. It couldn't be! The vision of Hale standing next to Erik floated in his mind. A small, muscular man with short blond hair and daunting blue eyes. That boy from the Nest bore a striking resemblance!

He leaned back in the chair and considered the implications. The House of Les would have a strong claim to the throne if there was proof the boy was somehow related. The Court considered Tirate the rightful heir, but if Erik or that horrid little dragon were seen inside the city, that claim could be challenged and the Court could opt to pass it to the boy. Erik was a threat that he already planned to eliminate. The dragon however, had proved more difficult to kill than he'd imagined, so this time he'd take a different approach. Kill the boy and the dragon dies, and any challenge from the House of Les dies with him.

He picked up a quill and dipped it into the ink pot. Fortunately, he'd had the foresight to make sure the spy he'd sent was also a well-trained assassin.

***

Boris found Ammon idly sitting in his tent while Fulgid lay at his feet, chewing on a clear rock. Kyle had just left a tray with a single steaming mug that filled the tent with its powerful aroma.

Boris inhaled deeply as he stepped inside. "Ready for some sword work son?"

Ammon barely nodded.

Boris sat in a chair opposite of Ammon and eyed the cup wistfully.

"So, what's wrong? You've been moping around like a neglected dragon since the recognition of your House and induction into knighthood two days ago."

Ammon's eyes barely lifted as he snorted softly. "You'll probably think I'm crazy."

Boris reached over and took the mug from the table. There was no sense letting it go to waste if he wasn't going to drink it. "I've seen crazy before. I'm not sure you qualify for that."

Ammon pulled his legs up to sit cross-legged on the bed. "Ever since I can remember I've been an orphan. I have a few faint memories of my mother's face, but little else. In the past few weeks my life has drastically changed, and I'm having a hard time believing any of it is real! Does anyone really expect that a simple tender could suddenly change to a knight and the head of a House? If what Erik tells me is true, then eventually I'll be king too! Just two days ago I learned that the people who were my family are all dead and I'll never get to know who they really were. I had always hoped that maybe I might have a relative alive somewhere. Even if I never found them, at least I had some hope."

Boris nodded sympathetically and swallowed the last of the contents in the mug.

"That's true Ammon, but you could also have lived the rest of your life and never have learned anything. Erik truly believes you are the last of a good family who just happened to be a powerful House in the Royal Court. So now you own lands and businesses that will provide income for you for the rest of your life. Maybe you should think of what you will do with your life because of that family. By accepting that, you carry on who and what they were, and then as long as you survive they aren't completely gone."

Ammon watched as Fulgid bit down on the rock and crushed it into tiny pieces with a loud crunch. "Yes, I know. I'm grateful, I really am! I just can't help but wonder how much simpler my life would be if I were the son of a merchant or a farmer or something. I know absolutely nothing about politics and even less about being king!"

Boris chuckled. "Well, in a way you are. Your house owns several farms in the southern country. Rather large ones too if I'm not mistaken, not to mention three or four very profitable warehouses in Gaul. As far as being a king, I have always thought the best politicians were the ones who weren't really politicians."

Ammon looked up hopefully. "I own farms? What kind of farms?"

Boris placed the empty mug back on the table. "Well, they're more like plantations really. Some of the best coffee plantations in all of Gaul."

Ammon smiled for the first time in days.

Boris laid a hand on his shoulder and winked. "Why don't you take a break from practice today? A man can't focus if his mind is elsewhere, and you my friend," Boris stood and stretched "are definitely elsewhere!"

Ammon nodded. "Thank you Boris."

"Thank me tomorrow when your training is twice as long!"

***

Ammon watched Boris leave and let the words sink in. He owned a plantation, which sounded just as good as a farm even though he didn't know what kind of vegetable coffee was. Still, if he could make a simple living with it, he'd be happy, and he could just tell Erik he didn't want the rest. He just had to figure out how to say it without sounding ungrateful.

He stared at the ceiling for awhile but couldn't concentrate. His mind kept wandering back to the plantation. He shook his head and sighed. "Come on Fulgid, lets go for a walk."

He lifted the tent flap and stepped out and Fulgid followed, still crunching on bits of rock. Nearby, Kyle was in a heated argument with the Maise, the head cook, over the preparation of food. Behind the cook stood her three assistants, including the pretty young woman that had smiled at Ammon during his escape from the palace.

She turned and curtseyed to him as he walked past, and Ammon couldn't help but notice her fair skin was as light as the white apron around her narrow waist. A sharp contrast to the black hair tied neatly in a loose bun. He blushed as he bowed clumsily then stumbled as he hurried away. Fulgid's ears twitched irritably and a tiny grumble rose from his throat. Ammon looked down in surprise at the little dragon bounding beside him. In his lessons Theo had told him most knights never married because of an intense jealousy felt by their dragons.

Halfway across the camp Fulgid was still growling and Ammon was glad they were out of earshot.

"Fulgid, hush!"

Softly, the little dragon growled again. "I said hush!"

A moment later came another almost inaudible, growl. Ammon rolled his eyes and shook his finger at the dragon. "Stop trying to get the last word!"

As they walked, Ammon became too distracted to notice Fulgid's last faint growl. Everyone he passed immediately stopped whatever they were doing and bowed until he went by. The first few times it was simply embarrassing, but it quickly became annoying instead. If this how he was going to be treated, he'd rather be alone!

With a sudden mischievous grin, he turned around and headed back towards The Wall. When he came to the crevice, he quickly looked around to make sure no one was watching, then picked up and lit one of the candles that Theo left on the ground after he'd retrieved the second saddle. He dropped to his knees and followed Fulgid into the hole. He was looking forward to exploring the cavern filled with crystals. He hadn't had time to look at them very closely before, and besides, it was much cooler in there than in the hot morning sun. Over an hour later he finally he emerged in the cavern covered in dust and dirt and he smiled in excitement.

Light was streaming from the small hole in the ceiling and reflected off the crystals, splashing a multitude of colors in every direction. He marveled at the hues of red, blue, and green as he made his way along the wall, careful not to step on any of the smaller formations.

The various sized and shaped crystals seemed to burst forth from the stones like flowers in a field. Most were yellow, but a few had blue, red, and green tints to them. Some were as big as pillars, but most were small enough to easily carry. In one spot he found a rock covered with filaments as thin as a spider's web and he was careful not to disturb their fragile existence.

The floor was littered with the broken shards of pieces that had fallen from their places and Ammon scooped a handful into his pouch. When he returned perhaps he would place them around the lanterns in his tent, and maybe he'd give one to the pretty young cook if Fulgid would let him get near her.

He watched as Fulgid scampered about investigating all the crystals within reach of his nose. Occasionally he'd find a small one to crunch between his teeth. Ammon shook his head at the dragon.

"You realize you're eating rocks don't you?" Fulgid ignored him as he searched for the next one to chew.

The wall turned in slightly, and Ammon followed it as it rounded a sharp corner strewn with rubble. The cavern extended down, like a large hallway, big enough for three men to walk side by side without touching and tall enough to ride a horse through. Curious, Ammon wondered if another cavern lay nearby, and he carefully made his way down an incline almost as steep as a staircase.

As the light dimmed, he held the candle up and followed the descending tunnel for a while. There were no crystals now, just the black stone walls and endless darkness beyond the candlelight. He was about to turn back when he heard a steady rushing sound. Standing still, he held his breath and listened. Wind maybe or perhaps water, but it was definitely coming from further down. With his curiosity piqued, he and Fulgid continued down. The passage lead straight down without twisting or turning for quite a ways before suddenly splitting in two. Both passages were roughly the same size and shape; the one to the right led back up at a steep incline, and the one to the left continued down towards the rushing sound that was now even louder.

Choosing the passage on the left, he continued, the candlelight flickering steadily on the walls. The noise steadily grew until it was almost a deafening roar. It definitely wasn't the wind, it had to be the fast moving water of the Olog River! The passageway began to lighten as he descended, and soon he blew out the candle. Sunlight reflected in where the passageway ended out the sheer walls of a canyon with the raging Olog flowing between.

The opening ended several feet above the swift water, and Ammon could feel the spray as it passed. He sat on the edge, pulled off his boots, and dangled his feet in the cool mist. Despite the raging current, it was peaceful here, and he sighed as he watched the water go by. As he sat tossing stones into the river, a brown speck caught his eye as it floated past. It no sooner got past the entrance of the passageway than it jerked and went opposite of the current, disappearing beneath the surface.

A moment later it happened again and this time Ammon recognized it as a cork that someone was using as a fishing bob! The camp must be just on the other side of the wall of the passage! Jumping to his feet, he held tightly to the wall and leaned out over the water as far as he dared. The river rounded the corner sharply, but he could just barely see the tips of fishing poles waving back and forth. The wall to the passage couldn't have been more than the thickness of his hand. He was in the hole!

Ammon almost giggled with delight. He could fish all he wanted with the privacy he desired, and yet was only inches away from the camp! He just needed to get through the crevice with a fishing pole and enough wood for a small fire! Rubbing his hands together, he looked down at Fulgid who lay hanging over the edge, snapping his jaws at the water splashing by.

"Come on Fulgid, we'll gather some firewood, and tomorrow we'll have ourselves a little picnic!"

He pulled his boots back on, lit the candle, and climbed back up the tunnel only stopping briefly at the fork in the passageway.

"We'll have to explore that another day. If we're gone for too long they might start looking for us."

Several hours later, he emerged from the crevice covered in dirt and trying to look as innocent as possible while collecting sticks and shoving them into the hole. When he though he had enough to cook a good sized fish, he and Fulgid headed back to camp. It was long past the midday meal, and both of them were hungry. Perhaps he could sneak something off into his tent.

Ammon knew most of the camp fished in the morning, so there would be a few poles lying around unused, and he quickly found a suitable one. His stomach was growling and he didn't feel like walking back to the crevice, so he went back to his tent. His tent was less than a pace-width away from the sheer rock face of The Wall, so he reached behind and leaned the pole against the stone and walked back nonchalantly.

He was about to go find the head cook and see what he could scrounge from her before supper when he saw Kyle out of the corner of his eye, striding towards him. The man would have a fit if he saw the dirt on Ammon's clothes and would lecture him while brewing more of that vile black bean-juice for him to drink. Quickly he turned the other way to make his escape and barely walked past the entrance to his tent when the flap suddenly opened and the pretty young cook stepped out. Stunned, Ammon stopped in mid step.

A look of surprise flashed in her eyes and then she smiled brightly and curtseyed. "My Lord, I've been waiting for you."

Feeling his face grow hot Ammon stammered. "Hi, uh, you've been waiting for me? Whatever for?"

She looked past Ammon at Kyle as he approached and smiled sweetly. "Yes, Lord, I thought maybe we could…talk?"

Ammon's mind raced. Talk? About what? What could he possibly talk about with this girl? Fulgid growled menacingly at his feet and he looked down at the little dragon peering suspiciously at the girl.

"Oh!" She quickly stepped away, pulling her skirts and apron back in alarm. "Is he viscous? Will he bite?"

Ammon shook his finger at Fulgid. "Shame on you! Be nice!"

Growling once more, Fulgid turned and lithely hopped onto Ammon's shoulder. He protectively wrapped his tail tightly around Ammon's waist and eyed the girl suspiciously.

Ammon fumbled for words. "He's uh, he's harmless. He just doesn't like strangers."

The girl tilted her head and looked curiously at Fulgid, but kept a safe distance away. Kyle finally reached them, his great bulk huffing and puffing as he tried to talk between gasps.

"Sire, you missed your midday meal! I tried to find you but Knight Boris said he gave you the day off from your sword practice!"

Ammon blushed again, this *sire* thing was getting ridiculous.

"I'm sorry, Kyle, I just went for a walk. I'll ask the cook for something to tide me over until the evening meal, don't worry."

Kyle made a short bow and eyed the young lady for a moment. A large smile slowly spread across his face and he looked back at Ammon.

"Yes, sire, I see you're in quite suitable company for such a quest!"

With a blatantly obvious wink, he bowed once more, and scurried off towards the king's tent.

The girl giggled softly. "Pardon me for saying so sire, but what a funny little man! If you'd like, I'm sure I can find something to satisfy you."

Ammon's stomach growled before he could answer.

"Come!" she said, grabbing his hand and carefully avoiding Fulgid's protective tail around his waist. "I'll fix you something myself"

Ammon followed silently as the girl led him across the camp. She chattered on in an endless stream, an expert in the rumors about the camp. Occasionally she pointed at someone and with hushed tones described the scandalous events of a blacksmith who argued with his wife because she spent too much time staring at the knights, or an errand boy caught stealing gold. Dazed, Ammon just listened politely and smiled.

Her name was Athaliah, but everyone called her Liah. At the cooks tent, she flitted from pot to pot like a honeybee in a field of flowers, picking out vegetables and bits of meat and placing it onto his plate. As she handed him the food, Fulgid clung stoically to his shoulder and watched Liah suspiciously. Ammon offered the little dragon a piece of meat but the dragon ignored it, his golden eyes fixated on the woman as she fluttered past. He waved the meat in front of the dragon's nostrils.

"You sure you don't want some, Fulgid?"

Liah stopped and looked at him. "I'm sorry, what did you say?"

Ammon shook his head. "I was asking Fulgid if he wanted some meat, but he won't take it." Fulgid's head peered over his shoulder, his scales glittering in the sunlight. "He's probably just full. He's been chewing on rocks all day, no doubt he's swallowed some."

Liah wiped her hands on her apron and sat down on the log to Ammon's right. Her voice was soft as silk. "He really is quite pretty. Like living gold!"

Ammon felt Fulgid slowly creep over his shoulder and beneath his chin.

"You should see him in the firelight; it's like a million candles all at once."

Ammon reached up to scratch the dragon's ear and found it pinned tightly to his head. Through the link he could feel the distrust oozing from Fulgid; equal parts of distrust and dislike.

Liah smiled and reached out to touch the shining scales, and Ammon felt Fulgid growl as his entire body tensed. Ammon was about to stop her when Maise, the head cook appeared from the side of the tent standing in front of them with a sharp frown on her face and a plump hand on each hip as she looked down her nose at Liah.

"I sent you to peel potatoes nearly two hours ago, and here you sit! That pot is still empty and you'll be there 'til midnight if that's what it takes!"

Liah jumped to her feet, her face clouded with anger. She said nothing as she took a large knife from one of the tables and disappeared behind one of the tents.

Maise dipped her head at Ammon. "I'm sorry sire. If she's been a bother to you I'll have her dealt with. She's only been under my charge for a year or so and she seems to think she's above of her station; above everyone's station!"

The large woman shook her head in frustration and picked up a bit of meat from the plate beside Ammon. Before he had time to think, she held it out to Fulgid who happily took it from her fingers. Ammon's jaw dropped.

Maise smiled down at the two of them. "In all my years, I've never seen such an adorable beast! His color is truly magnificent! Mark my words sire, this one will make history! I'd stake my best rolling pin on it!"

Ammon didn't agree or disagree. He was too shocked at the sudden change in Fulgid's behavior. His body had relaxed and he was licking his lips as if to ask for another morsel from the cook. Ammon stood and assured Maise that Liah had not bothered him in the least and that he'd actually enjoyed her company, which was the truth.

Maise only nodded as she stuffed bits of meat cheese into a small loaf of bread and handed it to him. "Supper will be ready soon sire. Will this keep you both until then?"

Ammon smiled. "Yes, thank you."

Fulgid devoured both portions before they were out of sight of the cook.

Ammon strolled back to his tent with Fulgid riding high on his shoulder, snapping at any horse flies that ventured to close. He sighed. If all dragons responded this way when a girl showed interest, he could certainly see why the knights stayed single. The thought of never getting married suddenly occurred to him. He certainly wasn't ready for that yet, but when the time came he wanted to be the one to make the decision, not his dragon. Perhaps there was a way to make Fulgid accept Liah? Maybe if he saw her on a regular basis Fulgid would get used to her and…

The little dragon's tail suddenly slapped Ammon lightly in the face. Stunned, he looked up to see the dragon staring back at him.

"AMMON!"

It had been awhile since he'd heard that golden voice echo inside his head and he smiled as he concentrated his thoughts into words. "FULGID!"

The dragon put his nose so close to Ammon's face that it touched. "AMMON TRUST FULGID!"

Ammon stumbled. There was no mistaking what he'd heard; the voice was as clear as a bell. For the first time he heard more than just his name! Stunned, he stared at the little dragon for several minutes until he realized Fulgid was waiting. He focused on the golden eyes and spoke into the clear bubble nestled deep inside his head.

"AMMON WILL TRUST FULGID!"

Fulgid relaxed and went back to chasing the horseflies that buzzed around their heads.

Ammon couldn't decide if he should tell Boris and Theo what happened. He'd mentioned to them before that Fulgid had called his name and they simply dismissed it as he'd just felt the dragon's emotions. He frowned. How can you prove something no one else can hear? The more he considered it, the more realized it would be best to keep it to himself rather than risk losing the trust and respect that he had developed with them.

They walked towards the landing field where Theo was busy stripping the saddlebags from his dragon, Ebony. The black dragon was crouched down so Theo could reach the girth buckles, and as they approached, she turned her huge black face towards them. Fulgid leapt from Ammon's shoulder and raced across the field. Ebony lowered her head to the ground and Fulgid skidded to a halt in front of her. Standing on his hind legs, he stretched to look into her eye.

Over a week ago Ammon had learned Ebony was the dragon that had laid the brood of eggs Fulgid hatched from. Even more surprising was that Boris' dragon, Ellis was the sire, and Ammon couldn't help but wonder how big Fulgid would grow with such large parents. Theo had taken it upon himself to teach Ammon about dragons, and according to him, the offspring usually resembled the sire more than the dam. Color however, was not something anyone had ever been able to predict reliably, and in Fulgid's case, none of the rules applied.

Free of the saddle, Ebony rolled in the grass sending clods of dirt flying into the air. Fulgid followed closely, doing his own version of rolling.

Theo snickered. "Like mother like son, eh?"

Ammon nodded and smiled as he helped carry the saddlebags to a large tent on the side of the landing field. Just inside, Shane sat at a table busily making a list of the supplies they still needed. The camp population had swelled far beyond the original two hundred knights as each day Theo and the others brought back more refugees. Although no one had actually said the words yet, a war was coming. Ammon didn't want to think about it, but it crept into his thoughts often. It was going to happen, it was only a matter of time.

Their camp was in a fairly safe area, protected by the rough terrain that would slow any sizable army to a crawl. Unfortunately, that same terrain limited them to whatever supplies could be flown in by dragon. The woodland wildlife and river supplied some food, but not nearly enough. It was already late summer, and soon the leaves would start to change color, and the nights would turn cool. The thin tent walls wouldn't provide much insulation to the coming cold, and the dragons needed a warm place as well or they would perish. Everyone knew they'd have to move against Tirate soon or find another place to spend the winter.

Shane looked up from his papers with a broad grin. "Ammon! Nice to see you! Have you come to rescue me from the confines of my tent and paperwork?" He laughed heartily. Looking around the floor he added. "Where's my little dragon?"

Since the day they arrived at the camp, Shane had taken on a grandfatherly position to Ammon and called Fulgid *his* little dragon. Ammon didn't mind, it was rather comical to see the old man doting on Fulgid as if he were a favorite child.

"He's out romping in the field with Ebony, probably terrorizing grasshoppers and field mice."

Shane leaned back in his chair and smoothed back the few strands of gray hair he had left on his head. "Plenty of those to be had, for sure. Too bad we can't feed a camp full of people with them." He looked up at Theo and sighed. "We're getting into a bad situation, Theo. A few more weeks and we'll have exhausted all our supplies completely. Without a massive raid on the palace, we'll be hard pressed to save ourselves, never mind retake the city. The daily supplies you bring in are barely enough to feed one or two dragons a day. Time is running out, quickly."

Theo tossed his gloves on the table. "I know, Shane, I know. We can't get anywhere near the city now. Tirate has his defenses placed deep into the surrounding woods. By the time we see them, they've already let loose a volley of shafts and we're hard pressed to avoid being shot out of the sky. I keep heading further and further up the river to the outlying towns to get supplies. Each time I go, I find he's hidden more of those confounded crossbows in the woods. As hard as dragon scales are, they'd punch right through. We're defenseless against them!"

Theo sank into a chair and the two men started to discuss rationing. Even Ammon knew that wouldn't help much. It might prolong the inevitable by a week or so, maybe less. The only true options were attack Tirate or find a place where food and shelter were available, and soon. Unable to contribute to the conversation, Ammon excused himself.

Fulgid was outside waiting for him and followed him back to his own tent. Lost in thought, Ammon decided he would investigate that second passageway in the morning. Perhaps he could find more saddles or something that would help their situation. He wasn't hungry after all the food given to him by Liah and Maise, so he decided to go to bed early. He would get up early while everyone still slept. Maybe he'd be back before breakfast was over if it was a short tunnel.

He lay down on the cot with Fulgid, and he let his mind wander as he drifted off to sleep. Eventually his thoughts turned to Liah's smiling face and then the clear voice whispered gently. "TRUST FULGID!" He thought no more of her as he slept.

***

Late that night, a shadow slipped into the storage tent and searched through the supplies for one particular bag of flour sealed with a strange wax seal imprinted on it. Carefully replacing it with another bag, the shadow left the tent and found a secluded spot to remove the hidden scroll in the seam of the bag. Lighting a small candle, the figure read the coded orders before burning the paper and crumbling it to ash. Silently, and with practiced stealth, the figure moved back into the camp. The orders to kill King Erik were no surprise, but killing the boy with the dragon was. Not that it made any difference, it was just another job. The big problem would be trying to get past that lizard of his without getting caught.

Chapter 9
The Lost City

The stars were still shining brightly when Ammon left his tent with a small sack over his shoulder. Fulgid followed close behind him as he hurried all the way to the crevice. He took one of the candles from the sack and lit it before he tossed the sack into the hole and crawled in after Fulgid. Pushing the sack in front of him, he slowly and tediously climbed until at last he exited into the crystalline cavern. As he walked he held the candle high, and the flickering light danced across a million facets that cast shadows in all directions. He carefully picked his way across the floor until he found the opening in the wall to the passageway.

He covered ground at a fair pace and reached the split in the tunnel fairly quickly. He paused to light a fresh candle before heading up the unknown passage. Unlike the

156

steep descent of the tunnel leading out to the river, this passageway was mostly straight with just a barely perceptible incline. After an hour and a half of walking and several more spent candles, he could finally see a dim light ahead and he quickened his pace. Fulgid stayed diligently at his side the whole time, only stopping occasionally to sniff the air. As Ammon got closer to the light source, he found the passageway had caved in. Large boulders blocked his way except for a tiny fist-sized hole near the top where a thin ray of sunlight streamed in. Ammon climbed the rubble and began to pull enough of the smaller rocks out of the way for him to squeeze through.

Fulgid scurried out first and waited for Ammon to follow. With his eyes closed to keep out the falling dirt, Ammon shoved his way through the hole and wiggled his way out, tearing a large hole in his silk shirt in the process. He sat with his feet dangling in the hole and opened his eyes as a light breeze blew warm air across his dusty face. He was sitting in the middle of a steep grassy hill surrounded by trees and a few large boulders. He stood up and shook the dirt from his hair as he looked around.

The hillside overlooked a lush green valley and spread across the entire area was the ruins of a giant city unlike anything he'd ever seen. Massive buildings covered in vines stood taller than any building in Gaul, their high domed roofs surrounded what was obviously a palace in the center. Its high walls and spires were unmistakable. Ammon smiled. This was even better than a few old saddles! This was shelter for the winter with room for dragons and all!

The temptation to roam the ruins in the early morning light was almost irresistible, but he decided to go back and report his discovery. This could very well delay the war between the king and Tirate until the knights were ready. He slid back through the hole with Fulgid and nearly ran the entire way back. The sooner everyone in the camp could get to a shelter and find food, the better. He practically tumbled onto the ground when he finally exited the crevice at the camp.

Breakfast was still cooking, and most of the camp were still in their tents preparing for the day. He wiped his dirty hands on the tattered remains of his shirt. He should have just enough time to wash and change his clothes before the meal was served. Then he could tell both Erik and Boris while they ate. He tossed his sack over his shoulder and grinned as he jogged back towards his tent with Fulgid bouncing at his heels.

As he got closer, he saw a group of men heading down to the river, and he remembered the fishing pole he had stashed behind his tent. He still had time to bring the pole back before he changed his clothes. No matter what was on the other end of that tunnel, meals had to be gathered and people needed to be fed. He dropped the sack by the entrance of his tent and hurried around to the back. As he rounded the corner, he barely avoided running headfirst into Liah who was crouched beside the tent wall. Fulgid instantly started growling. Surprised, Ammon backed up a step.

"What are you doing back here?"

Obviously startled, Liah straightened and smoothed a fold in her dress with her left hand.

"Lord Ammon! I didn't expect..."

She reached over with her left hand, grabbed his arm and pulled him closer. Her blue eyes gazed up at him and she smiled. Suddenly a snarling Fulgid charged past, striking Liah squarely in the stomach and knocking her back. Stumbling, she tried to regain her balance, but her feet became tangled in the line of the fishing pole, and with a loud shriek, she fell flat on her back. Ammon watched in horror as Fulgid pounced.

***

Before he left his tent, Boris washed the sweat from his face with a damp cloth and pulled a clean shirt on. After finishing his routine hour of sword practice with Theo he was looking forward to breakfast with Erik. "Why don't you join us this morning Theo? Perhaps you can suggest some ideas we haven't thought of yet."

Theo chuckled as they walked towards Erik's tent. "I seriously doubt I could come up with anything that you haven't already considered."

Boris shook his head. "If only we had more time…"

A loud scream pierced the air from behind Ammon's tent just as they were passing by and, with a speed that belied his size and age, Boris bolted around the side and skidded to a stop just in time to witness a strange sight.

Ammon, covered in filth, was down on his knees and desperately trying to pull his golden dragon off of a screaming bundle of rags that was spouting an impressive array of curses and insults, punctuated with squeals of anger. Bits of shredded cloth floated in the air and fell like snow all around them.

With a tremendous bellow usually reserved for battle, Boris charged, shoving past Ammon to grab Fulgid by the scruff of the neck. With a yank, he removed the dragon and held him at arms length. Fulgid stopped squirming and looked at Boris innocently. Ribbons of torn cloth hung down from his claws and teeth, while the weeping mass of rags at Boris' feet wailed and screeched as if still under attack. He looked over his shoulder to see Theo help Ammon to his feet. The bewildered looking young man was panting for breath and equally covered in shreds of dress.

With a voice like cold steel, Boris growled. "Would someone like to tell me WHAT is going on here?"

Ammon just looked up and spread his hands. "I don't know! I found Liah behind my tent, and the next thing I know Fulgid is attacking her!"

Boris handed Ammon the little dragon who was once again growling at the girl laying on the ground. "Dragons don't attack without reason. That's one of the first lessons you learn about dragons. You'd know that if you had paid attention." He turned to the girl lying on the ground and offered her a hand. "Now little missy, perhaps you can explain what you're…"

A flash of steel whipped past Boris' face a split second before Fulgid shot from Ammon's arms and once again onto the girl. Boris fell against the stone in surprise. A neat slice from his ear to the tip of his chin appeared on his lower jaw. Reaching up, he touched the side of his face and stared in disbelief at the crimson stain spreading across the front of his shirt. With a shout, Theo leapt forward, grabbed some of the torn apron from the ground and pressed it tightly to the wound.

Boris took the rags from him. "I'm ok, but by my dragon's teeth, what is going on here?"

The two stared down at the girl on the ground. Fulgid's razor sharp teeth were completely wrapped around her wrist, and in her hand lay a large knife almost as long as her forearm. Every time she moved, the dragon tightened his jaws a little tighter until she stopped. After a few moments of struggling, she finally held still, a look of fierce defiance dancing in her eyes.

Theo lifted the rag from Boris' neck and inspected the wound. "She nearly took your head off, another inch and she would've slit your throat."

Boris snorted. "Bah, I've cut myself shaving worse than this, but I have to say, looking at her condition, I think I got the better end!"

Theo laughed lightly and patted Boris on the back with a grin. "Time for you to go see your seamstress friend again! Don't worry, I'll take care of this pile of linen for you." He jerked his thumb at Liah.

Boris genuinely chuckled as he held the cloth to his face. "Well, Ammon, that dragon of yours saved both our bacon today!"

Confused, Ammon stared at the blood soaked cloth. "Saved us? What just happened? I don't understand!"

Boris exchanged glances with Theo. "She's an assassin Ammon. If Fulgid hadn't intervened, you'd be dead right now."

Ammon shook his head. "Liah? She wouldn't hurt me! She wouldn't hurt anyone! She's just the cook's helper! There has to be some mistake!"

Boris sighed and pointed to the tent wall where Liah had been waiting. "Then why would she slit the back of your tent open this early in the morning when most people are still asleep? I'm sorry Ammon, but with a knife like that, she was here to kill you. There is no denying it."

Ammon looked at the back of his tent where a long vertical slice in the tent wall gently fluttered in the light morning breeze.

Boris turned to Theo. "I saw Kyle going into the king's tent as we headed over here. He would have yelled if anything had been amiss, but I'll check on him after I get stitched. I suppose we'll all be late for breakfast." He gently squeezed Ammon's shoulder then walked away.

In disbelief, Ammon searched Liah's face and she sneered back at him and spat. Almost instantly she squealed as Fulgid tightened his jaws around her arm. Nauseated and unable to bear watching any more, Ammon turned and walked away. He just wanted to pick up the fishing pole; how did things go so wrong from there? Theo said knights rarely ever marry. Perhaps that wasn't such a bad thing after all.

Ammon quietly accompanied Boris to the seamstress' tent. They made a quick stop to inform Maise about her helper, and Boris picked up two mugs of the foul black drink and handed one to Ammon as they walked down past the rows of tents. The seamstress was a short but pleasant older woman who rolled her eyes at the gash in Boris' face before rummaging through her box of sewing supplies to find a sharp needle.

Ammon watched her handiwork with the thread and sipped at his mug until it was dry. This time he didn't even care how bad it tasted as long as it took his mind off what just happened. The seamstress insisted that Boris not talk while she worked, so Boris listened as Ammon told him about the passageway leading out the other side of the mountains to the city ruins. Boris' eyebrows raised higher and higher and Ammon couldn't tell if it was from his discovery or if the seamstress had sewed his face that way.

When she finished and had put away her sewing kit, Boris stood. "Thank you again, Mabel." Stooping down, he kissed her gently on the cheek.

The woman looked up at him and firmly planted her hands on her hips. "Pah! You can thank me by not doing it again! I won't always be around to sew you up Boris! Just remember that!"

She shoved a roll of clean cloth into his hands and barked instructions on keeping the wound clean and bandaged. Before he could leave, she made him promise to return every day to let her examine the stitches until they were removed. Boris nodded his head obediently, and she shooed them both out of her tent.

Boris muttered to himself as they walked back, and Ammon decided not to ask questions. It seemed he was just as confounded by women as Ammon was.

Kyle had breakfast waiting for them in the king's tent, and Erik's eyes widened in concern at the sight of the fresh stitches in Boris' face. "Theo told me what happened. Are you alright?"

With a half smile, Boris sat down and picked up his fork. "Don't worry. It isn't as bad as it looks." He winced as he attempted to chew a few bites, then reluctantly pushed his plate away. "Anyway, Ammon has been exploring again, and I think you should hear what he's found this time."

Erik peered over his cup at Ammon and raised an eyebrow. "Exploring again, eh? You seem to be very much like Boris and his brother were when they were your age; always looking for mischief and usually finding more trouble than they could handle! Well, what sort of treasure have you found this time?"

Ammon glanced at Boris. It was hard to believe the man ever did anything to break the rules or found something he couldn't handle. Turning back to Erik, he cleared his throat and described everything he'd seen in detail. When he was done, the king pointed his fork at Boris.

"I think you should take some men and investigate these ruins as soon as possible. If the wall by the river is that thin, you may be able to make a hole big enough to walk through wearing all your armor. I'd like you to take Ammon and Fulgid with you, as they seem pretty adept at finding things. Besides, despite how small he is, having Fulgid would be helpful."

He turned his fork towards Ammon and continued. "I've noticed none of the other hatchlings seem anywhere near as mature as Fulgid is. His reaction to that cooking girl shows his perception of a threat is as acute as a full-grown dragon. Ammon, make sure you pay attention to how Fulgid is feeling, he won't lead you astray."

Ammon nodded and Erik dropped the fork on his plate and frowned. "I'll deal with the assassin myself."

Ammon cleared his throat. "Sire, uh, what will happen to her?"

A long silence filled the tent. Finally the king spoke; his voice hard as steel. "The penalty for attempted assassination is death."

Ammon felt the blood drain from his face, and his stomach felt like he'd been punched. "Is that really necessary? Couldn't she be punished another way?"

Erik sighed and looked up at Boris who was studying the contents of his mug. "According to Theo, they found several more knives on her, including several high quality throwing spikes. She is undoubtedly a professional assassin and given another chance, she would not hesitate in the least to kill you, or me, or anyone. It would be dangerous to keep her alive, Ammon."

Ammon slumped in the chair. "But she didn't kill me!"

Erik studied Ammon thoughtfully. "I suppose the crime was committed against you, therefore you should have some say in the matter. Without the luxury of a prison to hold her, the only other option I have is to put her under constant supervision. I think I know of one place we can put her where she can be watched day and night and perhaps work off some small portion of her penance."

Boris frowned. "What do you have in mind?"

Erik smirked as he picked up his fork again and stabbed at a sausage on his plate. "We've had two hundred dragons confined to this one area for weeks and not a single wheelbarrow in the whole camp. When you consider that each pile is as big as a full-grown man, and all we have are a few small shovels? I think we can keep that young lady busy moving manure for quite some time. Besides, in an open field surrounded by dragons she could hardly leave without them noticing."

Boris laughed and slapped the table with his hand so hard his plate jumped. "Aye, now that just might be a fate worse than death!"

***

Ammon flipped open the flap to his tent and walked inside. Fulgid was stretched out on the cot with his head on the pillow and bits of shredded cloth still clinging to his body. With a deep sigh Ammon flopped down beside him and began to idly pick away at the threads wedged between his scales.

"You were right Fulgid. I don't know how you knew, but you were right."

Fulgid curled his head around and placed it on Ammon's lap. Large amber eyes peered up sympathetically. Ammon pulled him onto his lap the rest of the way and scratched his ears.

"I just don't understand why all this is happening to me? I never asked for any of it! All I ever wanted was to live a quiet, peaceful life."

The dragon's nose gently touched his. Ammon smiled and nodded. "Yes, with you."

A feeling of joy rippled across the bubble nestled deep within his consciousness, and Fulgid yawned contently before sliding off his lap and rolling onto the pillow.

"Don't get too comfortable, Erik wants us to show some of the knights the ruins."

He pulled out the glittering armored vest from under the bed and held it up. The edge of each scale had been carefully wrapped in leather then sewn in an overlapping pattern over a heavy cloth. There had only been enough scales to make a vest, but the next time Fulgid shed he should have enough for a full suit of armor. Then it would be practically impervious to arrows or knives unless one managed to slip past the stitching.

He slipped the vest over his head and pulled it down into place. "Well, dragon, ready to go exploring?"

Fulgid hopped to the floor and waited as Ammon belted on his new scabbard and slid the dull gray sword into place. He stepped out of the tent and into the sunshine where Boris and Theo were waiting with two other knights.

Boris whistled at the sight of the vest as it sparkled in the light. "Boy, you'll be visible for miles in that getup!"

Ammon smiled down at Fulgid sitting at his feet. "Yeah, but I'll be the safest one there!"

Boris touched his bandaged face and grinned. "Aye, that's probably true. At least against maidens with bad intentions!" He slapped Ammon's shoulder playfully and nodded to the two other knights. "This is Chanel and Cen, they'll be accompanying us. Now, show me this tunnel of yours. I wish to see a city!"

Ammon lead the way down to the riverbank and pointed to where the Olog River plunged violently through the large hole in the mountain wall. Boris looked at the river for a moment and spoke softly to Ammon.

"Men have rode this river and fallen through that opening never to return. No dragon has ever been able to fly high enough to make it over the mountains before the cold turned them back. It has always been said that beyond these mountains is the end of the world, the natural boundary at the edge of creation. It has been many years since I've adventured outside of Gaul. I'm looking forward to seeing this new world."

Ammon watched the river rush past. He doubted anyone could survive those waters to make it to the other side. Yet someone had built a city there, a city that now lay in ruins. Who were they and what happened to them? As his curiosity grew a twinge of excitement tightened in his stomach. The sooner they got there, the sooner they'd find out.

Boris ran his hand along the stone leading down to the river's edge, occasionally thumping it with his fist. He thought for a moment, then picked up a good-sized rock and heaved it at the wall. It struck hard, and a hollow crunch sounded as a small hole appeared. A few more tosses and the rock went clear through.

Boris examined the hole with interest. "Look at the marks on the stone. See how smooth it is at the bottom compared to higher up? The level of water must have been much higher at one time. Over the years the river must have changed course, and as the river shifted, the spring floods knocked down and covered the tunnel entrance until nothing could be seen. Looking at it now, there is no indication of a tunnel on the other side, just the appearance of a sheer face of solid rock."

He picked up another stone and used it as a hammer to widen the opening until they could step through. Once inside he whistled as he looked around.

"Someone made this tunnel! See the chisel marks? And it's big enough for a dragon to crawl through, although it'd be a bit tight for Ellis."

Ammon nodded as he looked at the marks on the stone in wonder. They hadn't been visible in the candlelight. "The whole tunnel is this size or bigger all the way out to the other side to where the opening caved in."

Boris slapped him on the shoulder with a grin. "Well, let's go see it! Lead the way!"

They lit their lanterns and followed Ammon up the tunnel with Fulgid bounding just ahead of them. Within hours they reached the other end, and Fulgid perched himself on a boulder and watched while Ammon and the others took turns clearing the exit. Once they had removed enough rocks around the opening that they could all climb out, the little dragon scampered out first.

Once more, Ammon stood on the grass of the hillside looking down at the ruins of the city in amazement. The others were strangely quiet, cautiously checking their armor and swords before beginning their descent into the city with Fulgid frolicking ahead of them. As they walked, Boris gave instructions to each of them to follow once they entered the ruins. He and Ammon would take the lead, choosing the path through the city. Chanel and Cen would follow behind them and watch the rooftops and windows for movements. Theo would bring up the rear in case they were followed. Boris wanted Ammon to pay particular attention to Fulgid, as he'd likely be their first warning of any danger. With firm grips on the hilts of their swords, Ammon and the four men followed the golden dragon through the decayed city's gates.

***

Tirate gritted his teeth as he watched his men struggle against the current as they floated the barges down the Olog. He already lost two men to the river and a third had been left behind on the riverbank with a broken leg. Transporting the heavy crossbows down the river was risky, but it was faster than having it carried across the harsh terrain of the wasteland. He watched as his men on the riverbanks eased the barges downstream using long ropes and pulleys. He had to get into position before Erik's dragons had time to react.

The scouts had located a clearing up ahead large enough for them to unload the smaller, portable weapons, and from there it was only a two-day march to Erik's pitiful camp. The dragons couldn't escape over the mountains and with his crossbows lining the river and dispersed throughout the woods, Erik was neatly trapped between Tirate's hammer and the anvil of the mountains.

He smiled and felt the skin stretch across his face as the new scars slowly healed. It was time to remove those beastly dragons from the world altogether. With any luck, they'd all be extinct in less than a week. Just the thought of what was to come made him giddy. If his assassin hadn't already taken care of his dear Uncle Erik and the boy, then his new weapons surely would. His laughter echoed into the trees and was swallowed by the roar of the mighty Olog River.

***

Derek reluctantly plucked an arrow from his quiver and laid it across his longbow. As much as he hated killing, he was a skilled archer with an uncanny ability to move his massive body silently through the thickest woods. Although he preferred eating fruits and vegetables, the camp would benefit greatly from the wild boar he'd been tracking since yesterday. The boar had made a well-worn path that crisscrossed all over this area, and now Derek could hear the distant sounds of movement coming from down the path. Patiently he waited. Eventually it would show itself and start rooting for grubs under the tree stump twenty paces away. Derek checked the tension of the bowstring. His aim had to be good, very good. A wounded boar was not something he wanted to deal with; they were dangerous enough as it was.

Leaning behind a large boulder, he slowly peeked over the top and frowned. It wasn't a boar that came down the pathway, it was two men dragging a wheeled skid with a large canvas bundle tied to it. As they got closer he could hear them curse at each other as they strained to pull the wagon over the rocky terrain.

He cupped his ear and listened to them as they talked. It was difficult to hear the entire conversation, but what he did hear was enough to make his eyes widen.

"…stuck out here in the middle of nowhere! Left here to be sucked dry by bloodthirsty mosquitoes I tell ya! We'll not be seein the inside of a pub until winter!"

"Oh shuddup, will ya? I'm no happier about it than you are, but Tirate wants these dragon killers set up and in place for the attack. Now unless you'd like to be on the front line with the rest of the squadron…"

"NO!…I mean, no, this is fine!…It's just that they took all the good food and left us with dried rations! Not even a drop of ale! We can't live on that! A man's gotta have sumthin else!"

The words slowly sunk into Derek's brain. A squadron armed with dragon killers? He leaned back against the rock and tried hard to think. It was always so much easier when someone simply told him what needed to be done. He'd always needed help to figure out things that seemed to come naturally to everyone else, but now he was alone. He knew what he'd just heard must be important. Anything named dragon killer had to be bad. He ran his massive fingers through his thick white beard and wished Boris or Theo were with him.

With a deep sigh, he decided the best thing he could do is bring all the information he could back to the camp. He drew back his bow, peered around the rock, and aimed at one of the men. With a soft thunk the arrow sank deep into the man's boot and he fell to the ground with a scream. A second later the other man lay beside him with a matching arrow in his foot and the two howled in pain.

Soon Derek was striding through the woods dragging the skid behind him with both men gagged and tightly strapped atop the canvas. If he hurried, he could make it back to camp by the end of the day. Boris would know what to do with them. At least he wouldn't have to kill any boars today. He puckered his lips and began to whistle the repeating three notes of the only tune he knew. It helped to pass the time and after a few hours of walking he wondered if the two men tied to the skid liked the sound. Every time he started the song over, they grunted and groaned past their gags.

Chapter 10
Crystals

It was obvious to Ammon as they passed through the gates of the city that it had been many years since it had been abandoned. Trees nearly as big as his waist had forced themselves through the cobblestone streets and collapsed buildings had blocked off entire roads with their moss-covered stones. Fulgid strolled leisurely ahead as if nothing were unusual. A few squirrels chattered noisily at them, and once they startled a deer grazing on a patch of clover, but otherwise the city appeared lifeless.

They crossed a large square to a dusty fountain standing in the center. The once-polished marble basin was overflowing with dead leaves and dirt. Grass grew up so high it nearly hid the small dragon statue in its center. Theo's voice echoed down the empty alleys as he hurried to join them. "This place is huge! It has to be at least twice the size of Gaul!"

Boris nodded in agreement. "At least twice as big or bigger, and this is just the southern side, we've yet to even reach the center where the palace is." He shaded his eyes from the sun as he looked up at the unusual architecture of the tall buildings. "My question is, what happened to the people?"

Ammon felt his heart skip a beat. He'd been so fascinated by the ruins, it never occurred to him to wonder what happened to the people who built it. How many people had lived here? He peered at the rows of blocky buildings that stretched as far as he could see. There was easily room for thousands, and this was only part of the city!

Boris pointed inside one of the broken doorways that had rotted off its hinges. "Look, you can see there is, or was…rotting furniture still inside. We passed a blacksmith shop a few rows back. Did you notice the rusted tools still hanging on the walls? Have you ever known a blacksmith to leave his tools behind when he moved?"

Ammon pointed up one of the long streets. "There aren't any remains of any wagons in any of the roads…"

Boris stroked his moustache thoughtfully. "Which means they left in a hurry and didn't have time to take much with them."

Cen leaned forward and cleared his throat. The tall, thin knight was perhaps in his thirties, but his face carried the lines of a man much older. His narrow jaw sported a rather unfortunate beard, and he nervously fingered a tiny cross medallion that hung around his neck. "What would cause an entire city to flee so suddenly?"

Boris shrugged his wide shoulders. "The gates were rotted, but not broken, so I doubt it was an invading army. Whatever happened, it was a long time ago, judging from the size of the trees growing in the street." He paused. "I doubt whoever or whatever caused it is still here. There is nothing left of any value but crumbling buildings and rotting wood. Still, I'd like to see the palace; there may be something of use there."

They walked in silence towards the center of the city. Every street they passed looked the same as the last; dilapidated buildings and roads filled with brush and trees growing from any place the roots could work between the stones. When they reached the palace, the thick wooden doors of the main entrance still stood haphazardly against each other.

Boris smoothed his moustache with his thumb and chuckled. "Should we knock or just go in?" He kicked at the latch and jumped back as the doors disintegrated into a pile of dusty fragments, leaving only the rusty iron hinges hanging in midair. Boris grinned as he stepped over the splintered door. "Maybe I shouldn't have knocked after all!"

Ammon followed him inside and gasped. The palace was in considerably better shape than any of the other buildings they'd seen so far. Large and well built, the high quality craftsmanship still held the elegant stone walls firmly in place. Towering above them was a graceful domed roof lined with massive ivory colored beams, and along the walls, sunlight streamed through the colored glass of unbroken windows. Furniture was neatly placed throughout the room, and although rodents had chewed through most of the leather cushions, the wood remained solid. A thick coating of dust blanketed everything, muting the colors to a dull gray.

Theo whistled softly in surprise. "This is bigger than the Hold in Gaul!"

Boris nodded and smiled at Ammon's confused look. "The Hold is where we keep the dragons during the winter to keep them warm." He ran his fingers through the layers of dust on one of the tables. "I haven't seen anything that appears threatening in the least. Lets look around a bit to see what we can find."

Ammon followed Fulgid down a hallway and into a large room with a long table surrounded by chairs blanketed with cobwebs. High above them hung a crystal chandelier, unlit for decades. Tapestries covered the walls except for the far end where a large fireplace with an ornate mantle dominated the room. Above the fireplace hung a painting, and Ammon felt his jaw drop as he got closer. The others had to see this!

He ran to the door and yelled for the others then climbed onto a chair and cleared away the cobwebs he could reach until they arrived.

Boris got there first; the rest followed closely behind him. "Did you find something, Ammon?"

"Yes!" Ammon jumped off the chair and pointed at a finely painted picture above the mantle. An incredibly lifelike portrait depicted a noble looking knight astride a large, black dragon, standing on its hind legs with its wings partially spread. A stream of fire spewed from its mouth over a pile of oddly shaped gray rocks.

Boris coughed as he waved away the dust floating in front of his face. "There is an ancient myth about fire-breathing dragons that is mentioned in some of the oldest records of the palace library, but this is the first time I've actually seen it in a painting. Imagine what a tremendous military advantage that would be if it were possible."

He rubbed his jaw thoughtfully. "There was a dragon fountain in the square, and now this. This civilization had, or was at least familiar with dragons, and if they had dragons, then there must be a landing field and some sort of Hold for wintering them! If we can find it and it's still usable, we'll have a place to wait out the winter while we prepare against Tirate!" He turned and walked quickly towards the door. "Check every window you can find. If there is a landing field you should be able to see it, and that will lead us to the Hold. The sooner we find it, the sooner we can get back."

Ammon ran from room to room, scrubbing the dust from the windows before peering out. Fulgid trotted behind, occasionally chasing a surprised mouse across the floor. Ammon grumbled. "I don't even know what a landing field looks like. How am I supposed to find it?"

Three rooms later, Ammon heard distant shouts. As he stuck his head out into the hall, Theo rushed past. "Cen found the landing yard!"

Wiping cobwebs from his face, Ammon gladly gave up his search and followed Theo down the hall to a room at the end. Boris was already there, peering out the window at it. "That's it alright, overgrown as it is. The Hold should be close to the palace, so we could very well be standing several floors over it. Find the stairs leading down and hopefully we'll be in the Hold!"

They roamed the halls until they found a winding stone stairway leading deep below the palace. They paused to light their lanterns and followed the steps to the bottom.

The Hold was even larger than could have imagined, and even Boris stood looking at the rows of dragon chambers with awe in his voice. "This is incredible! There must easily be over a thousand chambers here! Have that many dragons ever existed at once?" He patted Ammon on the shoulder and watched as Fulgid curiously sniffed around the chambers, sneezing in the dust. "Ammon, I think you've found us our winter quarters! We must get back and inform Erik. The sooner we get everyone here, the better!"

***

It was well into the night when they finally emerged from the tunnel tired and hungry. Workers had cleared the entrance to the tunnel, widening it considerably. Torches were placed at the end, and the moment they stepped out, a young page ran to notify Erik. Plates of food were brought for them and set at a table by the entrance while they waited.

Ammon eased into a chair beside Boris, and Fulgid climbed onto his lap. The little dragons ears twitched back and forth and the feeling of unease drifted through the bubble in the back of Ammon's mind. He looked around as he picked at the food and spoke quietly. "Fulgid is nervous, something is wrong."

Ammon carefully studied everything around them as they ate. The men waiting for them wandered aimlessly about, and the cook wrung her apron between her hands like a piece of dough. A nearby blacksmith reached for wood for his fire and jumped when a cricket leapt from the grass.

Boris' eyes squinted. "Something is definitely askew. Erik is on his way, we'll find out soon enough."

They were nearly finished eating before Erik came into view of the firelight followed by the hulking giant Derek, who dragged something large and covered in canvas behind him. They started to rise but Erik waved them down. "Sit men. It is good you got back when you did, and I hope you have better news than I do. Derek found two of Tirate's men a day's walk from here. They were pulling this along behind them."

He nodded to Derek, who reached over and pulled back the cloth, exposing a large crossbow on a collapsible pedestal. Bundles of steel-tipped shafts as big as three fingers lay neatly stacked on either side.

Erik looked grave. "Derek was wise enough to bring back the men back who were with this contraption." With a curious glance, he looked up at the giant man. "I don't know exactly what he did to them, but by the time they arrived they were more than willing to talk as long as we promised to keep him away from them."

Derek grinned sheepishly and shrugged his shoulders.

Erik continued. "Anyway, from what we've learned, Tirate has an entire squadron of men less than a days march from here, all armed with more of these devices. He's peppered the whole countryside with them. We're trapped here unless you've found a way out."

Boris stood and with a slight bow, gestured towards the tunnel entrance. "My king, we have not only found you a way out, but we have found a place to winter the dragons. The only access appears to be through that tunnel and it would be easily defensible against an attack. The city there appears to be completely abandoned and the condition of the palace is acceptable with some work. It is large enough to easily accommodate all of us in the camp and more. We can start moving the camp and the dragons right away."

Erik visibly sighed with relief, the strain showing plainly on his face. Placing a hand on Boris' shoulder, he smiled. "Well done, Boris. Would you see that preparations begin immediately? The sooner we begin, the better. I'll be in my tent, let me know how quickly we can be underway."

Boris looked down at Ammon and Fulgid. "Once again, you've done us all a great service, and for that, I thank you." He strode away from the table and almost immediately his booming voice began barking orders.

Ammon pushed his half-finished meal in front of Fulgid and watched as the little dragon wolfed it down and sniffed around for stray crumbs. "You deserve all the credit, all I did was chase after you."

***

Within an hour, tents throughout the camp were being pulled down and packed away as word spread quickly of the move. Ammon went back to his tent to pack the few belongings he had. He was already wearing his armor, sword, and ring, and what was left could easily fit into his old sack. He picked up a small bag and a handful of crystals he'd collected from the cavern tumbled to the floor. Fulgid pounced as they scattered, grabbing one with his teeth and crushing it with a loud crunch.

"Fulgid no!"

He reached for the dragon, but it was too late, in one gulp the dragon had eaten the entire crystal.

"Why do you keep eating these? It can't be good for you!"

A golden voice bubbled up, ringing through his head like wind chimes. "HOT!"

Ammon shook his finger at the dragon's nose and scolded. "That's not hot, it's sharp! Now don't eat any more!"

Before Ammon could gather the rest of the crystals, Fulgid had managed to swallow two more. He threw his hands in the air in frustration and rolled his eyes. Theo once told him dragons were as stubborn as mules but he was beginning to think the mules took lessons from dragons.

By morning, a steady stream of people filed into the tunnel, following the trail of torches to the other side of the mountains. At regular intervals, a knight would enter the tunnel with his dragon crouching down and wings folded tight against its body. Erik, Boris, Theo, and Ammon watched the steady procession from the riverbank.

Boris squinted at the sun climbing into the sky. "I'd say we should have everyone through by mid morning as long as there aren't any problems. Ellis will have a tough time squeezing through, but as long as his saddle and bags are stripped off, I think he can do it. Before I remove them, I'm going to take a quick flight to see how close Tirate is. We don't need any unpleasant surprises."

He turned and placed a hand on Theo's shoulder. "Keep them moving, I don't want anyone left behind. Ditch equipment if you need to and supplies if you must, but not a soul gets left behind. I'll be back shortly."

Ammon watched the number of people entering the tunnel. It was amazing how quickly the camp had grown from a few hundred knights with their dragons to over five hundred men, women, and children of the palace staff. Most had flown in to the camp in the first week as the dragons were sent to pick up refugees of Tirate's rule. They had left almost everything behind to escape and now they shuffled past, looking at the tunnel suspiciously before entering. Some of the children cried, and more than a few paled as they peered into the dark depths of the long passageway. None spoke of what lie ahead.

Erik paced in small circles, his brow furrowed with concern as he watched his people disappear into the mountainside. Ammon could feel the tension in the air, and even Fulgid seemed agitated. He lay on the ground swishing his tail and pivoting his ears, listening to every sound.

As the hours passed, the stream of people thinned to a slow trickle, with only a few dragons left with their riders. Theo strode quickly towards them, dipping his head respectfully to Erik.

"My King, we are ready for you to go. As soon as Boris is back, we'll be ready to block the entrance from the inside."

Erik peered up into the sky, his blue eyes scanning the horizon. "No Theo, not yet. A king's duty is to protect his people and a king's right is to be first in battle and last to leave. Our threat comes from behind, and safety lies on the other side of the mountain. I will stay until the last man goes through."

Theo sighed. He looked at Ammon and shook his head. "I suppose you won't leave either?"

Ammon smiled. He would wait until Boris returned, and they'd all go together.

Suddenly the blast of a horn sounded, and Ellis' great wingspan appeared above the distant tree line, flying faster than Ammon would ever believe a dragon could. Once more the horn blasted, and within seconds the great dragon was circling over them with Boris shouting down.

"Tirate pushed his army on through the night; he'll descend on the camp any minute! I'll hold him back while the rest get through the tunnel!"

Theo sprinted towards the tunnel, barking orders to the few stragglers at the entrance. The few knights and dragons left began to lope like giant horses towards the opening. One by one they squeezed in until only Theo's dragon, Ebony remained. Erik stood as still as a stone, watching for Boris. Ellis' massive shape rose over the treetops and the shouting of men followed close behind him as they burst into sight. Several groups appeared pulling the large-wheeled crossbows behind them and they worked frantically to ready the weapon.

Ellis suddenly flipped upside down and dove towards them with Boris hanging from his saddle, his long sword drawn and held over his head. A man atop of the crossbow barely managed to leap aside as Boris' blade sliced through the bowstring. With a loud crack, the bow snapped back and hit the man in the back of the head, tossing him to the ground where he lay in a crumpled heap, unmoving.

Ellis rolled upright as his powerful wings pumped the air and he gained altitude. Wheeling in midair, they dove again for another attack. A thin, black streak shot through the air and struck Ellis in the chest and a loud, ear-piercing shriek filled the air. Ammon watched in horror as Ellis tried to regain control with one wing flapping uselessly and the shaft of the large bolt jutting from his side. Boris had somehow been thrown from the saddle and hung upside down by one foot in the stirrup. He flailed wildly beneath Ellis as they fell to earth in a rapidly spinning spiral. With a sickening thud, they crashed onto the steep riverbank and slowly rolled down towards the raging river until they stopped, half-submerged in the roiling current. Out from the trees, a dozen men charged toward Ellis and began pushing the helpless dragon further into the water.

With a fierceness in his heart he'd never felt before, Ammon drew his sword and charged across the ground with Fulgid running beside him. He barely recognized the danger he was putting himself in, his thoughts were blurred by the fury he felt through the link with Fulgid. The tiny bubble in his head boiled and flowed through him like fire. Engulfed in rage, he struck at the closest man with a wild swing of his sword. The man easily blocked the blow with his own blade and pushed Ammon back, sneering as he attacked. The training Boris had drilled into him became instinct as the man slashed down. As the blades connected, Ammon jumped aside and used the momentum of the strike to carry his own sword in a backward arc that struck the man across the back of his legs. With a scream, his opponent dropped his sword and crumpled to the ground.

Almost instantly, another man rushed forward and Ammon gasped for air as their swords clashed again and again. With each blow he felt his breath coming harder and harder. Sensing his fatigue, the man raised his sword high and brought it down in a crushing blow. Ammon blocked the strike and reeled as the force of it sent painful jolts through his arms. Grinning, the man struck once more and this time Ammon let his sword drop, letting the man's blade glance harmlessly off his armored vest. Without resistance, the empty blow threw the man off balance and as he stumbled, Ammon raised his sword and lunged forward piercing the man's stomach. Shock filled his eyes as he fell to his knees and Ammon pulled his sword free.

He spun, expecting the next attack, but none came. Theo stood several paces away, eyeing him curiously as he slowly sheathed his longsword. Fulgid prowled nearby, his eyes glowed white-hot and lips pulled back in a fierce snarl. Groaning men lay scattered haphazardly about and there was shouting coming from the trees.

The riverbank was empty except for the deep claw marks in the earth leading down the steep embankment. Boris' longsword lay half buried in the mud beside a large crimson stain in the grass. Ammon rushed to the water's edge and felt his heart sink as he saw Ellis' body rolling in the turbulent whitewater, then disappear down the hole in the mountain.

"Boris!" The roar of the water carried away the sound of his cry. He was too late.

With tear-filled eyes, he retrieved the engraved blade from the muck and clutched it tightly to his chest. Swallowing the lump in his throat, he called to Fulgid and followed Theo back towards the tunnel where Erik stood waiting.

Erik's voice was barely audible when he spoke. "Come. It is time to go."

As they moved further in, Theo coaxed Ebony to strike the roof of the tunnel a few times with her tail. Each time there was a loud crash as the entrance collapsed into a pile of rubble and dust. Slowly they moved up the tunnel together. There was no fear of being followed now. It would take Tirate's men months to clear out that debris. Erik put his arm around Ammon and in the dim torchlight, Ammon could see tears streaming down his cheeks from the loss of his oldest and dearest friend. Ammon's own cheeks glistened wetly as he carried Boris' longsword close to his heart.

***

The ruins were at a higher elevation than Gaul and early mornings already had the taste of autumn in the air. With oncoming winter just months away, they had little time to prepare for the cold and unknown weather patterns of this strange region. Dragons, knights, men, and women helped in gathering firewood from the large forests surrounding the city.

Because of his experience with furnaces in the Nest, Erik placed Ammon in charge of the heating system. He spent days with the blacksmiths directing the repairs of the multiple furnaces in the Hold beneath the palace. He couldn't help but marvel at the clever design of the palace builders. Although most of the rooms had fireplaces, it was unlikely they would be needed except in the coldest weather. The heat produced from the furnaces to keep the dragons warm also traveled through small channels to the upper floors, keeping the entire palace at a comfortable temperature.

Today he decided to check how quickly the firewood supply was building. Beside each of the dragons quarters was a large room for firewood, and Ammon directed each to be filled to the ceiling. The builders wouldn't have built rooms that size for wood storage if most of it were a waste of space. After two weeks, only a third of them were filled. He shook his head and frowned. It had to be brought in soon or it wouldn't be dry enough to burn. He wandered through the hold until he found Theo splitting wood with a rusted axe.

His taunt arms flexed as he sank the axe deep into a chunk of wood, and even in the cool air, his bare chest glistened with sweat. His lean frame shifted fluidly, wasting no movement as he deftly cracked the wood apart with precise blows and tossed them aside. He paused as Ammon approached and knuckled his back before wiping the sweat from his face with a rag.

Ammon picked a waterskin off a nearby stump and handed it to him. "Theo, is there any way we can get the wood in faster? I'm concerned that it won't season fast enough before the cold weather starts, and we don't know how soon that will happen here."

Theo paused to take a long drink. "I know we need more firewood, but the men are doing the best they can. I already have more than half of them working on it now. Most of the rest are out hunting, trying to bring in enough food to keep us and a few hundred dragons fed through the winter. Fortunately, this region seems pretty rich in game, so the hunting has been good." He gestured to the dragons quarters with one hand. "Anyone who isn't hunting or gathering wood are here making the place livable."

Ammon sighed. "If you can think of any way…"

Theo hefted the axe again and smiled. "Don't worry. The wood and the food will be in with time to spare. Have faith."

Ammon nodded and headed back to his rooms. He knew they were doing everything they could, but he felt restless. The day they arrived at the ruins of this city he'd asked Erik for permission to locate the Olog River on this side of the mountains. He wanted to find the bodies of Boris and Ellis and at least mark the site with some sort of memorial, but Erik had refused him. He was needed here, not just for repairing the furnaces, but because he was now officially the heir to Erik's throne.

Erik's eyes had looked at him with sympathy and understanding, for Boris was his closest friend. "As heir to the throne, your life is no longer your own. You have a responsibility to the people, to the Knights of Gaul. You can no more wander off on a quest any more than I can."

His life was no longer his own. As he walked the hallway to his chambers, those words echoed over and over in his head. He closed the door to his room and picked up his sword. He found he could release some of his frustrations practicing with it, and today he felt more apprehensive than usual. Fulgid lay quietly on the windowsill, watching as Ammon worked at the exercises Boris had taught him. The strange gray sword felt less awkward now. The blade whistled through the air with increasing speed and accuracy, cutting through the tiny targets of acorns he hung on strings from the ceiling. When he finished an hour later, Fulgid happily devoured the split acorns scattered across the floor.

He dipped a towel into a washbowl and wiped his face with cool water as he walked around the room. His quarters were situated next to Erik's and were well appointed. A freshly stuffed mattress lay across a large bed and his golden armored vest hung inside a beautiful oak wardrobe. Desks, tables, and chairs in the sitting room had been pushed aside so he could practice his sword, and in the corner near the fireplace where he stood, was a washstand complete with an uncracked looking glass.

He turned to stare at his reflection, a sight he'd not yet become accustomed to seeing. He'd never seen himself except in the distorted images of rippling pools of water and curved lamp reflectors. Looking back from the glass was a young man with shoulder length blond hair and sharp blue eyes set squarely above the high cheekbones and determined jaw of a tanned face. Erik said he had many of the characteristics of his father, yet he could not recall a single memory of the man. With a sigh he turned away. Looking at the strange face in the glass made him feel odd.

A tap sounded at the door and he opened it to find a young pageboy looking up at him in awe. Ammon and Fulgid had become almost legendary after his attack on Tirate's men in the failed effort to save Boris. Someone had overheard Theo discussing the fight with one of the other Knights and the story had spread through the palace staff like wildfire. With each telling, the battle got bigger and the two men he fought grew to dozens. Before long it was an entire legion, and no matter how many times he corrected them it never changed. One odd consistency in the story was that his eyes glowed white as he charged into battle. No doubt they meant Fulgid's eyes, which did inexplicably glow at times. The story had taken on a life of its own and now everywhere he walked people gave him a wide berth. Erik said it would pass and that this was not a bad thing. The loss of Boris had struck a deep wound in their morale and the people needed a hero. Their view of Ammon filled that void.

It took the pageboy a moment to speak. "Uh…Lord Ammon! The king requests your presence in his chambers right away!"

Ammon tossed the damp towel over the back of a chair and looked over at Fulgid chewing on a bit of acorn. "You coming?"

Fulgid snatched another bit of acorn and loped out the door in front of Ammon. The page followed close behind, staring wide-eyed at the little dragon who swaggered along the hallway as if the palace were built for him. Reaching into his pocket for an acorn, Ammon handed it to the boy and nodded towards Fulgid. Timidly the boy tossed it and giggled with delight as Fulgid snapped it out of the air with a crunch.

Outside the doorway, Ammon waited for the page announce his arrival. Fulgid pressed against the back of his knee to get his attention. Although he was the size of a large cat, the dragon had taken to riding on Ammon's back most of the time, and today was no different. Ammon bent down, and Fulgid gracefully leapt onto his back, wrapped his long golden tail around his waist, and rested his head on Ammon's shoulder.

The page opened the door and bid him to enter. Erik sat in the center of the room on his makeshift throne, a heavy wooden chair padded with multicolored pillows. Theo and Cen stood on either side, and in front of them, on a small chair, sat what appeared to be a pile of dirty rags topped with a shock of tangled silver hair.

Motioning for Ammon to come closer, Erik spoke up. "Ammon, I thought you'd be interested to hear this. It appears our uninhabited city had a resident after all. One of the hunting parties saw movement in a window of a partially collapsed building near the north gate and decided to investigate."

Leaning forward, Erik raised his voice. "Miss? Miss? Can you hear me? How came you to this ruinous city?"

The bundle of rags moved slightly, and a voice creaked irritably. "You've invaded a dead city! It belongs to the dead, nothing here to take! Go home!"

Erik looked up and exchanged glances with the others. "Invade? Not hardly, my dear woman. Unfortunate circumstances have led us here to seek shelter for the coming winter!"

The silver hair atop the rags bounced with cackling laughter. "Aye, and you're just out here on a picnic with a few hundred armed men?"

Theo's face began turning red, and his voice was hot as he snapped. "Mind your manners! You speak to a king!"

Erik held his hand up. "Peace, Theo. This woman has every right to be suspicious. If anything, we are her guests. Uninvited as we may be."

A thin, bony hand gripping a twisted walking stick jutted out from the rags and thumped the stick soundly on the floor several times. "King? Pah! Guests? You come unannounced from beyond the impassable mountains, move into the city, and call yourself guests? Ha! Invaders I say!"

Erik sat back, tapping his fingers.

Sensing the growing frustration, Ammon stepped forward. "If I may ask, ma'am…what city is this? To what country have we come? We are not here to take…your…city. Only to take shelter for the winter so we can return home in the spring. We thought the city was abandoned and found no sign of anyone here until now."

Without looking up, the heap of rags shuddered soundlessly. Her low voice sounded weary. "Abandoned? No, not abandoned lad." Picking up her head she pointed a knurled finger at Erik. "Leave this place king. It is not a place of happiness or a place to rest. All of you!" Slowly she shook her finger at each one of them. "Leave this place to crumble in peace. This city should not be…" Her eyes suddenly widened as they fell on Fulgid, who lay motionless on Ammon's shoulder.

Rising from her chair, she stood shakily and hobbled towards Ammon. Peering up, her old eyes focused in disbelief on Fulgid. "What is THAT?" Her voice half whispered, half screeched.

Ammon protectively turned his shoulder away. "That's my dragon!"

The woman followed him, reaching out her wrinkled hand towards Fulgid's head. "Is it real? Is it really that color?"

Ammon instinctively, but gently grabbed her wrist. Her attention turned from Fulgid to Ammon's face and she let out a ragged gasp and staggered back. Theo and Cen rushed forward and carefully guided her back down to her chair. Her eyes never left Ammon and Fulgid.

"How can this be? I gave up so long ago! So very, very long ago…"

Erik stood up, his patience at an end. "Theo, Cen, please return this woman safely to her…home. She has obviously has nothing worth telling us, and I'm tired of waiting."

Theo and Cen gently lifted the woman to her feet, but her shrill voice rang out to Erik as he walked away. "Oh my dear king, I do indeed have something to say!" She looked once more at Fulgid and her wrinkled face began to smile. "More than I ever thought I'd live to say! But this old woman needs a drink to wet her throat, it's been many years since I've told this story."

Within minutes several pages arrived with clay mugs and a pitcher of water on a small table. Picking up the mug with shaking hands, she took a long drink. Fulgid jumped to the floor and sniffed at the woman's feet while Ammon eyed her suspiciously. When she had drained the mug, she wiped her mouth on her tattered sleeve and cleared her throat.

"I am Sasha Celest. My grandchild and I have lived alone here for many years. How many? That I do not know exactly. Five decades at least. How and why does one measure time when there is only yesterday, today, and maybe tomorrow? You are in the great City of Laton, the crown jewel of the DoTarian Empire. What you see is all that is left of a once great nation!" She snorted softly. "At least we thought of ourselves as great." She mumbled something unintelligible beneath her breath.

Erik sat teetering on the edge of the makeshift throne. "Tell me, Sasha, what happened to all the people of Laton?"

The old woman cackled as Fulgid climbed back up onto Ammon's shoulder. Suddenly she closed her eyes and whispered:

"A dragon gold,
Our fate does hold.
A lost son shall return.
The common man
Will rule again,
To yield his life for all.

A sliver heart,
The strength to start.
The courage to endure.

Two lands unite,
The curse to fight,
And lead us all from ruin."

Confused, Ammon looked at the others, then at the old woman who was now casually drinking from the water pitcher. After several large gulps, she set it back on the table and looked up at him with a raised eyebrow.

"What's your name young man?"

"Ammon."

Erik cleared his throat expectantly.

Ammon winced. Erik insisted he use his entire formal name now. "I am Ammon of the House of Les."

There was a long silence and then, with some effort, she stood and faced Ammon, her head barely as high as his shoulder.

"Well, your Majesty, if you will excuse me, I'm a tired old woman and I need rest."

Ammon's jaw dropped to his chest. "I'm not...! Excuse me ma'am, but you have me confused with..."

The old woman waved him off as she shuffled out the door, but as she left she cackled.

"Must go home and have a talk. Yes, a talk! We have much to do for these changes to take place."

Exasperated, Erik flopped back in his chair. "Apparently women are just as difficult to comprehend in this country as our own!" He lifted a mug of water and stared into it. "Well, men, do you make of this?"

***

Frustrated, Ammon kicked at a small stone as he picked his way through the rubble strewn across the street from a collapsed building while Fulgid chased squirrels across the sunlit cobblestones. Erik decided that since the old woman had shown an interest in Ammon, he was probably their best chance to learn what happened to the City of Laton. On this cloudless day, he could have thought of any number of things he'd rather do than spend time listening to the rants of an insane old woman.

The truth was that he really wanted to look for Boris. The river couldn't be far from the city, Ellis' huge body would be easy to spot from the air and Boris would be somewhere nearby. A lump formed in his throat again as it did every time he thought about that day. Boris and Ellis deserved a ceremony at least, but Erik said it would have to wait until the palace was settled. He kicked another stone angrily. Instead he was being sent to see a crazy old woman instead of doing something meaningful!

The dilapidated house near the north gate was pretty easy to find from the directions that Theo had given him. There was no front door. In fact, there wasn't much left of the front of the building. A good portion of the wall facing the street had buckled and collapsed, and the rest of the building listed precariously to the left. Dark shadows loomed behind the windowless holes framed with broken and missing shutters. It wasn't clear what held the whole façade from collapsing in on itself, but he felt sure a strong wind might end its existence.

He hesitantly stepped over the rotted remains of a wooden beam that lay across the threshold and stood inside looking up at the sky through the roof. He had lived in worse conditions out of necessity, but he was puzzled why the woman chose this house. There were certainly other buildings in the city in better condition, although none as close to the gate as this one.

Fulgid scampered past to an inner doorway that was still somewhat intact. It hung at an odd angle, and the latch had long since fallen away and been replaced with a knotted rope. He took a deep breath and knocked carefully, half expecting it to fall from its hinges. There was a scuffle inside and a moment later the old woman peered through a gap in the door suspiciously before her eyes lit up with delight. Heaving the door open, the old woman nearly pulled it off its rotted frame as it scraped along the warped floorboards.

She stood aside and motioned quickly for him to enter. "Come in! Come in! Oh and you brought your little dragon! How delightful! Sit down right there and I'll bring you some tea!"

She motioned towards a lopsided stool beside an equally unsteady table. Like the exterior of the house, everything within the room seemed on the verge of collapse. He eased himself onto the stool and it creaked dangerously under his weight, and waited impatiently. Sasha pushed a cracked mug filled with steaming tea in front of him and sat down with her own mug, slurping it noisily. Fulgid busied himself by climbing in and around the sparse furniture, sniffing among the numerous shelves that lined the walls from floor to ceiling. Hundreds of bottles and jars were crammed into the room from one end to the other, filling the shelves and every nook and cranny.

Ammon eyed the tea doubtfully and cleared his throat. "Ma'am, King Erik asked me to come here. We have some questions to ask you about this city…"

Fulgid jumped up onto one of the lower shelves, rattling jars and knocking a few to the floor. Ammon started to scold him, but the old lady held up a withered hand and motioned for him to be silent. Turning on her stool she watched him with keen interest, occasionally cackling gleefully.

"It has been many years since a young dragon has graced my home! See how he sniffs? He smells it! He knows it's here somewhere! You watch! He'll find it soon enough I wager! Hee hee!"

Ammon sighed. Fulgid might bring down the whole wall as well as everything on the shelves, but the old woman certainly didn't seem concerned about it. Fortunately, the shelf was low enough that the jars fell harmlessly to the floor without breaking. What she expected Fulgid to find in that mess was beyond him! He lifted the mug and cautiously took a sip. He was fairly certain there was no useful information to get out of Sasha; the woman was obviously afflicted with dementia. Living alone for decades in these ruins probably caused it.

A burst of honey enveloped his tongue as the tea passed his lips and his eyebrows rose in surprise. It was a welcome change from the black brew Kyle served him each morning, and he wondered if he could obtain some from the old woman. At least then his trip here wouldn't be a complete waste of his time. For now he contented himself to sip it quietly and let the old woman delight in Fulgid's activities.

Jar after jar rolled to the floor before Fulgid found a particularly large one sealed tightly with wax. With one quick swipe of his claw the dragon broke open the seal and the old woman clapped her hands.

"Oh how clever! He has the Gift of Finding doesn't he!"

After unsuccessfully trying to get his head into the narrow neck of the jar, Fulgid pushed it off the shelf and it rolled into the middle of the floor.

The old woman leaned close to Ammon and whispered. "Now that he's found it, lets see if he knows what to do with it!"

Ammon put down his cup and watched Fulgid leap down from the shelf. "Do with what? What is it he's found?"

The woman put a bony finger to her lips and hushed at him. "Just watch!"

The little dragon circled the container once before putting both front feet into the opening. Within one quick jerk he sent the jar spinning into the wall, shattering it into pieces. Ammon could see clearly now what was inside as the light reflected off the half dozen or so tiny crystals that lay on the floor in a heap.

"Fulgid! NO!"

The dragon had already crushed one in his jaws and was swallowing the shards. Ammon tried to get up from the stool, but dozens of the jars had rolled under his feet and he stumbled. As he regained his footing, the old woman reached across the table and grabbed his sleeve with an iron grip.

"Stop being foolish, he knows what he's doing!"

Bewildered, Ammon's eyebrows rose in disbelief. "Knows what he's doing? He's just a baby! Those shards will cut his insides to ribbons!"

The woman's grip held fast. "You don't know much about dragons do you? Their insides are just as tough as the outside! Besides, those crystals are important to a dragons diet, I only wish I had more!"

Ammon eased himself back onto the stool. "Important? How?"

The old woman rolled her eyes as she released her grip. "Don't they teach young knights anything about dragons where you come from? How do you expect him to protect himself from Kala-Azar if you don't let him have calentar?"

Ammon looked at Fulgid happily chewing the last crystal. Deep in his mind the bubble glowed like a ray of sun as the golden voice in his mind chimed. "Trust Fulgid!"

Ammon gritted his teeth. "I do trust you, it's her I'm not sure about!" He jerked his thumb at Sasha who sat with her cup half to her lips.

She looked quizzically at Ammon, then at Fulgid. Slowly, she put her cup back down. "You don't know about calentar crystals?"

Ammon shook his head. "I've only been linked for about a month and only by accident. I'm just learning about dragons and this is the first time I've ever heard of that Kala-whatever, but I've seen those crystals before in the mountains. There was a huge cavern filled with them."

The loud snort from the frail old woman made him look up from watching Fulgid. The shock on her face was evident, even beneath the years of wrinkles. "You've never...heard...of Kala-Azar and you have an entire cavern of calentar?"

Sighing, Ammon shook his head. "No, I've never heard of it. I'm only here because King Erik wants to know what happened to this city. You're the only one here we can ask! What happened?"

The old woman stared silently at Fulgid as he sniffed out the last bits of the crystal shards. "How many dragons came with you?"

Ammon shrugged. "About two hundred I think."

Sasha's hand slapped the table so hard that it made Ammon jump. "Bring me to your king, I must speak with him at once! The danger is great to us all!"

Ammon led the way back to the palace. Surprisingly, the old woman kept pace with him, pushing him to walk faster. It still took them nearly an hour to reach the Erik's chambers, and when the page that announced them let them pass, both Erik and Theo stood waiting.

Erik seemed annoyed at being disturbed as he shoved papers aside at the desk and sat down. "Well, Ammon, have you learned much from our friend here?"

Sasha pointed a finger at Erik, her old voice creaked in a high pitch as she spoke. "Tell me what you know about the Kala-Azar and calentar!"

Erik and Theo exchanged glances and Erik shrugged. "Are the Kala-Azar the people who drove out the residents of Laton?"

Sasha slowly sank into a chair, placing her head into her hands. Softly she whispered. "No, not again, please not again!"

Erik looked up at Ammon. "Would you please explain to me what this is about?"

Embarrassed, Ammon stammered an apology and took the old woman by the arm and tried to pull her from the chair. Maybe he could get her back to her shack and that would be the end of it. With any luck Erik wouldn't think he was too much of an idiot!

Sasha slapped his hands away and looked up fiercely. "You have no idea what I'm talking about do you? None of you do!"

Silence filled the room before Erik sighed and pulled the papers on the table back in front of him. "Ammon, would you be so kind as to escort our...lady...back to her home? We have much work to do."

Sasha stepped closer to Erik, her voice on the verge of screeching. "You must know! How could you not know about the slugs?"

Ammon gently but firmly pulled on her arm and half dragged her to the door, her voice continued to get louder and louder in a fevered pitch.

"You'll all die before winter! Listen to me, please! You must listen!"

The page closed the door behind them as Ammon led her down the hallway. Outside the palace Sasha wrested her arm away from Ammon and grumbled under her breath. Turning sharply she faced Ammon with a bony finger pointed inches from his nose.

"You! You must learn and teach the others! It's the only way they'll listen! In the library of the palace you must find the history, but you must work quickly! Yes, very quickly! Who knows how long before they wake!"

Ammon walked next to the old woman, listening politely as Fulgid bounded from building to building chasing squirrels. He had no intentions of doing any of the insanity the woman was ranting about. Erik asked him to escort her home and that's all he intended to do. As they rounded a corner past the rubble of a collapsed wall, Fulgid ran past into the shell of an empty building across the street.

A blood-curdling scream erupted from the shadows of the house and Ammon jerked to a stop as Sasha gripped his forearm tightly, her face pale. "No! By the dragons teeth, no!"

Fulgid slowly backed from the building with his back arched. With each step his claws raked the ground and ripped gouges deep into the paving stones. He growled fiercely through razor sharp fangs, and his eyes glowed white with intense fury. Ammon drew his sword and took one step before Sasha pulled him back.

"Fool! You cannot fight it with that!" she nodded at his sword.

Ammon pulled his arm free. "Fight what? What is in there?"

Fulgid growled even louder as something emerged from the doorway. A gray head as big as a melon emerged from the shadows and moved slowly into the street. A pair of long black mandibles protruded from the sides of its gaping maw and clicked as they opened and closed. Its fat, bulbous body was as big around as the chest of a horse and it rippled as it moved like a gelatinous bag of water. The color of wet slate, it was as long as Ammon was tall, and the reeking scent of rotting meat permeated the air. The legless body slid forward like a giant worm, its mandibles clicking as it stared at Fulgid with unblinking black eyes.

Gagging at the putrid smell, Ammon pointed his sword at its head. "What *is* that thing?"

Sasha looked up at Ammon, fear in her wide eyes. "Kala-Azar!"

With surprising speed, the slug suddenly lunged forward at Fulgid who quickly leapt to the side, raking the flank of the creature with his claws. Long shallow slices appeared on its bulging rolls, and as Fulgid neared the back of the creature, he sank his teeth into the stubby tail. Like a fat whip, the short tail thrust upward and flung Fulgid tumbling through the air and into the side of a dilapidated building. The wall teetered unsteadily for a brief moment before it crumbled down on top of the dragon, covering him with stones.

With a shout, Ammon leapt forward with his sword high above his head and brought it down on the creature's back with all his might. The gray blade bounced back in his hands so hard he barely kept his grip. He stepped back again in disbelief. It was as if he'd struck a thick piece of leather with a stick, the sharp sword hadn't even left a mark.

The grotesque head turned towards Ammon, mandibles open wide, and its slug like body rippled as it flowed towards him. Without taking his eyes off the creature, he yelled to Sasha. "How do I kill it?"

Sasha's voice was filled with terror. "You can't kill it with a sword! It will only die with fire!"

Ammon's brain raced frantically. Fire? Where would he get fire quickly? He had to do something, Fulgid may be hurt under that pile of rubble and he wasn't about to let some slimy…thing eat him! The slug advanced towards him slowly, and Ammon backed up until his back was against the wall of a building. The only warning he had was a tiny twitch of the lumpy tail, he faked a move to the left before jumping right and hit the ground on his shoulder before rolling to his feet. Two loud thumps echoed behind him, and as he turned he saw two large holes in the wall, one where he'd been standing and another to the left of where he'd been. The edges of the holes sizzled like boiling oil as they steamed.

Sasha yelled to him again. "The saliva is like acid! Don't let it touch you!"

Ammon moved to the middle of the street and faced the giant slug. A few rocks in the pile from the collapsed wall tumbled away as Fulgid climbed out, his eyes shining like white hot metal. Ammon could feel the fury building inside the dragon as Fulgid deliberately stalked forward. Ammon called to him. "Fulgid! Back away!"

Fulgid snarled, and the Kala-Azar turned its ugly maw back towards the angry little dragon. Fulgid stood up on his hind legs, head back and mouth open, and the slug shot forward with incredible speed.

There was a sudden flash and Ammon was knocked onto his back by a tremendous blast. Instinctively he raised his hands to protect his face and felt his palms begin to blister. In seconds it was over and he sat up, blinking against the heat coming up from the street. As his eyes focused, he could see a massive scorch mark that blackened the entire area where the Kala-Azar had been. Paving stones hissed and cracked with loud pops and thin tendrils of smoke drifted up from where weeds once pushed up between them. Fulgid nonchalantly walked up and sat next to him as Sasha hurried to his side.

Standing over him with hands firmly planted on each hip, she looked down and said, "Now do you believe the danger?"

Painfully climbing to his feet, Ammon looked around for his sword. The blast had knocked it from his hands and thrown it several paces away. He retrieved it and slid it back into the scabbard then dusted bits of ash from his armor. The pungent smell of burnt hair and sulfur filled his nostrils and stung his eyes.

"What caused it to explode like that?"

Sasha cackled. "HA! The Kala-Azar didn't explode! Your little golden dragon incinerated the filthy vermin! I thought you said you'd never heard of calentar?"

Ammon rubbed his forehead with blistered fingers. "I haven't. How could Fulgid have caused that explosion?"

"Humph!" Sasha hobbled down the street, her walking stick tapping the blackened stones in rhythm to her step. "Come, I have a salve for those burns."

His mind reeling, Ammon followed, keeping a wary eye on the vacant doorways. What caused that thing to explode? There was nothing flammable around and certainly nothing that would burn that hot and that quickly! The increasing pain of his burns soon took over his thoughts, and by the time they arrived at Sasha's home he could think of little else.

Fidgeting uncomfortably on the rickety stool, Ammon closed his eyes and clenched his teeth while the old woman rubbed a clear, foul smelling paste on the burns. Despite the odor, the salve had an immediate cooling effect, and the discomfort eased considerably. As he relaxed, he opened his eyes and was surprised to see a small hooded figure eyeing him suspiciously from the doorway. Shorter than Ammon and with facial features obscured beneath the hood, he guessed the figure to be a boy barely into his teenage years. The deerskin shirt and breeches hung loosely on a thin frame, and slung from his shoulder was a hunters bow and quiver.

Mumbling incoherently to herself as she applied the poultice to Ammon's hands, Sasha suddenly looked over her shoulder at the boy "El, get me the box of bandages."

El slipped the bow from his shoulder and propped it against the wall before pulling a brown box from the shelf and handed it to the old woman. Ammon began to wonder how many others were hidden in the city as Sasha wrapped his hands. Suddenly it dawned on him that if the number of jars, pots, and bottles in the room were filled with various medications, then Sasha must have enough to treat a small army. Perhaps Sasha wasn't as crazy as she appeared. She may have avoided answering their questions to protect the residents still living in the city. If she thought they were invaders, it was reasonable to assume others would too and would remain hidden until they were assured of their own safety.

Satisfied that every blister was covered, Sasha wiped her hands on the tattered remains of her clothes and stepped back as Fulgid leapt into Ammon's lap to investigate the wounds. Ammon flexed his hands gingerly. He could still move them but with the bandages and poultice he'd have difficulty handling his sword.

The old woman pulled down a couple large woven sacks from a shelf and tossed it to the boy. "We're moving to the palace. I'll need all the jars from the third shelves, we'll come back for the rest later."

Without a word, the boy started filling the sack with everything off of the shelf. Sasha turned back towards Ammon and lifted his chin between her thumb and forefinger. Speaking over her shoulder she announced.

"Too bad you didn't see him before the burns, he's got a pretty face to be sure."

The boy stiffened for a brief second with a jar in his hand before snorting and continued.

Despite his bandaged hands, Ammon carried two large bags filled with liniments over his shoulders and the boy carried two more. Fulgid walked beside Ammon carrying a small jar in his teeth and the old woman walked ahead of them with pockets bulging. When they arrived at the palace, Theo met them in the hallway, and Ammon briefly explained what happened and showed his wounded hands.

Theo nodded with concern. "Erik will want to hear this entire story, as do I! As soon as you can, meet me in his chambers. I'll inform him you are coming."

Sasha insisted that first she find a room near Ammon's where she could store her medicines. She looked at three different rooms before choosing one directly across the hallway from Ammon's. He wasn't terribly fond of the idea of having her that close to him, but her ointments seemed to be soothing the burns, so he reluctantly agreed. Besides, it would be easier to keep an eye on her if she were nearby.

Once inside her room, Ammon dropped the bags onto a table and excused himself. "The king wishes to see me."

Sasha never looked up as she pulled the jars from the bag. "Yes, yes, go, speak with him, tell him everything mind you! I'll be there soon to explain the Kala-Azar. El, are you sure you got everything from the third shelf?"

Ammon rolled his eyes and left with Fulgid trotting beside him. Before entering Erik's chambers, he checked himself over quickly and dusted off a few bits of ash from his vest. The armor had very likely saved him from burns across his chest as well. Looking down at Fulgid, he marveled at the thought of a fireball that powerful coming from such a tiny dragon! Could Sasha's claim be true? How big would a fireball from a full-grown dragon be?

Ammon had barely started to tell what happened when Sasha arrived. He decided it would be best to just describe the events he witnessed and let her fill in the rest. Sasha plucked a crystal shard from her pocket and dropped it on the table. Erik picked it up and eyed it doubtfully.

Sasha pointed a bony finger at Fulgid who sat quietly at Ammon's feet. "DoTaria has known for thousands of years to give calentar to dragons to make them breathe fire. How your civilization has managed this long without it is stunning to say the least. Without calentar, dragons have no defense against the Kala-Azar except to flee. That, my king, is what has happened to all of DoTaria.

For centuries these mountains were mined for the crystals and eventually the mines were depleted. The Kala-Azar are drawn to dragons like flies to rotting meat. The more dragons in one place, the more slugs appear. When the calentar mines ran out, there were over one thousand dragons here. In less than a week, hundreds of them were slain. To survive, the remaining dragons scattered across the countryside, and the people of Laton scattered with them. Eventually the slugs disappeared or went into hibernation, nobody really knows where they came from or where they went. Occasionally they still surface, hunting anything that moves and killing any dragon that stays in one place too long. The presence of a few hundred dragons here has awakened the slugs once again, and soon they will return! This whole city will be crawling with the loathsome things!"

Erik turned the crystal in his hands thoughtfully. "Dragons that breathe fire? I have a hard time believing this myth told to children. Yet Ammon is a truthful young man, and there was no denying the burns on his face and hands. There is no doubt something caused the people of Laton to leave, and leave quickly. Everywhere we look are signs of a people leaving in a hurry, yet no signs of a battle. To think a force of a thousand dragons are forced to flee from these Kala-Azar slugs. Are they that difficult to kill?" He placed the crystal down on the table, sat back and crossed his arms. "Where do we find this calentar if the mountains have been mined out?"

The old woman stepped closer. "Ammon told me of a large cavern with crystals! If you find that deposit, you'll be able to defend yourselves, at least for a little while!"

Theo bent down and picked up the crystal. "It's true. I've seen the cavern myself. It was filled with these. Tons of it. How much does each dragon need to produce this...fire?"

Sasha rubbed her hands together gleefully. "Tons of it you say? Are you sure? Each dragon only needs a fistful, but they must have it everyday! It takes at least a week of feeding before they can produce the fire! You must show me this cavern at once! Before the slugs return your dragons must be ready!"

Erik looked doubtfully at Theo, then at Ammon, and finally at Sasha. "Alright, I will send a few of my knights to go with you as soon as you're ready. If this calentar works as you say, perhaps this may be our key to return home as well!"

Theo followed Ammon out into the hallway. "Do you really believe it was Fulgid that caused the fireball?"

Ammon shrugged and held up his burned hands. "I did not see it, but I don't have any other explanation."

***

Sasha leaned heavily on El as they reached the entrance to the tunnel, and Ammon shifted the bundle of the empty sacks on his shoulder as she studied the entrance carefully. "I thought I knew of every mine on the mountain, but this is one I've not seen before!"

The opening had been cleared to make room for the dragons during their escape, and once inside, Theo and Ammon lit the torches along the walls as they made their way deeper inside. When they finally reached the entrance to the cavern, the reflected light from their torches on the crystals lit the entire cavern up like the morning sky. Fulgid leapt about from rock to rock, the lights twinkling off his brilliant scales.

Sasha stood in the middle of the cavern gaping in astonishment. "Tons of calentar! More than I ever dreamed of! Do you know what this means? Do you have any idea?"

Theo shrugged his shoulders. "Does this mean these are the type of crystals you talked about?"

Sasha held her hands high and cackled gleefully. "Calentar! Enough to last an army for hundreds of years! A thousand years or more! Don't you understand?"

Theo and Ammon looked at each other blankly. Mildly irritated, Sasha threw an empty sack at them. "It means the return of the dragons to Laton! We can take back the city and drive the Kala-Azar back to whatever pit they came from! We will not hide from the slugs anymore!"

Ammon shook one of the sacks open as he began filling it with bits of crystals shards. "You mean the Laton dragons are still out there somewhere?"

The old woman's shrill voice echoed through the cavern. "Yes! The whole city is out there! Scattered across the land!"

Theo paused after he placed a particularly large crystal into one of the sacks. "Sasha, just how many dragons out there would come back because of these crystals?"

The old woman picked up a fist-sized crystal and held it up to the torchlight. "Not as many as once was. I'd guess about twelve hundred or so now, maybe a few more. They've continued to breed even though they're scattered far and wide. The furthest is about a weeks flight from here."

She tossed the crystal to Ammon who jumped to catch it. Stepping over the pile of bags she stood in front of Ammon looking up at him curiously. "You and your golden dragon! Just as it was written!"

Before Ammon could ask what that meant, a full bag of crystals suddenly struck him in the back of the leg and nearly knocked him to the ground. "Hey!" Rubbing his calf, he looked up as El snatched another bag and turned away to fill it. "What was that for?"

Sasha looked quizzically at El, then at Ammon and grinned.

**

Fulgid led the way back out of the tunnel carrying a couple small bags of calentar on his back. Ammon, Theo, and El each struggled under the weight of the bulging sacks they carried. Sasha had filled so many pockets in the rags she wore that she rattled with each step. As they headed down the steep slope to the city, Ammon walked beside her, offering his arm at the more treacherous spots while El steadied her on the other side. He kept a wary eye on the boy. For whatever reason, El seemed to disliked him and he wasn't going to give the boy a chance to hit him from behind with another sack of calentar.

He studied the boy as they walked. It was difficult to say what El looked like with the hood always drawn tightly over his head. Even his facial features were carefully hidden from view. He was shorter than Ammon by nearly a head, yet moved with the grace of an experienced hunter. Perhaps the strangest thing Ammon noticed was that El never spoke or looked anyone in the eye. Suddenly it occurred to him that perhaps the boy was disfigured. Sasha's comment about Ammon's *pretty face* would certainly explain the boy's attitude towards him! He suddenly felt pity and decided to ignore the resentment and be friendly, as Boris had been to him. In time El's attitude would change.

Theo struck up a conversation with Sasha and Ammon took the chance to walk a bit closer to El. Speaking quietly so only the boy could hear he asked. "What did she mean when she said, 'as it was written'?"

The hooded head turned slightly but said nothing and moved away to be closer to Sasha. Ammon looked down at Fulgid and shrugged. "I tried."

Fulgid suddenly bounded forward, cut in front of El and tripped him with his tail. Ammon stopped in mid-step watching helplessly as the boy stumbled down the steep hillside. The heavy sack of crystals swung wildly on his back as he desperately tried to slow his descent. With an undignified stop, he crashed into a small clump of saplings. Even from a distance, Ammon could feel El's eyes glare at him from beneath the hood before he stomped off. Fulgid pranced back to Ammon's side, the picture of innocence.

He looked down at Fulgid and tried not to smile. "Was that really necessary?"

The little dragon yawned as if nothing had happened, and strolled ahead.

***

Once inside the palace, Sasha ushered them to her quarters where she could prepare the crystals. She produced a large brass bowl and pestle from a pile of her belongings and squinted at Ammon. "Before your king will agree to giving his dragons calentar, he will likely want a demonstration and your dragon is the only one that has had enough to make fire. You must bring him to the courtyard, away from anything that will burn and show him."

Ammon rubbed his bandaged forehead, remembering the heat of the blast. He wasn't sure this was such a good idea. "How do I make him breathe fire?"

Sasha filled the bowl with crystals and stopped to look at Fulgid. She grabbed a few small shards from the bowl and tossed them into the air. The dragon jumped and snatched them from midair with a loud crunch. She grinned.

"Dragons are empaths. They understand the feelings and needs of their links. If he feels you need fire, he'll produce it. You just have to let him know you need it."

***

It was nearly time for the evening meal to be served, and Ammon stood nervously in the center of the large courtyard. The dragons were already in the hold eating their meal, while the knights impatiently mingled at the edge of the courtyard waiting for everyone to arrive. Fulgid lay contently on his back, soaking up the last few rays sunlight, completely oblivious to the growing crowd around him.

Erik's clear voice rang through the courtyard. "Knights of Gaul, I've summoned you here to witness a demonstration of sorts. According to the…resident…of Laton, our dragons can breathe fire by consuming this." He held one of the crystals high above his head. "We've all read the myths of fire in the ancient books, and there may be some truth to it. Young Ammon and his dragon have apparently already used it in defense against one of the slug-like creatures responsible for the desertion of this city. Of all of us, only Ammon has seen these so called dragon-killing slugs, but I feel it is unwise to dismiss any potential threat. Ammon…you may begin!"

Ammon watched nervously as the crowd made a large circle around him. He had only expected to have to demonstrate in front of Erik and perhaps Theo, but Erik thought it best to show every one of the knights the technique. Now they all stood waiting impatiently for him demonstrate while Fulgid lay lazily on his back with his legs in the air. Ammon wiped the sweat from his palms on his breeches.

"Fulgid, please! Lets get this over with!"

A loud snore from the little dragon suddenly broke the silence of the courtyard, and muffled laughter rippled through the ranks of the knights. Embarrassed, Ammon looked toward Erik and Sasha. The old woman impatiently waved for him to continue. He reached down and rolled Fulgid onto his belly and the dragon opened one eye and looked up at him sleepily.

"Please, Fulgid, just blow a few flames and we can both go off to dinner!"

Fulgid yawned and flicked his tail unappreciatively.

"Fulgid, please?"

The golden dragon slowly sat up, ignoring the crowd surrounding him and focused on something in the distance. His ears swiveled back and forth as if listening to the murmur of the Knights.

Ammon shrugged his shoulders and turned to Erik. "I don't think he'll…"

HISSSSSSSSSSSSS…

Ammon gripped the hilt of his sword and spun towards the noise. That wasn't a noise he'd ever forget for as long as he lived. Fulgid's back was arched tight, and he bared his teeth as a loud growl rose from his throat. Someone in the crowd shouted and all eyes watched in disbelief as a large gray Kala-Azar appeared at the end of the court, snaking its way towards Ammon. The rippling hide of its bulbous body glistened wetly as it lurched forward. Unblinking black eyes fixated on Fulgid and clicking mandibles around a gaping maw dripped acidic saliva onto the cobblestones.

Knights scrambled for their weapons, and soon volleys of arrows streaked across the courtyard to strike harmlessly off the side of the creature. Theo's authoritative voice commanded his men to draw their longswords and prepare to attack.

"Stop you fools!" Sasha's unmistakable screech halted them for a moment.

"Your swords and arrows are useless! Without the fire even your dragons cannot defeat them!"

Useless or not, Ammon wouldn't let Fulgid face the slug alone. He drew his and faced the oncoming slug with determination. Fulgid moved to the right, drawing the attention of the slug and Ammon slowly raised his blade. This time he would try impaling the beast rather than slicing at it. As soon as the slug turned, Ammon pounced, driving the tip of the sword into the back of the bulbous head.

Like a spring, the blade bent, then sprang back, sending Ammon reeling backwards. The slug swung its thick tail with surprising speed, striking him on the hip, and he crumpled in a heap several paces away. Fulgid growled loudly, and the black eyes returned its attention to the little golden dragon. Fulgid backed up slowly as the slug followed, its hissing growing louder and louder until it became a high pitched sound that sent shivers down Ammon's backbone. He tried desperately to stand up but found he could barely move his leg. He watched helplessly as Fulgid drew the Kala-Azar further back.

Finally, the dragon stood up on his hind legs and Ammon instinctively covered his face and turned away before a deafening roar and blast of heat sent him tumbling across the stones. Moments later a set of hands gripped his shoulders and pulled him roughly across the cobblestones. Intense pain enveloped his entire body and the sound of running footsteps and shouts slowly faded from his hearing before he passed out.

***

When he opened his eyes, he was shirtless and laying face down on the bed in his room. He rolled to his side and instantly felt the burns on his back come to life. He stifled a groan and pushed himself up to a sitting position and looked around. Fulgid lay curled on his pillow, watching Ammon intently. Laying next to the fireplace were the tattered, charred remains of his shirt. Through the bedroom door Ammon could see Sasha perched on the edge of a chair in his sitting room. She had the large brass bowl between her feet and was crushing calentar with a long pestle. She was talking softly with someone, and smiled when she saw Ammon sitting on the edge of the bed.

He stood up and instantly felt the swelling in his leg and hip from where the slug had hit him. He shook his head as he limped to the wardrobe. His old leather shirt from the Nest would not have burned so easily but Kyle would never let him wear that again. He pulled one of the silk shirts out with a heavily bandaged hand, and with his back to the door, he leaned against the wardrobe to ease the weight from his bruised leg. He winced as he slid one arm through the sleeve and struggled to pull it on the rest of the way.

Bemused, Sasha sat and watched for a moment as he wrestled with it. "Go help him El, the man is burned and bruised from head to toe and won't even ask for help getting dressed! He's either proud, stubborn or ignorant…but most likely all three!"

Ammon felt a set of hands firmly pull his shirt where he could reach it, and he carefully slid his arm through the sleeve. "Thanks El, I appreciate…"

He turned to face the boy and froze in shock. El's hood was down and a shock of long black hair spilled out in waves. Deep brown eyes gazed up at him through long eyelashes and a small nose and sharp defiant chin framed red lips. He gasped. El was most definitely *not* a young boy, but was a girl about his age. He blushed and pulled his shirt

206

closed, his bandaged fingers fumbling with the buttons. El rolled her eyes and pushed his hands away as she buttoned up his shirt.

Still in shock, Ammon grasped for something to say. "Um, thank you, I uh, I'm sorry, I didn't know you were, I mean I thought…"

El roughly buttoned the last button of his collar and looked up at Ammon with a smirk. "You thought wrong." Curtly she turned and walked back to the sitting room. As she walked away, Ammon noticed the bandages covering the palms of both her hands.

"What did you do to your hands?"

She only sniffed loudly and sat down in one of the chairs without saying a word.

Sasha looked up from her bowl of powder. "She dragged you away from the hot stones that dragon of yours cooked the slug on, then beat the flames out of your shirt with her hands." She shook her head and returned to inspecting the powder. "Mild burns, but bad enough to warrant bandaging. Quite painful too I'd wager." She grinned crookedly. "The way she acts towards you, she'll likely let you roast next time."

Ammon stepped into the sitting room and looked at El. She sat leaning back in the chair with her legs crossed, staring at her boots as if he wasn't there. He still wasn't over the shock that she was a girl. He cleared his throat. "Thank you, El. You didn't have to do that. I know you don't particularly like me for some reason, and for that I'm sorry. I just want you to know I appreciate what you did."

El sat for a moment, furiously wiggling her toes back and forth before looking up from the floor. "Yes, well I hate the smell of burning toad."

Ammon's eyes narrowed as he forced a smile at her. "Well maybe you should keep your hands out of the fire then."

Shock spread over her face as her jaw dropped, and Ammon turned his back and walked back into the bedroom to find his boots. So much for his peace offering! Sasha roared with laughter.

Ammon stamped his boots on and then inspected his armored vest. It was covered in ash but otherwise was unharmed and he slipped it on. The burns he had on his back would likely have been considerably worse if he hadn't been wearing it. If these slugs were going to start appearing regularly, he was going to wear it to bed at night. Fulgid followed him out to the sitting room just as Erik opened the door and came in.

"Ammon! I was just coming to ask Sasha to notify me when you awoke! How do you feel son?"

Ammon held up his bandaged hands and shook his head. "Rather helpless at the moment! I can't even button my own shirt!" He felt his face turning red again.

Erik gently placed a hand on his shoulder. "No, not helpless by any means. From what Sasha has told me, that thing would have killed quite a few of us if not for you and that dragon of yours." He frowned for a moment. "A creature that preys on dragons is something we've never encountered before, and this ability to breathe fire? I could only have dreamed! This truly is a different world on this side of the mountains. I only wish Boris were here to see it."

Sadness tilted the corners of his eyes as he watched Sasha grind more of the crystals into powder. "Ammon, I hate to ask this of you, but I have no other choice. Until the dragons have had enough calentar to produce fire, Fulgid is our only protection. If just one of those slugs gets into the Hold it would be disastrous. I need you and Fulgid to guard the Hold. Sasha thinks the slugs will come for the dragons first, so we have to protect them. I don't know how else to do it. You and Fulgid will have to be our guard for a week."

Ammon sighed and nodded. He'd had a feeling this was going to happen. He knew the moment Sasha had told them it took at least a week to produce fire, and he'd started working on ideas then. He motioned Erik to sit at the table and he eased into a seat, then he laid out his plans.

Chapter 11

Guard Duty

All ten of the massive doors leading into the Hold were shut, and every dragon except for Fulgid had been moved deep inside against the thick stone walls. A small cot, table, and several chairs were centered just inside the entrance so Ammon and Fulgid could quickly reach any of the doors should the slugs break through. Piles of firewood soaked in lantern oil surrounded the entrance of each door as well. If multiple attacks came, the guards could simply throw a torch on the pile and create a wall of fire that would last until the wood burned away. An occasional attack would be easily turned back, but a constant invasion would be difficult to hold for long. Until the calentar took effect on the other dragons, all they could do was hope for the best.

The first day started out uneventful. Theo brought him several books from what was left of the palace library and a large mug of that foul black liquid. Ammon thanked him, but after Theo left, he sat idly turning the pages with bandaged fingers. He'd never learned to read, and he stared blankly at the strange markings on the pages as he flipped past looking for pictures.

A voice from behind startled him with a mocking tone. "It figures you'd be the type to be interested in politics."

Turning his head, he looked up to see El standing beside him. Embarrassed for being taken off guard so easily on his first day of guarding the Hold, he fumbled for something to say. "I...I'm not. I hate politics." He said truthfully. It was true. Every time Erik discussed politics his thoughts drifted to the plantations Boris had told him about. Someday he needed to learn what kind of fruit coffee was.

El dropped a bag down on the table and pointed a finger at the book he'd been looking at. "Then why read that?"

Ammon shrugged. "Theo brought it to me."

She sat on the edge of the table, picked up his mug and sniffed it. "How can you drink this stuff without cream and honey?"

Ammon shrugged his shoulders. "Never had it that way." He watched her suspiciously. This was the most talkative and the most friendly she'd been towards him. She was up to something.

El turned the bag upside down, and several jars and bundles of bandages spilled out onto the table and she muttered sarcastically. "I would have thought a rich boy like you would have been raised on cream and honey from the day you were born."

Ammon threw his head back and barked a laugh. "Me? A rich boy? What in the world would make you think that?"

She slammed one of the little pots down onto the table so hard the lid popped off. Crossing her arms she sneered at him. "Oh I don't know, let me think. Perhaps because we're about the same age and you've already linked a dragon, although it's one unlike anything I've ever seen or heard about. Then there is the fact that every person I've met, including the knights call you sire. You're king drops in to visit you in your own chambers and talks as if you are an equal! You strut around here in that gaudy golden armor with an Honor blade on your side that you couldn't possibly have earned already. What else could you be but a rich boy? Am I supposed to think you are just an ordinary peasant?"

Ammon felt his temples starting to throb as his stomach started to boil. Irritated, he raised a bandaged hand and pointed a blistered finger at El as he leaned forward in his chair. "A bare two months ago I was an orphan working in a nest with no more than a handful of copper talons in my pocket!" He thumped his fist against his armored vest. "As for this? I accidentally linked to the dragon that was supposed to belong to the heir of the throne! He wanted to use Fulgid to overthrow King Erik, but I got him instead! Now he wants me dead! He already sent an assassin to kill me but failed, then chased us into the tunnel with an army, killing my friend and his dragon! I didn't ask for any of this, but it's mine to deal with and I'm going to make the best of it."

He nodded at Fulgid who lay curled on the pillow of the cot. "He's the closest thing to family I have, and now I wouldn't change it if I could. Whether you believe I'm a knight or a peasant doesn't really matter to me because it changes nothing! So why don't you just leave me alone? Go away, go spend your time with that old woman, or alone, or make friends with a Kala-Azar for all I care!" Ammon stood up and looked her in the eye. "Just leave me alone."

El slid off the table and scrubbed her palms against her breeches as she looked down at the small pile of jars. Suddenly she turned on her heel and stalked off, fists clenched at her sides. Ammon sat down with folded arms over his chest and watched her walk towards the small side entrance door of the Hold where Sasha was giving a guard a small jar of ointment. Fulgid lifted his head from the pillow and gave a low growl.

Ammon snorted. "I agree! That girl could drive the patience out of a rock." For some reason El easily irritated him, but he didn't know why.

Fulgid growled again, this time much louder, and Ammon peered over his shoulder at him. He was now standing on the pillow, head down and the golden eyes were starting to glow white. Ammon jumped to his feet and followed Fulgid's gaze. He was staring at the small door near Sasha and the guard. El was still walking towards them and was now directly in front of the door. Leaping from the chair he drew his sword and shouted as he ran. Fulgid streaked past him.

"Slugs! Slugs at the door!"

El stopped and looked back in confusion as Ammon screamed at her to get away from the door. Before she could take a step, the thick wooden door behind her shuddered violently. With a loud creak, the bottom of the door began to fold inwards until, with a horrifying crack, it burst open. A fat bulbous body slipped past and started slithering over the firewood barrier.

Ammon yelled to the guard as he ran. "Light it! Light the fire!"

The guard grabbed a torch from the wall and hurled it onto the oil soaked wood. In seconds the entire barrier burst into a wall of smoky flames. El stood frozen a few paces away, watching in horror as the slug writhed in the inferno. Squirming back and forth, it lurched headfirst into the barrier and broke through, tumbling over the burning logs and rolling onto the floor at El's feet. Fulgid skidded to a stop in front of the slug and stood up on his rear feet with his head back. Ammon raced past at a dead run and flung himself at El, knocking her to the floor. As they slid to a stop he pulled her beneath him and shielded her as a tremendous blast roared behind them. When he looked up again the slug was disintegrated, leaving nothing but blackened scorch marks on the stone floor.

Ammon rolled over and jumped to his feet as he patted at the smoldering bits of his shirt with his bandaged hands. The guards had gathered and were working to shut the door while others pulled the burning logs apart and smothered them with wet blankets. Ammon quickly checked the other doors and instructed the guards to rearrange the firewood barriers so they couldn't be knocked over so easily.

Satisfied that the doors were secure, he walked back to the table. It seemed Fulgid had the ability to sense when the slugs approached, and at the moment, the little dragon was relaxed. He eased himself into the chair and picked up the mug Theo had brought him earlier and took a long sip. The bitter drink was barely lukewarm but he didn't care, he needed to do something with his hands to keep them from shaking. After he drained the mug, he pulled one of the books closer and flipped it open. Black specks of burnt bandage flaked off his hands onto the pages.

He didn't look up when El sat down at the table. She reached across and carefully began to unwind the burnt bandages on his left hand. Neither said a word, and Ammon stared blankly at the book, occasionally flipping a page. When she finished, she started on his right hand. She worked silently as she applied the ointment and wrapped it with fresh bandages.

When she was done there was a long pause, then she spoke in a voice so soft it was barely audible. "I could teach you, if you want."

Ammon turned another page. "What are you talking about?"

With a tiny giggle, she reached over and tapped the book with a slender finger. "You have it upside down."

Ammon felt his ears grow hot, but before he could say anything, El got up and walked behind him.

"Let's get that armor off so I can look at your back. I'm sure the bandages need changing and you probably have new burns as well."

Ammon sighed reluctantly as she helped him slip the vest over his head and charred bits of cloth fell to the floor. El gently plucked the burnt threads from his back and spread the soothing ointment over blistered skin.

Softly, and very faintly he heard her whisper. "Thank you."

He gritted his teeth against the pain as she placed bandages against the blisters. "You're welcome."

Later that night Fulgid alerted him just before another slug burst through one of the doors, but the guards had the barrier burning before he got there. Each day the number of attacks increased and by the fifth day Ammon had completely run out of shirts. El replaced the burned bandages several times each day, and as the sixth day approached, she threw down the last piece of burnt bandage from his back in exasperation.

"You don't even need a shirt now, you're completely covered in bandages! The other dragons had better start breathing fire soon or this will never heal. I'm afraid you'll be covered in scars as it is!"

The worst of the attacks always happened after nightfall. Again and again the slugs pushed their way through the doors, sometimes two or three at a time.

Frustrated, Ammon watched the fires roar almost constantly with the wood they'd worked so hard to gather for the winter. The screams of slugs echoed through the smoke-filled Hold long into the night as Ammon and Fulgid blasted fireballs at any that managed to get past the barriers. An excited Theo came during one of the few lulls just as Ammon downed a fourth cup of the black liquid mixed with honey and cream that El had brought to him.

"Ebony just blew her first breath of fire! It wasn't nearly as impressive as Fulgid's, but it will be effective! Until now, the dragons have been sullen and quiet in the back. An hour ago Ebony started getting antsy, so I brought her up front. Since then two more have started acting the same way. By breakfast we will have enough help so you can rest!"

A wave of relief washed over Ammon. He was so tired that every bone in his body ached and each burn screamed against his skin. Even Fulgid looked miserable. His eyes were still bright, but he no longer bounded so quickly from spot to spot. Ammon knew they wouldn't have been able to keep going much longer. Theo's timing couldn't have been better.

He positioned Ebony and the two other dragons by the doors, and an hour later three more came to the front ready to fight. By the time El had brought Ammon and Fulgid their meal, there were enough dragons to man every gate. Ammon collapsed face down in his bed for the first time in days, and Fulgid crawled onto the pillow beside his head. Within minutes both of them were snoring in a deep sleep. He didn't even wake when El changed his bandages.

***

Ammon awoke to see Theo looking down at him. Blinking his eyes as he sat up and stretched gingerly, he winced against the pain as the bandages on his back pulled his skin.

Theo shoved a steaming cup into his hands and smiled. "It's about time you woke up. You've been asleep for two days. I was beginning to get concerned!"

Ammon's jaw cracked as he yawned and he took a sip from the mug. "I've been asleep for two days?"

Theo nodded. "I would have awoken you sooner but that girl El wouldn't let anyone near you. She threatened to personally feed anyone to the slugs if they bothered you." He chuckled and pointed at something behind Ammon. "And I believe her! I'd watch out for that one if I were you, Ammon."

Ammon turned and felt his jaw drop. El sat at a table on the far side of the room talking with Kyle. Fulgid was stretched out on her lap with his feet in the air. She was casually rubbing his belly and he was obviously enjoying it.

Theo tilted his head in wonder. "He woke up the next morning but you were still asleep and he wouldn't leave your side. El figured he was probably hungry and got him to eat some dried pork. You know it's rare that a dragon allows anyone else to feed it when it's guarding its link?"

Ammon shook his head in disbelief. Leave it to Fulgid to accept a woman who hated him.

Theo refilled Ammon's cup. "Anyway, we all would have been glad to let you sleep, but the Hold isn't exactly comfortable quarters for five hundred or so people and two hundred dragons. No one dares explore the palace in case there are slugs hiding inside and our dragons can't fit through the doors. None of the hatchlings that are small enough to go inside have been able to produce a fireball much bigger than your hand."

Ammon sighed. "So you need Fulgid to sniff them out." He jerked his thumb at El. "Maybe she could've got him to do it."

Theo put his mug down and looked across the room at them. "No, Ammon, she couldn't. Nobody could. A dragon's instinct is to protect its link. That is the only important thing to a dragon and nothing else matters to them. Don't let yourself be fooled into thinking otherwise."

Theo pushed the chair back and stood up. "Let me know when you're ready and I'll go with you. I don't think it'll take long, as dragons seem to have an ability to sense when the slugs are near. Fulgid should be able to lead us right to them."

Ammon yawned once more. "We can go now I guess. Then I'll get something to eat."

He steadied himself against the table as he stood. Every muscle and bone throbbed and his head ached. The two of them walked slowly across the room as Ammon worked the stiffness from his legs.

El looked up as they came close and gave Theo a dark frown. "Couldn't let him sleep a while longer eh? The palace has been here for thousands of years, it wasn't going anywhere." Theo shrugged his shoulders but said nothing.

El stood up and slung a sack over her shoulder. "Lets get this over with then, so he can get some rest." She turned to face the two of them before they could utter a word. "Yes, I'm going with you. I haven't been slopping goo and bandages on your hide just to have it burned off again. Besides, Sasha has asked me to stay near you. She seems to think there is something important about that gold dragon of yours." Ammon opened his mouth to protest, but she held up her hand and cut him off. "I will slap you if I have to."

Ammon's mouth snapped shut. When agitated, the woman could make Kala-Azar seem cute and cuddly.

The Hold doors were open now, and as they stepped out into the sunlight, Ammon could see the courtyard was completely blackened with soot. He looked at Theo questioningly.

"A few hours after you went to sleep all of the dragons had the fire. As soon as that happened we decided to go on the offensive. We threw open the doors and blasted our way out. There were hundreds of slugs across the courtyard descending on the Hold, all of them screaming at once. As soon as the first dragons could break through, we took to the air and burned them from above. By the time night fell, not a single one made it across the courtyard alive. I'm sure there are more hiding throughout the city and in the hills, but now the tables have turned and we're hunting them instead. We're combing the streets the best we can, trying to draw them out."

He looked quizzically down at Fulgid trotting beside Ammon. "You may be interested to know none of the dragons, regardless of age or size, have matched Fulgid's ability to breathe fire, at least not yet. We're hoping their abilities increase the longer they take the calentar."

As the three of them climbed the steps to the palace, a shadow flew overhead as several dragons circled. Theo shaded his eyes and watched them land in the courtyard. "Those must be the Laton dragons coming in from the countryside. Sasha asked Erik to send out riders with satchels of calentar and maps. Apparently she knows exactly where every one of them is. If what she says is true, in a few weeks there will be more dragons assembled here than the world has seen in many, many years!"

El sniffed indignantly. "It's true. You'll soon see!"

Ammon rolled his eyes and followed them wordlessly up the stairs to the palace. If this is how she was going to act, it was going to be a long day.

The palace interior looked much the same as it had before. They searched room to room and found two Kala-Azar hiding in Ammon's chambers. Fulgid made quick work of eliminating them, destroying the rugs in the process, but otherwise the only damage was a layer of soot covering everything. Another slug was waiting in Erik's chambers, and scrolls of paper and a good portion of the table were burned when Fulgid destroyed it. As they worked their way through, Ammon noticed that it was the places that Fulgid frequented where they found slugs waiting. Everywhere else seemed undisturbed, but to be safe, they decided to search it anyway.

As large as the palace was, there were places that had not yet been explored, and in one area they stumbled upon an armory. Ammon stared in wonder at the row after row of armor, shields, and swords. Theo walked down one of the rows and called out to Ammon and El. Holding his torch up to the dust-covered sword hanging on the wall, he pointed to the one Ammon wore.

"Look, it's the same odd style as the one you have, Ammon. I had thought perhaps your sword was one of a kind, but it appears quite common here judging from the number of them on these walls."

El snorted. "Common? Hardly!" She turned to Ammon and frowned. "I told you before it was an Honor Blade!"

Ammon shrugged. "Yes, I remember you saying that now. I was a bit…distracted…at the time though. So what does it mean?"

El squinted her eyes at him mischievously and smirked. "If you'd read that book you'd know." Embarrassed, Ammon looked away and she continued. "An Honor Blade is given only to royalty and to those knights who earn the right to carry one through great acts of courage or personal sacrifice. With it comes the responsibility to act as an authority figure. If there is a dispute, the bearer of the Blade acts as judge."

Theo rubbed his chin thoughtfully. "How do you know all this if the city was abandoned long before you were born?"

El shrugged. "Grandmother Sasha insisted I learn the laws, titles, customs, and traditions of the country for the day the dragons return. I always thought it was foolish because the dragons would never come back. I guess I was wrong."

A loud crash from behind startled them and they all spun around. Theo held the torch high over his head to cast the light further into the room. At the end of the row, Fulgid stood innocently next to a shield he pulled down from a suit of armor. They breathed a sigh of relief, and El picked the shield up and placed it back on its stand next to the armor as Ammon scolded the little dragon. Theo gasped and stood still as a stone with his mouth open. Ammon and El looked up at him, then at each other.

El jerked her thumb at Theo and whispered to Ammon. "What's wrong with him?"

Ammon stood up from where he'd been kneeling next to Fulgid. "Theo? What's the matter?"

Theo pointed at the wall behind them. Ammon turned and felt his heart skip a beat. A large portrait hung on the wall of a young man with bright blue eyes and shoulder length blond hair. The resemblance was so close that Ammon could have been looking in a mirror. Theo brought the torch closer as El dusted the name plaque.

Coughing from the dust, she read it out loud. "King Halos, House of Les." She stepped back, tilting her head at the painting. "It's definitely a striking resemblance to you, Ammon. Ammon? Now you look like you've seen the ghost!"

Ammon was staring down at the shield El had carefully hung back on the stand. He held up his bandaged hand and unwrapped his finger to expose the ring he wore. In the firelight, El could see the engraving was identical to the gold dragon insignia on the face of the shield.

El shook her head in confusion. "I don't understand. This is impossible, King Halos died over fifty years ago!"

Ammon felt sick. Whatever these coincidences meant, he felt sure it wouldn't lead to anything good. Despite his argument that they should leave things where they were, Theo insisted they bring them downstairs to the Hold where Erik had set up his temporary chambers. Ammon reluctantly carried the shield while Theo carefully hefted the large portrait down the hallway in front of them. El walked beside Ammon and Fulgid lost in thought.

"We should tell grandmother. She would understand more about this than anyone. She knew King Halos. He was the last ruler of DoTaria before the fall of the city."

Ammon only nodded, there wasn't much else he could do. He had a bad feeling about this. The look on his face must have been obvious because El patted his arm reassuringly before she left to find Sasha.

When they got to Erik's quarters, it was so crowded with people there was standing room only. Ammon held the door open, and Theo shuffled in with the portrait and they looked around curiously. Erik was in the far end of the room facing them with a broad smile across his face. Behind him, Shane was leaning against the wall and laughing hysterically. Ammon stood on his toes and strained to see over the shoulders of the people in front of him. He could just see the top of a bald headed man sitting in a chair facing Erik. Standing off to the side were four knights with strange looking armor. Although obviously still made from dragon scales, the overlapping design swirled in a whimsical fashion rather than in straight neat rows like typical armor.

Erik noticed Ammon and Theo in the back of the room and gestured for them to come closer. "You two are just in time! Not a quarter of an hour has past since these four honorable DoTarian Knights arrived carrying a rather large payload between their dragons. Perhaps you'd like to say hello to one of their passengers?"

The bald man turned in his chair. His face was covered with partially healed scratches and the remnants of a large bruise above his left eye still colored his forehead. One arm hung limp in a sling, and Ammon could see his leg was wrapped and braced with saplings. Despite all the injuries, there was no mistaking the familiar smile on the man's face. Stunned, Ammon let the shield slip from his hands and it rattled loudly on the floor. Fulgid suddenly bounded across the room and leapt excitedly onto Boris' lap.

"Aye! As happy as I am to see you, could you get this confounded oversized lapdog of a gilded dragon off of me before he breaks my other leg?" With his good arm he reached up and scratched Fulgid behind the ears.

Ammon plucked Fulgid from Boris' lap and placed the little dragon on the floor, then embraced his friend warmly as he struggled for words. "I...I thought you were dead! I saw you and Ellis fall, and I tried to get to you...I tried but I couldn't!" Ammon looked down at Fulgid as the words caught in his throat. "We tried, but the water pulled you away before we could get there!"

Boris reached up and grabbed Ammon's shoulder. Despite his injuries, the man still had a grip like iron. "I know, I saw what you did. Even if you had reached me there was nothing to be done. Ellis took a horrible hit, and when we fell my leg was tangled in the stirrup and pinned beneath him. Even if you'd have gotten me free, I wouldn't have left him there to the mercies of Tirate and his men."

Ammon felt the blood drain from his face. He wasn't sure how to ask about Ellis, but Boris just smiled.

"Yes, he's alive. The water swept us down the river and through that blasted hole in the the mountain." He shook his head. "Once you go into that hole it's complete darkness. The two of us were tossed and dragged over the rocks like rag dolls until we went over the falls. Once we hit the bottom of that, the water was much calmer and we floated out the other side of the mountains. Neither one of us were able to do much of anything but keep our heads above water. We were fortunate a couple of these lads were fishing on the banks and managed to pull us ashore."

He patted his heavily bandaged leg. "They doctored me up pretty well, but Ellis was in bad shape. It's a good thing they had some fair knowledge about dragons, or he wouldn't have made it. Who would have thought there were still people around with dragons on this side?" He looked up at Erik. "More dragons than we ever could have imagined! Although they'd never seen one as big as my Ellis!" he chuckled.

One of the knights rolled his eyes as he tore his gaze away from Fulgid. "And he won't let us forget it either! It took four dragons and a sling and carry the wounded beast here."

Boris nodded. "One of the roughest landings I've ever experienced too!"

The seamstress woman that had stitched Boris' face suddenly stepped through the doorway. "Here you are with a broken arm and leg and you complain about their landings? I've sewed you up enough times to know just how rough some of your touchdowns have been!" The woman stood glowering down at Boris, hands on her hips.

Shane buried his face with his hands as he tried to stifle a laugh, but Erik slapped his knee heartily. "Ha! She's got you there Boris! She's probably seen more of your insides than of your outer skin!"

Ammon was chuckling until the seamstress suddenly turned on him and poked a finger at his chest.

"And you young man! The way you go through shirts, it's obvious you take after him! Mind you I'm too old to be following the both of you around like a forsaken puppy, so you'd best start looking for someone with a needle to sew that pretty face of yours back up when you get cut shaving!" Ammon's jaw dropped and the room erupted in laughter.

Theo placed a hand on his shoulder. "I wouldn't let your man Kyle at you with a needle if I were you. He may be a decent man for taking care of your daily meals, but I've seen his stitching and it's nothing to brag about."

Laughter filled the room again and Kyle, who sat on a chair near the back, laughed the loudest as he pointed to the crude stitching on his shirt.

With his good hand, Boris gently plucked the bandages on Ammon's hands. "They told me you've been busy but it looks to me like you've been playing with fire! So it's true? The dragons really can breathe fire with these crystals?"

Ammon nodded, but before he could say anymore, Sasha entered the room followed by El. All four of the DoTarian knights bowed with a fist to their chest. Her voice creaked like a rusty hinge as she impatiently waved her hand at them. "Yes, yes, none of that now. Theo, El tells me you have found something of interest to show us?"

Theo jumped as if startled. "I'm sorry! I was so surprised to see Boris I'd forgotten about it!" He lifted the painting up for everyone to see. "We found this in one of the armory halls when searching for slugs. It's titled King Halos, House of Les."

El held up the shield that Ammon had dropped. "We also found this beside the portrait. It's the same insignia as what is on Ammon's ring."

Boris whistled. "By the dragons teeth, it's a spitting image!"

Erik rubbed his jaw thoughtfully. "How is this possible? Who is this King Halos?"

Sasha eased herself into a chair and took a deep breath. "Perhaps it is time to tell the story. I've suspected it since I first laid eyes on you, but please understand that I had to be sure. This land has already seen far too much angst in recent years to have their hopes dashed needlessly." A sad look came into her eyes and she cleared her throat.

"Halos of the House of Les was the last king to sit on the throne before the Great Fall. He was not just the ruler of this city, but of all DoTaria. He was a good king and a great man, and I consider myself blessed to have counted him as a friend despite our differences. In the last days when the calentar mines ran out, the dragons could breathe no more fire. Halos ordered the knights to scatter throughout the countryside with their dragons in hopes that if enough of them survived, they might one day find a deposit of calentar and return to fight the slugs. Once the dragons were gone, the Kala-Azar began to prey upon the people instead. He ordered the city abandoned and stayed behind with his dragon to draw the Kala-Azar away so the people could escape. He was never seen again. Killed by the slugs no doubt and his dragon too."

Theo and Ammon exchanged glances. Erik rested a hand gently on her shoulder and spoke softly. "I understand. I'm sorry, Sasha. It is the king's duty to his people to protect them the best he can, no matter the personal cost."

A tear trickled down her weathered cheek, and the years showed heavily in the creases of her face. A moment later she cleared her throat and continued. "The real question is something I've pondered since I first saw young Ammon. But to understand the present, you must first learn the past. You must have history records in Gaul, how far back do they go?"

Erik sat on the edge of his desk and frowned. "Most of the palace records go back only a few hundred years, some a bit further. The rest were consumed in a fire that nearly destroyed the entire city. The oldest records of anything in Gaul would be the Book of Dragons which was kept in the Nest at the time so it was unscathed. It lists all dragons hatched and who they were linked to, for over nine hundred years at least."

"I see. Interesting!" Sasha folded her hands on her lap and looked at Ammon curiously. "The records in the Laton library go back approximately two thousand years or more. Since coming back to the palace, I've been researching the histories and found some interesting events even I was unaware of. About nine hundred and seventy years ago, King Thaire of the House of Les announced his intentions to expand the DoTarian Empire. Under a misguided interpretation of an old prophecy, he sent men, women, and dragons out on a quest to explore and colonize the lands under his family's insignia of the golden dragon. Several of the groups never were heard from again, one of which was led by his youngest son, Ethanel.

Ethanel was well educated in subjects concerning the earth and was credited with discovering many calentar deposits with his dragon who had the unusual Gift of Finding. He spent many years directing the mines. About the time of Ethanel's disappearance, there is a notation of a tremendous shaking of the earth that caused significant damage to the city. Many of the miners were killed when the tunnels collapsed, and it was believed Ethanel was one of them."

She waved a long, bony finger between Ammon and the portrait. "Now I suspect Ethanel had tunneled beneath the mountains and discovered the land you call home. Intending to fulfill his father's wishes to explore, he led a group of followers and dragons through the tunnel and became trapped on the other side when the tunnel collapsed. Unable to return, he established a colony, which you now call the Kingdom of Gaul. Why he didn't try to tunnel back I can only guess. It may have been difficult to convince anyone to step back underground after such a violent upheaval of the earth."

Sasha paused. "What can you tell me about the families of Gaul?"

Erik sat with his fingers laced together under his chin, and it was a long moment before he spoke. "As I had said before, the oldest records of the palace only go back a few hundred years. The Book of Dragons is the oldest, but doesn't give much information except the names of those who linked. I know the House of Les was old, very old. The last of its members were thought to have died about fifteen years ago, until Ammon appeared. I knew his parents well and he has many characteristics of his father. He also possesses a ring with the House of Les family insignia on it, which he has had since a child. It is the same insignia you see on that shield in front of you."

Erik paused. "Considering the likeness of the portrait and the insignia, I think there is far too much coincidence here to simply dismiss. I have to believe what you say is true and that he is a direct connection between our two lands."

Sasha nodded in agreement. "I too, fully believe it. Ammon must be the soul living survivor and descendant of Ethanel, son of Thaire from the House of Les. You must realize of course the significance of this?"

Erik nodded slowly.

Sasha pursed her lips thoughtfully. "Of course you will wish to see the records yourself, but the bloodline cannot be denied its rightful place. You may place a challenge in front of the Hall if you want to contest this."

Erik stared at the portrait for a long moment, his brow furrowed in thought.

"No. No, I have no wish to contest it. The outcome would be the same regardless." He smiled. "Besides, I have my own reason for wanting this. I have no need to review the records, the evidence before me is sufficient."

Sasha folded her hands and tilted her head. "It is not without reservation that I also submit to it. After such a long separation, there will be differences between the lands. Hardship has torn DoTaria apart and there exists old feuds in the Houses that must be resolved. This unification will be a challenge beyond imagination."

There was a long, uncomfortable silence in the room as the two contemplated each other's words. Finally Ammon could stand it no longer. "What does all this mean?"

Erik looked up and studied Ammon's face for a long moment before getting to his feet. With a hand on Ammon's shoulder, he smiled a genuine smile. "It means that Tirate does not, nor ever had claim to the throne whatsoever!" He then slowly dropped to one knee, lifted Ammon's hand to his lips, and kissed the ring on his finger. With his head bowed, Erik's solemn voice echoed across the room. "I, Erik of the House of Thayer, swear allegiance to you, Ammon of the House of Les, King of Gaul!"

Ammon's eyes widened in shock as gasps erupted from everyone in the room.

Sasha knelt beside Erik and firmly grasped Ammon's hand and kissed the ring. "I, Sasha of the House of Celest, swear allegiance to you Ammon of the House of Les, King of DoTaria!"

One of the DoTarian knights dropped to his knees beside Sasha and grabbed her hand. "No my lady! This cannot be! Do not do this!"

Sasha turned and gave him a stern look. "Silence! Do not question my decisions or my motives, knight! I have waited many years for this moment, long before you were even conceived!"

Shamed, the knight hung his head and backed away, but not before Ammon saw him glance defiantly at him. Ammon felt his blood turn to ice and the hair on his neck stood on end. To make things worse, Boris painfully rose from his chair and knelt in front of him the best he could with his broken leg.

"Where the House of Thayer goes, so goes the House of Dejias."

To Ammon's dismay, one by one, everyone in the room knelt and proclaimed their alliance to him. He shook his head in confusion. This couldn't possibly be right! What were Erik and Sasha thinking? It seemed that the more his wished for a quiet, simple life in the country, the more it moved out of his reach. Even from across the room he could see the disgusted look on El's face as she quietly slipped out the door. Well, at least she would still treat him the same old way.

***

From the palace windows, Ammon could see a stream of people filing through the city gates. As news had spread across DoTaria of the newly found deposits of calentar, the population of Laton began to swell. A few of the original elderly inhabitants returned with their descendants to reclaim their dilapidated houses. They flocked to the city dragging the few scant belongings they owned and waited as the city was gradually cleansed of slugs.

DoTarian Knights both young and old arrived daily on their dragons, eager to claim their share of the calentar. Fulgid enjoyed almost legendary status amongst the people of Gaul and many of the DoTarian's, but a few cast cynical stares at the little dragon. Repairs had extended beyond the palace now to the city gates, streets, and buildings. The main roads were cleared and rubble removed by the ever-increasing number of hands moving into the city.

Ammon wrinkled his nose at the smell of an unwashed body, and he turned from the window as Sasha ambled down the hall towards him. "Ah!" she cackled. "You aren't so easy to sneak up on are you?" She squinted at Fulgid sitting on Ammon's shoulder and broke into a toothless grin. "Your new chambers are ready now! Come! Come!"

He sighed reluctantly and followed her down the hall. Since they'd moved out of the Hold a week ago and back into the palace, Erik and Sasha had insisted he should move into larger quarters. No amount of objecting could convince them otherwise, and finally he resigned himself to accept the fact that he had no say in the matter.

At the end of the hallway Sasha threw open the doors and stood aside as Ammon entered. The room was impossibly huge, with high rounded ceilings dotted with crystal chandeliers. Rows upon rows of highly polished tables and high-backed chairs completely filled the room except for a pace wide opening down the middle. At the far end of the room, on a raised platform was a heavily gilded throne encrusted with rubies, emeralds, and diamonds. Ammon could only stare at the gaudy chair and wonder just how uncomfortable it would be to sit on.

Somewhere they'd found cloth to make curtains for the giant windows overlooking the vast courtyard. The ornate tapestries that decorated the room had been removed, cleaned, and returned to the walls in all their original splendor. Dragons embroidered with gold and silver thread decorated each one, and glittered in the sunlight that streamed from the tall windows.

Ammon swallowed, and his voice was faint. "These are my chambers now?"

Sasha cackled and shook her head. "No! This is the Hall of Knights. This is where you meet to hear and judge disputes that cannot be resolved by those who carry Honor Blades. Here you dispense justice, bestow honors, and sadly, decide the occasional war. The king's chambers are in the next room."

The old woman motioned him to follow her down the long isle. A few paces to the right of the throne was another set of doors where Erik and Theo stood waiting. Swinging them open, she stepped through and waited for Ammon to enter.

Ammon blinked in disbelief. His chambers were bigger than the Nest! The sitting room was lined with overstuffed couches and chairs that surrounded large ornate fireplaces on each of the four walls. Beyond the sitting room, through another set of double doors was his living room. A massive fireplace dominated the length of one entire wall, big enough to burn entire tree length logs. On the other walls were hundreds of books neatly stacked on shelves that reached to the ceiling. Large oil lamps with clear crystal lenses stood on elegant stands beside numerous chairs and couches that would easily sit a dozen people comfortably. Near one of the windows was a long polished desk inlaid with golden dragons across its dark wood surface.

Behind the desk, another set of doors led to the bedchambers. The largest canopy bed Ammon had ever seen lay centered in the middle of the room and was covered with fresh sheets. Fulgid gleefully hopped from his shoulder onto the bed and curled up on one of the pillows while Ammon wandered around the room. Fireplaces located in the walls on either side of the bed would easily warm the room, and thick rugs covered the polished marble floor. A glass-paned door lead out to a balcony over the courtyard that overlooked the southern part of the city and the mountains. The view of the snow-covered peaks as they caught the sunlight was stunning. Overwhelmed, Ammon stood on the balcony and gripped the stone railing tightly. Erik's strong, thin hand squeezed his shoulder.

"Ammon…King Ammon…Your palace, your city, truly is beautiful!"

Ammon pulled his hands from the rail and clenched his fists. "Please! Don't call me that. I am not a king, or a knight, or…anyone! I'm just…me!" He faced Erik, his voice pleading. "I'm just an tender who accidentally linked a dragon! You know I can't do this! I can't lead this city…these people! I don't know how! You are the real king, you know how to rule and make decisions! These people should be following you, not me!"

Erik was silent as he looked out over the balcony at the mountains. A slight breeze stirred a few strands of white hair on his head, and his clear blue eyes were brighter now than Ammon had ever seen. When he spoke, his voice was low, but strong.

"Ammon, you must accept what you've become and who you must be. The ring, your lineage, the likeness of the portrait, all these cannot be mere coincidence. There are many reasons why I have chosen to surrender the crown to you, and in time you will understand. For now I simply ask that you trust in me. Your bloodline has provided a means for you to obtain the crown, but it is the qualities of your heart that make it right." Erik squeezed his shoulder once more. "I would be honored to act as your advisor if you'd let me."

Sasha puckered her lips and tilted her head thoughtfully. "A wise decision! All of you as advisors…and myself too of course! DoTaria is a large country with a diverse and complicated social structure. Ammon needs training and help to deal with the problems of rebuilding an entire nation with customs and traditions different from Gaul." She cackled gleefully. "A challenge for the young king! A challenge worthy of a golden knight!"

Ammon felt like crawling under the bed and wondered if they'd ever find him in a room this size if he did.

***

After they'd left, Ammon sat alone in his new chambers in an overstuffed chair and watched as Fulgid curiously climbed across the bookshelves as he investigated his new surroundings. His head throbbed dully as the stresses of the day seeped into his brain and an unmistakable feeling of loss crept into his chest. Never again would he spend hours fishing in the Olog with his next meal his only concern. He twisted the gold ring on his finger and sighed. Like it or not, they were going to make him king over both DoTaria and Gaul and somehow he was supposed to deal with it.

Fulgid jumped into the cold fireplace and clawed through the ashes. Finding nothing of interest, he hopped onto the bed and curled up on the pillow, leaving a trail of ash across the clean white sheets.

"Kyle will have a fit when he sees the mess you made." Fulgid rolled onto his back, spreading the ash deeper into the sheets. Ammon snickered. "I wish I was as carefree as you, Fulgid, but the responsibilities keep growing! By the dragon's teeth, I can't even read, and they want me to run a kingdom? How am I supposed to do that?"

A sullen voice at the doorway replied, "I'm supposed to teach you."

Startled, Ammon instinctively leapt to his feet and as he spun, his hand reached for his sword. El was standing just outside the chamber doors, her arms folded tightly across her chest and a dark expression on her face. The voice was the same, but other than that, Ammon would not have recognized her. She no longer wore her bland brown hood, shirt, and loose breeches that Ammon had always seen her wear. Before him stood an elegantly dressed woman in a flowing sky blue gown that swept the floor in waves. Embroidered down the front were vine like flowers and her ruffled lace sleeves stopped at her elbows, exposing browned, sun tanned arms. Her flowing dark hair hung down loosely in ringlets to her shoulders, but the smoldering dark eyes glaring back at him were unchanged.

Ammon stammered as he loosened his grip on his sword. "Oh, I…um…I…didn't hear you! You…look very nice! I didn't recognize you for a moment!" Ammon bit down on his lip to stop himself from talking.

El gave a stiff curtsey. "Forgive me, my King! I didn't realize how poorly I usually look!"

Ammon resisted the urge to smack himself in the head with his hand. "That's not what I meant! I uh…I meant you look beautiful!" He felt his face going red. What was it about her that made everything he said come out backwards? Clearing his throat, he tried to regain his composure. "What was it you are supposed to teach me?"

El barely hid a sneer. "I am to teach you to read and instruct you in political history, as well as the customs of this land."

Ammon frowned. "You were told to do this? By who?"

El lowered her eyes. "Grandmother Sasha has informed me it is my duty to educate you in these areas. I am to report to you each day at a convenient time where you can begin your studies. If this displeases you, I can relay that information to someone else."

Ammon closed his eyes and rubbed his temples. It was beginning already. Would everyone soon address him with the same feigned respect? "I don't care. If you don't wish to teach me I'm sure Sasha will find someone who will. I certainly won't make you do anything you don't want to, no matter what she told you to do. Tell her I relieved you of that duty, or make something up that sounds right. You can go now."

He turned his back to her and flopped back into the overstuffed chair. If he was going to be king then he'd make sure of at least one thing. Nobody would be forced to serve him against his or her will. He looked down at his hands and ripped the bandages off. Slowly he flexed his fingers, feeling the skin stretch where the blisters had been. He should be able to start practicing with the sword again soon. Maybe then he could work out some of his frustrations. In the meantime he had to find another outlet.

He looked at Fulgid stretched out on the pillow. "What do you think about escaping from this snooty palace for awhile and going for a walk? Maybe we can get out without anyone noticing and have some peace and quiet. Somewhere without all this confounded royal treatment."

"I'd love to."

Ammon jumped in surprise and turned in the chair to see El still standing there. "I thought you left?"

El shook her head. "I didn't. I think that walk sounds nice. If anyone asks I'll tell them it's part of your education. After all, you should know the city if you're going to be king."

Ammon stared at the pretty girl in front of him and wondered how he had ever mistaken her for a boy. "Only if you want to. I will not force you, or anyone to do anything for me."

El smiled a genuine smile. "Lets go."

As they walked down the long aisle of the throne room, Ammon noticed El walking uncomfortably. "Are you ok?"

El winced as she took another step and rolled her eyes. "These slippers aren't exactly made for walking, but it's how I'm supposed to dress now while inside the palace."

Ammon thought for a moment. "So you can dress any way you want when outside the palace?" El stumbled before nodding her head. "Aren't we going outside of the palace?"

El stopped and looked at Ammon for a moment before a smile crept across her face. "I certainly can't give you a tour dressed like this can I? Would you mind if I make a quick stop at my quarters before we leave?"

Ammon smiled back. "I'd be happy to wait." She really was quite pretty when she smiled. Idly he wondered why she had to wear those clothes inside the palace when everyone else was dressed normal. It certainly seemed absurd, but he shrugged it off.

He waited outside the chamber door with Fulgid while she changed back into her familiar shirt, breeches, and boots. This time she left the hood down, letting her hair hang loosely down her back. Before long they were outside the palace and wandering the still abandoned areas of the city. Green flags hung on the sides of buildings to indicate they had been purged of Kala-Azar and safe to enter. Fulgid ran ahead as they strolled through the alleys and peered into the ruins. Occasionally El found the remnants of a sign on the side of a building and pointed out individual letters, making Ammon repeat them afterwards.

As they walked from one building to another, El suddenly became serious. "Did you really mean what you said? That you would never force me, or anyone else to do something we don't wish to do?"

Ammon shielded his eyes from the sun as he looked over the street before them. "I'm being forced to become something…someone I'm not. I don't have a choice. If I have to be king, then I will surround with people who wish to be there, not those who have to be."

El walked on silently for a little while. "That isn't the behavior I expected from a king, Ammon."

He shrugged. "I hope that's a good thing?"

She laughed a little. "Yes, I think that's a good thing."

Ammon breathed a sigh of relief. "Good. I hope this means you don't hate me anymore?"

El held her thumb and forefinger up spaced slightly apart and grinned mischievously. "Maybe just a little."

Ammon groaned and plucked a piece of long grass from between the cobblestones and threw it at her. "You're impossible!"

They spent the afternoon exploring and searching for more signs and by the time they returned to the palace he was able to recognize several of the letters on his own. Fulgid loped ahead down the hall and suddenly he skidded to a stop in front of Sasha. She stood in the doorway of her chambers silently casting a disapproving eye at El's clothing.

Ammon stepped in front of El. "Good afternoon Sasha. I hope you don't mind that I asked El to change and help acquaint me to the city. It was quite a learning experience!"

Expressionless, Sasha looked at them both. "Indeed? I'm happy to hear this! Perhaps after she's changed into more appropriate attire, she can further that learning experience in your chambers with pen and ink!"

El's face dropped, and without a word, she slipped past Sasha and closed the door. Sasha leaned forward and dusted some imaginary dirt off Ammon's shoulder. "I don't know how old you think I may be, but I assure you I wasn't born within the last fortnight." With that, she turned and entered her chambers, closing the door behind her.

Flabbergasted, Ammon looked down at Fulgid. "What was that supposed to mean?"

***

Sasha closed the door behind her and smiled. The boy was quick. Just like Halos was. She eased her aching bones into a chair and sighed. She was tired now. At eighty-four years of age, she hoped she still had enough strength left to see her work through to the end. The events had already been set into motion and the prophecy was being fulfilled, although nothing like she'd imagined. It was only a few short weeks ago that she had been shocked to see a living gold dragon on the boy's shoulder. For centuries scholars had assumed the prophecy of the gold dragon was a metaphor for the House of Les. When Halos died with no heirs to the throne she had given up on the prophecies as mere fanciful stories.

Now this marvelous gilded creature roamed the palace hallways and a direct descendant of the royal bloodline was his link. Although young, the boy had already shown his leadership abilities when he took charge during the attack of the Kala-Azar. Unfortunately he was painfully shy and lacked the self-assurance needed to be an effective king. That would come in time of course, but time was something she had little of at her age.

The boy needed backbone to stand up against those who opposed him in the Hall of Knights, or he'd be over-run and useless as a king. The House of Les had led the DoTarian Empire well with a doggedly determined stubbornness and sheer will. Now more than ever, a strong leader needed to sit on the throne in Laton if they were going to rebuild DoTaria and heal the rift between the Houses. Within a week a gathering of the knights would occur for the first time in over fifty years, and getting the knights to trust a very young Ammon as their king would be a hard battle. Their perception of him as an outsider would only make it even harder. He needed to learn as much as he could about DoTaria as quickly as possible, but without pushing him too hard. He needed to want to learn.

She looked up just as El came out of her bedchambers wearing the blue gown. She was a beautiful girl, and the perfect way to capture the attention of the young lad. She smiled at her granddaughter. Yes, the perfect learning tool!

***

El stormed down the hallway towards Ammon's chambers, kicking at the dress as she went. The pale blue ruffles bounced and flowed with each stomp, making it all the more elegant. Hard as she tried, it was impossible to appear mad in the frilly outfit, and that made her even angrier. Her grandmother had no right to do this! Ammon's stupid plan to roam the city worked for one lousy day, and now because of him, she had to wear the stupid dress every time she left her chambers! Each protest she made had been knocked flat by the fierce old woman who suddenly decided El had no business climbing through broken buildings, or fishing, or hunting, or any other activities that would be difficult to do in a dress.

She had lived on the edge of wilderness her entire life, and this wasn't a change she thought she could, or would adapt to. Why her grandmother suddenly decided to force this upon her was even more frustrating. Until now she was allowed, and even encouraged, to learn how to provide for herself. Sasha had taught her to hunt, fish, and learn what vegetation was useable for food or medicinal purposes. Since the arrival of Ammon and the rest of the strangers from the other side of the mountains, her grandmother had been acting stranger than usual. Asking the old woman inevitably led to more questions than answers. She stopped at the entrance to Ammon's chambers and tried to quiet her anger. She knew it wasn't his fault, but it sure was easy to blame him. With a deep breath, she opened the door and stepped into the large sitting room.

***

Standing shirtless in the middle of the room, Ammon held his sword straight out and balanced on his heels. It had been awhile since he'd practiced with the sword because of his injuries, but the training Boris hammered into him came back instantly. Gracefully, he moved from one stance to another, each movement of the sword slicing open one of the many acorns suspended from the ceiling with string.

Fulgid waited patiently as they hit the floor, pouncing and devouring each one with a quick crunch of his golden jaws. With each stroke of the sword, he increased his speed until it was one long flowing movement. When the last few acorns were left, the sword whistled through the air sending most of them bouncing across the floor almost at once. Impaled on the tip of the sword was the last one and Ammon deftly pulled it off and tossed it to Fulgid.

He started to wipe the sweat from his brow and stopped when he realized the tender new skin on his hands had cracked and he was bleeding again. He slipped the sword back into its scabbard as he looked around for something to use as a bandage and saw El leaning against the doorway, her mouth open. Embarrassed, he quickly grabbed his shirt off the back of a chair and pulled it over his head.

El had recovered her composure by the time Ammon turned back around, and now she stood glaring up at him with her fists on her hips. "How do you expect those hands and the rest of your wounds to heal if you keep doing stupid things like that?"

She pointed her finger at a chair, silently ordering him to sit while she rummaged through the bag she was carrying filled with parchments and quills. It was the same bag she used to carry the bandages she frequently had used on Ammon, and there were still several bundles lying at the bottom along with a jar of ointment. Ammon sat quietly as she wrapped his hands and when she was finished, she sat back in her chair and looked at the small pile of paper and quills.

"Well, I suppose you won't be doing much writing today with those hands. Grandmother will have my head wrapped in a pretty little bonnet at this rate."

Ammon inspected his hands and flexed them under the bandages before carefully asking. "A bonnet?"

El snorted. "Don't ask. I wouldn't do it anyway, not for anyone."

Ammon recognized the dangerous tone in her voice and decided to divert her attention to something less volatile. "Well, lets go into the city and read more signs then. It's much more interesting than books anyway."

El slumped back in the chair. "I can't." she said ruefully. "I'm not allowed to wear anything but these horrible gowns!" She gripped the frills across her lap with both hands in dismay. "I'd never be able to walk through the rubble in this!"

Ammon thought for a moment. "What about inside the palace? This place is huge and many of rooms I've only glanced at as we searched for slugs. Surely there are things to read like the painting we found?"

El dropped the frills from her hands. "Yes, I suppose there probably is. It's rather boring, but better than reading The History of DoTaria." She stood up and gently pulled Ammon to his feet. "Come on, the stairs are just down the hall from here."

El took one of the torches off the wall, and Fulgid led the way up the stairs to the next level. At the top she pointed down the dusty hallway. "It's all bed chambers on this floor. During a Gathering there would be more than a thousand knights here at once, although my grandmother told me there hadn't been one that big in hundreds of years."

They continued climbing to the next floor where there were rows of similar, but smaller chambers. "These were the chambers for knights awaiting a Hatch. Directly above us are the Nests."

Ammon's eyebrows rose. "The Nests are above the palace? How strange! In Gaul, the Nest is inside a mountain above the city, the palace is some distance away."

El frowned. "That makes no sense at all! Wouldn't you want your knights nearby instead of in another building? What would happen if the eggs hatched and they didn't get there in time?"

Ammon shrugged and scratched his head. "The knights stay all night in the Nest during the new moon, from evening until they've all hatched, so that isn't really an issue. Let's go see the Nests! I'm curious how different they are from ours."

It was a short climb up one flight of stairs, and they stood in the middle of a long, wide hallway lined with doors. El opened the closest door and held the torch overhead, its feeble light was swallowed in the darkness. "Let's try the south wall. I noticed one of the dragon doors were open when we were roaming the city. We should be able to see in there with the daylight shining in." At the end of the hall a dim light came from beneath one of the doors. El held up the torch as she flipped the rusted latch to the side. "This must be the one!"

Ammon pushed his shoulder against the door and it slid heavily to one side. Cobwebs and dust stirred, and the torch flickered as a small breeze came through the dragon entrance. Leaves and twigs littered the corners from abandoned bird nests, but otherwise the layout of the Nest was similar to the ones in Gaul. A tender's room was located just inside the door, and beside it were several neatly stacked metal lined buckets. A heavy wrought iron poker and tongs lay in the corner thickly layered with dust. The furnaces in each corner of the room were built of stone and mortar, rather than carved out of rock, and the firebox doors were larger. Like the Hold beneath them, they were designed for firewood rather than coal, and Ammon suspected they worked just as well.

He smiled at El. "I bet there is a beautiful view of the city from up here!" He started to walk around the large sunken area in the center of the floor and as he went past he looked down. He froze so suddenly that El bumped into him and nearly knocked him over.

Taking a quick step backwards she mumbled. "Give a little warning would ya?"

"Give me the torch for a minute!" She started to protest but Ammon cut her short. "Give me the torch!"

She handed it to him and he knelt down and held it over the deep depression in the floor.

El gasped. "Are those…?"

Ammon nodded. "Eggs!"

The ladder had long since rotted away but the iron bolts that anchored to the side were still solid. Ammon handed the torch back to El as he removed his shirt. He twisted it tight, then tied the sleeves to the iron peg and carefully climbed down into the Nest. He ran his hand across each of the eggs and shook his head in disbelief.

"There are twenty-five eggs down here and they're still warm! They must have just been laid very recently! With everything that's happened it never occurred to me that it was laying season! We've got to get a fire started and bring up the temperature in here in a hurry!"

He scrambled up the side, ran to each of the furnaces and began wrestling with the doors. Two of them opened with force, but the others were hopelessly rusted shut. He grabbed armfuls of sticks from the abandoned bird nests and stuffed them into the furnace then shoved the torch in. The dried twigs burst into flames and he slammed the furnace shut. He dusted his hands off and looked at the huge dragon entrance and frowned. "We've got to close that to keep the heat in!"

The huge dragon door hung on massive brass hinges and opened inwards. There was just enough room for Ammon to fit between the wall and the door and he braced his back against the wall and pushed. The door creaked, but barely moved an inch. El dropped the torch and slid next to Ammon. With both of them pushing, it reluctantly began to move, slowly at first and then with a loud snap, the stuck hinges let go and the door swung free. They pushed it shut and jammed a few sticks under the bottom to keep it closed.

Ammon ran to the Tender's room, dragged out a chair, and smashed it against the floor. As he loaded the pieces into the furnace he turned to El. "Take the torch and find Theo! Tell him we need firewood, lots of firewood…and a blacksmith with tools to fix the other furnace doors! Hurry! If the eggs chill the dragons will die!"

El grabbed the torch and ran down the hall, leaving Ammon to sit in the darkened Nest with Fulgid. The only light he could see was from the cracks around the large dragon doorway, and the two glittering dots of Fulgid's eyes. He couldn't help but laugh as he recalled what had happened the last time he was in a Nest. So many things had changed since the day of Fulgid's hatch. It seemed almost surreal to be tending eggs once more. Fulgid stretched out across his lap and they listened to the wood crack and pop inside the furnace. It was incredibly peaceful.

The serenity of the Nest didn't last long. Soon Ammon could hear the thumping of footsteps coming down the hallway. With torches held high, El and Theo burst through the door with Derek following closely behind carrying a giant armful of firewood. Ammon stoked the furnaces while Theo and Derek peered down at the eggs in disbelief.

Theo rubbed his jaw thoughtfully. "I've never seen so many eggs in one place before! Ebony flew off this morning with a few other dragons, but I just assumed they went hunting! This far from home I wouldn't have thought any of them would have laid eggs this season!"

Ammon shrugged. "They must have felt this was close enough to a home for eggs! Anyway, I need to know where I can get a cot and a leather shirt and breeches, and some leather gloves too. These furnaces will have to be cleaned more often than the coal furnaces in Gaul."

Theo and Derek exchanged an odd look. Theo cleared his throat noisily. "Ammon…I'm afraid you can't be a tender to these eggs."

Ammon felt his heart skip a beat before he blurted out. "What do you mean I can't tend to them? I won't let them die! I'm a tender, this is what I do!"

Erik's voice echoed across the room from the doorway. "Ammon, you are not a tender of eggs, you are the king. This nation needs you as it's king. No one can stop you from visiting the Nest, but you have more important duties elsewhere. The egg you must tend now contains all of Gaul and DoTaria. I'm sorry."

Ammon's shoulders slumped as the realization sank in. Heartbroken, he looked down at the eggs. "Who will take care of them then? Who else here knows how to be a tender?"

There was a long silence before the rumble of Derek's slow voice boomed. "I could do it if you'd teach me. I don't have anything else to do and besides, people here don't like me."

The big man looked down at Ammon hopefully. Since arriving in Laton, he had gradually retreated to his room in the back of the Hold, rarely coming out. His great size and fearsome looks frightened most people, but something about him made the people of DoTaria exceptionally wary, and they went to great lengths to stay as far away as possible. Ammon sighed. He could see the sadness in Derek's face and knew this was a perfect job for him. He liked Derek, and as much as he wanted to do the job himself, the big, simple man needed a place where he felt needed.

"Yes, Derek, I think you'd be an excellent tender. Just keep those furnaces going, and I'll be back later to show you what else needs to be done."

Ammon turned quickly on his heel and strode from the Nest with Fulgid trotting beside him. He didn't stop until he entered his chambers and had closed the door behind him. With a disgusted grunt, he flopped onto the bed and stared at the ceiling. Fulgid curled around the pillow near his head and lay with his nose barely touching Ammon's forehead. A clear golden voice chimed from the bubble deep in his consciousness. "AMMON."

Ammon reached up and scratched the dragon behind his ears. "Yeah, I'll be ok. I just don't feel I'm who they want me to be."

Fulgid closed his eyes, enjoying the scratch. The golden voice spoke once more. "AMMON KING."

Ammon rolled his eyes. "You've been talking to Sasha and Erik haven't you?"

There was a soft tap at the door before it opened slightly, and El stuck her head into the room. "Ammon? May I come in? Who are you talking to?"

Ammon replied with a humorous snort. "You wouldn't believe me if I told you. Come on in."

El perched on the edge of the overstuffed chair facing the bed. Dust covered the hem of her gown and there was a large smudge on her left shoulder from pushing on the dragon door. Idly she tried flicking the dust off. "Are you ok? You looked upset when you left the Nest."

Ammon took a deep breath before answering. "Yeah, I'm ok. I'm just tired of everyone trying to make me into something more than who I am." He sat up on the side of the bed he looked down at himself with a snicker. "Looks like I've lost another shirt eh?"

El giggled, and it sounded like the tinkle of bells. She held out the ruined hem of her gown to display the dust and grime ground into the cloth. "If I keep company with you, I'll go through gowns like you go through shirts!" She stood up, walked to his wardrobe, and threw open the doors. She stood for a moment with a finger to her lips before reaching in and selecting a shirt. Holding it out for him to examine she said thoughtfully, "Here, why don't you try this one on?"

Ammon took it from her and pulled his arms through the sleeves. The light blue silk of the shirt nearly matched her gown. He stood after he buttoned it and grinned. "Well?"

El walked slowly around him as she inspected it, nodding her head slowly in approval. "Yes, I think it'll do nicely. I believe this may have been the nicest shirt you had in your wardrobe!"

Ammon looked down and felt his face redden. "You think so?"

El stepped closer and lifted his chin with her finger until their eyes met. "Yes, absolutely. Of course, it was the only shirt you had in your wardrobe, so that narrowed it down quite a bit. I'd suggest you ask your man Kyle to get more for you."

Standing so close, Ammon could smell the flowery scent of her hair. Her deep brown eyes looked back at him with more than a hint of mischief. He smiled as he wiped a streak of dust off her cheek with his finger. "I'd better ask him for quite a few."

For a long moment Ammon gazed into her eyes until Fulgid suddenly snored loudly on the pillow and they both burst out laughing.

El grabbed him by the hand and led him into the sitting room. "You have got to learn how to read, so let's get started."

Chapter 12
The Gathering

Ammon struggled to reproduce El's elegant writing with his ink stained fingers. It was hard to concentrate when there was so much activity just outside the balcony window. Each day more DoTarian dragons arrived, and he longed to be outside watching the great beasts as they landed in the courtyard. He would have gladly given up long ago but for the pleasant company of El.

She pushed away the paper and gave him a fresh sheet. "Try again. Remember not to press so hard on the quill this time!"

He nodded obediently. Although she said she could see improvement in his work, to Ammon it seemed all he produced were blackened sheets of paper. He dipped the quill in the ink and started once again.

The tip had barely touched the paper when suddenly the chamber doors flew open and Sasha burst in unannounced. Almost instantly, he felt El's demeanor chill several degrees like a winter wind. Her gentle instruction suddenly became harsh, and she moved her chair further away from his side. She was normally quite friendly and pleasant, but whenever the old woman was near, El's attitude changed to a cold, unrelenting teacher.

Sasha eased herself into one of the overstuffed chairs and sat staring at the two of them. Idly, Ammon wondered why she insisted so vehemently that El should be dressed as if for a royal ball, when she herself appeared like an unsuccessful street beggar.

Distracted, Ammon's quill smeared a large spot onto the paper, and El gave him a sharp rebuke. "Pay attention!"

Sasha's voice creaked as she spoke up. "Enough, El. He is done for now."

El lowered her head and softly said, "Yes, grandmother."

Sasha folded her hands across her lap and stared hard at Ammon. "The knights of DoTaria have answered the call for a full Gathering and will meet in the Hall today."

El had taught him enough to know a Gathering was a meeting between the knights of the Houses and the King. There had been a partial Gathering fifty years ago with Halos to discuss abandoning the city, but there hadn't been a full Gathering in centuries. The last one to occur involved a land dispute between the leaders of the two most powerful Houses. As the minor Houses sided with one or the other, they eventually refused to attend a Gathering out of disdain for each other. The rift continued even after the city fell and the people scattered across the countryside. Now the Knights were returning to reclaim their Houses, and the feud was being revived.

Ammon wiped his ink-stained hands on a cloth. He had to present himself before these knights with his claim to the throne. Ironically, he might have to argue to win the throne that he didn't want. "When do I meet with them?"

Sasha plucked at the rags of her dress as if wearing the finest gown. "Today. In about an hour."

Ammon's eyes widened. "You don't give much warning, do you?"

Sasha stood up and shuffled towards the door. "You've had a week to prepare. They're already filling the Hall. I'd suggest you wear something…appropriate." She walked out without a backward glance.

Ammon looked down at the papers in front of him where he'd been attempting to write his name. Sasha had decided it was the first thing he should learn to write and had instructed El to help him. It looked like Fulgid had played in the ink and walked across the paper. He picked up the quill and began to carefully trace the letters. If he concentrated, then he wouldn't think about the few hundred DoTarian knights he was about to meet. El sat quietly beside him, watching him write.

The hour passed quickly, and soon there was a knock on the door as Theo entered. He sighed and put the quill down. "Is it time already?"

Theo nodded and placed a hand on his shoulder. "You will do well, Ammon. The page will announce you to the Hall before you enter and then will show you to your seat." He started walking out the door and paused for a moment. "I will be nearby if you need me."

Ammon waited a few minutes after Theo had left before donning the gold vest and sword. He checked himself in the bedroom mirror before walking out to the sitting room. Fulgid slid off the bed and casually strolled behind Ammon as if looking for a more comfortable place to nap.

El was waiting for him and took his hand between hers. Softly she spoke, "I should go now."

He squeezed her hand gently. "Don't go…I mean…would you come with me? I mean, I might need your help...in case I have to write something?"

She tilted her head and looked up at him with a faint smile. "I will if you like."

Ammon nodded with relief. The thought of standing in front of a few hundred people made his stomach hurt and he didn't want to face that alone. They walked together to the Hall doors where the page was waiting, and as Ammon approached the boy, ducked out the door. A moment later the doors opened and El slipped her arm through his. They walked through together with Fulgid close behind.

A trumpet sounded as they passed through the tall arched doors of the massive Hall. Ammon's step faltered in surprise as he surveyed the room. Beside every chair stood a knight and more lined the walls on either side. He only expected a few hundred DoTarian's, but there was more! Much more! There were seats in the Hall for over a thousand, and there wasn't nearly enough chairs! He swallowed hard and forced his feet to keep moving, keeping pace with El. A collective gasp echoed through the Hall when Fulgid came into view, and a murmur arose as they gaped at the brilliantly colored scales. As if to draw more attention, Fulgid suddenly leapt onto Ammon's shoulder and stretched his neck to look down at the crowd as they passed.

Ammon followed the page to a row of chairs on the platform in front of the throne, and the boy motioned to a single empty seat beside Erik. Ammon leaned over and whispered to the page. "El is staying with me. Please find her a place to sit."

The boy smiled broadly and quickly brought another chair. When they were finally seated, Sasha stepped forward, and with a single motion of her hand, the knights sat down with a great rumble of heavy chairs moving into their places.

She cleared her throat and spoke. Her raspy voice rang clear across the Hall. "Knights of DoTaria! I have called this Gathering to the great Hall. The first in over five decades! A little more than a month ago, our brethren from the distant land of Gaul emerged from a tunnel beneath the impassible Southern Mountains. With them, they brought life and hope back to this dead city and back to DoTaria! With them comes knowledge of a calentar mine so rich it will provide us with an almost unlimited supply of dragon fire. A week ago, their dragons blessed our Nests with the first eggs laid in Laton in fifty years! But most of all, these honorable knights brought with them the fulfillment of the prophecy! They brought with them a direct descendant of Ethanel, son of Thaire, who was trapped in their land after the great cataclysm! As was Halos, he is of the House of Les, the last surviving member!"

She turned and pointed a crooked finger at the painting of Halos that now hung on the wall above the throne. The room erupted as men began talking and shouting. Sasha motioned for Ammon to stand. She held her hand up and waited for silence.

"Look at his face, at his eyes! He carries the crest on his ring! Can there be any doubt of his lineage? He is Ammon of the House of Les, King of Gaul! By his royal blood he is the rightful King of DoTaria!"

A short, squat man a few rows from the front stood up. He wore the same elaborate armor of the DoTarian knights, but with a velvet purple and yellow sash across his chest emblazoned with a black dragon entwined around a sword. His voice was coarse as gravel. "You expect us to believe the sudden appearance of this boy from an unknown land is somehow related to King Halos from a family line lost a thousand years ago? All I see is a boy that resembles a portrait and an oversized painted pocket dragon!"

Peals of laughter rolled across the room, and Sasha squinted at the man for a moment before speaking. "Roth! I should have known you would be the first to object. You still have the same lack of common sense you had as a boy when you stuck your finger in a hornets nest and were too afraid to pull it out!" The man's face reddened as more laughter echoed through the Hall.

He slammed his fist on the table. "Say what you will, Sasha, but you bring no hard evidence of his heritage, and I have no reason to believe this is the prophecy!"

Sasha grasped Ammon's hand and raised it over her head. "He bears the ring of the House of Les! A ring he had before he crossed the mountains! He carries a DoTarian Honor Sword, which he had before he crossed the mountains! He is already King of Gaul, and his dragon is a true dragon! It is neither painted nor gilded! Come forward and test his scales if you need more proof!"

With a deep scowl, Roth hesitated, then at the urging of a few others, drew a knife from his belt and came forward to stand before Sasha. Holding the dull black blade up he smiled as Sasha inspected it and nodded. He walked confidently towards Ammon and reached over his shoulder to grab Fulgid by the neck. Fulgid snarled and without thinking, Ammon grabbed his wrist and twisted, pulling the man off balance.

Sasha held her hand up. "STOP! Roth, are you really such a fool? You should know better than to touch a knight's dragon without permission! Consider yourself fortunate he stopped you before the dragon ripped your arm off!"

Roth snorted. "I would if it were a true dragon! Anyone can touch a Tasche dragon, but if you insist!"

Ammon released his grip. Roth rubbed his wrist and glared at him disdainfully. He did nothing to hide the sarcasm in his voice. "Permission to inspect your painted dragon, sir!"

Another round of laughter filled the room and Ammon smiled as he nodded and whispered to Fulgid. "Rest easy."

Roth gripped Fulgid firmly by the neck and scraped the black blade of his knife across the scales. The smirk on his face slowly disappeared as he pressed harder and harder, unable to leave so much as a scratch on the glittering scales. He gritted his teeth and his muscles began to strain as he pushed the tip of the blade hard against the little dragon.

Sasha turned back to the crowd. "It is as I said! The dragon's golden color holds true against an Honor Blade!"

Furious, Roth jammed the knife hard against Fulgid's scales, the clink of the blade ringing loudly. Without warning, Fulgid snatched the blade with his teeth and ripped it from the man's hand. With a snarl, Roth grabbed the hilt and tried to yank it free from Fulgid's mouth. A loud crunch echoed across the room, and Roth suddenly stumbled back with the empty hilt of the knife in his hand. Fulgid spit the remnants of the shattered blade onto the floor in tiny black pieces. Every man in the room stood up in shock as Roth reached down and picked up a piece from the floor. Even Sasha stood with her mouth gaping.

Bewildered, Roth turned to her and held up a piece of the shattered blade. "This...isn't possible!" He turned to look at Fulgid as the dragon sat quietly on Ammon's shoulder. "It just isn't possible! What kind of creature are you?"

Obviously shaken, Sasha did her best to regain her composure and turned back to the assembly. "Does anyone now doubt the distinct...difference of this dragon? Does anyone doubt this is the fulfillment of prophecy? He is the Dragon of Gold and Ammon is the rightful King of DoTaria! Speak now if you still have doubts!"

Silence filled the room as each knight looked at each other. Scowling, Roth gathered the pieces of the blade and returned to his seat, staring at Fulgid with obvious disdain.

Another knight stood and nervously cleared his throat as he addressed Sasha. "What about the division of the Houses? The rift between the two sides must be dealt with to the mutual satisfaction of everyone! There can be no true unity in the Hall unless the division is healed!"

Sasha stood silently as everyone waited for her to speak. In a tired and reluctant voice she spoke. "I have thought long and hard about the rift. This political tear has torn DoTaria in two. Those who began this foolishness have long slept in their graves while the living continue to perpetuate the problem. Halos and I had conceived a solution, but he died before it could be carried out. I now put that solution before the Hall. The two houses must merge as one, thus ending the dispute."

The room erupted into shouts until Sasha raised her hand for silence again. "If the two houses merge, than neither has more, or less of a claim to any of its possessions. They become one." With a long sigh, Sasha stood up straight and shouted. "I put forth to the Hall a motion to bind the two Houses in an alliance that will end this feud forever! I await the answer of the Hall."

For a long moment nothing happened. Then a single sword rose into the air, then another and another. One by one a sea of raised swords bristled above the crowd.

Sasha held up her hand again. "Then it is agreed by the majority of the Hall. A forced merger between Houses has not happened in more than a thousand years, but the unity of DoTaria outweighs the preferences of the individuals."

Sadly, she turned towards El with tears in her eyes. "And it outweighs the preference of individuals too." Stepping down, Sasha slowly walked down the aisle and out the door.

Confused, Ammon turned to El and noticed the tears rolling down her cheeks. "I don't understand? What was that…" Ammon winced as a sharp pain stabbed him in the shoulder. Fulgid's claws had pushed under the armhole of his vest and were digging into his skin. The little dragon's eyes were glowing bright white and his golden voice suddenly boomed in Ammon's head.

"WORMS COME! MANY WORMS!"

Ammon's eyes widened at the realization sank in. The Gathering had brought many DoTarian dragons to Laton, but few could defend themselves until they received a full weeks dose of calentar. They would have to depend on the Gaul dragons for protection. He leapt to his feet he shouted. "Listen to me!" His voice crashed across the large hall like thunder and all heads turned to him. "Kala-Azar are attacking, lots of them! Everyone must get to the Hold if their dragons are unable to breathe fire! There is no time to waste!"

The knights quickly emptied out of the room, rushing to bring their dragons inside the Hold. Ammon followed Fulgid as they raced to the courtyard.

Within moments Theo had assembled the Gaul dragons in a protective circle around the doors of the Hold. Seeing Ammon, he pulled him aside and lowered his voice. "What are you doing? What makes you think the slugs are attacking? Is this some trickery to get the DoTarian's to support you?"

Ammon grimaced. "No!" He knew there wouldn't be time to explain and Theo wasn't likely to believe him anyway. "Just trust me!"

The bells in the palace towers started ringing, a last call to safety for anyone that might still be left in the city. Stalwart, the Captain of the DoTarian Guard lumbered across the courtyard towards them. A stocky man with a thick moustache, he had the same hardened look as Boris did. He nodded curtly to Theo before he crossed heavily muscled arms and peered down doubtfully at Ammon. "Why raise an alarm when there isn't a sign of a slug anywhere?"

Ammon heard Fulgid's voice in his head once more. "WORMS COME...NOW!"

He looked around warily. Fulgid hadn't told him which direction they were coming from. "They're here!...I don't know where, but they're here!"

Theo and the DoTarian Captain exchanged glances and the big man cleared his throat. "Now...uh...sire...You may be the unconfirmed king of DoTaria, but you are new to this land. I've been fighting the Kala..."

He was interrupted by an unmistakable hiss that rose into an entire chorus of screams. The color drained from his face as an increasing number of glistening, bulbous bodies emerged from the trees at the edge of the courtyard. Stalwart shielded his eyes from the glare of the sun and watched as the squirming gray line steadily approached. "By my dragons teeth there must be hundreds of them! How did they get into the city without notice?" He laid a thick hand on Ammon's shoulder and lowered his head. "Forgive me, your highness! I doubted you. I won't do so again!"

Ammon shrugged the man's hand off and pushed him towards the door of the Hold. "Forget it. Now get inside! I don't want anyone out here unless they have a dragon with fire!"

Stalwart looked confused for a moment as he looked down at Fulgid. "But sire...that little dragon won't be able to protect you, and it is my duty as captain of the guard..."

Ammon cut him short. "Fulgid has more fire than any other dragon! If you must protect someone, protect my people in the Hold and get that door shut and barricaded with firewood!" Stalwart hesitated a moment, then reluctantly went inside and closed the door behind him.

Ammon drew his sword lthough he knew it was worthless against the Kala-Azar. It was the only defense he had if one of the slugs got past the circle of dragons. Dimly, he realized that he'd ordered Stalwart to protect *his* people. All this talk of kingship must be going to his head.

Outside the protective circle, a squad of Gaul dragons were flying overhead were already raking the approaching mass of slugs with streams of fire. The ear-splitting screams from the maggot-like creatures were suddenly cut short as intense fireballs rained down on them. Again and again, the dragons swooped low. As soon as one finished its dive, another followed behind, covering the ground with flames. Acrid smoke billowed into the air, and the stench of burning slugs made Ammon gag.

The cobblestones in the courtyard began to crack and explode from the tremendous heat, but through the columns of wafting smoke, Ammon could still see the endless writhing forms push forward. Oblivious to the horrid death awaiting them, the Kala-Azar plunged themselves into the flames.

Ammon wiped the sweat from his brow and frowned. "Fulgid, this makes no sense! No creature is so stupid as to throw themselves into an inferno to die! If they had any intelligence at all they'd retreat …unless…" A horrid thought came to him and he looked down at Fulgid whose amber eyes met his gaze. "Unless this is a distraction! But a distraction from what?"

Ammon turned his back on the invading slugs and studied his surroundings intently. The huge doors of the Hold were shut tight. It was unlikely there were slugs inside or he'd hear the commotion and people would be streaming out the doors. He turned his attention to the building itself.

The Hold was located in the very foundation of the palace. The massive structure was almost pyramid shaped, with each floor slightly smaller than the one below. Directly above the Hold was the kitchen and staff rooms. On the far side of the courtyard, a large ramp led up so supply wagons could be driven straight into the second floor. The third floor held his chambers and the Hall, and the fourth floor was the knights chambers and the armory. The fifth floor was just empty rooms for potential knights to wait in during a Hatch, and the sixth and final floor was the Nest.

Ammon tilted his head back and suddenly saw what they were after. Lines of Kala-Azar were somehow clinging to the sheer walls of the palace and were close to reaching the dragon doors of the Nest. Ammon tried to get the attention of the knights flying overhead, but they were so intent on protecting the Hold that they could hear nothing but the steady screams of dying slugs.

Desperately Ammon broke into a run with Fulgid racing beside him. Derek would never have left the Nest, even if he had heard the tolling bells. He would protect his eggs no matter what, or die trying.

Ammon bounded up the stairs with Fulgid running a few paces ahead. As he passed the fifth floor, his breath was coming in gasps, but he forced his legs to keep climbing. His heart pounded as he cleared the last steps and ran down the hall. He could already hear the Kala-Azar screams as he drew his sword, kicked open the door, and charged into the Nest.

The dragon door had been forced open and daylight streamed in through the opening. Derek stood between the door and the eggs with a Kala-Azar struggling between his massive arms. His muscles strained as it writhed and screamed, the deadly mandibles snapping viscously at his head. Fulgid streaked past as four more of the slugs pushed past the door. He barely skidded to a stop before he let loose a ball of fire as big as the door itself. Orange flames boiled out across the ceiling, scorching the walls and blackening the door. With a mighty heave, Derek threw the slug toward the open door and it bounced once before another of Fulgid's fireballs disintegrated it in midair.

Derek rushed forward and shoved against the door with all his might. The hinges groaned loudly as they reluctantly began to move. Ammon dropped his sword, put his shoulder to the door, and the two of them forced it closed. Just before it shut, a shadow passed in front of the opening and through the crack Ammon saw Theo astride Ebony fast approaching. Seconds later he heard a blast of fire strike the sides of the stone wall outside.

Ammon panted as he leaned back and wiped the sweat from his face. Derek hurried back to his eggs, checking each one carefully and talking soothingly as he patted the bone colored shells. Ammon could only smile and shake his head. The man had definitely found his calling.

Satisfied they were unharmed, Derek climbed out and his bearded face smiled crookedly as he picked Ammon up like a child and hugged him.

"Thank you, Ammon!" Without another word the big man set him down and turned to busy himself stoking the furnaces.

Ammon chuckled as he and Fulgid walked to the door. "You're welcome, Derek. I'm glad the eggs are ok." When he got back to the courtyard, Theo and most of the other dragons were waiting while a few still circled overhead.

Stalwart had come back out of the hold and was talking with Theo. "I've never seen so many at once! Strange beasts, they literally threw themselves into the flames by the hundreds!"

Ammon looked over the blackened and smoldering courtyard. "It was all a diversion. They were after the eggs."

Theo looked up at the scorch marks Ebony left on the side of the palace. "I would never have thought them to be a cunning creature, but to sacrifice hundreds for just a few dozen eggs? For what purpose?"

Stalwart snorted in disgust. "To end a dragons life before it can begin! They will do anything to kill a dragon, especially the eggs. If it weren't for dragons, the Kala-Azar would be unstoppable. A few years ago they wiped out an entire village to get to a single egg. We have been defenseless against them for fifty years, and keeping the dragon population up has been a challenge. Two or three dragons in one place for very long will draw them out within a few days. So as soon as the eggs are laid, we separated them and disperse them over a large area in hopes that some of them will live to adulthood."

Theo whistled softly. "It's amazing any lived at all! It seems as if they can pass through walls without being seen. I don't know how so many could sneak up on us so easily when guards are posted on the walls and buildings surrounding the palace. I'd understand one or two escaping detection, but hundreds upon hundreds?"

Stalwart nodded. "Most of the time you don't know they are there until they're upon you. Still, I've never seen so many at once, and it's likely we'd all be dead if our new king here hadn't raised the alarm." He peered curiously at Ammon. "Pardon me for asking, sire, but how did you know? We were all inside the Hall. You couldn't have seen them coming, and I was sitting in the front row near you, and your…uh…queen, so if anyone had come in to notify you, I'd have seen them!"

Ammon laughed nervously. "Queen? Oh she's not the queen, that's El, Sasha's granddaughter."

Stalwart looked at Ammon for a long moment with sympathy in his eyes. "Pardon me again, sire, but perhaps you don't understand what happened in the Hall today?" Ammon looked at him blankly and he sighed. "I was afraid as much. I suspect there are many differences between our lands. Perhaps I can explain. Tell me, who owns the palace in Gaul?"

Ammon frowned. "The king."

Stalwart nodded. "And who owned it before the king did?"

Ammon and Theo exchanged looks and Theo rubbed his chin thoughtfully. "It has always belonged to the king as part of the throne. Whoever holds the crown takes possession of it."

Stalwart tapped his temple with a thick finger. "That makes sense if you rule a small place like Gaul, but in a large nation like DoTaria it's a bit different. We call the throne The Seat of Power, and by law it is located in the palace of the largest city, making it the Place of Power. Occasionally that location changes as populations move from one place to another and the royal family owns a palace in each city. The last change is what caused the rift between the Houses.

Centuries ago this city was nothing more than a small mining operation owned entirely by the House of Celest. When a large deposit of calentar was found, the population grew, and Laton quickly became the largest city in all of DoTaria, which elevated the House of Celest to the most powerful of all the Houses. Because Laton was originally just a mining town, there was never a royal palace, and when it was announced that the Seat was moving to Laton, the House of Celest objected. They were willing to accept the throne, but they refused to give up the only thing they owned, the very land the city was built on. Without the land that was their birthright, their House would be dissolved to nothing. I suppose if they had owned land elsewhere like most Houses do, none of this would have happened."

Confused, Ammon began to rub his temples. Politics always gave him a headache. "So why didn't the Seat just use part of the palace and leave the rest to the House of Celest?"

Stalwart shrugged. "Because the law states that the Seat and the Place of Power must be one. There can be no division, it must be whole ownership, otherwise whoever owns the Place of Power could have too much influence on the Seat. The debate went on for years before the smaller Houses began to take sides. Each side demanding either Celest surrender their birthright, or the royal family surrender the throne to Celest.

The deep division might have led to war if the Kala-Azar hadn't suddenly become such a problem. Even after all this time there are still feelings of doubt as to the validity of either side as ruler."

Ammon felt as if his head was spinning. "Okay, but what does all that have to do with me?"

Stalwart flinched uncomfortably. "The merger Sasha proposed and accepted by the Hall combined the two Houses into one, effectively ending the dispute. Now the Seat rules at the Place of Power."

Ammon looked over at Theo. "Do you understand what he's saying?" Theo shook his head.

Stalwart grimaced uncomfortably before continuing. "The Hall has the ability to merge a House with another…in this case by marriage…if it decides it is for the greater good of the kingdom."

Ammon felt his jaw drop. The man couldn't be serious! "Are you telling me the Hall just…married me…to someone?"

Stalwart nodded. "Yes sire, I'm afraid so. You will be required by the Hall to merge the head of your House to the head of the House of Celest."

Ammon felt the heat rising into his face. "And who would that be may I ask?"

Stalwart looked away from Ammon to stare uncomfortably at the ground. "Uh…well sire, the head of the House of Celest would be the Lady Sasha."

***

Sasha slowly returned to her chambers from the Hold. It was strange that the attack of the Kala-Azar seemed almost planned. It definitely was not typical of the unorganized and random attacks in the past. She fervently hoped it was mere coincidence.

She pushed the heavy wooden door of her chambers open and entered the sitting room where a small pot of water steamed over the fireplace. A cup of tea would be welcome after such a stressful day. She lifted a poker and stirred the dying coals in the hearth. Her ancient ears barely heard the soft footsteps behind her and she turned to admonish El for trying to sneak past her again.

"I specifically instructed you to…gahh! No! No! It isn't possible! It cannot be you! NO…! Please NO!"

The wrought iron poker slipped from her grasp and fell noisily to the floor, unheard by anyone else in the palace.

***

Ammon was furious as he stormed into his chambers. How dare that crazy old woman do this to him! How dare this bloody Hall agree to it! Of what use was the power he possessed as king if he couldn't even decide who he married? Fulgid scurried past into the sitting room just as Ammon slammed the door behind him with a satisfying crash. If he knew how, he would immediately call another Gathering and renounce the throne and everything that comes with it. In fact, if Sasha had been there, he'd gladly have handed it to her and be done with it. Forced marriage was wrong, but being married to that crusty old pile of rags was more than he could handle.

He unbuckled his belt and tossed his sword onto the polished desk and sulked into the bedchambers. Fulgid walked beside him and suddenly stopped in mid step to stare at the balcony curtains. His ears swiveled and his head twisted to look at Ammon and then back at the balcony. Ammon carefully drew the curtains back to reveal El standing there, her tear streaked face was red and her eyes puffy.

With a snort, he walked back into the room and dropped into a chair and propped his feet up on a table. "What do you want?"

El sniffled, dabbing at her eyes with a small lace handkerchief. "I'm sorry Ammon! I wasn't...I didn't know! I mean, I knew she was up to something, but I didn't know what! Honestly, I had no idea! I can't believe she's done this to you!"

Ammon rubbed his temples with his fingers. "I nevered want to be king, but they forced me into becoming one. As if that wasn't bad enough, now they're marrying me off to a crotchety old woman old enough to be my grandmother! You know what, El? All I ever wanted was to live a quiet, peaceful life farming. When Erik said my life was no longer my own, I didn't fully understand what he meant until now. Married! Pah!"

El gingerly sat on the edge of the table by Ammon's feet. Her voice was so soft it was barely audible. "I'm sorry. I wish it were...I wish I could change it for you, but I can't. I'm sorry."

Ammon closed his eyes and swallowed. A hard lump formed in his throat. "You can't, El. It's already done. From what Captain Stalwart told me, all that's left is the ceremony, and I guess the Hall wants that done as soon as possible. Today!" He took a deep breath. "Perhaps it would be best if you go now."

She sat quietly for a moment, then nodded. Her fingers brushed his hand lightly and then she left without saying another word.

He sat for a long time with his eyes closed, resisting the urge to break something. Any minute now they'd knock on his door and they'd escort him back the Hall where he'd be forced to marry an insane old geezer. Queen Sasha. He ground his teeth. He'd be anything that this was what she had in mind all along! What would happen if he refused? It wouldn't matter; the merger would happen even if he weren't there.

He didn't move or answer when the page knocked on the door. After the second knock, the page opened the door slightly and announced the Hall was in session and waiting. With a slow nod, he acknowledged the boy, but sat a bit longer anyway out of spite. Let them wait a few more minutes. Besides, wasn't being late for your wedding was supposed to be good luck or something? If it was perhaps the floor would open up and swallow him whole.

The door swung open and Boris thumped his way in on crutches. He eased himself down on the edge of the bed and rubbed a knuckle across his thick moustache. "In all my years, I can't say I've ever met anyone who led a life quite like you. There are people who dream of excitement and pursue adventures with all their might, but never really find it. You however, seem to attract it like flies to a manure pit. You know, some people might consider you a very lucky man."

Ammon snorted and jerked his thumb at the door. "Lucky? Have you seen my bride?"

Boris nodded. "Aye. Well, there is that. Not exactly what you had in mind I'm sure. But perhaps she's more than what she appears? Let's hope so. If not you can always hope to go blind…and deaf. Losing your sense of smell probably wouldn't be so bad either."

He groaned as Boris' hardened face split in a wide grin. With a weak laugh Ammon spread his arms wide. "I don't suppose you'd be willing to take my place would you Boris?"

The big man's laughter boomed through the bedchamber. "No, I think not! She's much too old for my taste, but I'll tell ya what I will do. Once this ceremony is over, come down to the Hold with me. Mabel cooks almost as well as she can sew, and she's been pushing food down my gullet since I arrived here. There is enough leftovers to feed even that bottomless pit of a stomach of yours!"

Ammon reluctantly stood up and waited for Boris to get to his feet. "I think I'll take you up on that invitation Boris. At least for ten, maybe twenty years or so."

After Boris had left, he and Fulgid waited at the Hall door while the page announced him. Numbly, he climbed the steps of the platform to stand in front of the large, gaudy throne. A kings duty. A life not his own. The last glimmering hope of a life of farming finally faded away to nothing and he idly wondered if he'd ever see his plantations or find out what type of crop coffee was.

A thin old man leaning heavily on an elegantly carved cane stood unsteadily beside the throne. His back stooped low and his hands were twisted harshly with arthritis. He thumped the cane loudly three times against the floor and cleared his throat. When the room was silent he spoke in a frail voice. "As the next senior speaker, it is my duty to perform the ceremony of Merger by Marriage. The wisdom of the Hall has accepted and approved the proposal set forth by the House of Celest. The Merger of these two Houses will mend the rift and bring unity back to the DoTarian nation. Bring forth the Heads of the Houses! House of Les, step forward!"

Ammon hesitantly moved forward to stand silently beside the man. Ancient fingers reached down and grasped his wrist with surprising strength then forced his hand into the air. "I see before me, Ammon, House of Les! Now step forth the head of the House of Celest!" A long silence filled the room. Annoyed, he banged his cane against the floor. "I say again, House of Celest, step forward!" There was a long, silent pause, and he dropped Ammon's hand and in irritation motioned to one of the pages. "Go to her chambers and find her!" He shifted his weight from one foot to the other and mumbled just loud enough for Ammon to hear. "You're a braver lad than me to marry that lizard of a woman, I'll say that much!"

Several long moments later, the Hall doors opened and the page entered leading El who carried a small bundle in her arms. The page hurried up the platform and leaned forward to whisper in the ear of the speaker. The old man's eyebrows suddenly rose, and he stood up as straight as he could and shouted, "I have an announcement! This young lady has terrible news I'm afraid!" In a soft voice he coaxed El to come closer. "Go ahead my girl, tell them!"

Ammon could see El's face was pale and streaked with tears. She held up the bundle she carried and her voice broke as she spoke. "My grandmother Sasha…is dead! The Kala-Azar…" The bundle in her hands unraveled to reveal heavy blood soaked stains in the rags that Sasha had worn. "This is all that was left!" She sobbed. "She's dead!"

The Hall was silent except for her weeping and Ammon could take it no longer. He stepped forward and wrapped his arms around her, and as she buried her face in his chest, she dropped the rags on the floor. They stood there for a long time, with the whole Hall watching in quiet respect.

The withered old man finally stepped forward and gently separated them. His old voice creaked like a broken hinge as he spoke. "Listen to me, my dear. She lived her life the way she wanted and refused to change for anyone. I've never known her to even consider a compromise until she set this motion before the Hall, and that agreement still must be fulfilled. Now child, you must answer me. In the absence of your elder sister Eithne, do you, Eliva, represent the House Celest?"

El nodded and closed her eyes as the old man raised her hand with Ammon's and clasped them firmly together. Then from his pocket he produced a long gold and silver ribbon and in an intricate pattern, carefully bound their hands together. "Ammon, head of the House of Les. Eliva, head of the House of Celest. In the name of unity, the authority of the Hall declares your Houses as one! In the eyes of God and before the Hall of Knights and all of DoTaria, this union is forged and cannot be broken. As Speaker of the Hall, I declare Ammon and Eliva, House of Les-Celest, the rightful king and queen of DoTaria! The Merger is complete! Long live your majesties!"

As the speaker stepped back and bowed, the hall erupted in a deafening roar as the knights of both DoTaria and Gaul rose to their feet and applauded. Dazed, Ammon leaned down and spoke into El's ear just as Fulgid leapt onto his back and perched on his shoulder, "Could you tell me something?"

She nodded as she wiped a tear from her cheek.

He leaned even closer so only she could hear. "Did we…just get married?"

***

A large pile of paperwork lay neatly stacked in the center of the desk in front of Ammon. Several times a day a representative from the Hall brought him *important* documents that needed to be reviewed and signed. Each time he pretended to stare at it thoughtfully before placing it aside with a promise to look it over carefully. Later, Erik would read it to him and make his recommendations. He shook his head in wonder. How the kingdom managed to accomplish anything with so many projects that required approval was beyond him. If it was so important, why didn't someone just take care of it? Why did everything need to be written down as a proposal and presented to him before it could be carried out? If the roof needed repair, just get it fixed instead of wasting two days for a signature while the water poured in! It was enough to make him want to pull out his hair.

Fortunately, Erik was skilled at seeing through the *fluff* as he described it, to determine what the writer of the proposal wanted. Once, Erik laughed as he read off the price of twenty gold talons for the repair of a fountain in the square. At his advice, the document was sent back with orders from Ammon to strike the man's name from the palace workers. Although harsh, word would spread, and there would be less chance of another trying to overcharge the palace.

Today he was alone in his chambers with Fulgid, who had curled up comfortably on one of the overstuffed chairs. It had been a month since Sasha's death and the merger of El's House with his. He was relieved that it was

El instead of Sasha, but it still made him uncomfortable. He hadn't had the opportunity to find out how El felt about it yet, he'd only seen her once briefly since they were married. No sooner had the ceremony ended and she closed herself into her chambers and refused to see him.

He felt torn. Although it was true he had not been a willing husband, for reasons he couldn't explain, he wanted to see her again. He had grown to relish the awkward conversations with her and how his stomach fluttered when they talked. She teased him terribly, yet he enjoyed her company. It was all very confusing.

He leaned back in his chair and stretched as he gazed out the window. The morning sun streamed through a cool foggy mist rising off from the mountains in the distance. "Fulgid, I need to get out of this room for awhile. Want to go with me to the Nest and visit Derek?"

He knew he didn't have to ask. Fulgid liked Derek and at the mention of his name the little dragon was off the chair and bounding for the door, looking back to see if Ammon was following. "Just a moment, I have to wear my sword any time I leave my chambers remember? Palace rules."

He rolled his eyes as he belted it around his waist. Each day Boris and Stalwart came to instruct him in his sword lessons. At first the two men bristled at each other, each one interrupting the other's lessons as if trying to out do the other. By the end of the first day. they'd spent more time arguing with each other than teaching. As the days passed, they began to view each other with mutual respect, and both agreed that he should carry his sword anytime he was outside his quarters for both protection and as a symbol of honor to the DoTarian's.

He followed Fulgid out the door of the royal quarters and headed towards the stairs. The halls were crowded with various craftsmen who respectfully stopped working and bowed as he walked past. He acknowledged them as politely as he could and quickened his pace so they could return to their work. Repairs to the palace were progressing slowly but steadily as the scattered population began to return, bringing with them skilled workmen.

The fourth floor badly needed attention to make the knights quarters habitable, as well as most of the top two levels. Derek had taken it upon himself to oversee the repairs of the Nest using the few Gaul craftsmen that had accompanied them through the tunnel. Despite his gentle nature, the DoTarian's kept a respectable distance from him at all times and few would venture onto his floor.

Ammon knocked politely before entering the Nest. It looked far different now than the dark and dingy place where he and El had discovered the large clutch of dragon eggs a month ago. Oil lamps glowed brightly in every corner, casting a warm glow on freshly swept floors and walls cleared of cobwebs. On a large table near the tender's room was a mound of fresh fruit, blocks of cheese, and breads. He couldn't help but smile at the feast when he remembered the cold gruel he had lived on. A few well-placed words to the royal kitchen from him had insured that Derek would be well fed.

The big man was diligently stoking the coals of the furnaces, and Fulgid gleefully ran to greet him. Derek's broad face broke into a grin as he lifted Fulgid with a massive hand and plopped him onto the shoulder of his thick leather shirt. "Hi, Fulgid! Hello, Ammon!"

Ammon smiled. After the ceremony in the Hall, everyone would only address him as 'your majesty' or 'my king' and treated him as such. Derek however, acknowledged everyone in the same, simple way regardless of his or her position. Ammon liked that. "How are things here, Derek? Are they bringing you enough to eat? Do you want me to have more sent up for you?"

Derek scratched Fulgid under the chin with one huge finger. "No thanks. I barely have time to eat. I don't want to neglect my duties!"

Ammon chuckled. "I don't think you would ever neglect your duties, but you do need to eat properly so you can take care of those eggs."

Derek looked down at Ammon thoughtfully. "Yes, I guess I hadn't thought of that. I suppose I should eat more. Could you ask them to bring me more fruit? I don't like the taste of meat."

Ammon frowned slightly. He'd never known anyone that didn't eat meat, but Derek was undoubtedly different than anyone he'd ever met before. "I'll make sure to take care of that for you. Anything else I can do?"

Derek tugged thoughtfully on his white beard and nodded. "Could you look at the eggs for me? There is one that is much bigger than the others and it wasn't like that before!"

Ammon followed Derek down to the eggs to inspect the egg in question, and he whistled softly in surprise. The egg was almost half again larger than the others and was an impressive sight. Slowly he ran his hand down the leathery shell. It was warm and gave slightly to the touch. "It seems to be okay, just extremely large. Some hatchlings are larger than others, and the soft shell stretches as they grow. I don't think it's anything to worry about yet."

Derek gave a huge sigh of relief and gently rubbed the egg with a big hand. "I was worried! I want them all to hatch and be like Fulgid!" He reached above his shoulder to scratch beneath Fulgid's chin again.

Ammon knew it wasn't likely that all twenty-five of the eggs would hatch and was about to say so when a voice called from the doorway. "Derek? Are you in the Nest?"

Ammon's heart skipped a beat. He would know El's voice anywhere.

Derek grinned. "Oh that's El! El, I'm down here!"

Fulgid leapt to the floor and sat in front of Ammon as Derek squeezed past the large egg. Ammon could hear the clatter of the ladder as she climbed down into the Nest, but he couldn't see past Derek to see her. The big man stood in the narrow gap between the eggs, and Ammon couldn't get around without climbing over them, so he waited for Derek to move. He desperately wanted to talk to her, but what would he say?

Derek opened his massive arms and hugged her. "Now all three of you are here to visit!"

El's voice sounded confused, "Three?"

Derek nodded, his thick beard flapping up and down. "Yes! Ammon and Fulgid are here too!"

Faintly she repeated his name. "Ammon? Ammon is here? I'm sorry...I...I can't stay Derek! I'll see you later!"

Ammon pushed against Derek's back and tried to squeeze past. "El! Wait! Please?"

El stopped with one foot on the rung of the ladder and hung her head. "What is it you want Ammon?"

Derek moved aside and let him by. He groped for something to say. "I...I just wanted to...can we talk?"

El started climbing the ladder again. "There is nothing to talk about, Ammon."

Stunned, Ammon's head spun. Nothing to talk about? They'd been married a month and had only seen each other once the whole time! How could she say that? "El, what is wrong? Why won't you talk to me? What did I do?"

El climbed out of the Nest and stood up with her back to Ammon as she straightened her skirt. "Nothing. Nothing at all."

She started to walk away when Derek blurted out sadly, "You two don't like each other anymore?"

El visibly stiffened. She turned and spoke to Derek without looking at Ammon. "*Like* has nothing to do with it. *Like* has nothing to do with *us*!"

Dumbstruck, Ammon stood speechless as El turned and hurried away. Derek leapt out of the Nest and yelled to Ammon. "I'll bring her back! I'll bring her back so you can talk and like each other again!"

Ammon shook his head. "NO!" Slowly he climbed out of the Nest. Derek, looking confused, stood a few paces away with one of his large hands gently grasping El by the arm.

"Let her go, Derek. I said before that I would not force her to do anything against her wishes. I won't change that now."

El's eyes flickered at him for an instant, but otherwise she remained motionless. Ammon walked past them both without looking at their faces and Fulgid followed slowly behind, his amber eyes peered sadly over his shoulder at El until he passed through the door.

Ammon followed the stairs all the way down to the Hold. Theo and Boris were sitting at a table with Stalwart who was just filling a mug out of a steaming pot. Ammon pulled back a chair and Stalwart placed it in front of him. He peered into the cup briefly before taking a long swallow of the dark, rank liquid. "How long before we can leave?"

The three men exchanged glances and Boris slowly put his mug down on the table. "Leave?"

Ammon repeated himself. "How long before we can leave? Tirate will only strengthen his position while we're gone. Now that we have calentar, the Gaul dragons have a fighting chance against his arsenal and we can retake the city before winter." He was in the mood for a fight, and Tirate was the perfect person to take it out on.

Boris smoothed his moustache with his thumb and forefinger. "Well, Ellis started flying again yesterday for the first time. He's stiff, but he can fly. My arm and leg are healing but not nearly as fast. I'd be no match for anyone skilled with a sword. I could advise, but Theo would have to lead the fight. Otherwise, the only thing that is stopping us is the collapsed tunnel. Using the dragons, we could clear it in a few days I expect, but I'd be willing to bet Tirate has his men waiting on the other side to pick us off one by one as we came out. We'd never get our heads out of the tunnel long enough to use the dragon fire."

Ammon drained the cup and slammed it on the table with a thump. "I have a plan."

Chapter 13
The Kings Right

Stalwart's face clouded with frustration. "But sire, the DoTarian dragons should assist in your war…"

A wave of Ammon's hand cut him off. "As far as I'm concerned, Gaul is a separate country from DoTaria. If any of the DoTarian knights wish to help, we'd gladly accept, but it must be voluntary."

Boris nodded in agreement and held up his mug for a refill. "No offense, Stalwart, but this isn't your war."

Stalwart sighed as he poured more of the harsh black brew into each of their cups. "I will call another Gathering so you can speak with the knights as soon as possible, but as for me, I am Captain of the Guard and it is my duty to protect my king. I will accompany you, of that you can be sure."

Before he excused himself, Ammon sent one of the pages to have Erik meet him in his chambers and then followed Fulgid up the stairs. Erik met them in the hallway, and Ammon wasted no time as he described his intentions while they walked into his chambers.

He listened intently and when Ammon was finished, Erik sank into a chair and looked up at Ammon with a hard stare. "It's bold, it's daring, and I don't like it. There is far too much that could go wrong, but if anyone can do it, it would be you and that little dragon of yours.

Ammon, this crown was given…no…thrust upon you, and as its bearer you do have the right to begin this war. Tirate's actions certainly justify it, but just remember that war always has a high price and someone has to pay it. It might be you, or your friends, or it might be the dragons…inevitably, someone always pays."

Ammon studied Erik's penetrating blue eyes. The man had been the King of Gaul for most of his life and knew the weight of the crown. Still, Tirate was likely wreaking havoc in Gaul, and as king, it was Ammon's duty to protect and free his people. It had to be done. It was just a matter of when and how.

There was a soft knock at the door before a page entered to notify them the Gathering in the Hall was ready. Ammon looked in the mirror and adjusted his sword and golden vest before purposefully striding into the Hall. To his surprise, El was standing beside the throne, and she eyed him coolly as he approached.

He grunted softly under his breath. "What are you doing here?"

She sniffed at him. "You called a Gathering. I'm required, as queen, to attend."

"Oh. Well you don't have to stay, this won't take long." Ammon abruptly turned his back on her and faced the crowded room. He raised his hand in the same manner Sasha had done and the mummer of voices in the Hall faded. "Knights of DoTaria, as many of you know, the knights of Gaul and I were forced to flee from an invading band of cutthroats and mercenaries armed with dragon-killing weapons that, until now, we had no defense against. With the use of the calentar, we will return to battle against that army as soon as the tunnel is cleared. There is a small passageway just big enough to allow my dragon and I to pass through. I intend to sneak through and create enough of a diversion to make them think we're attacking from behind. The tunnel exit will then be left essentially unguarded, and the Gaul dragons can clear out the remaining debris and join the fight.

Captain Stalwart has asked that I include the DoTarian Knights in this battle, but I have refused his offer."

A rumble of voices echoed across the Hall, and El hissed behind him in a harsh voice. "Are you insane?"

He ignored her and raised his hand again for silence. "This is not your war, therefore I will only accept help from those who volunteer. If you wish to accompany us, please speak with Captain Stalwart as soon as possible. We begin clearing the tunnel tomorrow. Thank you."

Ammon turned on his heel and walked quickly back to his chambers with Fulgid close behind. At the doorway to his quarters he informed the page that he did not wish to be disturbed. Inside his sitting room he sat in one of the overstuffed chairs with Fulgid on his lap and scratched the little dragon's ears while he contemplating his next move. He knew it was risky, but he just had to keep Tirate's men busy long enough for the others to break through the tunnel.

None of the other hatchlings were small enough to fit through the crevice and none could match Fulgid's ability to throw flames. Aside from that, Fulgid could move so quickly Tirate's men would think they were being attacked by a large force on multiple fronts, and that would increase the likelihood they would turn their attention away from the tunnel.

Tonight, he and Fulgid would sneak out and make a quick pass through the crevice to make sure it was still open and to get a good look at the defenses in case there were any surprises. If anyone knew, they'd insist on sending an escort with him and he would rather not put anyone else in danger. It was one thing to take part in a war as part of an army, but quite another to be alone in the middle of an enemy camp. Besides, he had Fulgid to watch over him.

There was a knock on the door, but he ignored it. He had told the pageboy he didn't want to be disturbed and he meant it! When he heard the door open, he annoyingly snapped at the page. "I said I don't wish to be disturbed! Send them away!"

The door slammed shut and El's shrill, angry voice made Fulgid's head pop up from his lap. "So what are you trying to do, get yourself killed?"

Ammon put his hand to his forehead and tried to force his voice to be calm. This was not what he needed right now. "No, I'm just doing what needs to be done."

She hissed angrily. "So putting yourself in danger needs to be done?"

Ammon felt the last of his patience evaporate. "I have an entire country on the other side of that mountain that needs me to take care of it. That's where my home is and I intend to go back there as soon as I can. I would think you'd be happy! I'm saving you the trouble of having to run and hide every time you see me walk down the hall! I'll be gone for awhile, maybe a very long while."

It was quiet for a moment before El said softly. "Maybe forever."

Ammon nodded. "Maybe. Either way I'm doing you a favor. Now that our Houses have…merged…you can stay here in Laton as queen and run things with the full power of both Houses. As for me, Gaul is far away. Once it's freed from Tirate, I'll probably just stay there."

El came around from behind the chair to where Ammon could see her and shook a finger at him. "You could get killed!"

Ammon looked up from his lap where Fulgid lay with his ears back. Calmly he shrugged his shoulders. "That doesn't really affect you. You're still the queen, and if I die you can live your life anyway you choose."

El suddenly scooped up a small vase from the table next to her and launched it through the air. It sailed just past Ammon's head and smashed violently on the floor behind him. Stunned, Ammon turned to stare at the broken shards of pottery scattered over the floor. "What'd you do that for?"

El's face was red and she shook with rage. "Because you're thick as a brick! You think I want you to go?"

Fulgid slipped from Ammon's lap and sauntered into the bedroom. Ammon would have followed after him but El had moved closer and now loomed over him. He couldn't rise from the chair without pushing her aside. As he looked up her dark brown eyes glittered dangerously. "Uh, well, yes! Yes, I do think that!"

He never saw it coming, but he heard the slap as his ears rang and it felt as if his jaw had come unhinged. El put her hands on each arm of the chair and put her face close to Ammon's.

"Now tell me again! Do you still think I want you to go?"

Confused, Ammon rubbed his jaw, and from the corner of his eye, he could see Fulgid curling up on the bed. This didn't make sense! It wasn't long ago that Liah had tried to stab him and Fulgid nearly killed her. Yet here El had thrown a vase at his head and slapped him hard enough to rattle his teeth, and the little dragon was falling asleep! El moved her face just inches away from his.

"You know what El? I honestly don't know what you want, but I know what I see! You've avoided me like a bad stench since we married! None of what has happened is my fault! I'm just as stuck as you are! You want to get away from me, and I'm making it possible. What else do you want from me?"

Ammon flinched as El suddenly stood up and screeched. "Arrrgh! You really don't understand do you? We're married to each other now! Husband and wife! King and queen! It doesn't matter how you feel, or who you love! We have no choice! The Hall decided our fate and we have to live with it!"

Suddenly her behavior was beginning to make sense to Ammon. El was in love with someone and now, because of the arranged marriage, her dreams were dashed. The thought made him feel strangely sad and empty inside, as if someone was sitting on his chest. Still, she deserved to be happy. There had to be a way she could be released to love whomever she chose.

"El, I...I know a king and queen are married for life, but if I go to Gaul, then you are free to stay here and love whoever you please. I promise I would never interfere or make you do anything you don't wish to do!"

El stared at him for a long moment, then with a deep sigh, leaned forward and kissed him gently on the cheek. "I hope you find what you're looking for, Ammon."

Ammon watched her as she quickly walked out the door. Now he felt more miserable than before.

***

El made it all the way down the hall and into her chambers before she started to cry. Her heart felt like it would burst inside her chest, and the air in the room felt stale, so she stepped out on the balcony that overlooked the southern mountains.

For such a smart, observant man, how could he be so incredibly stupid? She had watched in awe as he commanded the knights during the slug attacks and was amazed as he took over the offices of the kingdom despite his inability to read. Less than an hour ago, he walked into a room filled with over fifteen hundred of the most powerful men in the world and without blinking an eye, calmly informed them that he intended to start a war and intentionally place himself directly in harms way. By refusing help from DoTaria, he deftly manipulated them into volunteering by the hundreds. Despite all that, he had no inkling of what she desired of him! Was it so difficult to understand that she wanted to live her life under her own terms? In this marriage they should choose to be together, not because the Hall forced them to.

She felt her stomach drop into a hollow pit as it suddenly occurred to her that maybe he wasn't so ignorant. Perhaps he really did know how she felt and he didn't feel the same? Was there was someone in Gaul and that was the reason he was trying to leave? Her eyes welled up once more.

She stayed locked in her chambers the rest of the day and tried unsuccessfully to force all thoughts of him from her mind. As the evening approached she perched on the balcony rail with her back against the wall and watched the fading sunlight cast long shadows across the city. Workers had cleared much of the brush and trees from the roads and many of the buildings boasted newly thatched roofs. She had lived here all her life and never really thought about how beautiful it was until now.

In the last few rays of sunlight, a brief flash on the streets below caught her eye, and she leaned forward to see what it was. A dark figure quickly moved from the shadows of one building to another, obviously trying to avoid being seen. Following closely behind was a small gold dragon.

She frowned as she watched Ammon's movements in the fading light. He was obviously heading towards the southern gate, which could only mean he was heading towards the tunnel. His insane plan to slip through some hidden crack to distract an entire army while the dragons and knights cleared the tunnel entrance truly frightened her. It would be too easy for him to be killed, and she seemed to be the only one who recognized the danger. Even so, work on the tunnel wasn't supposed to begin until tomorrow, and she knew from their descriptions that it took more than an hour to pass through to the other side.

She watched as he slipped around the corner of a building and out of sight. "What are you up to, Ammon?" She bit her lip in disapproval. If he was going to do what she suspected, he was likely going to get himself killed.

***

Ammon waited until after the evening meal before he strolled out of the palace, as if going for a leisurely walk. He knew it was unlikely anyone would question him about the bundle he carried under his arm containing the dark cloak. After all, as king, he could walk the city anytime he chose. He knew what he was about to do was risky, but he had realized after he thought Boris was dead that he couldn't stand the thought of losing anyone else. The information he would gather tonight would be invaluable despite the danger. Erik was right, war had a price, and he wanted to make sure the cost was as minimal as possible.

His plan was really quite simple. He would slip out the crevice after nightfall and stay hidden in the shadows. Although there were a few dark clouds building up over the mountains, tonight's full moon should offer enough light to see the layout of Tirate's defenses. It would take about an hour to estimate the number of men and the locations of the crossbows, then he would return back through the passage. He smiled smugly. With any luck, he'd be back before midnight.

Once outside the palace walls, he camouflaged Fulgid's gleaming scales with an old sackcloth, then slipped into the growing shadows of the buildings and hurried towards the gate. Fulgid trotted behind him, and as they crossed the sunlit square, he looked back just in time to see Fulgid's sack slip off. He paused for a moment and tied it securely back into place. He had thought one sack would be enough to cover the little dragon, but it left parts of him exposed. From a distance the brown cloth made Fulgid look like some sort of strange dog except for the golden feet poking out.

Once they passed through the gate, they sprinted into the cover of the trees and began the trek up the hill. It wouldn't take long to reach the entrance to the tunnel. A path had been cleared through the woods as the mined calentar was brought down to the palace, and the open trail made traveling easy. He slowed to a walk to conserve energy. He didn't want to be too exhausted to defend himself should something go wrong.

The entrance of the tunnel was lined with rows of glass-covered oil lamps, and at the end was a large pot filled with oil. Further inside was a large lamp with a very small wick that was left alight for lighting the other lamps. Ammon picked up one of the full lamps and held the wick to the tiny flame. A puff of smoke rose as it sputtered to life, and he pushed the protective lens into place and looked down the dark passageway. "Are you ready, Fulgid?" The little dragon paused to swivel his ears and looked curiously back into the woods and then trotted down the tunnel.

The light cast shadows on the stone walls that moved and twisted with the surface of the rock. Only the crunch of gravel under his feet and the click of Fulgid's claws made any sound as they walked. The oppressive weight of the mountain felt as if it were pressing down on him, and it was a relief when the tunnel opened up into the calentar cavern. Evidence of the recent mining lay about everywhere. Picks, shovels, and wooden wheelbarrows were scattered about, but the amount of crystals still seemed impressive as the lantern's light bounced and reflected on their surfaces.

One particularly large crystal, the size of a man, lay on its side atop a four-wheeled cart waiting to be pulled out. Ammon ran his hand over the smooth surface in awe. If each dragon needed only a handful a day, once pulverized, this crystal alone would be enough for many months. It was not the largest of the crystals either. Some of the bigger ones were as wide as a large oak tree and reached twenty to thirty feet up to the ceiling. Those crystals would probably last years.

He picked his way across the cavern to the small crevice and placed his lantern on the ground. He would have to make the trip in the dark. Any light seen coming from the hole would instantly give him away, and it would be difficult to carry anyway. He removed his sword from belt and laid it beside the lantern, then followed Fulgid headfirst into the blackness.

As the walls scraped against his back and shoulders, he realized the space felt narrower than before. The months of sword training and better food had built up his muscles noticeably, and it was a little more effort to work his way through the crevice. He squirmed his way down on his belly, and eventually he poked his head out from behind the rock in the face of the wall where their camp had been. Wrapped tightly in his sackcloth, Fulgid was waiting patiently in the dark beside the opening.

The moon lay partially hidden behind thick clouds that swirled past, and a rumble in the distance signaled a coming storm. Light from a multitude of campfires dotted the field where the dragons once resided, and rows of tents glowed from the lanterns within. Ammon silently climbed out the rest of the way from the crevice and pulled his dark cloak over him, careful to stay deep in the shadows.

The nearest tent was more than two hundred feet away and Ammon kept close to the wall where the shadows were darkest. He moved quietly towards the river and the collapsed tunnel exit. As he got closer, he could hear voices drifting over the sounds of the Olog River. He dropped to his hands and knees and crept closer with Fulgid beside him.

Fifteen small campfires arranged in a semi-circle surrounded the tunnel exit. Beside each fire sat several men and at least one of the big crossbows. Beyond them was another, larger semi-circle of fires and the shadows of more crossbows in the distance. Ammon pursed his lips in thought. With that many crossbows they could maintain a steady hail of the thick, spear-sized bolts raining down on the dragons emerging from the tunnel. The diversion he needed to create would have to be huge, big enough for all of the men stationed here to think they were under a major attack from another direction.

Fulgid's ears suddenly twitched, and he turned to look behind them. Ammon strained his eyes in the dim light but could see nothing. He turned his attention back to the fires and tallied up what he thought was a good approximation of men. Forty crossbows with two men each arranged in two semi-circles around the exit. From where he was, he couldn't count all the individual tents or fires in the field, so he guessed there were roughly two hundred tents. That number made sense if they kept the crossbows manned round the clock in three shifts. Satisfied that he had gathered enough useful information, he slipped deeper into the shadows and followed the wall back towards the crevice.

Fulgid crept slowly in front of him. His sack covering made a soft, whisking sound as he moved. Several times he paused to listen, his ears quivered uneasily at some unseen threat, and he would wait until it passed before continuing on. They were only a few yards away from the crevice when Fulgid suddenly squeezed himself tight to the wall, and Ammon did the same. A man appeared and walked towards them holding a torch high. Ammon held his breath and instinctively reached for his sword before realizing he'd left it in the cavern. The man veered off behind a pile of large boulders and the torch faded from sight. With a sigh of relief, he again moved forward and bumped into Fulgid.

"C'mon, Fulgid! Let's get out of here before we have any more close calls!" Fulgid looked back at Ammon, but didn't move.

The whisper of a familiar voice rose from the darkness in front of him. "Quiet! You'll get us both killed making that much noise!"

Ammon jumped in surprise and banged his head against the rock wall. "El? What are you doing here?" he hissed.

The voice was filled with irritation. "Trying to keep you from getting killed! Now will you please SHUT UP before someone hears you?"

Angry, Ammon moved past Fulgid towards the voice. "Dragon spit! El, I don't have time for this right now, we have to…ugggh!"

He was interrupted by a sudden, blinding pain in his right side that took his breath away and with an involuntary moan he fell face first into the dirt. The shadows around him rushed in as he tried to move. "El?"

    ***

El cursed something she knew was far from ladylike. Even in the faint moonlight she could see the arrow jutting out of Ammon's chest beneath his right arm. He lay motionless and she quickly placed her hand on his chest to see if she could feel him still breathing. The man with the torch was cautiously peering from behind a boulder some distance and was holding up his torch to see if he'd hit his prey.

With a low growl, a Fulgid started towards the man but he stopped with El's urgent whisper. "No Fulgid! If he yells the whole camp will be down on us in seconds! We've got to get Ammon out of here!"

Fulgid reluctantly turned back and gripped the shoulder of Ammon's cloak with his teeth and dug his claws into the dirt. Quickly, the two of them dragged Ammon the last few yards back to the crevice. When they got to the opening they backed into the hole and pulled Ammon in by his left arm. The arrow jutting from his ribs banged against the stone and a low moan escaped from Ammon's lips. Fulgid leaned across Ammon and neatly snapped the shaft of the arrow off with his teeth. Then he and El pulled Ammon in the rest of the way and began to gradually work their way up the crevice.

***

Pock was sure he'd seen a shadow moving along that rock face. To be sure, he ducked behind a boulder, dropped his torch, and fired an arrow at it. He was beginning to think that perhaps he was imagining things when it moved again and disappeared behind a rock. He drew his sword and approached cautiously. There were scuff marks in the dirt and a pool of blood leaving a trail behind a boulder. He shoved the boulder aside and held his torch up to the blood smeared on the edge of the hole. So it seemed he'd hit his target after all.

He smiled to himself. "Ah, so they are still in there, eh? Well that one won't live long if Grody's poison is as effective as he says it is!"

He picked up the broken shaft of the arrow and twirled between his filthy fingers. "Now if they be spying on us, then they must have some plans of returning after all! Lord Tirate will want to hear about this before he heads back to Gaul!"

He slid his sword back into its scabbard and chuckled gleefully. This kind of information could mean a few more gold talons in his pay! He turned and trotted back towards the tents, taking a shortcut through the brush rather than the cleared path. The faster he got there, the sooner he could tell Tirate.

He was about to step around a strangely shiny boulder when it suddenly moved. He jumped back in surprise and held his torch up to see a gray, glistening body and large mandibles that suddenly began to click eerily. Small unblinking black eyes stared up from the ugly head as it looked at him.

In shock, he dropped the torch and drew his sword to instinctively strike at the revolting creature in front of him. The blade bounced off harmlessly, and as it turned to face him, he stabbed and slashed at it with all his might. He almost had time to scream when, with a twitch of its bulbous tail, the strange creature suddenly launched itself at him with incredible speed.

***

Both El and Fulgid were panting heavily by the time they emerged hours later into the cavern dragging Ammon behind them. Her hands were numb and bleeding, and her knees and elbows were rubbed raw. It had taken far too long to pull him through the crevice without being able to check his wounds.

The lanterns they'd left behind produced enough light that she could see his face, and it scared her. His eyes were partially closed, and his face was terribly pale. His lips were bluish, and he didn't respond when she shook him. Fulgid paced the length of his body, stopping to push his limp hands with his nose. El spat out the dirt that had accumulated in her mouth. Curse the fool! How could he do such a stupid thing?

She pushed a stray strand of hair out of her face and then rolled Ammon gently onto to his left side. With her belt knife, she carefully stripped off the blood-soaked cloak and held the lantern up to investigate the wound. He was wearing his armored vest, but the arrow had passed through the armhole and struck him in the chest below his arm. Gently, she slipped her hand beneath the vest and slowly felt his back until her fingers found the tip of the arrow emerging beneath his shoulder blade. Judging from the angle, it had glanced off his ribs and spared his lung, but the injury was still quite severe. His breathing was shallow and ragged, and his body felt cold to her touch. She knew she had to do something and soon. With the amount of blood he was losing, there was no way he'd live long enough to get to the city.

She pulled back her hood and wiped her hands on her shirt. Although her grandmother had often been harsh and controlling, she truly wished she were there right now.

As a skilled healer, she'd know exactly how to remove the arrow and treat the wound. El hung her head. Her grandmother would also have told her she could do this herself. It wasn't like she had any other choice anyway. She slipped off the pouch she always carried from around her waist and emptied its contents on the cavern floor. Of the handful of tiny vials, she selected two, shepherd's purse and an ointment of leopard's bane, and then she looked around the cavern.

Near the wall the miners had stacked a pile of firewood beside a large barrel of drinking water. Several mugs and a small pot hung on a metal rack over a blackened ring of dead coals with a makeshift chimney that rose up to the ceiling and out of sight. El quickly arranged some kindling and struck a small fire, then dropped the shepherd's purse into the pot and left it to boil.

She turned back to Ammon and gently propped him into a sitting position. Carefully, she used her belt knife to reach underneath and cut away at the heavy fabric that held his armored vest together. The blade dulled quickly against the dragon scales, but she kept at it until she could peel it back from his side. Then she pulled off the remains of his blood-soaked shirt and ripped it into strips. She spread a thick layer of ointment across the cleanest ones and put them aside.

When the tea was ready, she poured a cup into a mug and forced it into his mouth. Weakly, he shook his head and murmured, but she pushed it past his lips and waited until he swallowed it. When the cup was empty, she reached behind him and grabbed the arrow tip with trembling fingers. "This is going to hurt, Ammon, but it has to be done. I'm sorry." He screamed as she yanked it out and then went limp and slumped forward. She eased him down to his left side and wrapped his chest tightly with the ointment-soaked bandages and strips of cloth. Fulgid anxiously hovered nearby, nudging Ammon's hand with his nose and looking at El expectantly.

She wiped her hands with a rag and shook her head at the little dragon. "I've done all I can for now. It seems I spend most of my time patching him up, and does he appreciate it? I doubt it!"

She tossed the rag down and looked thoughtfully at the four-wheeled cart loaded with the large crystal. "Fulgid, could you help me move that?" El knew that dragons were intelligent, but it still surprised her when Fulgid bounded over to help pull the heavily-laden cart closer to the crevice. Then, using every bit of her strength, she pushed the crystal over the side and it slid down the hole and out of sight, slamming and banging until it came to a sudden stop with a sickening thud.

She dusted her hands off in satisfaction. "Nobody will be following us up through there and Ammon won't be going down either. Two problems solved at once."

Gently, she lifted Ammon onto the cart and draped his cloak over him. Then she used the heavy leather cargo straps to tie him on securely and hung the lanterns on each side of the cart with the rest of the tea. She gripped the handle with both hands while Fulgid tugged on one of the leather straps, and they began to pull him up the long tunnel. It was a long trek back to Laton and the sooner they got there, the better it would be for Ammon.

It was deep into the night when they finally reached the tunnel exit and she could hear the rain long before she could see it. The dark clouds that were gathering when they left had turned into a raging storm. Cold winds whipped the hillside and sheets of rain lashed deep into the tunnel opening. Streaks of lightning split open the sky with a deafening roar.

El groaned in frustration. If she tried to pull Ammon through that he'd freeze to death before she even got near the city! She moved the cart deeper into the tunnel away from the wind and blocked the wheels with stones. Ammon's face was pale and he was shivering violently beneath the cloak. She frowned and tucked the cloak tighter around him as she mumbled to herself. "Somehow I've got to find a way to keep him warm. His hands and face are as cold as ice! We need a good fire, but with this rain, where will I get dry wood?"

Fulgid busied himself pushing a few melon-sized boulders against the wall with his nose. She rubbed her sore back as she searched the tunnel. There were a few wooden wheelbarrows she could burn but those wouldn't last long. The only thing left was the cart Ammon lay on and she'd need that to get him back to the city.

A sudden explosion of flame and a blast of heat behind her made her jump with a yelp of surprise, and she spun to stare wide-eyed at Fulgid. The little dragon was spewing a steady stream of fire against a mound of rocks that steamed and hissed as they began to glow. Tiny flakes of stone popped and bounced against the tunnel walls as the warmth washed over them.

El grinned. "Fulgid, you're a genius!"

She maneuvered Ammon closer to the glowing stones and felt the heat radiate into her own body. She had been warm while pulling the cart, but once she stopped, the cold and damp had quickly begun to sink into her bones. Fulgid hopped onto the cart and curled up on Ammon's legs, his amber eyes faintly reflected the glowing rocks as he stared at Ammon. She studied him curiously as she gave Ammon another dose of the strong tea. She knew from her studies that dragons were loyal and intelligent, but she couldn't help but wonder if they all were as smart as he was.

As the night dragged on, she forced dose after dose of tea into Ammon and hoped to hear him at least mummer faintly in protest each time. She sat close and watched him breathe. It was still shallow, but not as ragged as before, and his skin had warmed to the touch. Outside, the storm still rumbled but was starting to ease up. She would wait until daylight as long as Ammon appeared to be stable. If she slipped in the dark and injured herself, it would be that much longer before she could get Ammon home again. She placed her head against his good shoulder and closed her eyes wearily.

She didn't realize she had dozed off until she was startled awake by Ammon's voice. He was mumbling incoherently, and she quickly pulled back the bandages to inspect the wound. Around the wound the skin had turned an angry red, and his eyes were open and stared blankly into the darkness. She frowned. It shouldn't be showing signs of infection this bad already, it was too early! He strained weakly against the leather straps that kept him from falling off the cart. She was glad she had left them on. Even in his fevered state, he was strong enough that she couldn't have held him down for long. She pushed another cup of the tea past his lips and wondered how long before dawn.

As his fever grew, he began to ramble almost constantly, once even reciting the letters from his lessons. She couldn't help but smile. He had indeed been paying attention after all! She listened as he talked aimlessly, deep in conversation with Fulgid she thought, or maybe Erik.

"...how am I supposed to know? ...not...good with people. ...someone else? I'm in her way...simple tender...farmer."

She shook her head. Simple was definitely not the word she'd use to describe him.

His voice grew louder, almost shouting. "...what would I say?...I love her? She'd just laugh...throw another vase."

El almost fell over in shock. Did he just say he loved her? Or was it the delirium of fever? She reached over and brushed a few strands of hair from his eyes. His hand reached up and grasped hers. Briefly he looked at her as if to notice her presence for the first time. "Hello, El. Eliva. I like that name. Can we walk through the city again today? Queen Eliva. My queen..."

His eyes gradually lost their focus, but he continued to hold her hand. His queen? A tear formed in the corner of her eye, but she didn't let go of his hand to scrub it away. In all her life she had never cried as many times as she had in the short time she'd met him. She sniffed and whispered gently to the incoherent man lying on the cart. "You'd better live through this after all these tears! You hear me? You'd better or...or I'll...I'll kill you myself!"

As dawn finally broke, the storm slowed to a light drizzle. El fashioned a small harness from a piece of rope and attached Fulgid to the cart. Then the two of them pulled it down the muddy path as fast as she dared. She didn't stop until she reached the palace where a group of concerned knight's carried Ammon up the stairs to his chambers. Theo and Stalwart met them in the hall as they rushed by, and she quickly explained what had happened then hurried down the hall, shouting as she ran. "Get him into his bed and get a fire going in his room, I'll be there in a moment!"

She rushed into her quarters to get more of the medications she'd need before running to Ammon's chambers and shooing the anxious knights out the door. "You'll be no help to me standing in my way! I'll call if I need you!"

Once they were gone, she put a pot of water over the fire to boil and set about preparing proper bandages and sorting through the teas and poultices scattered on the desk. This time, she vowed, she would not leave until he was better and until he'd told her exactly what she wanted to hear, his *queen* was going to make his life very difficult.

**

With a yawn, El arched her back and stretched wearily. She had spent every moment of the last few days nursing her still-unconscious husband. Although she had been treating the wound aggressively, the infection was still wreaking havoc on his body. As the fever waxed and waned, she bathed his face with cool water and listened to the ranting of his tortured dreams. An agitated Fulgid paced the length of the bed, hovering over Ammon and nuzzling his hand hopefully. He refused to eat or sleep and allowed no one but El near the bed to tend to Ammon.

El had her belongings brought to Ammon's chambers along with every book she could find in the palace library on medicinal cures. She had also sent for the entire collection of jars and bottles and the stacks of handwritten books from Sasha's dilapidated house by the north gate. In the short lulls between Ammon's fevered spikes, she immersed herself in the books, desperately searching for anything that might help. If Ammon's body weakened any more from the fever, the infection would kill him.

Each day Erik came to ask if there were any improvements, and today was no different. El was sitting at a desk piled high with tattered books and foul smelling jars when he entered carrying two steaming mugs. With a concerned look, he placed one in front of her and glanced into the bedroom. She sat back and nodded with gratitude before slowly sipping its contents.

Erik sniffed one of the jars before making a face. "How is he doing?"

She pushed back a stray strand of dark hair from her eyes and looked at Ammon sleeping fitfully in the bed. "The same. He's not getting worse, but he's not getting better either. Whatever this is, it happened too quickly to be an ordinary infection. I've already tried everything I know, but nothing seems to help. My grandmother knew of more treatments and cures than I'll ever learn, so I'm going through her notes now." She pointed at a teapot steeping beside the fireplace. "That's one of her elixirs mixed with two others I found listed in a book in the library. I've been giving it too him every few hours since yesterday morning. If it works, then hopefully we'll see results tonight. If not…" She felt her voice choke.

They both eyed the young man lying in bed grimly. Soaked in feverish sweat, his blond hair lay on the pillow in thick strands. Blue eyes stared blankly at the ceiling while his lips quivered, mouthing soundless words. Erik placed a fatherly hand on her shoulder and smiled. "I will take care of the matters of the palace until you can both resume your roles. If there is anything I can do, please let me know!"

El nodded with appreciation. "Thank you, Erik."

After he left, she pushed the empty mug aside and climbed into the bed beside Ammon. She leaned against the headboard and gently pulled his fevered head onto her lap and began dabbing his face with a cool, damp cloth. As she wiped his face she studied his half-open eyes. She had always been attracted to tall men with dark complexions and commanding attitudes. Ammon however, was exactly opposite of that. His blond hair, blue eyes, and lightly-tanned skin were quite different from anyone she'd ever seen before. He was only a little taller than she was, and his muscular frame moved with a grace very much like his golden dragon. He was painfully modest and gentle, yet had shown he could effectively command those around him. Men seemed to want to follow him and his strangely-colored little dragon. She laughed ironically and leaned her head back. Not just men it seemed, despite her efforts, she was drawn to him just as much as they were.

She yawned. Perhaps it was all part of the prophecy, although she hated the thought that her life might be already planned out for her. Her eyelids began to droop. Maybe tomorrow she'd send someone to the library…to find the book of prophecies…tomorrow.

As sleep finally overtook her tired body, she sank to the pillows with Ammon's head still on her lap and her fingers laced through his hair. She hadn't noticed that Fulgid had stopped pacing and now lay curled beside her on the pillow.

***

Ammon fought in a void. Through the murky, sluggishness of his fevered mind, he struggled against the invisible bonds that held him down. What or why he fought, he didn't know. Perhaps it was the stubbornness in him that refused to give up or give in. So within that void he struggled and strained, grasping desperately at the slippery, fleeting memories that flashed past with faces and names he knew but couldn't quite remember. With each endless minute, he fell deeper into the blackness. How long he had been lost, he couldn't say, time had no meaning. Maybe he'd always been there, maybe that's all there is— darkness eternal and infinite. No, that couldn't be right.

There was something…someone he couldn't quite remember…and so, he fought.

Suddenly during that silent struggle, a sliver of golden light pierced the darkness. It shone so brilliantly that it was almost painful to behold, but Ammon grasped at it with every fiber of his being. Slowly, ever so slowly, the light grew to envelop him, surrounding him in a gilded bubble of warmth and light. Light! Oh such blessed light that fractured the impenetrable blackness and cradled him in its protective womb! Ammon let the glow wash over him, through him, like he was no more than a ribbon of silk in the wind.

***

Ammon awoke feeling like the mountains had fallen on him. The world spun dizzily the moment he tried to lift his head, so he lay still and tried to recall what happened. Something moved slightly on the side of his head and gently tugged at his hair. Instinctively he tried to reach for it, and as soon as he moved his right arm, a shock of pain in his chest made him groan involuntarily and he gasped. Suddenly a cool cloth appeared and began to dab at his forehead while another hand stroked the side of his head. Confused, he tried to speak but his mouth was parched and his tongue felt like wood. He swallowed several times and worked enough moisture into his mouth to finally croak. "What happened? Where am I?"

The cloth lifted and the outline of a face appeared above him, but his eyes couldn't focus enough to see who it was. He heard the splash of water as the cloth was dipped and again applied to his face. Weakly, he tried to push himself up, but again the pain wracked his body, and he lay back down with a grunt, blinking. He licked his lips and tried again, louder this time. "Where am I? What happened to me?"

Once more the face reappeared and a hand felt his forehead. He heard El's voice exclaim excitedly. "The fever has broken at last! Thanks be to God! Ammon, how do you feel?"

Ammon thought for a moment as he became more aware of how uncomfortable he was. Every bone in his body seemed to ache except for the few that simply screamed in agony. His eyes were blurry and there was a taste in his mouth like someone dumped refuse in it. "I feel…like I swallowed a slug…whole! What happened, El?"

She moved slightly and he realized he was lying with his head on her lap. "You don't remember?" The flat tone of her voice indicated she didn't approve much of whatever happened. She moved again and the room slid into a sickening spin. He groaned loudly and the movement stopped. "Would you like me to stay in this position?"

He swallowed hard and squeezed his eyes shut. "Yes, please…"

A moment passed and then the cool, damp cloth returned and began to gently wipe his face. Her voice softened. "I guess I should have known your fever had broken. Fulgid got up an hour ago and ate something for the first time in days. He must have sensed you were getting better. You had me quite worried, you know. I tried every kind of herb and mixture I could find to treat you and nothing seemed to work. For awhile I thought…we thought we'd lose you."

Her voice became stern for a moment. "I've worked too hard to lose you like that, so you'd best not do it again, you hear me? And you owe me a new knife for the one I ruined trying to get that stupid armor off you!"

Ammon again tried to force his eyes to focus as he fought down a wave of nausea. He had no idea what she was talking about, or why she tried cutting his armor with a knife, but if he owed it to her, well, that was that. He'd buy her a whole armory of knives as long as she didn't move his head again. "I'll get you a new knife. Better than the one you had, I promise."

He heard El laugh softly. "You owe me more than just a knife. A queen ought to at least have a ring to show she's married don't you think?"

Ammon knew there was only one suitable answer simply by the way her hand suddenly gripped his hair firmly and pulled his face toward hers. She made him say yes three times before she relented. He lay there quietly and wondered what happened to make him wake up weak, in pain, and held captive by a woman who demanded a wedding ring and a good knife from him.

Chapter 14
A Sword, Knife, And Ring

Ammon struggled unsteadily to his feet and waited for the pain to subside. It had been nearly a week, and he was only now just barely able to move on his own and what little stamina he had was quickly depleted just walking across the room. The wound was healing slowly, and the muscle spasms in his side were excruciating. His right arm hung limply in a sling making it virtually impossible to even dress himself, so El became his constant companion, graciously helping him with even the simplest tasks.

If that wasn't humiliating enough, he learned the news of El rescuing him had spread through all of Laton. Curiously, she never mentioned it in front of him though, not even when Stalwart came to find out what he'd learned about Tirate's defenses. He was surprised to learn she had information of her own to offer. Apparently, while he was checking the placements of crossbows around the tunnel, she had gone the other way and found more of the dragon killers hidden in the tree line. He reluctantly conceded the plan would have been doomed even if the crevice were still open. They would have to come up with another plan to retake Gaul.

Stalwart visibly sighed with relief. "I must say I'm glad to see you won't be doing this. I'd much rather see a plan that didn't place our king at such risk. With all respect sire, next time will you please let one of my men do the reconnaissance?"

Ammon could see the smirk on El's face, and he rolled his eyes. "I had Fulgid with me for protection, it was just bad luck that I got shot. Anyway, it doesn't matter now, El blocked the crevice and no one will be passing through."

Stalwart grinned. "Aye, and it was good thinking too. Luckily for you, she was there, or you'd be dead. Dragon protection or not."

Ammon decided not to argue. She had indeed saved his life and risked her own to do it, but on the other hand, if she hadn't been there in the first place, he might have made it back unscathed. There was no way of knowing, so it was better to just drop the whole issue. Instead, he asked Stalwart for his ideas to retake Gaul. Stalwart gave numerous scenarios, all of which meant heavy losses, and Ammon rejected each one politely. He would not allow hundreds to go to their deaths, especially in a war he couldn't guarantee to win. It had to be a sweeping victory with minimal loss. Unrealistic or not, that is what he insisted upon.

When El rose to prepare a fresh pot of the horrid tea she forced him to drink every hour, he leaned forward and whispered to Stalwart. "May I ask a favor of you? I need to replace the knife El ruined when she cut off my armor, and…I also need to know where to get her a…ring."

A grin broke across Stalwarts face and Ammon thought he would burst out laughing. His eyes twinkled as he looked past Ammon to the fireplace where El was busy stoking the fire beneath the kettle. "Do you still have what is left of your armor?"

Confused, Ammon nodded. "Yes. It's in my wardrobe, why?"

Suddenly serious, Stalwart turned his gaze back to Ammon. "Are you strong enough to ride a dragon for a short distance? An hour or so from here?"

El returned to the table carrying a mug and placed it in Ammon's hands, motioning him to drink. "No, he can NOT go practice fighting on the back of a dragon!"

Stalwart shook his head. "No my queen, I wasn't meaning that. Could he just ride for a short distance? You would need to come too, if that makes a difference."

El frowned down at Ammon who sat forlornly staring into his mug. "What for?"

Stalwart grinned so wide Ammon thought his face might split in two. "Tradition my lady! One that hasn't occurred in many, many years!"

El fiercely placed her hands on her hips and tilted her head. "He can barely stand and you want him to go gallivanting around on a dragon? No, I think not! Not until he can walk to the courtyard by himself. Only then will I let him go."

Ammon placed the mug down in front of him and looked determinedly at Stalwart. "Captain, I'll meet you in the courtyard first thing in the morning."

Stalwart grinned even wider, and suddenly leapt to his feet and bowed. "Sire, I will retrieve the item from the wardrobe and have it prepared…and I'll see you both in the courtyard tomorrow morning!" He hurried into the bedroom and returned a moment later with the torn vest draped carefully over his arm. Smiling broadly, he rushed out the door.

El glared down at Ammon with her arms folded in front of her. "I'd beat you senseless if I wasn't the one who'd have to patch you back up again. Now tell me what is so dragon-fired important that you need to do this before you can even walk?"

Ammon shook his head and looked up at her truthfully. "I honestly don't know! Tradition I guess?"

El grabbed the mug from the table and shoved it back into Ammon's hands. "Drink!"

***

When the morning church bells tolled, El stubbornly refused to help Ammon into his clothes. She watched with amusement as he struggled to dress himself and only sniffed disapprovingly when he finally buckled on his sword. His unsteady legs shook as he descended the three flights of stairs to the Hold with El biting her lip in apprehension.

"You cannot do this Ammon! This is just some foolish tradition that isn't worth risking injury to yourself when you aren't healed yet! Now be reasonable and let me get you back to your bedchambers where you can rest!"

Determined, Ammon shook his head and continued on, certain he could hear El grinding her teeth in frustration. He was breathing heavily by the time he reached the crowded courtyard and a grinning Stalwart winked at him approvingly until a sharp look from El wiped the smile from his face.

Ducking his head slightly, Stalwart cleared his throat. "Ah, good morning! I'm glad to see you up and about, sire! My dragon Loyal and I will carry you both on our trip."

A strange box-like seat mounted behind the saddle straddled the neck of Stalwart's dragon, and with considerable effort, Ammon climbed in to sit on one side with Fulgid. Red faced and still grumbling, El sat on the other and refused to look at him. Stalwart swung into the saddle and looked back to wink at Ammon as he patted a leather pouch tied to his belt. After strapping himself into his saddle, he raised his fist into the air and dropped it sharply. One by one the Laton dragons leapt into the air followed closely by the dragons from Gaul. Waves of dust stirred across the courtyard as they climbed higher.

From the air Ammon could see Laton clearly. Newly thatched roofs surrounding the palace drew a stark contrast to the ruins in the rest of the city. The old protective wall that had originally encircled the small mining town before it had become a city was now integrated into the sides of buildings or torn down. Its replacement that now surrounded the city was easily visible with its thick ramparts and high guard towers.

The great palace with its partially repaired roof dominated the city, and Ammon felt his breath taken away by the sheer beauty of it. Reaching over, he touched El's hand and could see the sight had the same effect on her. Smiling in wonder, they watched the landscape pass beneath them as the dragons flew east to a distant mountain with a thin tendril of smoke trailing from the top.

They circled once high above the strange mountain before landing, and as they passed over, Ammon looked down in amazement. At the top of the mountain was a massive steaming crater and the bottom of one side a dull red glow radiated from deep within the bowels of the earth. The rest of the crater floor was flat and wide enough for them to land. As they approached, Ammon could feel heat coming up from the ground and the stench of sulfur hung heavily in the air.

"What is this place, Stalwart?" He mumbled in awe as he looked around.

A small group of people were already waiting there as they skidded to a stop on the blackened-rock surface. Oddly enough, most appeared to be blacksmiths waiting patiently beside their tools and large wooden barrels filled with water. Stalwart swung out of his saddle and tossed the pouch to the blacksmith who immediately opened it up and dumped its contents into a strange clay pot. The glittering golden scales tumbled in, clinking as they fell.

Stalwart turned to face Ammon. "You asked me to obtain a few items for you, and that's what I'm doing."

El helped him climb down from the box seat and held his hand as they walked over to a large rock and sat down to watch. The blacksmith lowered the pot down on a long chain through one of the holes in the crater floor that spewed sulfurous smoke while another man positioned three different sized wooden boxes filled with clay, each with a hole bored in the top.

Every ten minutes or so, the blacksmith would pull up the pot with his thick leather gloves and peer inside.

Each time he'd shake his head and lower it back down into the hole a bit lower than before. After nearly an hour, he pulled it up and nodded his head with satisfaction. The pot glowed bright orange and the air around it shimmered from the heat as two blacksmiths, placed a long metal bar through each handle of the pot. They carefully tilted it with the utmost care and slowly poured its contents into the holes of the clay filled boxes. The liquid was so bright that it was painful to look at and showers of sparks flew in every direction as it was poured.

Boris and the other knights from Gaul watched in fascination. Although it was interesting to watch, Ammon had questions he'd wanted answers to. The first of which was what did any of this have to do with what he'd requested from Stalwart?

After the boxes had cooled a bit, the blacksmith tipped them over and cautiously broke them apart with a hammer. The first box was long and thin, and as they chipped away the clay, it revealed a bright, golden sword unlike anything he'd ever seen. Quickly the blacksmith picked it up with tongs and hammered and filed a sharp edge onto the blade. When he was done, he dropped it into a barrel of water and as steam roiled out in all directions he moved onto the next two boxes. They were smaller and Ammon was too far away to see the objects clearly as the blacksmith worked. Each received a similar treatment like the sword did before it was placed in the barrel.

Once they had cooled and removed from the barrels, Stalwart wrapped them in soft towels and brought them to Ammon. The first thing he presented was the sword and as Ammon pulled back the cloth it glittered like a golden mirror in the sun. It was still warm to the touch, and as he lifted it, he was surprised at how elegant it was. An image of a dragon ran the length of the blade on either side, and the pommel was molded to resemble Fulgid's head with two small diamonds inlaid for eyes. He laid it across his lap and lightly touched the edge of the blade with his fingers. It was hard to believe such a beautiful work of art was actually a weapon!

Then Stalwart placed another bundle on his lap and smiled as he whispered in his ear. "Here are the items you requested of me. There has never been anything other than honor blades made this way so this will be unique."

As the knights began to gather around, Ammon turned to face El. He slipped his hand into the cloth and withdrew a golden knife with tiny dragons etched on the blade. Taking El's hand in his, he gently pressed the handle into her palm. "To replace the one you ruined to help me."

El gasped as she stared at the knife in her hand and shook her head. "No! Ammon I cannot take this! This is an Honor Blade! You cannot just give these away! These must be earned!"

He smiled. "You risked your life to save me. You dragged me through the tunnels and back to the city, then nursed me back to life. If anyone has earned that blade, it is you. Please…will you take it?"

El's face reddened as she quietly tucked the knife into the empty sheath on her belt. "Thank you, Ammon."

She reached over to hug him, but he gently stopped her as he reached into the cloth once more. "Wait. I have one more thing to give you that according to Stalwart has never been made before. Ever."

He slipped the ring onto her finger and her jaw dropped as she held it up to the sunlight, watching it sparkle. The blacksmith had etched a tiny dragon encircling the band, making it very similar to the ring Ammon wore.

Tears welled in her eyes. "Ammon…I…"

He gently kissed her cheek. "Good, I'm glad you like it."

Fulgid appeared at their feet and stood on his hind legs to sniff at the ring. With a disinterested snort, he casually sauntered off towards the blacksmiths unguarded lunch beside the water barrel.

Stalwart chuckled. "Apparently he isn't as easily impressed as the rest of us!" There was a ripple of laughter from the knights before he continued. "There is more to these gifts than you know. They were created from your dragon's scales and forged in the heat of this mountain.

This is how honor blades have been made since the first dragon descended from Heaven. But not one blade has been cast since the Scattering. After the last generation of sword makers died off, the knowledge of forging these legendary blades was lost. Only after our recent return to Laton was this knowledge regained through volumes of books in the armory. According to legend, once forged, an honor blade is unbreakable. This has always been accepted as fact until your dragon shattered one in the Hall.

Since that day there have been long discussions and numerous theories, but there is one thing of which we all agree. Fulgid is undoubtedly not a tasche dragon, and the blades and ring forged from his scales should have strength beyond imagination. They will never bend or break and the edge will forever remain true."

Ammon frowned. "A tasche dragon?"

El giggled. "Don't they have pocket dragons in Gaul?"

Ammon shook his head and Stalwart's eyebrows rose. "No? Well you should consider yourself fortunate. They are a cousin of true dragons and don't usually get much bigger than a cat. Some call them hearth or pocket dragons and believe them to be good luck, but the truth is they're a nuisance that will eat you out of house and home."

Ammon held the golden sword up and studied it once more. "Some day I'd like to see these tasche dragons, but for now I'd like to discuss these honor blades. I can think of a number of knights who deserve one and I'm sure you know of quite a few?"

Stalwart smiled and nodded. "Indeed I do, sire!"

***

The ride back to Laton was quiet at first. Ammon watched as El's eyes drifted from the stunning countryside to the golden band on her finger. She apparently had forgiven him for making the trip because she smiled genuinely as she clasped his hand between hers. Fulgid stretched his neck out to lay his head atop both their hands and gazed up at El with shining amber eyes. Like music floating in the wind, his golden voice sang from the bubble deep in Ammon's head.

"ELIVA NICE!"

Ammon chuckled quietly to himself. Perhaps most knights never married because of their dragons, but Fulgid seemed quite content to have El around. "Yes, she is."

El tilted her head quizzically at him. "She is…what?"

Ammon glanced at Fulgid, still resting his head on their hands. "He said you're nice."

Concerned, El reached over to place her free hand on Ammon's forehead and felt for fever. "Are you okay? I knew this was too much. You haven't recovered enough to be out yet!"

Ammon shook his head. He wasn't going to start off their marriage by hiding things from her. "I have to tell you something nobody else knows." He leaned closer. "Fulgid can actually speak. Not out loud of course. Somehow he can talk to me through the link, I hear his voice in my head. I don't know how he does it, but he does!"

Lines of worry crossed El's face and she looked eagerly ahead as they approached the city. The moment they landed, El called out to the men waiting in the courtyard. "Come quickly! Carry him inside and up to his chambers!"

Ammon sighed and waved off the cluster of men hurrying to his side. "No, no, I'm fine. I can do this myself."

El gripped his arm tightly. "You may be able to order them around, but you can't tell the queen what to do. You will let me assist you up the stairs!"

He smiled and nodded. That was an argument he knew he would not win. It was a long, slow climb up the stairs and El didn't release her grip until he was seated comfortably in one of the overstuffed chairs in his sitting room. He was too tired and out of breath from the exertion to complain as El fussed over him, and he watched as

Fulgid followed her into the bedchambers. He knew she didn't believe what he'd told her about Fulgid, but how could he prove it?

***

Frustrated, El stoked the fire and put a pot over the flames to make tea. At least Ammon didn't have a fever, but he had obviously pushed himself too far if he was hallucinating. She pulled down several small clay pots of herbs she'd left on the mantelpiece and found the little red jar she was looking for. It was a potent painkiller that would also make him quite drowsy. "This will help him to do what he should be doing right now, sleeping!" She murmured under her breath as she dropped several spoonfuls into a cup.

Ammon's voice called from the next room. "El, I don't need to sleep. I'm perfectly fine, just a little sore."

El almost dropped the jar before she could put it onto the table. He was on the other side of the sitting room completely out of sight! He couldn't possibly have seen or heard what she was doing!

His laughter rolled into the bedchamber. "El, don't look so surprised, after all, I tried to tell you!"

Her mouth snapped shut and she spun around. There was no mirrors anywhere, so how could he have known? Bewildered, she sat on the edge of the bed beside Fulgid who lay sprawled across the blankets, watching her.

Ammon called out again. "I told you he could speak."

She jumped to her feet and backed away from the bed. This couldn't be! It had to be some sort of trick!

Fulgid lay still, then looked at the door as Ammon came into the bedchamber.

"I'm sorry, I didn't mean to frighten you. I just couldn't think of any other way to prove it to you. Fulgid would never harm you. He has accepted you as part of me."

She shook her head fiercely. "No! Dragons cannot speak! I can show you dozens of books written about linking, and what you say isn't possible!"

Ammon winced as he shrugged his shoulders. "Well, you know I can't read, but do any of those books mention a gold dragon?"

She stared hard at Fulgid. "No...no other colors but black and gray...but...but the books say dragons only sense emotions!"

Ammon gently placed his hand on her shoulder, and she turned her to face him. "Fulgid is not black or gray. He's different than all other dragons and has been from the very beginning, but he won't hurt you, ever. You have my word...and his." He pulled her close and hugged her tightly. "Trust me."

She sighed. She did trust him and there was no doubt that Fulgid was unusual. Was it really possible the little dragon actually could communicate through the link? At first she couldn't help but believe he was still delusional from the illness, but that didn't explain how he could know what she had been doing in the next room. She peered into his face and could see the pain in the corners of his eyes. The long ride had taken a toll on him, and he badly needed rest. Her questions would have to wait.

"You'll have to tell me more about this later, after you've had some sleep. Now go sit down!" Ignoring his protests, she shooed him back to the sitting room.

Fulgid still lay on the bed, and El turned to face the little dragon. Quietly she spoke, so Ammon could not hear. "Well, unusual or not, it'll take the both of us to keep him out of trouble so he can heal, and it will be much easier if you help. So can I count on you or not?"

Fulgid sat up on the bed, his deep amber eyes looked at El then through the door as Ammon limped painfully back to his overstuffed chair. In one fluid movement, the dragon dropped to the floor and leapt up onto the table. With his teeth, he gently picked up the red clay jar and dropped it into her palm. Stunned, she stared at the jar in her hands and back at Fulgid. If there had been any doubt before, it was gone now. She opened the jar and hurriedly scooped several spoonfuls of white powder into Ammon's cup before pouring the tea. Fulgid sat quietly with his tail wrapped around his feet and watched. She put the cup on a tray and paused to lean over and kiss the little dragon on the nose.

"Thank you, Fulgid!"

Soon Ammon was stretched out and sleeping peacefully in the soft cushions of the chair. Satisfied that he was resting comfortably, El settled herself into a chair beside him and sighed. Fulgid climbed onto her lap and curled up as she scratched behind his ears. "I think we're going to get along just fine."

***

The days of forced rest were beginning to wear on Ammon. Despite El's best intentions, he felt confined as if his clothes were too tight. An overwhelming urge to stretch and escape the confines of his bedchambers gnawed at him, making him restless. The wound in his side still ached, but he was sure a bit of exercise would help. Shortly after breakfast one morning he announced his intentions of to visit Derek in the Nest.

El rolled her eyes as she tried talking him out of it. "You hardly need to bother checking up on him. You know those eggs couldn't be better cared for."

It was true, but he missed his frequent trips to the Nest. He sat fidgeting and scratching until El finally relented on the condition that she accompanied him to make sure he didn't overexert himself. He agreed eagerly, and as they readied to leave, he stopped at the bedchamber door and looked in. Fulgid lay stretched out on the bed. "Aren't you coming with us to see Derek?"

With a muffled groan, the dragon rolled onto his back and stuck his feet in the air. Ammon chuckled. "Alright, sleep in if you like, but Derek will be disappointed!" Arm in arm, he and El left his chambers and slowly climbed the stairs to the Nest.

Derek was sitting on the edge of the Nest dangling his tree trunk sized legs over the side. One of the Gaul Knights sat beside him and both turned their heads as they entered. He had met most of the knights of both Gaul and DoTaria but barely knew more than a dozen by name. However he knew this particular knight simply because Tashira was the only female.

Derek jumped to his feet as they approached and ran to grab a few chairs from the side of the room so they could sit down. "How are you feeling, Ammon? Shouldn't you be in bed resting? Would you like a cup of tea?"

Ammon shook his head and wheezed. "No thank you, Derek, we just came to visit and see how you were doing."

Derek stood uneasily, shifting from one foot to the other. "I'm okay and the eggs are doing well! I turn and clean them just like you showed me, but I'm still not sure about that big egg, it keeps getting larger and larger. Are you sure you don't want a cup of tea? I can put honey in it for you!"

Ammon rubbed his aching chest, and again shook his head, as he winked at El. "No thank you, I've had more than I can stand lately! Now, about that egg, it's still getting bigger?"

Derek's eyes shifted towards the Nest. "Yes, it keeps growing, but the shell is still soft and there are no marks on it. Are you sure you don't want tea?"

Tashira spoke up from her seat on the edge of the Nest. "Yes, Derek, I think tea for King Ammon is a wonderful idea!"

Derek practically ran to the back for his teakettle and Ammon and El looked questioningly at Tashira. She shrugged her shoulders and swung her feet up to sit cross-legged facing Ammon. "He's been terribly worried about you since you were injured. If you don't let him do something for you he might just explode."

Ammon grunted faintly and rubbed his chest. "Yes, I suppose so. Though I swear if I have any more tea I'm just as likely to explode myself."

Tashira snorted, and her tightly braided ponytail swung back and forth as she shook her head. "Wait until you see his teacup!"

Derek returned with a cup so large that Ammon had to grasp it with both hands. As he struggled to find a way to hold it, he whispered to El. "This isn't a teacup...it's a flaming soup bowl with a handle!"

El nodded absently as she stared curiously at Tashira's gray dragon scale armor. Ammon shrugged and tried unsuccessfully to sip the tea. He was finding it increasingly harder to breathe and his chest seemed to tighten more with every breath. Perhaps El had been right, it was too early for him to roam about.

El left her seat to kneel beside Tashira. "Excuse me, but I've never heard of a female knight before. Are they common in Gaul? Is their training different and was it difficult to link with a dragon? Do you always wear your armor?"

The two quickly became so immersed in conversation that Derek had to call their names repeatedly before they heard him. When they finally realized it, the big man simply pointed a huge finger at Ammon sitting lopsided in the chair. The large teacup slipped from his hands onto his lap and spilled to the floor in a steady stream.

"He don't look so good!"

Ammon felt like there were iron bands around his chest, squeezing the air from his lungs with each painful gasp. The wound in his side throbbed mercilessly and the skin around it felt as if it would burst. He forced his eyes open to see El beside him, her face clouded with worry. He tried to focus on his breathing, but each labored breath became more difficult than the last.

El's voice was frantic. "We need to get him downstairs quickly!"

Tashira placed a hand on El's shoulder and nodded to Derek. "He can carry him to your chambers easily. I'll stay here and tend the eggs for him." With a firm but sympathetic grip, she took El's hand between hers. "Take good care of him El. We need him…and you. We can talk more later."

Derek reached down and effortlessly scooped Ammon up into his massive arms as if carrying a baby and followed El quickly down the stairs.

Ammon faintly muttered between gasps. "Need…Fulgid!"

As they burst through the chamber doors El waved a hand at the couch for Derek to lay him down, but Ammon weakly shook his head and pointed to the bedroom.

"Bring me…there…quickly!"

Frowning, El nodded to Derek and the big man strode into the bedchambers and stopped. El whisked past and froze with her mouth open.

Fulgid lay stretched on his side across the center of the bed. The blankets, sheets and mattress were completely shredded beyond recognition and feathers littered the floor of the entire room. A low groan came from the little dragon and he slowly raked his claws down the covers, making fresh slices.

Ammon spoke softly but clearly. "Put me down beside him, he needs me."

Obediently, Derek gently laid Ammon next to the Fulgid as if placing a newborn in a crib.

Ammon placed a pale hand on the golden neck and whispered. "I'm here now."

El stepped forward, confused. "Ammon? What is wrong with…?"

Ammon held his hand up and shook his head. "Please!" He returned his attention to Fulgid. "It's alright my friend, we can do this."

Fulgid stretched himself across the mattress, sank his claws deep into the mattress and moaned pitifully, writhing in pain. After a few minutes he stopped, and his tongue hung from the side of his mouth as he panted, then it started again, and he cried out louder and longer than before. Once more he rested before he gripped the bed and released an ear-piercing howl of agony that ended sharply with a loud crack like the breaking of stone. He squirmed and wiggled as another muffled crack rose from beneath his body. Finally he arched his back sharply and a pop sounded across the bedchambers as the scales covering his body suddenly split apart, revealing a layer of shiny new scales underneath. Moments later he stepped out of his old skin, leaving behind a small mound of scales on the shredded mattress.

Sweat beaded across Ammon's brow and he draped a hand over the exhausted dragon, scratching him gently behind the ear. "It's over my friend. It's over."

***

Tirate paced in front of the palace window overlooking Gaul. The latest report Diam had given him was not what he wanted to hear. He knew it was too much to hope for that Erik and his accursed dragons had perished when the cave collapsed. The events of that day still haunted him as rumors spread of a golden knight with glowing eyes and a gilded demon that killed dozens of men. He knew those numbers had been greatly exaggerated, but with each new telling the story grew as it spread through the entire kingdom. He was sure it was that boy from the Nest, but he seriously doubted the timid youth could wield a sword well enough to kill anyone.

That miserable mutant dragon was certainly capable of causing considerable damage. He rubbed the deep scar on his face as he recalled his last encounter with it. He had severely underestimated the tenaciousness of the beast, a mistake he'd never make again. At least he had the satisfaction of knowing Boris was dead. The first victims of his dragon killing war machines. Many of Erik's knights were skilled at warfare, but none so much as Boris Dejias. His death would have severely demoralized the rest and robbed Erik of a superb military leader. The big question was, where did they go?

He had expected any attempt to return would have been made already. It was now mid-fall and although the daytime temperatures were still warm, the cooler nights would start to affect the dragon's ability to fly. Even if they had found a cavern inside the mountains big enough to hold of them, they still would need a steady supply of food and a way to keep warm. He had his men comb the countryside and there was no sign of the nearly two hundred beasts. He had to consider the possibility that if they hadn't moved by now they may already be dead.

But suddenly there were bizarre reports coming from the north. Each day one or two men would suddenly go missing from their posts, leaving behind nothing more than bloodstained clothing and sometimes a broken sword. He suspected that somehow that little mutant dragon found a way out. No full-grown dragon could make these attacks without being seen.

In a sadistic way, it made him happy to think it might still be alive. He wanted revenge for the pain and embarrassment he had suffered. He wanted to skin it alive and fashion a suit of golden armor from its shining scales to replace the steel it had shredded. It would be months before the blacksmiths could make him a replacement, he had them all busy fashioning hardware for the crossbows. He had no other choice but to use bits and pieces from the armory to make a complete suit. It fit poorly but at least it was made mostly of dragon scales, so if he ever did meet the little beast again it wouldn't have such an easy time tearing his flesh.

A faint stirring behind him reminded him that Diam was still waiting for his orders. He turned sharply on his heel, pulled back the chair, and sat down at his desk. He selected a quill and spoke quickly as the tip scratched across the paper.

"I want the debris cleared from inside the cave. If the boy and his mutant are still alive we'll go in after them. I won't sit back while they pick us off one at a time. Our crossbows are more than a match for a dragon. If he's alive, then there may be others. If they try to escape while we clear the rubble then have the guards pick them off the moment they exit."

Diam wrung his hands and cleared his throat meekly. "Yes sire, but your guards are…reluctant…to enter the mountain. At least willingly."

Tirate finished writing and placed the quill back in its holder. He sprinkled sand over the script and blotted it dry before handing it to Diam. "That is what this is for. Since I increased taxes to pay for the mercenaries, the prisons are full of those unable to pay, and more arrive every day. This document gives you authorization to use them as laborers to pay their debt. If you need more, I have a list of those who supported Erik's regime. Have them arrested under whatever pretenses you feel appropriate. Let Erik's own people die clearing the way."

"An excellent plan sire! I shall start immediately!" Diam bowed as he shuffled backward toward the door so he didn't see Liah until after he'd bumped into her. He turned sharply and his eyes widened in surprise. "Oh, I'm sorry my…Queen! I beg forgiveness!"

Liah sniffed and brushed at her gown as if an animal with mange had rubbed against her. Her voice was icy as she leveled a hard stare at the man. "If you ever do that again, I'll have your head cut off and hung in the square."

Diam visibly paled, and he bowed low once more before quickly leaving.

Liah sauntered around the desk and began to rub Tirate's shoulders. "I don't how you tolerate that man. I don't trust him. If you like, I could…remove…him for you."

Tirate never raised his eyes from the document he was reading. He reached over his shoulder and lifted her hand from his shoulder, then twisted it down, forcing her to crouch beside his chair. His voice was cold as steel. "How many times have I told you never to stand behind me? Diam is my secretary and will remain that way until I have no further use for him. Just as you may remain queen as long as it serves my purpose. Now leave me. I have work to do."

He released her and she rose to her feet, rubbing her hand. With only a hint of mockery, she curtsied and briskly left the room. He rubbed his eyes in aggravation. She could have tried to kill him easily enough. He knew her knife was hidden just inches from her grasp in the hem of her dress, but it would have been too obvious who did it. It was a risk to keep her nearby, but right now he needed her. With the news of a golden dragon reappearing in the north, some of the Houses began to question if he had indeed linked with that dragon after all. The elaborate hoax was beginning to crumble, and until the new mercenary troops arrived, he couldn't possibly quell an uprising.

His sudden, unexpected royal wedding to a stunningly beautiful woman quickly redirected the public's attention perfectly, and the protests had temporarily quieted. If they rose again he'd have to find another distraction. Perhaps he'd announce she was with child. As much as he hated children, eventually he would need an heir.

***

Liah stormed into her bedchambers and slammed the door. The man had no idea how close she came to slitting his throat. Frustrated, she drew one of the knives from behind her belt and threw it at the door where it sank deep into the wood with a solid thunk. The only reason she hadn't killed him a dozen times already was because she liked the prestige and adoration of being a queen, a much better position than her previous employment. Until now, she had merely been just another assassin for Tirate until the fiasco with that horrid little dragon and that insufferable boy. That was her first and only failure, and the memory of being forced to shovel tons of fly-infested dragon dung was almost more than she could bear. If she ever got the chance to repay that insult, she would be sure to make it painful.

She shivered at the thought. If Tirate's men hadn't attacked Erik's camp so quickly, she probably would have been discovered hiding beneath the dung. As soon as she realized there was a battle looming, she covered herself in the largest pile she could find and waited.

She looked at herself in the mirror and adjusted her hair. She was beautiful and she knew it, but that day in the woods was beyond humiliating. It had been no small feat to convince Tirate's men to bring her to him, especially covered as she was with filth. The miscreants had thrown her in the river headfirst before they would agree to it. If she'd had any knives, she'd have stabbed every one of them.

She flashed a brilliant smile into the mirror as she thought about the things she could now do as queen. Once Tirate had taken care of that horrid little golden beast, maybe she'd ask for a necklace made from its scales. As for Ammon, the boy was pretty enough to look at, so maybe she'd have him as her personal slave. When she tired of looking at him, she'd send him out to shovel manure for the rest of his life.

She dabbed a little powder to the end of her nose and gazed at her reflection. She had always taken particular care of appearance, but her nose was by far her favorite feature. Powder and paints could disguise many flaws, but a badly shaped nose could never be hidden. Many men had been led to their doom with no more than a wink of her eye, and her looks had been the key to becoming the queen of Gaul, the most powerful woman in the world! Never again would she touch a shovel, not for the rest of her life!

***

Ammon sat beside El patiently and waited as Boris eased himself into a chair in front of the breakfast Kyle had spread before them. The flames in the huge fireplaces of the royal sitting room crackled and popped, sending tiny sparks up the chimney. The first frost of the year covered the windows, but inside the palace was quite comfortable. Below them in the Hold, the furnaces churned out a steady supply of heat that radiated up into every room, and the numerous fireplaces added extra warmth. Neither Ammon nor El felt any affects of the chill outside, but the cold seemed to effect Boris, and he moved stiffly. Fulgid seemed to particularly enjoy the warmth as he lay stretched out in front of the fire snoring contently.

Boris wasted no time devouring his meal, and when he finished, he leaned back in the chair and patted his stomach. "Between Kyle and Mabel, if I keep eating this well I'll soon be as big as Ellis."

Ammon and El exchanged glances and tried to hide their smiles. Since Boris' return, Mabel had taken it upon herself to feed and care for him. Now that his health had returned, he was quite capable of doing it himself, but she still insisted on doting over him. It seemed everyone but Boris knew her true intentions. He poured himself a steaming cup from a large pot of black liquid and gestured at Fulgid in front of the fireplace.

"Speaking of getting bigger, that dragon of yours still hasn't grown much since his last shed has he?"

Ammon looked over his shoulder and shook his head. Even stretched out as he was, his body still wasn't much bigger than a large cat with a tail that was easily as long as the rest of him. "I think his tail has gotten longer but the rest of him seems about the same. How big do you think he'll get?"

Boris placed his mug on the table and smoothed his thick moustache with his thumb. "Hard to say. Dragons shed a few days after hatch and again about six months later. His first shed was very late, but his second one was pretty early. It shouldn't happen again until he's a year old. Most hatchlings his age are the size of ponies and he hasn't changed much, so it's possible he may not get much bigger. I'll be honest with you though, he doesn't seem to follow any of the typical patterns of dragons, so who knows?" He took a long sip from his mug. "I was told you have enough scales for your armor now?"

Ammon nodded. "Between the last shedding and what was left over from making the blades and El's ring, I had just enough. A few weeks ago Stalwart took them somewhere to have the armor made, but it's not done yet.

He insisted it be made in the DoTarian style, so I'll be interested to see what it looks like."

El patted his hand. "It's for decoration purposes only! No more arrows for you dear."

Between Boris' chuckles Ammon protested. "I've been told that as king, I have the right to be first in battle and last to leave."

El rolled her eyes. "That makes no sense at all. If the king dies, who will direct the rest of the battle?"

Boris held up his hands. "Don't get me involved in this argument! I'm learning that arguing with a woman is dangerous. Even if you win, you still lose!"

El shook her finger. "That's right, and the sooner you learn that Ammon, the easier life will be for you!"

Ammon couldn't help but laugh. "It's bad enough that you and Fulgid conspire against me, now you want to change an ancient tradition?"

El mockingly ignored him as she turned to Boris. "He still hasn't learned yet, but I expect he'll come around soon."

Boris grinned and shrugged his shoulders. "Mabel has done the same thing with Ellis. All these years he never allowed anyone to go near him but me, and suddenly she's feeding him and rubbing his nose like a pet! He's been corrupted I tell you! In the prime of his life too!"

"Perhaps he knows something" El began sweetly. "After all, he'd have to accept her if you two were to get married."

Boris sat forward so suddenly he nearly dropped his mug. "Married? Me? Uh...ahem...I.... Well, we really should begin our morning discussion now don't you think, Ammon?"

Ammon hid his laughter with a cough as El softly giggled. "Uh, yes, I suppose we should get on with it. Whenever your ready, Boris."

When Ammon had been too weak to leave his chambers, Boris, Erik, and Stalwart would take turns having breakfast with him in his sitting room to discuss the issues of the rapidly growing city. Eventually it became a morning ritual of problem solving that he looked forward to. Traditionally DoTarian queens were not involved in any decision making, but he insisted that El participate, and she frequently proved to be quite adept at finding solutions that nobody else had thought of.

Boris ran down the list of issues. "The problem of the leaky roof is ongoing. There simply aren't enough materials to repair and replace all the cracked tiles over the palace. We're looking into placing thatch on top until enough tiles can be made, but even that won't stop the worst leaks.

The good news is there are far fewer incidences of slugs. Apparently they hibernate or something in the winter. The colder it gets, the more infrequent the sightings are. We've already got a years supply of calentar ground up and in storage. Before snow falls we'll make a few more trips to haul out some of the larger crystals and keep them in storage as well."

El delicately crossed her legs and balanced her teacup carefully on her knee. "Boris, when did you say the adult dragons usually shed?"

He looked at her quizzically, confused at the sudden change of subjects. "Well, adult dragons shed annually in the fall, most after the first frost, give or take a few days. Is there a reason you ask?"

El smiled brightly. "There is your new roof! With roughly fifteen hundred dragons in the hold there should be enough scales to cover the entire palace and some left over for anything else you need!"

Ammon and Boris looked at her for a long moment. Boris softly grunted. "By my dragons teeth, she's right and what a roof that would be! It'd last forever, or at least until the building rotted out from beneath it!"

El frowned into her cup. "You should also continue to bring out calentar daily. It's the only known deposit right now, and we don't have the ability to dig it out quickly if the tunnel collapsed for some reason. A years supply would quickly disappear if there were no more to be had easily.

To get it out now while the Kala-Azar hibernate would be safest."

Boris tapped his finger against his chin and nodded. "Aye, I'll agree with that. I'll have the workers keep hauling it out and grinding it up. They wouldn't have much else to do once the snows came anyway."

There was a soft knock at the door as Mabel arrived to accompany Boris back to the hold, but Boris insisted he stay a bit longer to watch Ammon's sword practice with Stalwart. Although his arm had mended nicely, he was still unable to wield his sword yet and begrudgingly forfeited the duty to the DoTarian captain. He grumbled irritably as Stalwart entered the room. "There was a time I'd be back on duty within just a month or so."

Mabel settled herself in the chair beside Boris and patted his knee. "That was before you got old and feeble dear. Now be quiet and watch the man practice."

Despite the chuckles of everyone in the room, Boris' cheeks reddened but no words found their way past his lips.

Ammon tried to concentrate on his movements and force his sluggish muscles to react. The injury and weeks of sickness had robbed him of much of the hard-earned muscle he'd gained, and El had refused to let him practice until she was sure he was completely well. Several times he'd picked up the sword when he thought she wasn't around, but the woman seemed to have eyes everywhere and chastised him every time.

When her reluctant blessings finally came, he worked twice as hard to regain his skills. He no longer dangled acorns on string to practice. Instead, Stalwart tossed them with the expectation that he could block them with the sword before they touched his body. As his muscles loosened, he began to flow with a smooth grace. Stalwart handed a bag of acorns to Boris, and the two of them threw the nuts with increasing speed from opposite directions. Faster and faster the acorns flew, and Ammon began to sweat as pieces of split shells bounced across the room. When the last one had been thrown, Ammon stood panting. Only a dozen or so had actually managed to hit him and Fulgid was busily searching out the rest, crunching happily as he found them.

Stalwart tossed a towel to Ammon and nodded his approval to Boris. "The boy is a natural. How long did you say he has he been training? I have full-fledged knights that don't handle a sword this well. If he can keep learning at this pace he'll be one of the finest swordsmen I've ever seen!"

Boris agreed. "He definitely has the knack for it." He frowned for a moment. "I have a question. With the Kala-Azar scattering the knights across the countryside, how did you train the new recruits?"

Stalwart picked an acorn off one of the chairs and tossed it to Fulgid before he sat down. "I couldn't personally train each one. We scattered into small groups of two or three. The trainees rotated through each group and trained with each knight until they reached a level of competence that satisfied their teacher. It wasn't easy, and occasionally we lost a group and their dragons when the slugs caught them unawares.

You can't imagine how hard it was on us all. Most knights are too young to remember Laton when it was a shining city. I myself had just barely been recruited at the time. As the calentar mines began to run dry, King Halos assigned us to different areas of the country with orders to change to a new location every few days. The idea was to keep moving so the slugs couldn't keep up. We all expected to return to Laton in a few weeks after more calentar was found, but it never happened. Fifty years later, here we are."

Ammon mopped his face with the towel. "So calentar isn't found anywhere else but here in Laton?"

Stalwart spread his hands. "There were small deposits scattered throughout DoTaria, but those were depleted centuries ago. That's why Laton became so important when a large deposit was found. Once that was gone, few dared come back to attempt digging another mine. For some reason the slugs were thicker here than any other area and have a nasty habit of popping up out of nowhere. I always suspected they hibernated underground in old abandoned mines."

Ammon threw a sharp look at Boris, but he put his hand up before Ammon could speak. "I know, I thought of it too. I have a couple knights bring their dragons to the mine every morning to blast the inside with fire in case a slug appears. The tunnels are searched end to end before workers are allowed in."

Ammon sighed in relief. "Perhaps it would be wise to keep a dragon at the mine all the time, just in case."

Chapter 15
A Lily In The Dark

From his balcony Ammon watched as workmen hauled load after load of black and gray dragon scales out of the Hold. High above him on the palace roof, dozens of men worked feverishly as they plastered a thick, black glue to the back of each dinner plate sized scale and carefully tapped it in place. Everyone knew the heavy snows of winter would come all too soon.

Already the temperatures had grown noticeably colder, and the leaves on the trees changed from deep green to bright orange and red, with a few drifting lazily to the ground. As the morning sunlight reached the mountains, it revealed a patchwork of color that spread over the hills like a giant quilt as far as he could see. His breath hung lazily in the crisp air, and the chill raised goosebumps on his arms. He sighed contently and stepped back inside to the warmth of his chambers and closed the glass doors behind him. Perhaps when El got back he would ask her to walk with him outside one more time before the weather turned poor.

Lately it had become increasingly difficult to find time alone with her. Each morning she left for several hours to meet with the female knight Tashira. When he asked where she went, she simply replied that if the king was first in battle, than the queen should be beside him. It wasn't until later when he realized what she meant. It had started with a simple lesson of how to use the knife he'd given her for protection, but it soon expanded to several other areas of weaponry. His protests were met with a burning look, and he quickly decided to leave well enough alone. Still, the thought of her in a battle made him very uncomfortable.

By the time she returned, he was waiting in the sitting room with a wicker basket from the kitchen and a light cloak over his armor to keep out the chill. Still dressed in her hooded shirt and breeches, she accepted the invitation without hesitation and slipped her arm around his as they walked towards the door. With a grunt, Fulgid reluctantly left his spot beside the fire to follow them and soon they were headed out into the brisk air towards the mountains.

Despite the chilly air, the sun felt warm in the cloudless sky, and Fulgid romped ahead chasing squirrels through piles of fallen leaves. After weeks of hectic activity in the palace, the woods seemed so peaceful with just the sounds of singing birds in the trees and the crunch of stones beneath their feet. The road leading to the tunnel was well worn from the heavy traffic of the miners and loads of calentar, and it made for easy traveling. Soon they were within sight of the opening, and Ammon pointed past it at the wide field above. He knew the views of the city from the hilltop were impressive, and it was a perfect spot to have their meal.

Suddenly there were panicked shouts of alarm from the entrance of the tunnel, and they quickly exchanged glances as they broke into a run. Ammon recognized one of the Gaul Knights named Chanel trying unsuccessfully to calm several workmen who were gesturing frantically at the tunnel. They hurried closer just in time to hear one of them say "Kala-Azar!"

Ammon grabbed the nearest frightened man by the shoulders and demanded. "Where?"

Stuttering, the miner finally spit out. "The Gaul side tunnel!"

Chanel loosened the longsword on his back and eyed the entrance suspiciously. "My dragon is nearby, we'll head down and investigate immediately."

Ammon shook his head. "No. That end of the tunnel is collapsed and your dragon is too big to maneuver around. If he got into trouble there wouldn't be any way to help him. It would be faster if Fulgid and I went down. He's small enough to move around down there easily, and he has more fire than any other dragon."

After a long pause Chanel reluctantly agreed. He turned to El and bowed. "Your highness, I've already sent a messenger on horseback to the palace to alert them. Would you please let them know when they arrive…that…uh"

El stood with her hands on her hips and one eyebrow raised as she glared at him. Chanel's face began to turn red and he cleared his throat. "I'm sorry…uh…you're going down too aren't you? Of course you are! I will accompany you then!"

Ammon chuckled softly to himself. It seemed he wasn't the only one unsure of El's role as queen.

Their footsteps echoed as they walked, and Chanel's voice was little more than a whisper. "The miner said he heard slugs moving down here, although I can't imagine how they got in. Two dragons came and checked the entire tunnel this morning. We haven't seen a slug since we started having regular frosts at night."

Ammon threw back his cloak and drew his sword. His golden armor reflected the lantern light, sending tiny dots of light into the shadows. "According to Stalwart, slugs have a way of showing up in places you don't expect. So be prepared, they could be anywhere!"

They moved slowly through the tunnel, letting Fulgid inspect every inch until they reached the end where the roof was collapsed. Ammon held his lantern up high and studied the rubble. Piles of boulders reached to the ceiling, and Fulgid leapt from one to the next, sniffing between each of them.

Ammon shook his head. "If there were slugs down here, Fulgid would know. His reaction is pretty obvious."

Chanel kicked at a small clod of dirt. "Then I'm glad I didn't bring my dragon down. He wouldn't have appreciated having to back out all the way up the tunnel for nothing."

Ammon agreed. "I'm sure. I don't know what the miners heard, but at least we know it wasn't..."

Several fist-sized rocks suddenly rolled down between them and Ammon raised the lantern again. Fulgid had climbed to the very top of the pile and was forcing his nose behind a pumpkin-sized boulder. With a quick shove, he sent it tumbling, and they all jumped to avoid being hit.

Ammon watched as the little dragon clawed at the stones. "Fulgid, what are you doing?"

Fulgid pulled his head out of the hole he made, and the light from the lantern fell onto the dirty face of a small child, frozen in terror.

Ammon nearly dropped the lantern as the three of them scrambled to pull stones away. When she was free he reached in and gently lifted her out and carried her down the pile and set the trembling girl on her feet.

Wide-eyed, she stared at Ammon and Fulgid with her lip quivering, until finally she whimpered. "Are you going to let your dragon eat me?"

El put her face down close to the girl and gently pushed her hair out of her eyes. "No! No, sweetheart, why would you think that?"

Fat tears began to stream down the girl's cheeks. "The men...the guards said we have to move rocks so they can kill dragons before they ate us up! Please! I don't want to get ate!"

The three adults looked at each other in stunned shock. El sat on a boulder and lifted the girl onto her lap. "What's your name?"

Trying not to sob, the child sniffed and rubbed her nose with a dirty hand. "L...Lily! M...my name is L...Lily."

El took a small handkerchief from her pocket and wiped Lily's nose. "Well Lily, dragons don't eat people. See that one right there? His name is Fulgid, and unless you're a squirrel or an acorn, you're very safe. He would never hurt you, ever."

Fulgid lay quietly, his head flat on the ground between his front feet and gazed up at the little girl with amber eyes.

Lily tilted her head and half buried her face against El's shirt. "I…I'm not an acorn, b…but he scares me! The guards said a gold demon dragon and a gold knight are killing everyone!"

El pointed up at the hole where the little girl had been. "Lily, Fulgid doesn't want to kill anyone. He even helped pull you out! Fulgid is a nice dragon and only kills slugs and protects us from anyone who tries to hurt us."

Lily made a face. "I don't like slugs, they're…slimy!" She looked down at Fulgid who still hadn't moved. Pushing herself up against El, she whispered, "Is he really made of gold?"

Ammon smiled as he reached down and scratched Fulgid behind his ears. "No, he's not made of gold, but it looks like it, doesn't it? You can pet him if you like, I promise he won't hurt you!" Lily shook her head fiercely. Ammon knelt down beside the little girl. "It's okay, you don't have to! Lily, can you tell me how you got stuck in that hole?"

Shyly the little girl nodded. "The guard man pushed me in and said crawl around and tell me what you see, but a big rock fell behind me and I couldn't get out!"

El pointed at Fulgid. "Well you're safe now. We didn't know you were in there, but he did. He found you all by himself!"

The little girl sniffled and looked up at El's face. "He did?"

El nodded her head. "He sure did!"

She looked at Fulgid on the ground and meekly said "Thank you Fudlig!"

Fulgid slowly crawled forward on his belly and carefully laid his head on El's knee. Lily pulled back, frightened, but El held her close. "It's okay! Look…he likes to be scratched behind his ears...see?"

Cautiously, she reached out with El's hand and timidly touched Fulgid with a tiny hand. The dragon let out a long sigh and closed his eyes. Suddenly Lily giggled. "I think I like dragons that don't eat me!"

While El kept Lily occupied, Ammon pulled Chanel aside. "Tirate's men can't be too far behind if she climbed through. We need a guard placed here until we've figured out a plan." He frowned as he watched Lily scratching Fulgid's ears with both hands. "If they're using children to crawl through the narrow parts of the tunnel, than they're probably forcing others to dig. That will make things much more complicated. I don't want a single innocent harmed. It's Tirate and his men I want."

Chanel nodded. "I'll stay here. If anything happens, I'll notify you immediately."

"Thank you." Ammon turned and dropped to his knee beside the little girl on El's lap. "Lily? Would you like to come to the palace and have tea with us? You can tell us all about what those guards are doing!"

Lily's eyes rounded as she looked at El. "You mean a real palace? With kings and queens and everything?"

Chanel chuckled as he whispered controversially. "You're sitting on the lap of a queen right now, and the man in the golden armor is the king!"

Lily gasped, jumped to her feet and looked back and forth between them. Nearly bursting with excitement she nodded enthusiastically. "Yes! Oh yes, yes, yes! Please! May I?"

She reached up and gripped El's hand while Fulgid walked close beside her and they walked up to the tunnel exit. Outside a group of miners were waiting and Theo had just arrived with Stalwart and several other knights.

Ammon patted one of the minors on the back good-naturedly and gestured to Lily. "Here is your Kala-Azar! Not exactly what any of us were expecting to be sure!"

He smiled at the puzzled faces of Theo and Stalwart and pointed into the tunnel. "Chanel is guarding the tunnel by the cave-in. Tirate is making children crawl through the rubble to find the other side. We need a plan, and fast!

They must be close to coming through so we'll need dragons standing by. In the meantime we've invited Lily to the palace for tea, and I'd like you to join us as I'm sure she has some very interesting things to tell us!"

Fulgid strode forward with Lily proudly resting her hand on his head. Lily gasped in delight at the view of the city. Its freshly painted stone walls gleamed in the sunlight, and the newly topped spires stretched to dizzying heights. When they passed through the city gates, Fulgid marched straight down the center of the street, and Lily stared in awe as people stepped aside and bowed their heads. Ammon couldn't help but grin as Lily waved to everyone as if she were a member of royalty.

He leaned towards El and gestured discreetly at the dirty rags Lily was wearing. "Don't you think our guest would like to…freshen up…a bit? I'm sure Seamstress Mabel could find her something more suitable to wear while I send down to the kitchen for tea."

El nodded knowingly. "Why yes of course! A lady always makes sure to attend a tea dressed appropriately! I will make the arrangements myself!"

The moment they entered the royal chambers Ammon sent one of the pages to find Mabel and arrange for fancy tea and sweet pastries to be served. When Mabel arrived carrying bolts of cloth and other materials, El promptly shooed him from the bedchambers and closed the door. He chuckled at the flurry of activity on the other side of the wall and wondered if he'd recognize the little girl when they were finished with her.

Fulgid was stretched out comfortably by the fire in the sitting room and he knelt to scratch his ears. "You saved that little girl's life and who knows how many others today."

Fulgid rolled lazily onto his back and yawned as the familiar voice chimed in Ammon's head. "LILY HATCHLING HAPPY."

***

Lily felt like a princess as she sat between King Ammon and Queen El at the largest table she'd ever seen. The queen looked so different now than she did in the dark tunnel. She couldn't help but gaze up at the beautiful woman beside her in awe. The queen's dark hair hung down in ringlets that looked like they'd never been tangled and her brown eyes seemed so soft and gentle! It was hard to believe that the queen herself helped to make her a pretty velvet green dress to wear to the tea party! She fidgeted excitedly and beneath the table the queen gently squeezed her hand.

King Ammon sat on her other side. His hair was almost the same color as his shiny gold armor and his eyes seemed to see everything and were as blue as the sky. His face was kind like Queen El's, and he smiled each time he looked at her. When he put his hands on the table, she could see that they were covered in pink scars, and she shuddered. She had marks like that once before on a man who used fire to make metal things. She hoped it didn't hurt.

Without a doubt though, the most amazing thing Lily had ever seen was the little dragon. It was hard to say his name, but he didn't seem to mind. He sat in the chair with her with his head resting gently on her shoulder. His breath tickled her ear and made little wisps of her hair flutter when he exhaled.

Never before had she felt so special or so important. Before the guards took her and the others away from Miss Garret, she had always been just one of the orphans. Miss Garret gave them whatever clothes she could find and fed them what she could. Lily was always careful never to ask for very much because Miss Garret was quite old and very thin and needed to eat too.

As she looked across the huge table, she saw more food than she could ever imagine in one place. Her mouth watered, and she very cautiously snatched a big round cookie from one of the plates and slipped it into her pocket. She was sure Miss Garret would like one of them, and no one here would ever know they were missing! Suddenly, she felt guilty. Stealing was wrong, and Miss Garret would be mad, even if there was more here than they could ever eat. Sadly, she pulled the cookie from her pocket and put it back.

King Ammon suddenly leaned over and whispered. "You can keep that if you want. I can get lots more from the kitchen. Besides, this is just a snack until the noon meal is served. You can eat as much as you want, whenever you feel hungry ok? Just tell someone and they'll bring you something to eat."

She felt a little frightened for a moment. Those blue eyes really did see everything! He winked and smiled as he pushed the platter of cookies closer to her, and the fear melted away. Oddly, she wondered where all this food came from when Miss Garret always had such a hard time finding any. There must be a lot of food in this big, beautiful city!

More men came into the room and bowed respectfully to the king and queen before they took their seats at the long table. She couldn't help but stare in surprise. They acted very different from the guards in Gaul. These men didn't spit and swear, and they smiled as they passed a teapot to each other instead of drinking that awful smelling ale. They all dressed a little like King Ammon except their armor was black or gray and wasn't shiny like his was.

Mabel, the woman who helped make Lily's dress, came in holding the arm of a man who limped when he walked. He was a big man with thinning hair on his head and a large white moustache that flowed down on either side of his mouth. Mabel helped him to his chair before settling herself beside him.

King Ammon stood and the room quieted almost at once. "We have a surprise guest with us today from Gaul. Lily, would you please stand?"

El nodded encouragingly and helped her to stand in the chair so everyone could see. Her knees felt weak.

The king put his hand on her shoulder. "Lily, would you please tell us how old you are?"

Everyone was staring at her. "I'm four!" She stammered meekly.

Queen El gently took her hand and smiled. "It's okay, don't be nervous, you are with friends here. Can you tell us how you came to be stuck in the tunnel?"

As she looked at the faces around her, her stomach began to hurt and a lump was building in her throat. She wanted to make the King and Queen happy and tell them everything, but the words just wouldn't come! Suddenly there was a reassuring nudge behind her from the little dragon, and when she looked down at him, she felt a surge of courage.

She spoke quietly at first, then louder as she gained confidence. "The guards came and told Miss Garret she was under rest 'cause she didn't have taxes. So they put us all in a big wagon. Then they put us on a big raft and made us hold on while we went down the river, and I thought we would fall in the water. One of the guards fell in, and they didn't help him, and I think he sank. Then we got off the raft, and the other guards gave us shovels and told us we had to dig in the tunnel. Lots of grownups and kids were already there digging, but I was too small, so they made me crawl 'tween the rocks with a candle and tell them what I saw. The guards wouldn't help though, even with the big rocks. They sat on the wagon with the big bow and arrows. They made us pull it into the tunnel 'cause they said monsters were on the other side that would eat us and they had to shoot them.

Yesterday they put me behind a big rock, and my candle went out, and I couldn't see. I asked them to give me another but the guards yelled at me and said no, and I couldn't find my way out! I tried but then I couldn't hear them anymore, and I sat in the dark for a long time. Then I heard noises so I squeezed through and got stuck behind a rock until...until Fudlig found me...and now I'm having tea!" She settled back down into her seat and wondered why Queen El was crying.

Chapter 16
Stolen Heart

Ammon crouched behind a boulder downhill from the tunnel entrance and examined the odd arsenal Stalwart had provided. The arm length arrows, which the DoTarian's called coda, were tipped with clay vials filled with oil and a small wick and had been designed for fighting against the Kala-Azar. When shattered, the vial blanketed its target with burning oil, and when several struck from multiple archers, the results were devastating. Grimly, he peered around the edge of the rock and watched. There was little sign of the two hundred plus men waiting motionlessly in the woods, or of the entire fist of dragons hidden beyond the rise of the hill.

Suddenly he heard El's voice behind him and he spun on his heel. "Any sign of them yet?"

Embarrassed at being taken off-guard from behind so easily, he shot an accusing glance at Fulgid who greeted her happily. "What are you doing here? You're supposed to be at the palace!"

She rolled her dark eyes beneath her hood. "I told you if you insisted on going to battle then I'd be there too. Now, has there been anymore movement in the tunnel or not?"

He shook his head in disapproval at the full quiver of coda slung over her shoulder. It was obvious she intended to stay for the fight. He placed a hand gently to her cheek and pleaded. "Please, El, I don't want you to get hurt. If you go back to the palace where I know…"

El placed a stern finger to his lips and nodded towards the entrance where there were movements in the shadows. "I can take care of myself. Besides, dear, who will watch out for you?"

He groaned inwardly. It was too late to argue now. All he could do was watch and wait for Boris' signal. Not a single shot was to be fired until they were sure no one was left in the tunnel. From the shadowy entrance a small boy suddenly tumbled out into the open as someone shoved him from behind. He sobbed as he rose to his knees and looked around in wide-eyed terror. As the minutes passed he looked towards the tunnel questioningly. A moment later a thin man in ragged clothes stumbled into the daylight, waving a sword awkwardly over his head.

Ammon ground his teeth angrily and Fulgid growled faintly. Bait. They were using the people of Gaul to draw fire from anyone hidden in the brush. A coarse looking guard strode cautiously from the shadows and roughly retrieved the sword from the thin man and impatiently shoved it into his scabbard. A moment later a tattered group of men, women and children emerged, straining heavily against a thick rope. One by one the massive crossbows were dragged into the open and arranged in a semicircle around the entrance while guards loaded thick steel tipped bolts into the firing mechanisms.

He estimated there were approximately one hundred guards and at least three dozen enslaved workers. A burly bearded man in a chain mail shirt appeared to be in charge as he directed the placement of the crossbows and pushed the workers into a group near the tunnel entrance. Ammon smirked. The guard had unwittingly done them all a favor by separating the people of Gaul from Tirate's men.

He carefully notched a coda onto his bow and turned his attention to the brush where Boris lay hidden beneath a layer of leaves. When the signal came, a cloud of arrows rained down upon the guards from every direction as they scrambled to take cover. Ammon lit the wick of the cota with a small lantern and with careful aim, loosed it onto the nearest crossbow just as a guard attempted to swing it into position. The mechanism was suddenly engulfed in a burst of flames as the burning oil splashed across it, then the flames doubled as a shot from El found its mark. Three more streaked from the woods, and in desperation the guard dove to the ground, beating out the flames of his burning shirt. With a loud crack, the tense bowstring snapped as it burned and sent a shower of sparks high into the air.

One by one the crossbows blossomed into crimson flames as the guards sought shelter. Ammon began to lay a volley of coda between the guards and the huddling civilians, hoping to create a protective wall of fire between them. Only a narrow gap remained when a small boy, unable to control his fear any longer, suddenly burst from the group and ran terrified towards the woods. In a heartbeat, the guard wearing the chain mail recognized it as a chance for escape and grabbed the boy as he passed. With the child as a shield, he pressed his sword against the boy's throat and backed towards the tunnel entrance.

Ammon drew his sword and raced to block his escape. With a sneer, the guard tossed the child aside and lunged at Ammon with his sword. Ammon's golden blade easily deflected the strike, and his counterstroke sliced the chain mail armor open like a ripe fruit. As the man stumbled back in surprise, El suddenly appeared and fiercely wrapped her arms protectively around the boy. Fulgid streaked past and began to blast fire on the remaining crossbows while the knights charged up the hill to drive a wedge between Tirate's men and the tunnel. The desperate guard seemed to realize his escape was in danger and he launched into a vicious attack on Ammon. As they exchanged blow after blow, both began to breathe heavily from the exertion.

A scream from El momentarily distracted Ammon, and from the corner of his eye he saw El fighting with two men. One was struggling to hold her while the other was bleeding badly from where El's golden knife was buried to the hilt in his shoulder. Ammon gritted his teeth and leapt forward to fight with renewed effort. Suddenly on the defensive, the burly guard desperately tried to block the frenzy of blows that rained down on him. Ammon's eyes burned in fury, and his blade arched down in a golden blur as it sliced the guard's sword in two. Shocked, the big man collapsed to his knees and surrendered. Moments later two DoTarian Knights dragged him off to join the rest of the captured men. The battle was over.

Ammon looked across the smoking battlefield. Fulgid was herding several of Tirate's men towards the rest of the prisoners by snapping at their feet. Boris was nearby binding the wrists of a man with a thin trickle of blood on his forehead and covered in dirt. El was nowhere to be seen. He felt his stomach tighten. She should have stayed at the palace! He made a quick circle around the clearing and stopped when he saw the little boy.

"Did you see where El went? The woman who was protecting you?"

The boy nodded and pointed to the tunnel. "Two men took her in there."

Ammon felt his heart sink and his eyes began to burn as he broke into a run towards the entrance. He was just a few strides away when an iron grip on his shoulder jerked him to a stop.

Boris spun him around. "Ammon, stop! Listen to me! They'll be guarding that tunnel, you can bet on it. You go down there and...Ammon? Your eyes! What happened to your eyes?"

The stunned look on Boris' face was unmistakable, but that didn't matter right now. Ammon had to get to El! He tried to pull away, but Boris' grip tightened. "You'll just get yourself killed, and then who will help her? Think about what you are doing! You have to use yours brain this time, not your sword!"

He looked up at Boris helplessly, and the concerned older man squeezed his shoulder. "We will get her back. I vow to you that we will get her back! For now I think you should come back to the palace. I'd like someone to look at those eyes of yours!"

Ammon stared back at the tunnel where Fulgid was pacing just inside the entrance. Tendrils of fire and smoke drifted from his nose and mouth and his eyes glowed furiously white.

***

El winced and tried to ignore the itchy feeling of dried blood on her temple. With her hands and feet tightly bound and draped over the back of a mule it was impossible to see what was around her, but at least she could hear. Flies swarmed around her, but her hood was over her head so at least they were off of her face. The steady clopping of another set of hooves and the thud of boots in the dirt told her there was at least one man on foot walking ahead.

As they headed down a steep embankment, she heard a low groan followed by a string of curses. The footsteps paused for only a moment. "Shuddup, Ross an quit yer moanin! We're almost there and ya can find someone to yank out that bloody knife! Ya should'a let me pulled it back at camp, but instead ya insisted we git to Gaul and let that herb witch yank it. Ya best remember to pay me that twenty talons to drag you here, and I been thinkin that I ought to keep that fancy knife too! It's only fair for all the walkin I'm doin. Yer lucky Tirate had a trail cut, but even so I'll be clear through these boots quick, and I paid good money for 'em. So that there is the deal. If ya die before we get there I'll take it out of ya hide! I swear I will!"

The only answer from Ross was another curse and a longer moan. El smiled grimly. At least she'd given one of them something to remember. Judging from the shadows passing beneath her, she must have been unconscious for quite a while. She bit her lip in frustration. She had to find a way out of this predicament or Ammon would never let her leave the palace again. He meant well, but he was simply too overprotective. She was perfectly capable of taking care of herself, and escaping from this would only prove it. She strained to lift her aching head, but all she could see was boulders and brush. So this was the land Ammon was fighting to reclaim? Men were so strange.

It was well into the night when they arrived at the palace gates. At the door, a guard picked her off the mule and tossed her over his shoulder like a sack of grain. El stared at his back from beneath her hood. If she'd had any feeling in her feet at all, she would have kicked him. At least if she tilted her head, she could see where they were going. Before they went in, two more guards pulled Ross off the mule and dragged him in behind her, ignoring his groans. Once inside, a woman wearing a gaudy crown on her head and dressed in a long crimson gown met them at the end of the hallway.

The lead guard stopped and bowed. "My queen, Lieutenant Pru and Captain Ross have brought back a prisoner from the tunnel in the Wall."

He moved aside as the queen casually stepped forward. "King Tirate is asleep, therefore you will report your findings to me. Was the tunnel opened and did you succeed in killing the vermin dragons and their knights?"

Ross only groaned as the two other guards held him up, but the second man spoke up. "Queen Liah, we opened the tunnel, but were attacked by a thousand men an dragons that wit fire shootin' from their mouths! We lost all the crossbows we sent through in a terrible battle! Ross an me, we barely escaped through the tunnel with our lives! We been travelin' hard all day an night to bring news and so Captain Ross can git treated. This here boy snuck up and stabbed him durin' the fight."

El's stomach lurched as the guard flipped her off his shoulder and held her up in front of him. The queen reached over and yanked back the hood exposing the dark locks of hair that spilled over her shoulders.

The queen's voice was as cold as ice. "You mean to tell me the entire squadron sent into the tunnel armed with twenty dragon killing crossbows was wiped out? And you two imbeciles managed to survive this...massacre... from the fire breathing dragons and one thousand men?"

Obviously shocked to learn El was female, Pru stared and stuttered. "Uh, yeah...I mean...er...yes yer highness!"

The queen casually reached out and grabbed the knife protruding from Ross's shoulder. With a quick jerk, she plucked it out and promptly plunged it into the center of his chest. She calmly stepped back as he slumped to the floor and coolly did the same to Pru. As the man slowly collapsed, she wiped the blade on his shirt and held up the knife to inspect the edge. "Take their bodies out and dump them in the river. I will not tolerate failure of any sort."

She twirled the blade in one hand and grabbed a handful of El's hair with the other. With a cold smile she held the knife against El's throat. "Thank you for the pretty knife." She released her grip and nodded to the guard. "Take her to the cells. I will question her in the morning."

The guard dragged her into a small dark cell and cut the ropes binding her wrists and feet before slamming the door shut. She lay on the floor for a long time until the circulation returned to her limbs and she could finally stand. A trickle of light drifted in through a tiny barred window that allowed just enough illumination to see the four bare stone walls of the cell. The thick iron-strapped wooden door looked new, and after a brief study of her surroundings, she slid to the floor with her back against the wall. There was nothing she could do now but wait.

***

El awoke from a fitful sleep to the rattling of keys in the lock, and she quickly scrambled to her feet. As the door swung open, a guard stepped in followed by Liah, who now wore a dark blue velvet gown. The gold knife was tucked neatly into her belt, and El felt her face heat with anger.

Liah looked down over a perfectly powdered nose and sniffed with disdain. "Tell me girl. What happened on the other side of the tunnel? What is on the other side?"

El sneered at the woman. "You already heard it from your own men, just before you killed them that is."

The woman snarled. "You could very easily be next! Now tell me what is on the other side!"

El crossed her arms defiantly. "I have nothing to tell you."

Liah's eye suddenly gleamed and she smiled. "Oh good! For a moment I was afraid you would be boring! I always enjoy a challenge, but still, I wonder how much sport you will be?" She snapped her fingers, and two more guards rushed into the tiny room and pinned El tightly against the wall. Once she could no longer move, Liah grasped El's left hand and held it up so the glittering ring on her finger caught the dim light.

"I wonder how your husband will feel once he finds out where you are? I'll come back to visit again soon, then maybe you'll tell me all about who you are and what you know about the other side of that tunnel."

One of the guards pried open El's fist and roughly removed the ring from her finger before leaving her crumpled in a heap on the floor. The cell door slammed shut with a thunderous crash, and their footsteps slowly echoed away. As she rubbed the bruised skin where her ring had been, she felt the tears welling up. Try as she might, they wouldn't stop.

***

Ammon paced the hallway while Boris interrogated the prisoners. So far the news had been grim. Although twenty crossbows had been destroyed or captured, the guards said if their attack failed, the next squadron to enter the tunnel would use men, women, and children from Gaul as shields. There would be no way for the dragons to get past without killing scores of innocent people, and even then they still had to face more of the great crossbows. Inside the narrow confines of the tunnel there was no way to avoid the deadly bolts, and even if they managed to break through, they'd be shot down the moment they came out into the open.

Ammon could hear the bitter twang of crossbows and the trill of bolts loosed against their targets as Stalwart's men tested the range of the captured machines in the courtyard below. All around him was a frenzy of activity as every knight and able bodied man in the palace prepared for battle. Steel blades were sharpened while fletchers worked tirelessly to fill every quiver available.

Below them in the Hold, dragons snorted black smoke as they echoed the agitation from their links. Even Fulgid was restless and snubbed at the food Kyle waved beneath his nose. Everyone was ready to charge through the tunnel and into battle the moment the word was spoken. Almost everyone. As desperate as he was to get El back, he could not lead these men to slaughter in that passageway. Another way had to be found.

Boris emerged from the prisoner's room and with a silent nod, Ammon followed him up the stairs to the royal chambers. Stalwart, Erik, and Theo were already waiting as he and Boris entered the sitting room. As they took their seats, Ammon crossed the room to stare out the window at the whitecapped mountains. There had to be another way to get to Gaul.

With a sudden jerk, he spun on his heel. "Do we have any maps? Maps of those mountains?"

Stalwart nodded slowly. "Aye sire, we do, but if you're thinking of flying over them, I'm afraid it won't work. In all the histories of DoTaria, there is no mention of anyone crossing over." He shrugged. "The slopes are too steep to climb and the dragons can't tolerate the cold at those altitudes for very long or they get sluggish. If they're exposed too long, they fall into a deep sleep and eventually die."

Ammon shook his head. "I still want to see the maps myself."

Stalwart got up, and from one of the many shelves in the sitting room, selected a large book. He brought it back and spread it open on the table. Erik lowered his voice and gently offered to read it, but Ammon waved him off.

"I'm able to read a little now, but maps are more like pictures than words."

Centered on the old map was Laton. Like a spider's web, roads lead away in every direction towards long forgotten cities and regions. The river Olog emerged far to the east of the city from beneath the jagged drawings of a mountain range that extended completely across one side of the map. To the west was a mountain with a small anvil drawn on the side and smoke coming from the top. "This is where the Honor Blades are made?"

Stalwart nodded. "Aye, there are three smoking mountains in DoTaria and that is the closest."

Ammon looked for the others. The rest formed a line, each one closer to the mountains than the last. Ammon drew a line with his finger from the first to the last. "What if the dragons warmed themselves at each one before trying to fly over the mountains?"

Stalwart turned the map and looked at it. "That would get you a bit further, but it's hard to say what is beyond the mountains shown on this map. You might make it to the other side, or you might end up frozen on the side of a mountain for all eternity too. There is no way to know until you get there, and by then it's too late to turn back."

Boris rubbed briskly at his moustache. "I'd be willing to try it myself, but Ellis wouldn't be able to do it. He's already having a hard time with the cold at his age. I'd wager most of the older, more experienced dragons would have the same problem. Younger dragons are slightly less affected by the cold."

Ammon looked at the men around the table. "We have to get over those mountains. They won't be expecting an attack from behind. Once the tunnel is open the rest can come through and it's on to Gaul…and El."

Boris sniffed. "I suspect I already know a few who'd volunteer, I just have to put the question to them."

Stalwart shook his head disapprovingly. "This is an insane plan, and the chances that it will fail are too high!" He dropped a heavy fist down onto the table with a thud. "Phaw! But no more than a straight on attack through the tunnel I suppose. I know many of my knights will gladly volunteer. They've become quite fond of queen El and are itching to get her back. Besides, this scoundrel Tirate deserves to taste the fury of DoTarian dragons!"

Ammon looked at Fulgid sitting quietly beside him and took a deep breath. "Then let's get started. I'm going with them." He held up his hand before they could object.

"That was not a request, it was a statement. It is my right as king."

Boris and Stalwart glared at him in surprise and Ammon stared back coolly. He was going no matter what they said. El was on the other side, and he was going to get her back or die trying. His knuckles cracked as he clenched them in fists. If so much as a hair on her head was harmed…No, It was better not to try to think of that now, he needed to keep a clear head. He forced his hands to relax and turned to Erik.

"I'll leave the day to day operations of the palace to you until I return. Boris and Stalwart will maintain the cities defenses in case Tirate's men try to advance through the tunnel, or if the Kala-Azar return, which isn't likely in this cold. I want men and dragons ready to move through the tunnel at a moment's notice. Once we're on the other side, I don't know how long we can hold them until reinforcements arrive. I'll send someone through the tunnel to notify you. How long before you can have those volunteers? I want to leave within the hour."

Ammon braced himself for an argument as Erik stood up, but he only bowed with his fist to his chest. "It will be as you say, King Ammon." After a pause, Erik smiled. "I do believe you wear the crown well. I would prefer you sent others over the mountains, but under these circumstances, I fully understand your desire to accompany them. I only ask that you take as little chance with your life as possible. I believe you have the potential to be one of the greatest kings that ever lived, but you have to live long enough to do so."

Boris cleared his throat, obviously unhappy with Ammon's intentions. "Theo can have riders ready within the hour, although I…oh we'll just have them ready." He nodded to Theo, and the thin man hurried out to assemble the Gaul knights.

Stalwart grinned at Boris for a moment, then turned to Ammon. "I'll have my men ready as well. Please excuse me."

Boris cleared his throat and leaned towards Erik. "Would you mind if I have a private word with the king for a moment?" Erik just smiled and nodded, then patted Boris on the shoulder as he left.

When they were alone, Ammon turned back to look out the window and felt Boris' intent stare on his back. "You don't approve of me going."

Boris sighed and Ammon could hear the chair creak as he leaned back. "No, Ammon, I don't. You don't know if this will work. You could very well just lead yourself and the others to an icy grave, and that won't help get El back. If you die up there we won't know until you don't come back, and then what? Besides, twice now in the midst of a battle your eyes have changed color and no one has yet been able to tell me why, although Stalwart has a theory. He tells me there is a condition called Rage when the eyes of a linked knight will change, but it's always been a permanent condition and always leads to madness. The last thing we need is for you to go mad."

Ammon stared at the snow-capped mountains in the distance. "I have not gone mad, and whatever happened to my eyes had resolved before we got back to the palace. Besides, we both know that El is the best person to treat something like that, and she's in Gaul. Now, let me ask you something, Boris? If the king did nothing but sit on a throne directing others to do his bidding, would you, or any knight, truly serve with all your heart or just because it is your duty? I refuse to send anyone to do something I wouldn't do myself. Isn't that what leadership is? Besides, El has been gone for two days, and we haven't come up with anything better than charging through the tunnel to certain death. I don't want this fight, but I can't turn away." He turned to face his friend. "Tirate wants this war and will stop at nothing until we give it to him, including enslaving every last person in Gaul."

Boris looked down at his outspread hands. "Aye, many prefer to follow a king who leads rather than pushes, but leadership also requires sending others into dangerous situations for the good of the whole. You are my king and I

338

will follow you. That doesn't mean I have to like this plan of yours. As far as Tirate, well, I doubt slavery is the worst he's done in Gaul. For now, let's just hope he doesn't have El yet."

***

Ammon strode purposely down the hall with Fulgid by his side and mumbled quietly to himself. El was alive. He knew it with every bone in his body. She was alive, and he was going to bring her back and out of harms way. Once she was safely back, he was going to find a way to make her listen to him. There would be no more of this queen's right nonsense, he would lock her in the palace if he had to.

He pushed the door open that led out to the courtyard and stopped, his mouth agape. The early afternoon sun beamed down from a cloudless sky over a crowded courtyard of knights and dragons. Theo appeared beside him with a broad grin spread across his face. Puzzled, he nodded his head at the gathering. "What's going on? Is this a send-off?"

Theo chuckled. "No, sire. You asked for a few volunteers to accompany you over the mountains, and this…" He gestured with his hand in a broad sweep. "This is less than half of the ones who demanded to be allowed to go!"

He felt himself gasp. There were dozens of them! "Half?"

Theo laughed. "Oh yes, and there would have been a whole lot more, but we put a limit on how many could go. We thought fifty ought be more than enough."

He rubbed his forehead in disbelief. He expected no more than six at the most. How was he going to lead fifty dragons over an unexplored mountain range and expect to sneak up on the encampment surrounding the tunnel exit? "I thought only the younger dragons could go because of the temperatures?"

Theo nodded. "These are the younger ones. I wish we could send some of the more experienced riders, but the temperature affects dragons more once they reach about the age of twenty, so that was one of our requirements. Believe me, there was quite a lot of argument over who should go. It seems no one wants to be left out of giving Tirate's army a taste of dragon's fire." Theo put a hand on Ammon's shoulder. "Besides, we all want El back as badly as you do."

A slender knight in dragon armor approached them, and it wasn't until the feminine voice spoke before Ammon realized it was Tashira. Nodding respectfully to them both she turned to Ammon. "Argent will bring you and your dragon for the first part of our journey, sire."

Confused, Ammon looked around. "Argent?"

Tashira nodded. "Argent is my dragon."

Ammon's eyebrows rose in surprise. "You mean she's coming?"

Theo's grin slowly melted. "Ah, well...yes, of course! Tashira is the most experienced knight in the group."

Ammon raised his hands. "What will happen once we reach the other side and engage in battle?"

Theo cleared his throat. "When you go into battle, you be very, very glad that she is on your side."

Tashira's voice strained through clenched teeth. "We should reach the last of the fire-mountains and make camp by sundown. We'll make our first attempt at a flyover in the morning."

Ammon sighed and nodded. It was obvious Theo trusted her and Boris must have trained her. Hopefully once the battle started she could hold her own. He felt a tug on his sleeve, and he looked down at Lily's tear-streaked face.

"Are you gonna bring Queen El home?"

He brushed a few wisps of stray hair from her face and knelt down beside her. "Yes, Lily, Fulgid and I are going with all these dragons to bring El home and stop those men who put you in the tunnel."

Lily looked at Fulgid who sat patiently waiting beside him. Her little hand reached out to pet him on the head. "Are you gonna come back soon?"

Ammon smiled. "I'll be back, but it might be a little while. Will you be alright until then?"

Lily sniffed but didn't answer. He rubbed his jaw thoughtfully for a moment. "Lily? Could you do something for me? It's pretty important…"

Lily's eyes grew large and she nodded.

"Good! I need someone to watch over a friend of mine. He works all by himself up in the Nests and sometimes he forgets to eat. His name is Derek, and he's very nice, but some people are afraid of him because he's so big. Queen El and I often visit with him while he watches over the dragon eggs, but while we're gone, he'll be all alone. Do you think you could keep him from getting lonely? Maybe you could bring him some fruit from the kitchen? I think he would really like that!"

A grin slowly spread across the little girl's face, and she threw her arms around his neck and squeezed tightly.

"Lily, I have to go now, so you take care of Derek for me ok?" She nodded again.

Theo laid a hand over his shoulder. "It's time to go."

He rose to his feet and followed Tashira to her dragon, a sleek gray that eyed Fulgid curiously. She patted her dragon's side affectionately. "You'll be able to socialize with him later, Argent, right now we have work to do."

She walked slowly around the dragon checking each buckle and strap carefully. When she'd made a full circle she stopped and turned to face him with her arms crossed. "That was a lovely thing you did back there."

Ammon felt his eyebrows raise. "Huh?"

She looked down and kicked at a stone with her toe. "Telling Lily to watch over Derek. That was very sweet."

Ammon smiled. "Well, I thought maybe something good might come of it. Who knows?"

She laughed quietly. "Lets get mounted!"

He climbed into the saddle behind Tashira, and Fulgid hopped up to perch between them, twitching his ears at the other dragons in the courtyard. From where Ammon was sitting he could see the whole group. Shane was methodically checking every saddlebag, making sure each had the correct supplies.

The large cook Maise followed behind him, passing out small sacks filled with meat pies and cheese. She handed two bags to Ammon and huffed. "You've finally put on a little weight, but you're still too thin!" Her eyes narrowed at Fulgid for a moment, then she smiled and handed Ammon two more bags. "He looks thin too!" She hurried off to catch up with Shane.

Tashira leaned back, tapped her nose and gestured towards them. "There's one man with a ring in his nose who's too blind to see it."

Ammon watched the pair in confusion. A ring in his nose? What was that supposed to mean? He shrugged and decided not to pursue it. He had far to many other things to worry about right now.

The courtyard was cleared of everyone but the dragons, and the riders turned their attention to Ammon. Tashira leaned back as if to check the tightness of the saddle girth and whispered. "They're waiting for your signal to take flight!"

Of course! He was the one leading the dragons this time so it only made sense! Mimicking the way he had seen it done before, he raised his fist over his head and pulled it down sharply. The force of Argent's leap shoved Ammon deep into the saddle as the great wings pumped the air. Steadily they began gaining in altitude and the rush of the wind blew back his hair. Below him he could see the dragons taking off in pairs, and soon the entire squad was airborne, forming a giant spiral as they circled upward.

Fulgid gripped the edge of the saddle with his claws and beat his own small wings, as if to push Argent faster. Once high enough to clear the top of the palace, they headed towards the horizon in single file.

Fulgid settled down with his wings tucked back against his body and Ammon absently scratched him behind his ears. Below them the ground slipped past at a breathtaking speed and they flew steadily towards the snowcapped mountains in the distance. He knew she was alive, he could feel it. "I'm coming El! Hold on, I'm coming!"

***

The sun had just dipped below the horizon when they finally arrived to circle over the last of the three smoldering mountains. Even in the fading light, the glimmering peaks seemed impossibly high and forbidding. He forced away his own self doubts as he stared up at the bleak, ice-covered ridges. This was the best chance he had to save El's life. He had to make it work. He drew a deep breath and wrinkled his nose at the strong sulfur fumes. Tonight they would camp on the top of the smoking mountain where the dragons could warm themselves. If the weather held, tomorrow they'd make their first attempt to cross over.

As the camp settled, Ammon watched as the knights removed large, flat stones tied together with leather straps from their saddlebags and stack them around the steaming vents. When strapped to the sides of the dragons, the heated stones would help them to ward off the cold and could easily be cut free once their warmth was gone. No one had ever tested them before, so there was no way to know how well it would work.

The meal was served in silence with only the occasional deep rumble of the earth beneath them. Only Fulgid seemed immune to their somber mood as he bounded from knight to knight, staring at them with unblinking amber eyes until they surrendered a portion of their food. When he was satisfied that not a single morsel was left, he climbed into Ammon's bedroll and fell quickly asleep, filling the small tent with snores. For Ammon, it was a long time before sleep came.

When morning came, he lifted the tent flap to find Tashira waiting outside with a cup of strong, black liquid. He ignored the bitter taste and gulped it down to force his body awake. They broke camp quickly, and once the heated stones were strapped into place, Ammon took his place behind Tashira. Argent's deep wing strokes swirled the rising smoke from the vents into the bitter morning air. Already the temperatures were noticeably different, and as they flew towards the mountains, puffs of steam blew from the dragon's noses. A frigid gust of wind sent shivers through him as they steadily gained altitude.

The pale sun did little to warm them, and he pulled his cloak closer to block the cold. The ground beneath them gradually changed from sparse trees to barren rock and then to featureless snow and ice as they headed towards a notch between the two nearest mountains.

Bit by bit Ammon felt Argent's speed lessen as they struggled against the thinning air and icy temperatures. They skimmed just a span or two above the ground as they labored up the steep slope. He looked back and watched the line of dragons that followed, their wings beating sluggishly. Ahead of them the mountain continued upward, but in the featureless snow, it was impossible to judge the distance to the top. As they crested each rise hoping to have reached the summit, their eyes met only an endless sea of white rising ever higher and higher.

He could hear Tashira coaxing through chattering teeth "Come on, Argent, just a bit further now!"

With each passing minute their speed slowed drastically, and he could hear the others behind them shouting encouragement to their mounts as they struggled to keep up. In the reflected glare of the cold sun, he saw the top of the next rise far up the slope and knew they'd never make it. He tapped Tashira on the shoulder, but she shook her head as if she'd already read his mind.

"We've already past the point of no return. They're too cold to make it back, and if we stop, they'll never get moving again. We have no choice but to keep going and hope we make it."

He turned to see one of the dragons following behind drop slightly and its belly struck the surface, sending up a burst of snow. It struggled mightily and barely managed to keep flying. It wasn't going to work. In despair, he realized Boris was right, he had led them to die on a mountainside with El held captive on the other side. It was a gamble he had chosen, and El, the knights, and their dragons would pay for his mistake.

Fulgid suddenly stood up on his hind legs and pointed his muzzle into the air. With a sudden blast, he loosed a tremendous fireball over their heads and Ammon had to duck to keep from being singed. "Fulgid! By the dragons teeth what are you doing?"

Fulgid ignored him and let out another, even larger fireball.

Bewildered, Ammon looked back to see the dragon behind them suddenly emerge through the flames that still hung in the air. He gasped as he realized what was happening. Heat! "Tashira, do you see what he's doing?"

With a large grin she nodded and leaned forward to speak to her dragon. "Go ahead and let one loose Argent!"

Although brief, the heat washed over them as they passed through the flames, and with each blast, the warmth began to slowly soak into his bones. The dragon's wings began to beat faster, and the peak drew steadily closer until he could see the crest clearly as they approached.

With an exhilarating rush, they passed over the top and glided down the other side with increasing speed. Beyond them lay another, smaller mountain, and they easily flew over with bursts of fire blossoming around them. Beyond each peak lay another, lower mountain and finally the snow gave way to rock. Finally the ground below them dropped away as they passed over the Wall and from their great height, he could see the twisting Olog River in the distance, and he choked back a gasp. They made it! He threw his arms around Fulgid and squeezed him in a bear hug while the riders behind him cheered. They crossed over without losing a single rider!

They quickly descend into a small clearing and stripped off their cold weather garb while the dragons rested. Tashira gathered the group together and carefully recounted her plan of attack once more. There was no room for error, and it wouldn't take long before Tirate's men realized they were just a diversion. Ammon stood quietly and listened as Tashira assigned tasks to each knight. Despite his earlier misgivings, Theo was right. She was quite knowledgeable in the tactics of war, much more so than he.

It was mid-morning when they took to the sky with the sun on their backs and codas notched in their bows. Ammon rode with Tashira at the head of a fist of five dragons. They would be the first to draw blood as they swooped down hard and fast to cleave through the outer ring of crossbows before heading towards the heavily guarded tunnel. The rest of the group would be causing as much havoc as possible, destroying crossbows and disarming anyone carrying a weapon.

When they reached the edge of the encampment, Ammon grimaced. It was larger than he had thought, but fortunately, the semi-circles of crossbows had been drawn in closer to the tunnel. On Tashira's signal, the dragons dropped from the sky and Ammon felt his stomach sour as bile rose in his throat. Beside him, Fulgid's claws gripped the saddle harness tightly. His golden ears were pinned tight against his head, and above his curled and snarling lips, his eyes glowed white. The wind pressed hard against their chests, and ahead of them, the ground rushed towards them in a blur.

As they leveled out, Ammon drew his bow and loosed the first coda. It struck its target and fire spread across the thick wooden planks of the crossbow. In confusion, the guards lounging beside it leapt to their feet with a shout. One of them reached for a pail of water as the other broke into a run towards the camp. Ammon fumbled to notch his bow, but before he could take aim, the man fell to the ground with Tashira's arrow planted firmly in his back. His companion barely had time to drop the bucket before he met the same fate with only the fletching of her arrow protruding from his chest.

He felt sick to his stomach as Argent swept past the dying man. Around him he could hear the screams of men and the shouts of alarm. As the outer ring of crossbows fell to the dragon's fire, men scrambled in panic towards the center of camp. The few brave enough to stand their ground turned their crossbows and shot blindly into the sun, sending volleys of deadly bolts high into the air. As they swooped towards another crossbow, Argent suddenly flipped upside down. Ammon could hear arrows whizzing past as he hung helplessly from the lap belt of the saddle. In a single, fluid movement, Tashira drew her long sword, and as the ground rushed past their heads she held it in front of her with both hands. With one, neat stroke, the blade sliced through the string of a crossbow as they passed overhead. The sudden violent release of the drawn bow knocked one man over, while another crumpled in a heap beside the now useless device.

Just as they turned upright, a hail of arrows bounced off Argent's sides and Ammon's armor. The dragon's wings beat furiously as they gained altitude and moved out of range. Ammon looked down at the leather strap that held him into the saddle. An arrow had sliced into it deeply, nearly severing it in two. Argent wheeled in the air as he began his next dive.

He leaned forward and screamed into the wind to Tashira. "My belt is breaking!"

She twisted around in alarm just as the belt snapped and he was violently ripped from the saddle. Desperately he clawed for something to hold onto and managed to grab one end of the broken belt and held on. He felt Argent try to slow his descent as he dangled from the strap beneath him. With each backstroke of the dragon's wings, the belt slid further through the loops, and Ammon looked down at the treetops rushing towards him. Argent spread his wings once more and the belt suddenly came free. For a moment he felt weightless and he screamed as he plummeted to the earth. "Nooooo!"

Suddenly something dug into the shoulders of his armor and he felt his speed slow. He glanced up to see Fulgid desperately beating his small wings. Although the little dragon was not able to fly yet, it slowed his descent, and they landed in a tumbling heap. Ammon gasped for breath and lay still for a moment before he opened his eyes to see Fulgid standing on his chest looking down at him in concern. He sat up and tested each arm and leg in disbelief. Once again the dragon had saved his life. "Thank you, my friend!"

He jumped to his feet as Tashira circled overhead and signaled to her. With a wave of relief, they flew off to rejoin the battle. He drew his sword and trotted towards the encampment with Fulgid on his heels. At the top of a small hill, he suddenly found himself facing half a dozen men desperately trying to repair one of the crossbows.

With a curse, one of the guards hefted one of the crossbow bolts like a spear and cautiously approached Fulgid while another drew his sword and charged Ammon. Ammon lifted his golden blade and stepped aside just as the bigger man threw his weight into his sword strike. As the larger man stumbled past, Ammon slashed down, leaving a wide gash across the guard's back. Infuriated, the guard spun, swinging his sword wildly. As the man closed in, Ammon raised his blade, and they met with a loud clash. With each sword locked at the hilt, Ammon quickly twisted his around, and the tip gouged deeply into the man's arm. He jumped back yelling a string of profanities, then lunged forward only to find himself staring in shock at the golden hilt buried deep in his chest.

Ammon pulled his sword free and turned to see Fulgid had already made short work of the others. On the ground a man lay howling as he held a mangled and bleeding hand tightly to his chest. Beside him two others lay face down in the dirt while the rest ran frantically towards the center of the camp. With Fulgid loping beside him, Ammon gave chase, stopping only after meeting three more guards desperately trying to reload a smoldering crossbow. What little courage the guards had left failed when Fulgid loosed a ball of fire that completely engulfed their machine and they left their swords in the dirt as they fled with Fulgid in pursuit.

Ammon tossed the swords into the flames and turned just as a thin and shirtless man silently appeared from the bushes. Intricate black lines of a tattoo darkened one side of his tanned face beneath a matted and dirty beard. In his hand he wielded a heavy knife with a curved blade and he snarled words buried so thick in a guttural accent that they were unintelligible.

The barefooted man cautiously approached until Fulgid suddenly returned. With a snort, tendrils of smoke billowed from the little dragon's nostrils, and the color drained from the tattooed face. In one quick step he disappeared silently into the bushes just as quickly as he appeared. Ammon probed the bushes with his sword but the man was gone. He shrugged his shoulders and jogged down the path towards the camp. He had no time to wonder about such things right now. There was a battle to be fought.

As the morning wore on, Ammon muscles ached with fatigue. Although Fulgid did most of the fighting, he often found himself crossing swords. Most surrendered after Ammon's golden blade sliced through the soft metal of their homemade weapons, but a few mistook his small size and youth as an easy kill. It didn't take long before they learned how well he had been trained. They battled their way across the field, and Fulgid incinerated any crossbow they found. Once they reached the center of camp, it was easy to distinguish the guards from those who had been forced into labor by the filthy rags they wore. As they were freed, the laborers took up the abandoned swords and followed him into the fight.

As the number following him grew into a small army, they began to cover ground more quickly. Tirate's men saw the approaching mass and retreated towards the Wall. Few were foolish enough to raise their swords against the ones they'd held captive, and those who did met a quick and decisive end.

Most of the crossbows were already abandoned or destroyed from the relentless attack of dragons. Ammon's ragtag army pulled down and set fire to the rest before they chased down and captured the remaining guards, and by noon there were only sporadic fights that ended quickly. As Ammon approached the tunnel entrance, a dozen dragons keeping watch over a group of prisoners greeted him. The surviving guards sat dejectedly on the ground by the river with hands and feet bound tightly. He watched as a fist of dragons moved into the tunnel to remove the remaining crossbows. The large mechanisms were too big to turn inside the tunnel, so dispatching them from behind would be a simple task.

He wiped his sword clean and looked at the tree line in the distance. It would be foolish to assume no one had evaded capture. Word would reach the men hidden in the woods, and they would attempt to prepare themselves for battle, but it wouldn't help them much. He slid the sword back into its scabbard and gazed at the devastation. With over a thousand fire-breathing dragons circling over their heads most would either run or surrender. At least they would if they were smart.

Then it was onward to Gaul and Tirate.

***

Ammon heard Boris' booming voice long before he emerged from the tunnel leading a long line of dragons. He grinned broadly at the sight of Ammon and Tashira waiting nearby. "I'm relieved to see you made it over the mountains! You certainly made good time too. We weren't expecting to hear from you for at least another day!"

Tashira nodded. "If Ammon hadn't had the idea to use dragon fire for warmth, we never would have got over the peaks. The camp is secured but there is no sign of El."

Ammon felt his stomach knot. If she wasn't here, then she must be in Gaul. "It wasn't my idea it was Fulgid's."

Boris eyed the little dragon as he circled the captured guards and growled menacingly. "Figured that all by himself, eh? It seems he's more intelligent than most dragons are at his age."

The three stood in silence for a moment until Ammon's patience broke. "What do we do next?"

Boris patted Ammon on the back. "I wish I could say things will be easier from here on, but that'd be a lie. The real battle has not yet begun. Tirate has had plenty of time to build up his defenses around the city, and I'm sure the woods are peppered with his men."

Ammon gestured at the growing number of dragons around them. "They can fly above the range of the crossbows in the city and hit them with coda. In the confusion Fulgid and I will go in and find El."

Boris shook his head. "We can't get close enough for an accurate shot and if you miss you run the risk of burning down the city. I'm sure there are bows hidden in the woods around Gaul too, so we'll have to take the ground around the city first. Ammon, you shouldn't put yourself in danger when we don't even know if El was taken there yet."

Ammon stared at Boris, and the older man's steely blue eyes calmly returned his gaze. He knew Boris was right, but he had to do something. He gripped the hilt of his sword in frustration and walked towards the group prisoners. "Which one of you is in charge?"

Every eye peered at him with silent disregard.

"Tell me! Who here is in charge?"

One of the men in the front spat on Ammon's foot and a chorus of chuckles followed. In an instant, Ammon's sword was in his hand and the razor sharp tip pricked the soft skin of the man's throat. A few men in the front row exchanged nervous looks as their fellow guard gagged, his face suddenly pale.

Ammon forced himself to speak calmly and clearly. "I'm going to cut out your tongue and feed it to my dragon. After that, I will do the same to each and every one of you until I get an answer. Now I'm going to ask one more time, which one of you is in charge?" He punctuated his question with a slight twitch of the blade and a tiny droplet of blood appeared on the man's neck.

One by one their eyes turned to a large scraggly bearded man with dark stains covering his shirt and a purple bruise forming over his eye. The man snarled at the others and murmured a curse under his breath.

Ammon gestured to a few of the knights standing uneasily nearby. "Bring him to me."

With his hands still bound tightly behind him, two knights dragged him to the front. Ammon felt his eyes begin to burn as he grabbed the man by his beard and forced him to look up. "Where is she?"

The big man twisted and tried to pull away as he snorted. "I dunno what you're talking about."

Ammon twisted the filthy beard tightly around his fingers and pulled up, nearly lifting the man off the ground. The months of hard training had strengthened his arms and his muscles bulged against his armor.

"The woman you captured on the other side of the tunnel! Where...is...she?"

The man's face twisted in pain, but still he sneered. "I know the knight's code of ethics, and this ain't very knight-like behavior! You can't do anything to me! Now what would your captain Boris say if he were alive to see this?"

Boris' voice spoke from behind Ammon. "Ammon? This is not..."

Ammon turned his head only slightly, but never took his eyes off the man in front of him. "He's going to tell me where El is, or I'm going to kill him."

The big man's eyes flickered in surprise at Boris and then he smiled.

With fist to chest, Boris lowered his head. "As you wish, sire." Without another word, Boris walked away.

The bearded guard watched him leave, obviously confused.

Ammon pulled his face closer. "King Eric has passed the crown to me! I make the rules now, and I will kill you if you don't answer me, is that clear?"

A flicker of fear flashed in the man's eyes. "Alright! I'll tell you what ever you wanna know! But I know nothin 'bout any woman! Two days ago Ross came back through the tunnel with a young boy and a knife in his shoulder. He and Pru took him to Gaul for questioning. That's all I know! I swear! Nobody else has been out of that accursed tunnel!"

Ammon released the man and shook the hairs from his fist as he walked back to the tunnel entrance. Boris was leaning against the inside wall quietly talking to Theo and Tashira. They became silent as Ammon got closer.

Boris never took his eyes from the ground as he asked quietly. "Did you kill him?"

Ammon could feel the tension resting on that question. "No, he's back with the others."

Boris raised his head and looked out at the river flowing past the entrance. "Would you have?"

Ammon picked up a stone and threw it into the water rushing past. Would he kill someone to get El back? Hadn't he already done that in the battle? It was different though, in battle they fought back, whereas this man had been tied. "I don't know Boris, I really don't know. I just...I need to get her back."

Boris laid a firm hand on Ammon's shoulder. "Ammon, I know you will do what you need to do. El has to be found and brought back. But you have to remember you are a king and a knight, therefore you must hold yourself to a higher standard than anyone else. If you use whatever means necessary to accomplish your goals, then you aren't much different than Tirate and his men."

Ammon defiantly looked Boris in protest, then sighed and hung his head. "I just need to get El back, that's all. I just have to get her back."

Theo and Tashira each placed a hand on Ammon's back and Boris squeezed his shoulder. "We will soon. You gave Tashira an idea of how we can make our next move, and I've already sent for the reinforcements!"

As the three of them began to smile, Ammon hoped whatever they had planned was going to work.

Chapter 17
Return To Gaul

Liah could hear Tirate shouting as she neared his chambers, and she paused in the doorway to listen with a faint smile. For some reason she derived great pleasure in hearing the man scream in frustration, although she had no explanation as to why. She pressed her ear to the door and delicately wrinkled her nose. Apparently the battle near the tunnel had begun, but no information had come forth yet about how badly Erik's forces were beaten. She curled her lip and twirled the gold knife expertly between her fingers. Perhaps it was time to visit the girl in the cell again, if only to see her reaction when told all the dragons were dying in a hail of crossbow fire. Her husband was surely captured by now, or soon would be.

She knew from her own network of spies that anything that emerged from the tunnel would be shot within twenty paces. No dragon or army would ever come out of there alive. She strolled down the hallway towards the prison cells and contemplated what the girl's reaction would be. That was the true enjoyment of the game she played with her victims. The slow, painful elimination of hope would break even the strongest will.

As she rounded the corner, she bumped into a tall figure walking the other way. "You clumsy fool! Watch where you...oh! It's you, Devan!"

The tall, well-dressed man flashed a brilliant smile and bowed elegantly. "Please pardon my oafishness, my queen! Although I cannot truly apologize for an act that brought me so close to your fair beauty!"

Momentarily forgetting her objective, Liah felt her cheeks redden under the gaze of Devans cool green eyes. This wasn't the first time the captain of Tirate's guards had made her blush. "I grant you your pardon, captain, but I expect better behavior from you in the future."

Devan pushed back a stray lock of his dark hair and casually rested his hand on the pommel of his bejeweled sword. "Nothing would bring me greater pleasure than to learn such changes in my behavior beneath your capable guidance my queen, but alas, my duty first requires me to meet with your husband to discuss some matters of importance."

Disappointed, Liah stepped forward and rested her hand on the captain's muscular arm. "Well, if you must!"

"Yes, I must. Perhaps another time? Until then my queen." Flourishing another bow, Devan strode down the hall.

Liah watched until he was out of sight. With a great sigh, her thoughts turned back to the girl in the cell. As handsome as Devan was, he couldn't provide the hours of entertainment she derived from her prey. This one had proved to be surprisingly tough, showing only a hint of weakness after her ring was removed and placed on Liah's finger. Later, the girl had actually smirked, claiming Tirate's defenses would fall quickly beneath an onslaught of thousands of dragons.

At the entrance to the cells, she nodded to the guard and waited while he brought a lantern and unlocked the door. The girl stood defiantly in the corner, making no attempt to hide the bruises covering her arms and face.

"I thought you'd like a little good news. It seems your friends have decided to come through the tunnel, and King Tirate's men are killing them as fast as possible. By this time tomorrow, they'll all be dead. All except for one, I've left strict orders with my men to spare your husbands life. I want him alive. I want to repay him for what his dragon and friends did to me." She held the dragon ring up to the light and smiled. "However, his dragon will be chopped up and fed to the palace dogs."

She waited but the girl stood still as if nothing was even said. Disappointed in the lack of reaction, Liah stepped forward and slapped her across the face. El barely winced and kept her chin up and eyes focused.

With a sniff, Liah turned on her heel and walked out. "I'll be sure to tell you when he arrives."

The cell door slammed behind her with a ringing echo as she stomped down the hallway. The girl was infuriating! Locked in a dark cell for days and the girl showed no sign she was about to break! One way or another she would find the weak spot, and when she did, she would savor that moment for a long, long time.

***

El waited until the footsteps had faded down the hall before she sank to the floor and put her head on her knees. She knew Ammon wouldn't blindly lead the dragons through the tunnel to their deaths, so Liah had to be lying. Even if the dragons could get past the tunnel, Liah had gleefully explained how hopeless an attack against the heavily fortified city would be. She cursed. All the knowledge she'd learned from Liah of the palace defenses was worthless unless she could get it to Ammon, and he was on the other side of the mountains. She shook her head and rubbed her eyes before any tears could form. As much as she wanted to be rescued, it was foolish to think it would happen. At least Ammon and the rest were safe in Laton and out of Tirate's reach.

She closed her eyes and thought about the days she shared with Ammon roaming the city with his golden dragon. It seemed like such a long time ago.

***

The sun was just dipping below the horizon when Boris came to Ammon. "We're ready to begin."

Ammon nodded gravely as he stood on the riverbank with Fulgid. He looked down the long line of hatchling dragons evenly spaced along the tree line. He raised his arm and dropped it sharply, then watched as the little dragons and their knights slipped into the woods as silently as shadows.

Fulgid looked back at him impatiently before charging ahead and quickly disappearing into the brush. As darkness settled, the night was punctuated with sudden shouts of alarm and the pungent smell of the burning crossbows. With only the light of the stars, Ammon picked his way down the paths cut by Tirate's men and helped to gather the prisoners. By morning, a large swath of the woods were hunted clean, and after a small meal, he and Fulgid napped under a tree while another group of hatchlings forged ahead.

The next night was the same. A piercing shout or scream in the darkness and the crash of terrified guards running blindly into the woods as they were herded straight to where Ammon and the knights waited. Before the sun rose over the city of Gaul on the third day, Ammon stood peering through the trees at its tall buildings and high walls. With each breath he could feel El's presence getting nearer, and Fulgid paced around him, eager to begin.

A short distance away and out of sight of the city, a landing field had been cleared, and all the dragons of Gaul and DoTaria gathered together for the assault. When the morning light touched the rooftops, the dragons took flight and began to circle high above the city, out of the range of the crossbows. Ammon watched as a single dragon left the swirling beasts overhead and swooped down to drop a parcel onto the palace grounds.

Hoping everyone's attention was focused on the growing mass of dragons flying overhead, Ammon looked down at Fulgid and nodded. In an instant, the little dragon was streaking towards the city and the golden bubble in Ammon's head rang.

"TRUST FULGID, FREE ELIVA!"

Ammon watched him race away. "Be careful, Fulgid!"

***

Tirate grumbled irritably as he stumbled from his bed to answer the pounding on his bedchamber door. He stifled a yawn and growled. "This had better be important!" He threw open the door and stood back as a wide-eyed guard stumbled in. "What is it? Are they finished killing the dragons already?"

The guard shook his head wildly and held out a crumpled note. Tirate held it up to his bleary eyes and read it aloud. "By order of King Ammon, House of Les-Celest, sovereign ruler of DoTaria and the colony of Gaul, you are hereby ordered to surrender immediately and without conditions. Those who comply peacefully will be given leniency. Resistance will be dealt with severely. An immediate response is expected."

Tirate chuckled before tossing the paper into the fireplace. "You woke me up for that? It is a joke? DoTaria? Never heard of it, and there is no King Ammon, I am the king. Find whoever wrote that and have them flogged. Now, as long as I'm awake, tell the kitchen to have my breakfast sent up, and be quick about it."

He shoved the man out the door before he could protest and slammed it shut. King Ammon? Now that Erik was dead and his army crushed, did the old king's supporters really believe an insane plan like this would work? He pulled a shirt over his shoulders and drew open the curtains of the window overlooking the courtyard. He squinted through the glass at the overcast sky and scowled. Rain would ruin his plans to travel north to view the decimated remains of the dragons. He yawned again as he looked up at the dark cloud swirling above the city. Suddenly a bright orange burst of light blossomed in the sky and he blinked his sleepy eyes into focus.

"What the...?"

He pushed the window open and stared up in disbelief. It wasn't possible! The sky was black with dragons! Hundreds, no, thousands of them! He watched in horror as the maelstrom of flying creatures overhead belched fire and smoke as they circled. He closed his eyes and shook his head violently.

"No, I'm dreaming! I must be dreaming!"

Hesitantly he opened his eyes to see a steady stream of dragons joining the cloud. He quickly backed away from the window and ran for his armor as he shouted to the guards posted outside his door. "Get every man to his post! I want every crossbow manned and ready!"

He fumbled with the buckles of his breastplate as he tried to put it on. Why hadn't the northern guards notified him that Erik had broken through and where did all these dragons come from? His hands froze as the realization sank into his sleep-fogged brain. They didn't tell him because they were probably dead. All the time, planning, and gold he'd invested in putting crossbows in the north woods…was gone!

***

Liah awoke once more to Tirate's shouts across the hall, and she pulled a pillow over her head to drown out the sound. Didn't the man know how to talk in a normal tone? Especially this early in the morning? The pillow did nothing to muffle the sounds of boots stomping past her door as men ran down the hallway. In frustration, she threw her covers back and slipped a silk robe over her shoulders. It was obvious she'd never get back to sleep if she didn't intervene now. She yanked open her door and screamed at the men rushing past, then watched in disbelief as they ignored her! This insolence was intolerable! She'd have every one of them whipped until they screamed for mercy! She reached out and grabbed the nearest guard as he rushed by and her arm was nearly pulled from its socket before he stopped.

"What is the meaning of all this! Tell me!"

The wide-eyed guard pulled loose from her grip and shouted back as he continued down the hall. "We're under attack by dragons! Thousands of 'em flying over us!"

Thousands? Liah rolled her eyes. The idiots Tirate hired could barely count to a dozen, nevermind a thousand. She crossed the room to her window and drew the curtains, then stumbled back as a sickening feeling hit her in the stomach. After all the work she had done to get this far, how could this happen? How could Tirate let this happen? What was he waiting for when he had all those crossbows?

Her eyes narrowed. This was that girl's fault! It was probably her husband leading these beasts even though she was a hostage. The fool! She grabbed the golden knife and stormed down to the cells. Tirate would deal with the dragons soon enough, and since they were going to attack, then the girl's life was forfeited! It was a simple matter to carry out that particular task right now.

At the entrance to the cells she frowned in disgust. In all the excitement, Tirate's men had left the cells unguarded. Obviously Tirate should have let her take control of all prisoners. She picked up a key and a lantern at the guard's station then walked down and unlocked the heavy wooden cell door. When it swung open, she put the lantern on the floor and glowered at the girl. "It appears I have no more use for you anymore."

She expertly twirled the knife in one hand, and with the other, flashed the golden ring on her finger. "Your dragon friends have come after all, and although I am quite sure Tirate can hold them off, if by some chance they manage to succeed, I'm sure your husband would be upset by my…somewhat less than gracious hospitality towards you. It is a shame though, I do so enjoy our little talks."

For the first time, the faintest hint of fear flashed across the girl's face and Liah couldn't help but smile with satisfaction. She took a slow step forward and focused intently on the girl's eyes. Over the years she'd become exceptionally skilled with a knife, and by watching the eyes, she knew exactly how her victim would react. As she moved her prey tensed to fight. So she still had some spunk left in her after all! Too bad there wasn't time to drag this out a bit longer. It would have been quite…entertaining.

In a feigned move, Liah slashed the knife in front of her and forced her victim back. At any moment the girl would charge and she would slip the knife between her ribs and it would be over. No matter how many times she did this, she still felt a thrill go down her spine. Steadily she backed the girl into the corner until there was no place left to go. She watched the eyes closely, any moment now…suddenly El smiled.

Confused, Liah braced herself for a lunge. Nobody ever smiled at her just before they died! Strangely, the girl leaned casually against the wall and crossed her arms just as a faint scraping noise whispered through the open door.

Instinctively Liah spun, ready to stab whoever was behind her, but it wasn't a man or woman that met her eyes. Of all the things she could have seen, nothing horrified her more than the sight of the accursed golden dragon standing in the doorway with its teeth bared and glowing eyes. Before she could even think about defending herself, it streaked across the cell and knocked her to the floor, ripping the knife from her hand. Laying on her back she froze as razor sharp teeth hovered menacingly a hairsbreadth away from her face.

El reached down and picked up the knife then stood over Liah twirling the blade just as she had done earlier. Liah felt her eyes widen. "You wouldn't dare!"

El smiled sweetly and pointed the sharp tip at Liah's throat. "Get up."

The little dragon slowly withdrew, and she cautiously stood up. She brushed the dust off her silk robes and straightened her hair, then stuck her delicate nose up as regally as she could. With her hands on each hip she announced, "By the right of marriage to King Tirate, I am the Queen of Gaul. To kill me is an act of treason!"

The girl leveled the knife at her throat and spoke slowly and deliberately. "Tirate has no right to the throne, by birth or any other claim. The House of Thayer has even submitted to Ammon, House of Les-Celest, ruler and king of DoTaria!" She suddenly reached out and jerked the ring off from Liah's finger. "Which makes me the queen by right of marriage. You however, are the unfortunate wife of a traitor and a scoundrel who will likely be hanging in the square before nightfall."

Liah felt her mouth drop open. "Ammon is a…king?"

El's smile grew even wider. "Yes he is. This tiny little outpost you call Gaul is merely an ancient colony of the greater kingdom of DoTaria!"

The dragon twitched his tail impatiently towards the door and El nodded. "Yes, Fulgid, I think it's time we leave now." She backed up until she was in the hallway and started to close the cell door.

Liah nearly threw herself against the door in desperation before it closed. "Wait! You can't leave me here like this!"

The girl paused and sighed. "You're right, I can't just leave you this way." She tucked the knife into her belt and motioned for her to come forward. Relieved, Liah quickly stepped forward and was about to pass through the doorway, when suddenly a fist struck her in the face hard. She toppled backwards from the force of the blow and landed in a heap on the cell floor. She brought her hands to her face and sobbed as she heard the door slam shut. "No! How could you? You broke my nose! YOU BROKE MY NOSE!"

***

El threw the keys onto the guard's desk as she followed Fulgid out, stopping only briefly to throw her arms around Fulgid and hug him tightly. "Thank you my dear little dragon! Thank you!"

He snorted out a tiny puff of smoke before loping down the hallway and she ran to catch up. He stopped at a large doorway that led through an empty kitchen and down a dark staircase to the street. Above them on the palace walls, she could hear men shouting as they scrambled to their stations. She couldn't help but smile as she looked up at the massive swirling cloud of dragons overhead.

They hugged close to the walls and shadows and finally slipped down an alley that emerged onto a narrow street to the front of an abandoned inn. Above the boarded up windows hung a faded sign depicting a sliver dragon curled around a mug of ale. Fulgid pushed the door open with his nose and went in, and El cautiously followed, closing it behind them. Inside the common room it was dark and dusty and obviously unused but Fulgid marched straight to a room in the back. At the doorway he paused to wait for her, and she grasped the latch and whispered. "I hope you know where we're going!"

The door swung open and light spilled out from numerous lamps within. A small ragged looking group of men and women looked up in surprise as Fulgid sauntered into the room, his golden scales glittering. El paused a moment before clearing her throat. "People of Gaul! The dragons have returned!"

***

Ammon paced impatiently as he eyed the city in the distance. It had been nearly an hour since Boris had delivered the demand for surrender and so far the only response had been the sudden closing of the gates. "How much longer should we wait?"

Boris studied the city walls in the distance, making careful note of the movements of men in the guard towers. The seriousness in his voice was unmistakable. "We've waited long enough." He knelt down and cleared leaves and twigs from a patch of dirt before drawing a rough map of the city with a thick finger.

"When I left here with Eric, there were crossbows mounted atop the city walls above each gate and spaced about four or five paces apart all along the perimeter walls. The palace appears to be similarly armed as well. We should be able to break through the outer city wall fairly quickly and then…"

"Wait…" Ammon's attention was suddenly pulled away as he peered intently through the trees. "She's free!"

Boris frowned. "What are you talking about?"

Ammon smiled as the tiny bubble in the back of his mind nearly burst with pride. "Fulgid has El!"

Boris rose slowly to his feet and carefully wiped the dust from his hands. "Ammon…I know this has been difficult for you…"

Ammon slapped Boris on the shoulder. "Fulgid has her out of the palace and they're hiding somewhere in the city, now it's our turn!"

***

Even inside the dimly lit room, the flickering flames reflected brilliantly off Fulgid's golden scales and drew shocked stares from the men and women. After a long moment of silence, an elderly man stepped forward. His rusted mail armor clinked softly as he adjusted the antique sword at his hip. Faded emerald eyes set deep within a weathered face peered curiously at Fulgid, then at El. His voice was cracked but he spoke with authority.

"The dragons have returned ya say? Aye, that any fool could see that just by lookin, but what good is it to us? Good King Erik has died and left Tirate on the throne to persecute the innocent! Every day one of us disappears never to be seen again, and fewer and fewer are fortunate enough to escape to the countryside. Now with the dragons here to serve him, no place will be safe!"

An elderly woman fiercely grabbed his arm from behind. "Meader! Shush! Yer gonna get yerself tossed in the block!"

The old man patted her hand but straightened his stooped back defiantly. "Aye, I probably will, but I'm tired of livin' this way. A man ought have a right to say things."

El shook her head. "You don't understand! The dragons have returned to overthrow Tirate! Erik is alive and well…but…" She paused for a moment and wondered how to explain Ammon's rise to power. Quickly she decided this was not the time or place. "Erik has allies from a foreign land to help him reclaim the thrown. Tirate's reign has ended!"

Gasps of hope echoed throughout the room and the old woman stepped closer to touch El's sleeve. "Erik is alive? Can this be true?"

El nodded gently. "Yes! I have no doubt that Erik and the DoTarian king have Boris preparing their attack this very moment!"

A murmur rumbled through the room and all of them crowded around her. Meader nearly knocked her over as he jumped forward. "Did you say Boris is with him?"

El regained her balance and nodded again. "Yes, Boris Dejias, Captain Knight of the King's Guard."

Meader's leathery face broke into a broad grin. "In that case my dear, not only are the dragons welcome, but we'll even invite them in!"

***

Mounted atop Ellis, Boris barked out the last of his orders before he turned to Ammon. "I still don't like you being in the midst of this. Your sword training is far from complete and this is no time to find out what you haven't learned yet."

Ammon patted the gold sword at his side. "It's a king's right. As I said before, I won't ask anything from these men that I wouldn't do myself."

Boris shook his head in disapproval. "Then do me a favor? Don't get killed. I don't want to be the one to face the wrath of the queen if that happens!" He winked, then raised his fist in the air and signaled the others to take flight. One by one the rest of the dragons joined the swirling mass above the city.

Ammon watched as the black cloud of dragons seemed to move as one towards the western side of the city, leaving only a few stragglers behind. He counted to ten, then turned to the impatient young knights and hatchlings waiting behind him and waved them to follow. Wordlessly they moved rapidly across the open field towards the east gate while overhead the sky thundered with the roars of dragons. As they got closer he could hear the steady twang and the whistle of bolts cutting through the air. They were within fifty paces of the gate before the distracted guards noticed their approach and swung their crossbows towards them.

"Scatter!"

The word had barely left his lips before the first bolt hit the ground in front of a hatchling, spraying them all with the dirt. The little dragons moved with surprising speed as countless shafts seemed to materialize around them. Still, they were slowly driven back, unable to penetrate any further.

The guards atop the wall gained confidence with each shot and began to taunt them in hoarse shouts. Ammon waited until both of the gate crossbows were fired at the same time, then with a quick wave of his arm he signaled to the small group of dragons still flying over the eastern side of the city. With terrifying speed they descended, their claws ripped the half-loaded machines from their wooden mounts before they landed inside the gates. The panicked guards dived for cover, abandoning the first few crossbows atop the walls on either side of the gate. The rest of the wall defenses desperately tried to swing their heavy mechanisms around before a scorching blast of dragon's fire engulfed them.

As the smoke billowed over the wall, Ammon raised his sword. "To the gate!"

A moment later Theo unlatched the massive doors from within and waved them inside. The hatchlings raced ahead of their knights and disappeared into the streets and alleys. Soon puffs of smoke and flames began to appear as the hatchlings found more of the hidden crossbows.

Theo smiled and placed a hand on Ammon's shoulder. "Now that you're inside I will join the battle at the west gate. Good luck!"

With practiced grace, he swung into Ebony's saddle and nodded to Ammon as the big dragon spread it's wings. With a powerful leap they left the ground leaving swirls of dust to mingle with the smoke.

Just as Ammon was about to join the others, he heard the whistle of a bolt pass overhead and the sickening thud as it struck its target. He turned in horror as he watched Theo's dragon plunge out of sight beyond the city walls.

"No!" He raced past the gate to see the large black form lying in the field motionless.

Obviously dazed, Theo was just climbing out of the saddle and when he saw Ammon approaching he waved him away. "Go back! There is nothing you can do here! Just…keep…going."

As Theo's words trailed off Ammon swallowed hard and turned back towards the city.

***

A long string of curses spilled from Devan's mouth that surprised even the coarse men around him. The last thing he'd expected to see when he rose this morning was a massive swirling cloud dragons over his head! He spat on the floor in disgust. Tirate had assured him there were no more than two hundred, an estimate easily off by over a thousand.

Just as disturbing was the sight of Boris and his dragon swooping over the courtyard to drop the letter demanding their surrender. He had personally witnessed Boris' dragon drop from the sky and fall into the rapids, then disappear into the Hole. Already rumors were spreading among the men that it was the ghost of the captain coming back to seek revenge. He was a bit more practical than that however. Obviously the man had somehow survived and it was his job to deal with it.

He watched as the cloud of dragons overhead suddenly shifted towards the western gates and the men around him scrambled to meet the inevitable attack. He frowned and grabbed at the men in vain as they rushed by. "Stop you fools! Can't you see it's a diversion? Use your heads! Gather some men and get to the east gate!"

Frustrated, he shook his head and stepped into the guardhouse where a stout man snapped to attention. With a casual salute, he eyed the leader of his elite soldiers. "Get your men together and assign them to places along the palace walls. Today they'll earn the extra gold we've been paying them."

***

El tested the weight of the sword in her hand and studied the blade doubtfully. The small polished blade had been designed for a child to carry during formal ceremonies and never intended for combat. Meader had carefully sharpened the blunted blade to a razor sharp edge.

"Use it only if you have to." He cautioned. "It's made of soft metal and won't fair well against a real sword, but it's better than nothing."

She nodded in agreement and cast another curious glance Meader's corroded armor. He noticed her stare and chuckled.

"This armor wasn't always rusty, and I wasn't always this old."

The old woman behind him cackled. "You ain't getting any younger either!"

Meader's leathery face split into a toothless grin. "Nope, but I still can show them guards a thing or two 'bout fightin! Now listen, I got a man watchin your dragon friends. Looks to me like they plan on drawing attention to the west side and Tirate's men are all runnin that way to fight. We might be able to take out a few by the east gate while they're busy over there. We gotta go now though, while they're confused!"

El followed as the group spilled out the door and quickly dispersed into the shadowed alleys. Fulgid loped protectively beside her, his ears swiveling warily in all directions. As they neared the gate she could hear the shouts of the guards and the frequent twang of crossbows. Cautiously, she peered around the corner of a building and felt her heart leap for joy. She had a clear view of the gates at the end of the street. They were open wide and Theo and his dragon were just flying over them. Ammon was standing in the entrance, plainly visible in his gleaming gold armor.

She was about to run out and greet them when the whistle of a bolt pierced the air over her head. Her knees weakened as she watched the thick black shaft sink deep into the back of Theo's dragon. The enormous creature dropped like a stone beyond the wall and out of sight.

The clicking sound of a crossbow crank echoed down the dark alley and El pressed herself tightly against the wall. A low growl at her feet drew her attention to the glowing white eyes of the golden dragon. With ears flat and fangs exposed, Fulgid stalked down the alley.

"Fulgid! No!"

The furious little dragon ignored her and disappeared down the alley. She hesitated for only a moment then gripped the handle of her sword tightly and followed after him.

The narrow alley turned sharply to the left and ended at a stairway that led up to a platform where two men hurried to reload a crossbow. Fulgid's claws cleaved deep gashes in the wood as he raced up the stairs with incredible speed. The guards didn't even have time to draw their swords before the dragon fell upon them. As razor sharp fangs sliced through their armor, El turned away.

It was over in moments and Fulgid walked back down the alley leaving little behind but the broken and splintered remains of the crossbow and two dark forms that lay motionless atop the debris. El felt her stomach reel as she followed Fulgid back to the street. She had always known about the fierceness of dragons, but to actually witness that fury was sobering.

Before they reached the end of the alley they heard the rhythmic thrum of boots striking the cobblestone. She reached down and scooped Fulgid up in her arms and slipped into a darkened doorway as an army of men marched past, heading towards the east gate.

***

Inside the city Ammon could smell the stench of burning crossbows and hear the sounds of sword against sword in the distance. The knights had taken their hatchlings and fanned out the moment they'd entered the gates, searching out and destroying the guard posts atop the walls. Already thin wisps of smoke began to rise into the morning sky as they ripped their way through Tirate's forces. He should have been with them, but he couldn't leave Theo behind. He looked back at the man kneeling beside his dragon Ebony and knew Theo would not leave until the beast had drawn its last breath.

The sound of voices shouting pulled his attention back into the city. At the end of the long street, a group of heavily-armed men were gathering. His stomach knotted, and with a sudden grim determination, he sheathed his sword and ran to the gate. He threw his shoulder against the massive doors and pushed them shut before sliding the bolt into place. That should slow them down at least. He ducked into the guard tower, climbed to the top of the stairs, and peered through the window.

The company of men filled the street as they approached the gate with swords drawn and shields up. Behind the front row, a handful of men carried small crossbows notched and ready. As they got closer, he could hear a gruff voice bellowing orders.

"Get that gate open and finish off that dragon! The rest of you see what can be salvaged from the crossbows and find that man with the shiny armor! Send someone back and inform Devan the east gate is secured! Now go!"

Ammon pressed his back against the wall and scanned his surroundings. The guard towers were the first places the hatchlings had entered, and now little remained but shattered bows and broken arrows that littered the floor. He drew his sword and forced himself to breathe evenly as the sound of heavy boots trudged up the stairs. He struck the moment the man came into view, his golden sword sliced easily through the metal shield and into the armored body behind it. He withdrew the blade and used his foot to push the wounded man back down the stairs and prepared for the next one.

***

Meader hissed to El from across the alley. "Is that fella in the tower someone ya know?"

She nodded, not daring to take her eyes from the scene unfolding before her. "That is Ammon, King of DoTaria…and my husband!"

Meader's eyes widened. "The king is your husband?"

She nodded again. "Yes. My husband."

He rubbed thoughtfully at the scruff on his chin. "Well I'll be a dragon's fang! Guess there is only one thing to do then!"

El reluctantly tore her eyes away for a moment to watch the old man signal to the others with his hands. "One thing?"

"Ah-yup." A sly smile split across his wrinkled face. "Just one thing. Fight."

***

The head guard grumbled angrily as his men dragged another body out of the guard tower. He didn't have time for this. He'd already sent word to Devan that the gate was secured, but he couldn't get any men into the towers to check the crossbows because of this one man. The problem was that the tower had been designed to be defended from within. The narrow stairway made it impossible for more than one man to enter at a time and a single, well-armed man could hold off a siege for a considerable amount of time.

He grabbed the nearest man by his shirt. "Grab some wood and smoke him out or burn him alive, I don't care how you do it, but get me control of that tower!" The man's knees suddenly buckled, and he released his grip just as he fell face first on the ground with an arrow jutting from his back. Another arrow whizzed past to strike a man standing beside him. With a shout, he dove into the shallow recess of the gate and screamed. "Return fire, you fools!"

He grabbed a small crossbow from one of the fallen men and shot at a figure half hidden behind a building. The figure disappeared from view and the bolt harmlessly struck the cobblestones and rattled down the street. From rooftops and darkened windows, a steady hail of arrows pummeled them, and they fired back with the lethal crossbows until the street was littered with arrows. He cursed every citizen in the city as he wiped the sweat from his brow and gazed up at the buildings. Was this a pause in the fighting, or had they realized they were too outnumbered to succeed? After all, he had over six hundred men here, did they honestly think they could fight and win?

"They've given up for now, so get that gate open and make sure that dragon is dead! Then get that man out of the tower!"

Still holding up their shields protectively, a handful of men warily moved to the gates.

***

Ammon watched from the narrow tower window as Tirate's men struggled with the gate. Whoever had launched that brief attack had done little damage to the large detachment of guards. He shifted his position until he could see the street below. If only he had some of those arrows and a bow, he could stop them from opening the gate and at least protect Theo until help arrived. He gripped his sword in frustration. There had to be a way, but how?

In the back of his mind the familiar golden voice bubbled up. "WE COME. WE FIGHT!"

He pressed his face close to the window and smiled as almost a hundred men and women appeared out of the shadows and charged into the street. Behind them he could see El hurrying to join them with Fulgid racing beside her and his smile faded. What is she trying to do? Get herself killed? He took a deep breath, threw open the door of the tower, and attacked the guards waiting there.

Despite the ferociousness of his attack, the guards held their position and his arms began to tire as they began to surround him in groups of two and three. Even with Fulgid's help, he could see El's ragtag army wasn't fairing any better. They were hopelessly outnumbered, and it was only a matter of time before they were overrun. It would be long over before any of the dragons or hatchlings could arrive to help.

He set his jaw in determination and felt his eyes beginning to burn. If nothing else, he would find a way to save El. With renewed effort, he battled his way towards her, recklessly slashing his golden blade through the guards like a scythe. He was almost there when he saw a large man grab El roughly from behind and knock her sword to the ground. In an instant Fulgid was there, but the man instinctively held El in front of himself for protection with a knife placed to her throat. Fulgid skidded to a stop just a pace width away, fangs exposed and smoke trickling from his nostrils, ready to pounce at the first opportunity.

For a long moment the world seemed to stop as the three of them faced each other in a stalemate. Ammon forced himself to speak calmly. "Let her go and I'll let you live."

The big man chuckled. "Oh, you'll let me live? You're a funny little white-eyed boy, aren't you? All the dragons, except that little demon of yours, are on the other side of the city, and Tirate will hold them off with his crossbows! This little gathering you brought is all but defeated! The way I see it, this girl is my ticket to get that little gold beast back to Tirate!"

Ammon's heart raced as he tried to think of a way to free El without her getting hurt. Suddenly there was a thunderous crash from behind that sent him tumbling to the ground as shards of wood and debris flew in every direction. He rolled to his feet and looked up in surprise at Theo's dragon Ebony standing in the entrance. The heavy gate lay shattered, and the guard towers felled like trees as the angry dragon charged through. Beneath her right wing, the half-buried shaft of a crossbow jutted out, and a trail of dark blood streamed down her side. Before the stunned guards could react, dragon fire swept across the cobblestones leaving nothing but charred bits of smoldering armor.

Distracted, El's captor loosened his grip momentarily, and she slipped the knife from her belt and stabbed at his shoulder. With a scream he threw her aside and grasped at the wound, only to realize his mistake a moment before a massive fireball from Fulgid enveloped him.

The few guard that were left began to scatter in every direction, leaving behind a trail of discarded armor and weapons. Ammon turned to pursue them, but a wiry old man wielding a rusted sword gripped his arm and shook his head. "Let 'em go, they won't get far. Throughout the city are small groups like ours. Ain't no place in the city for 'em to hide. Besides, looks to me like your friend needs help." He nodded towards Theo and Ammon felt his heart sink.

Theo stood stroking Ebony's head as she lay on her side, drawing ragged breaths. El pushed past them and fearlessly climbed up the foreleg to inspect the wound.

Ammon hurried closer and put a sympathetic hand on Theo's shoulder. "How is she?"

His voice was almost inaudible. "Bad. Real bad." He looked up at El and cleared his throat. "Can you pull it out?"

El's darkened gaze met Ammon's for a brief moment before she shook her head. "No, it's too deep. If we pull it out she'll bleed to death, but I think I can stop some of the bleeding." She jumped to the ground and motioned to one of the women nearby. "I need hot water, as hot as you can make it, and clean cloth. Lots of them! Hurry!"

Theo leaned forward and rested his head against Ebony's snout. "I didn't ask her to do what she did. She crashed through the gate on her own as if someone had told her what was happening in here."

El touched his face gently. "I'll do what I can for her." She turned to take an armful of sheets from one of the women and paused. "Ammon, I can't leave. I'm needed here, but Gaul still needs you. Please…be careful!" She stood on the tips of her toes and kissed him lightly on the lips, then hurried away clutching the sheets tightly.

The thin old man sniffed and shoved a gaunt hand into Ammon's. "My name's Meader. Ya know, that's quite a woman you got there. She said you're some kind of king that's come here ta help? Well we're mighty grateful already! We might not be much of an army, but we're willin' ta follow you right through the palace gate! You just lead the way!"

Ammon looked grimly at the few dozen elderly men and women scavenging through the guards discarded weapons. He felt a slight nudge behind his knee and looked down to see Fulgid waiting patiently. His hand automatically reached to scratch behind the dragon's ears as he mumbled to himself. "If we at least had the hatchlings, we'd have a fighting chance."

Once more the bubble in the back of his mind rippled as the voice chimed in his head. "FULGID CALL!"

Ammon watched the little dragon, expecting him to make some sort of sound, but Fulgid sat quietly with his eyes half closed.

Meader cleared his throat politely. "S'cuse me sire, but what are we waitin' for?"

Ammon nodded towards Fulgid. "He's calling for the dragons to meet us here."

Theo opened his eyes slightly and frowned without lifting his head from Ebony's snout. Minutes passed slowly, then the distant sounds of shouting reached their ears. One by one, the hatchlings appeared, racing down the streets with their knights running breathlessly behind them.

As each one arrived, Theo's eyes grew wider and wider. "Ammon...how? How did you do that?"

Ammon hesitated. Nobody ever believed him before when he said Fulgid could speak, what if they didn't believe him now? The middle of a battle was not the time to put doubt in the mind of anyone. "I didn't do it. They must have decided to come back on their own!" Guilt washed over him. He knew lying to Theo was wrong, but what else could he do? "Now that they're back, I have a plan!"

***

Ammon led the group through the alleys and side streets up to the palace. The thick wooden door to the kitchen hung at an odd angle by its broken hinges, and one by one they climbed the narrow stairs. The long hallway outside the kitchen was deserted and his army followed him down towards the guard towers he stopped and spoke softly as they gathered around him.

"Try not to attract any attention and let the hatchlings spread out along the walls to take out the crossbows one at a time. Once we've been seen and the alarm is sounded, we'll all attack. Fulgid and I will go to the left and take out the nearest guards and crossbow. The next hatchling goes down the right side of the wall. Any questions?"

The young knights exchanged nervous glances in a mixture of eagerness and dread. He knew they were worried about their hatchlings. The decision to put them into battle without any training wasn't easy, but he knew Tirate would be expecting an attack from the full-grown dragons flying overhead, not from within the palace walls.

He pushed the tower door open slightly and pressed his face to the crack. The doorway led to a parapet that encircled the palace. On either side of the walkway was a shoulder-high battlement designed to protect the guards from projectiles. About every ten paces along the parapet a dragon-killing crossbow was mounted on a swiveling base so the guards could easily aim at targets overhead or on the ground below. Anyone trying to enter through the courtyard would have been shot to pieces in moments.

Two guards manned each crossbow, and he watched as the nearest pair shot a long bolt at a dragon flying overhead. The huge shaft fell harmlessly to the ground far outside the palace walls. He chuckled softly to himself. Stalwart had precisely measured the firing distance of the captured weapons and knew exactly how close they could fly and still be out of range.

He watched as the two men reloaded and counted. While one worked a crank on the side of the device, the other dropped a latch over the taunt bowstring and loaded the next shaft. About ten seconds elapsed. He whispered the information to the knights behind him, then took a deep breath and looked down at Fulgid beside him. "Ready?"

The amber colored eyes were already starting to glow.

They slipped out the door the moment the nearest crossbow shot off another bolt. The next shaft was just being laid into position when the guard noticed Fulgid and Ammon just a few paces away. Fulgid shot past, leapt over the crossbow, and struck the man in the chest, knocking him to the ground. Just as the other guard looked up from the crank, Ammon stepped forward and butted him between the eyes with the pommel of his sword. He crumpled to the ground as a line of knights and hatchlings rushed by to take down the next crossbow in line. Fulgid stood atop the guard who lay face down on the stones.

Terrified, the man suddenly shrieked and Ammon groaned. The next crossbow was already disabled, but the men working the third one in line had already swung it around and were aiming it straight down the narrow walkway.

A loud twang echoed across the yard as both knights and dragons pushed themselves tight against the stone battlements. The shaft bounced wildly against the walls, and Ammon dove behind the crossbow as it whizzed past. He heard a loud grunt and looked up just as Fulgid careened down the walkway. The bolt had passed through the guard Fulgid had been holding and hit the little dragon square in the chest.

He crawled on his hands and knees towards Fulgid, who lay curled up in a tight ball. Through their link he could feel a horrible pain in his chest, and he pulled the little dragon close and held him tight. "Are you ok?"

Slowly, the little dragon uncoiled and stood with his wings spread. Ammon ran his hand down the scales of the undamaged chest and sighed in relief. Fulgid's eyes flashed searing white and bared his fangs. His claws flexed and curled, and bits of stone broke beneath his feet. Slowly Ammon's feeling of relief was replaced by the rage that oozed through the link and burned his eyes. He gripped his sword tightly as the blinding fury washed over him and he struggled to keep himself from being swept away by the anger.

With blinding speed, Fulgid jumped to the top of the battlement wall and leapt fearlessly out into the space above the courtyard. Ammon stared after him in disbelief as Fulgid flew the length of the wall and blasted fireballs at each crossbow as he passed. A number of men at the far side of the yard tried to aim their bolts at the golden dragon as he darted back and forth. Fulgid was so intent on what he was doing that he didn't notice the men preparing to shoot, and Ammon looked around in desperation.

He stepped behind the loaded crossbow beside him and swung it around to point at the men across the courtyard. He pushed the release and watched the black shaft streak across the yard to strike the guard in the chest. The man slumped forward and the crossbow fired harmlessly into the air.

Ammon watched as the knights and hatchlings moved rapidly to disable the machines. As more of the guards aimed towards them, it was obvious they'd never reach the far side without taking heavy casualties. A dark shadow suddenly passed overhead, and Ammon looked up to see a massive black dragon swoop down with Boris hanging from the saddle as the beast flew upside down. They passed over one of the crossbows, and a sharp snap sounded as his longsword sliced through the bowstring. The steel tipped bolt clattered harmlessly to the ground as Ellis turned upright and they began to gain altitude.

Ammon quickly estimated the time it would take for the big dragon to make his next pass. Fulgid and the rest were steadily knocking out the guards, but there was no way they'd reach the last one before it was loaded and ready. Boris had bought them precious time, but they needed just a bit more. A scream sounded across the yard as one of the young knights fell, a thick shaft protruding from his leg.

Ammon charged down the walkway and past the wounded knight. Already his young dragon was standing over him protectively. There was no time to treat the injury now. Just ahead was a single guard desperately working the crank on the side of a crossbow while his partner lay face down on the stones unmoving. Before the guard could place a bolt in position, Ammon slashed down on the taunt bow with his sword and the gold blade sliced through the thick wood easily. Like a giant whip, the bowstring whistled past the guard's head and he stumbled back cursing.

The man drew his sword and looked down at Ammon with an air of self-confidence. He easily towered over Ammon and the hilt of his sword glittered with jewels. He smiled as he positioned himself. "Well golden-boy, you've picked the wrong man to play swords with. Must be your unlucky day today!"

Ammon held up his sword and wordlessly eyed the larger man. Up until now he'd been fortunate that he hadn't fought with a skilled swordsman, but it was obvious this man knew how to use a blade. The only advantage Ammon had was the dragon scale armor, but that wouldn't protect him from a stab or strike to an exposed area. They began to circle, each waiting for the other to move. Suddenly, his opponent struck like lightning, the sword striking a stinging blow to Ammon's side. Although it failed to penetrate through the armor, it felt as if he'd been punched in the ribs. The man twirled his sword, grinned and feigned a lunge. Ammon moved as if to block and was struck in the ribs on the other side by another stinging blow.

The man sneered, showing perfectly white teeth. "Come now, this isn't much game! Never send a boy to do a man's job. Shall we get this over with?"

Ammon forced himself to breathe evenly and focus only on the man in front of him and ignoring everything else. As if parting a curtain, a feeling of calm came over him, and the teaching Boris had hammered into him suddenly became clear again. With a blur, the fancy sword slashed down at his head and Ammon blocked it. The force of the blow pushed his sword down and Ammon followed it through, using its momentum to strike. The guard barely managed to bring his sword up in time to block Ammon's blow and surprise lit up his eyes.

"Aye, so there is some training in you after all! Never let it be said that Captain Devan shies away from a good fight! Let's see what you've learned!"

A flurry of blows rained down on Ammon, each one blocked by his sword and carried through into a strike. The delight on the guards face slowly began to change to concentration as sweat broke out on his brow and his breathing became labored.

"Not bad, boy! Not bad at all, but I'm afraid I've run out of play time and have to end this." He suddenly leapt forward and brought his sword straight down with all his strength. Ammon leapt aside and brought the hilt of his sword up to strike the man hard on the chin. He spun around and spat out a tooth angrily. "You'll pay dearly for that boy!"

The bejeweled sword whirled in his hand as he stepped forward quickly, driving Ammon back, step by step until his back hit the wall. Unable to move, Ammon blocked each blow. With the wall behind him, he couldn't swing his sword to strike back, and the larger man pounded furiously down on him. Suddenly Ammon lost his grip on the sword and it slipped from his hands and clattered to the stones several paces away.

The guard smiled and hissed through the gap in his teeth. "Never send a boy…"

He never finished his sentence. A dark shadow passed overhead and a large black claw ripped him from the parapet. Shocked, Ammon watched as the dragon holding the screaming man in his talons pumped the air with its wings and it climbed higher into the sky.

He picked up his sword and wiped the sweat off his face with the back of his shaking hand. A few seconds longer and he'd have been dead. He peered up at the dragon overhead. That knight and dragon saved his life and he owed him a debt.

The twang of a crossbow echoed across the yard, and a thick black shaft sailed overhead. Ammon felt sick to his stomach as he watched the bolt strike its target. With a nightmarish scream, the dragon howled and dropped the man it carried in its claw. He fell to the ground with a sickening thud, but Ammon couldn't take his eyes away from the scene above. The dragon squirmed and twisted in mid-air, then plummeted to the ground. With a loud crash, it landed in a heap in the center of the courtyard, its shrieks deafening as it thrashed about.

Ammon raced down the walkway towards the stairs while Fulgid flew up to the windows of the royal chambers overlooking the courtyard. A blast of fire suddenly lit up the dark window and a trail of black smoke began pouring out, billowing up towards the sky. Ammon frowned as he rushed down the stairs. There must have been another of the crossbows hidden inside. Whoever shot it would have had an easy target of anyone or anything in the courtyard. Curse Tirate, curse him to his grave!

One of the DoTarian knights met Ammon at the bottom of the stairs. "Sire, all the crossbows along the walls have been eliminated, we didn't know about the one in the window, I'm sorry!"

Ammon waved him aside with his hand. "Not your fault, nobody knew. Who is the wounded rider? Do you know?"

The knight's voice shook as he ran beside Ammon towards the dragon lying in the courtyard. "I believe his name is Cen, one of the Gaul knights. From where I was, I couldn't see how badly they were injured."

Ammon nodded as he ran. Angrily he gripped the hilt of his sword. If he hadn't lost his grip on his sword, Cen wouldn't have dived in to help, and this wouldn't have happened. This was his fault, nobody else's.

The black dragon lay still, his head twisted around to watch the man drooping in the saddle on his back. Ammon stopped in front of the man who sat gripping the saddle with one hand, and the long black shaft protruding from his belly with the other. The thin man's face was ghostly pale and his breathing was rapid and shallow.

He placed a hand on Cen's shoulder. "Let me get you down, and we can get you some help."

Weakly, the knight shook his head. "No, sire. I'm afraid there is no help for me." His voice was faint as he whispered. "Have we retaken the palace, sire?"

Ammon looked around at the burning crossbows and the prisoners being lined up in a corner of the courtyard. "Yes, Cen. The battle is over. Queen El is safe, the city and the palace is ours. We've won, and we all owe you...I owe you a debt of gratitude."

A tiny smile broke across the blue lips. "You owe me nothing, sire. A knight has...a duty...to his...king. It...has...been an...honor. I have only...one...request."

Ammon tried to swallow the growing lump in his throat. "Of course! Anything!"

Cen's shaking hand reached up and pulled the cross from around his neck and held it out to Ammon. "Take...this. Wear it...and...remember...who and what it stands for...Ask Captain Boris...It could be...the most important thing...you ever..do..."

Ammon took the cross from his hand, and as gentle as an evening breeze, Knight Cen slowly leaned forward and his breathing ceased.

Ammon felt the flutter of Fulgid's wings as he landed on his shoulder, and he wiped the moisture from the corner of his eyes. He turned to face the head of the great black dragon and placed his hand on its quivering nose. The large black eyes stared back, lost and alone. He stroked the nose gently and struggled for words, but nothing seemed to come.

The great beast stood up, its hollow eyes flickered from the still figure in the saddle to Ammon. He stood back and cleared his throat. "It's ok. I understand. We all do. Go in peace!"

The black dragon leaned back and leapt into the sky. It circled higher and higher, and then flew north towards the ice-covered mountains. Fulgid left Ammon's shoulder and followed behind him briefly as if saying his own good-bye, then returned to circle overhead. His golden scales shone brilliantly in the sunlight.

When Ammon turned around, Boris was standing beside him. They looked at each other for a long moment before Boris placed a thick hand on Ammon's shoulder. "It's part of war. Every knight knows it when they head into battle. Cen was a good man, he'll be missed."

Ammon could only nod sadly.

***

Stalwart was processing the prisoners as they were brought to the courtyard. He bowed as Ammon approached. "Sire, it appears you have succeeded in retaking Gaul. I think you truly have fulfilled the prophecy of reuniting!"

He looked at Stalwart earnestly. "Do you really believe in that?"

The DoTarian knight chuckled. "Well, to be honest...no. At least not until you started fulfilling it!"

Ammon rubbed his eyes wearily. Well if this prophecy was real, at least it was done now. "Someone needs to go to the east gate. Theo's dragon Ebony got hurt pretty bad. El is down there with them now.

Boris nodded. "I already know about it. Tashira has already headed down there with a couple dragons and a sling to bring them back here to the Hold. I think between El and Tashira, they'll heal her up good." He shaded his eyes and gazed up in the sky. "Don't you think you ought call down that little acrobat before he completely terrorizes the city?"

Ammon shook his head and watched Fulgid streak through the sky. "I doubt there are many left that don't already know about him, and as for the rest, well they should get used to seeing him. Besides, he just learned to fly and I think he's enjoying it. After today he deserves it."

Boris chuckled. "Well, I won't disagree with that."

Ammon sighed and fingered the cross in his hand. "Boris, I have some questions to ask you once everything is settled. But at the moment, I think it's time to speak with the man who started all this. Where is he?"

Boris pointed to a large group of men standing dejectedly in the courtyard. "There are at least a couple thousand men there, it'll take awhile to find him."

Chapter 18
He Who Runs Away

Tirate ground his teeth as he hurried down the hallway. Things were not going at all the way he had planned. The mercenaries and ruffians he'd hired as guards were abandoning their posts in droves. The sight of a thousand dragons flying overhead had unnerved them all. When the dragons started throwing fireballs from their mouths, even the toughest decided he didn't pay enough to stick around for the battle. Where those dragons had come was puzzling enough but the fire breathing had him completely baffled. How had they gotten past his defenses so easily? The carefully laid plans that he had started so many years ago now lay in ruins. Crumbled before his very eyes.

He entered the deserted royal chambers and threw open the doors of the large wardrobe. Hidden in the back lay a large sack filled with gold, clothing and a few other necessities in the event he needed to leave in a hurry. He buckled a sword around his waist and draped himself in a dull gray hooded cloak. Someone was going to pay for this, he didn't yet know who, but someone would.

He slipped down the empty hallway and rounded the corner by the kitchen just in time to see a line of hatchlings and knights follow the boy tender and that horrid gold dragon exit onto the parapet. He quickly ducked out of sight and pressed his back tight against the wall and listened. He could hear the boy giving orders and the other knights addressing him as…King Ammon? The boy tender? So, Erik had truly believed him to be the last descendant from the house of Les and passed the throne to him, sidestepping Tirate's lawful claim! He strained to listen and rolled his eyes in disgust. His hand twitched as he yearned to draw his sword, but he knew what that golden dragon was capable of and wasn't going to submit himself to that again. This time he'd plan it out carefully.

He backtracked down the stairs and opened the prison hall door and slipped inside. Once they passed, he'd slip out the servant's door and make his way out of the palace.

A woman's voice screeched from one of the cells loudly. "I hear you! Who's out there! Help me! I ORDER you to help me!"

Tirate's head snapped around. If he didn't silence her everyone in the hallway would come running! He drew his sword, picked the keys up from the guards desk and hurried to the only cell door that was closed. He quickly unlocked the door, drew back his sword…and stopped. Liah stood just inside, blood trickling from her broken nose.

He would have killed her instantly, but his curiosity of how she came to be in the prison with a broken nose was too much to resist. "Quiet!" he hissed. "What happened to you?"

Liah held her head high and tried to sniff regally, but it only made her wince. "That horrid, horrid woman broke my nose! I should have killed her the moment the guards brought her here from the tunnel!"

Tirate's suddenly felt his temple begin to throb. "What woman?"

Oblivious to Tirate's glare, Liah continued. "Oh you were too busy to talk to me about it. She told me she was Ammon's wife, and a queen! Imagine that, HA! Even wore that ridiculous gold ring with the dragon on it that Ammon had. She said she and Ammon ruled over some place called DoTaria, with a thousand dragons that breathe fire, or some such nonsense. Even I know dragons can't do that, so I figured she must have been crazy. She even said Gaul is just a tiny colony of that DoTarian kingdom."

Tirate's ears began to ring wildly and he could no longer hear the woman rambling. This so called queen was sitting in a cell directly under his feet and he didn't know? The key to holding off any attack or invasion and she didn't bother to tell him? "Where is she now?" He growled.

Liah suddenly seemed aware of the sword hovering near her throat. Swallowing hard, she motioned out the door. "That awful gold colored dragon came in while I was…questioning…her, and he knocked me down, then she broke my nose! All the guards were gone and I've been locked in here ever since! Why is your face so red?"

Tirate slowly raised his sword again. This woman had already proved more trouble than she was ever worth. Liah began to squeal loudly.

He lowered the sword quickly. "Be quiet I say!" If they heard her in the hallway, it would draw the unwanted attention of that dragon, and no matter how skilled with a sword, he didn't think he could kill the miserable woman before she screamed.

Liah began to sob. "I'll scream! Everyone in the city will hear me scream I swear! Just let me go and you won't have to worry!"

Tirate sheathed his sword. Of all the women in the world he could have married, this was certainly not his best choice. "Alright. Come with me, quickly. Don't make a sound…or else."

Stifling a sob, Liah nodded and followed him out of the prison and down through the servants quarters. At the end of the hallway he opened the door slightly and could see the yard was filled with small dragons fighting with the last of the guard that stayed behind. That miserable golden dragon was flying around, slowly ripping his forces apart. Escape through the courtyard was impossible, and it was just a matter of time before the rest of the guard were killed or surrendered.

He rubbed the scar on his chin and grinned. Perhaps he could at least inflict a little damage. He spun on his heel and climbed the stairs to the royal chambers. Mounted just inside the window was one of the large crossbows. From here, he could shoot almost anything in or above the courtyard. When he found his intended target he scowled. He could just barely see Ammon over the top of the parapet. If the boy had been a foot taller he could get a clear shot.

A moment later his scowl turned to a smile. The boy was fighting for his life against the best swordsman in his army. He leaned forward to watch the fight unfold although the walls obscured most of it. When Ammon was pinned against the wall and Devan raised his sword for the killing blow, he felt every muscle in his body tighten with exhilaration. It quickly turned to disbelief when a large black dragon swooped down from the sky and plucked Devan up in its claws. That accursed boy had wormed his way out of death again!

He snarled and once more aimed the crossbow at the boy, but still couldn't get a good shot and he was running out of time. His eyes followed the dragon as it started climbing into the air. At least he could kill one more of the beasts before making his escape! He swung the bow around, aimed and fired. The shaft streaked through the air and found its mark with deadly accuracy.

He almost shouted in elation but Liah's whining voice distracted him. "You idiot! They saw you! They'll be up here before we can get to the streets!"

Already several knights were pointing towards his window. He scooped up his bag and ran from the chambers with Liah whimpering behind him. When he reached the lower hallway, he stopped in front of one door and thought for a moment. Grimly, he opened it up and reeled back from the stench. This door led to a small stream that ran beneath the city used to carry away all the waste and refuse. It had to flow somewhere outside the city walls. He grabbed a torch from the wall, shoved Liah down the stairs and closed the door behind them.

Liah stopped at the bottom of the stairs and stared in horror at the muck rising past the ankles of her silk slippers.

"You can't possibly expect me to wallow through this like a common pig?"

He shoved her aside waded into the knee deep water without saying a word. As Liah tried to follow her feet stuck in the muck and she fell face first into the dark, foul smelling mud.

She shrieked and spat dirt out of her mouth. "Wait! Tirate, you can't leave me here!" She desperately scrambled to her feet and hurried after him while trying to wipe the black sludge off her velvet and silk clothes.

An hour later the two crawled out of a small hole on their bellies and into the sunshine. The underground sewer emptied out into a swamp not far from the bridge. Tirate looked at the broken hilt of his sword and tossed it into the mud. He had used it to pry back the rusted iron bars that covered the exit into the swamp. Wordlessly he trudged up towards the bridge.

Liah followed closely behind, a steady stream of complaints spilling from her lips. "I think I lost a slipper, but I can't tell through the layers of…whatever this is! Oh, I think I'm going to be sick…Tirate! Help me!"

He ignored her as they crossed the bridge and walked quickly down the road towards the south.

***

It was well past sunset when four darkly tanned and shirtless men with odd tattoos on their faces stepped out of the woods in front of them. Tirate threw his hand in front of his chest, palm up and fingers spread wide. "Bring me to Grody. Tell him his friend Tirate has come to see him."

The men eyed each other wordlessly and one of them pointed into the woods with the tip of his spear. Tirate walked into the woods and jerked his thumb at Liah. "Tell Grody I've brought him a gift."

The tattooed man smiled, revealing blackened and missing teeth. He grabbed Liah's arm and pushed her deeper into the woods.

Liah tried to wrest her arm away and screamed. "No! You can't do this to me! I'm a queen! You can't do this to ME!"

***

It was late summer in DoTaria and the night of the new moon. Ammon sat at a table in the corner with Derek and looked down into the Nest. Unlike the Hatches in Gaul, DoTaria actually invited guests to attend. He stared into the bottom of his empty mug and frowned. Only nine months had passed since they had passed over the mountains and fought to retake Gaul. Nine months of exhaustive searches and still Tirate was no where to be found. Erik now ruled over the city just as he had before, only with a new title of Governor under King Ammon. The people of Gaul had been reluctant to accept a new King, and keeping Erik in power made the transition easier.

He pushed the empty cup away along with his thoughts. Tonight was for celebrating, and he intended to enjoy it thoroughly. Boris eased himself into a chair at the table, and Derek offered one of his monstrous sized cups of the strong black liquid and Boris accepted it gratefully.

Ammon waited until after he'd taken a long sip. "Boris, where are Stalwart and Theo tonight? I wouldn't have thought they'd miss a Hatch this big. After all, this will be the first full Hatch DoTaria has had in decades!"

Boris blew at the steam wafting out of his mug and nodded. "Aye, they would have liked to attend but with the Kala-Azar so active lately, both here and in Gaul, we decided it would be best to have patrols out watching for the little beasties. Besides, I doubt Theo would ever leave Ebony alone when the slugs are active."

Disappointed, Ammon sighed. He certainly understood why Theo would stay with his dragon. Although El and Tashira had done everything they could to heal Ebony's injuries, she would never fly again and that left her vulnerable to the Kala-Azar. As if that wasn't bad enough, somehow the slugs had found a way into Gaul and seemed to be increasing in numbers.

He looked across the room at the Nest filled with eggs and smiled. "Derek, you've done a wonderful job here as both keeper and tender. Are you sure you wouldn't reconsider overseeing the Nest in Gaul as well?"

The big man shook his head, waving his white beard back and forth. "No. I don't want to leave Lily here without me. She can't go with me because she has to have schooling."

The little girl lay stretched out on a chair beside him, half-asleep. She smiled up at him and mumbled, "I wanna be with you poppa!"

His big hand ruffled her hair. "You oughta be asleep, it's late."

She yawned and rubbed her eyes. "But I wanna see the baby dragons!"

Ammon shook his head and laughed. The girl had Derek wrapped around her little finger.

The door opened and El entered the Nest. With a smile she waddled to a seat beside Ammon and eased herself down gingerly. Concerned, he placed his arm around her. "El, shouldn't you be in bed? The birthwife will have a fit if she finds out you're up here!"

El smiled and patted her swollen belly. "Ha! Who could sleep in this heat? I seriously doubt I'd get any sleep anyway, at least not until after the baby is born."

Boris chuckled and ran a thick finger across his gray moustache. "So have you decided on a name yet? I think Boris would be a fine name for a boy!" After a stern look from El he continued by clearing his throat. "Or perhaps Mabel if it's a girl, of course."

Derek raised an eyebrow for a moment and slowly asked. "What if you have both a boy and a girl?"

Boris roared with laughter, and El playfully slapped his shoulder. "If it's both, then Ammon can name them. He'll have plenty of time to think on it because he'll be taking care of them all night while I sleep."

Before Ammon could object, the door opened again and Fulgid sauntered in. The lanterns reflected off his scales, sending glittering spots dancing around the room. He hopped up on the table and sniffed at the empty mugs.

Derek grinned and reached over to scratch behind the dragon's ears. "Hi Fulgid! You come to see the Hatch too?"

Ammon yawned and stretched. "It should be any moment now, those knights better be ready!"

Fulgid moved to the side of the Nest and lay down against the wall, and Ammon and El followed to get a better view.

Derek and Boris brought chairs over for them all to sit on while they watched the largest hatch ever recorded. Twenty-five swollen eggs lay in the Nest, and against the wall on the other side stood twenty-eight hopeful Knights, all waiting impatiently for the Hatch to begin.

Finally, the ripping sound of tearing eggshells filled the Nest, and all attention focused on the depression in the middle of the room. One by one, tiny black and gray dragons clamored out of the Nest towards their chosen link. Time passed slowly, and as the last minutes of the hour closed, three of the eggs remained.

Derek stood at the edge of the Nest looking down sadly at them. Lily stood holding his hand, her face wet with tears. Ammon, Boris, and El left their seats and gathered around Derek.

Ammon stretched to pat him on the shoulder. "Derek, you did very well, you really did. Twenty-two eggs out of twenty-five is far above average! You should be very proud! We knew that large egg probably wouldn't hatch anyway, so don't be sad, this is a happy day!"

The big man wiped his cheek with a massive hand and sniffed. "I know, but I wanted them all to hatch."

El squeezed Ammon's hand, a tear forming in her own eye. "Maybe next time Derek. Next time there won't be so many eggs in one place, and maybe they'll all have a better chance."

The long beard wagged up and down as he nodded, and with a big sigh, he let go of Lily's hand and stepped down into the Nest to remove the shells. Moments later Ammon recognized the tearing sound of a shell opening and turned quickly to see. A ragged gap formed along the top of one of the eggs and within seconds, a fat black dragon scurried up the Nest wall to stand in front of Lily, staring into her big wondering eyes.

Ammon felt his jaw drop and he forced himself to blink. The girl had just linked! Before he could say anything, another very loud ripping sound echoed across the Nest. Derek was standing beside the large egg and watching in amazement as its sides began to split in every direction. As the shell peeled back, two dragons emerged one black and one gray. They clambered out the heap of eggshell and climbed up Derek's legs to perch on each of his shoulders, both competing to look him in the eye.

Boris let out a low whistle. "Twins? This is unheard of…and both just linked to him at the same time! It shouldn't be possible for more than one dragon to link to a single person! Theo will be sorry he missed this!"

Ammon gasped in amazement. Two dragons linked to one man and another linked to a girl barely five years old! He turned to El and shook his head. "El, can you imagine being linked to two at once! He'll have his hands f…. oh!…OH!"

El stood, eyes wide, looking down over her swollen belly at the glittering silver dragon sitting at her feet. "Boris? BORIS?"

Boris turned, reluctant to take his eyes off the two dragons on Derek's shoulder. "Yes? Oh! By my dragon's teeth!"

Ammon hadn't heard the tearing of the shell of the third and final egg over the noise the twins had made. Nor had he seen it climb out and stand in front of El, its chosen link. He looked at the dragon closely. It was definitely not gray. It was as shiny as polished silver and reflected the lights like a mirror.

Boris patted him on the back. "Well, it appears you are no longer the only one with a dragon of a different color!"

Dazed, El looked up at Ammon and put a hand on her head. She spoke softly. "She's hungry…and said our daughter will be born in two weeks!"

Ammon's knees felt weak as he turned to face Fulgid lying casually nearby. He could almost see the dragon smiling as the clear, golden sound of laughter echoed from the bubble in the back of his head.

END

A note from the author.

Thank you for reading Hatch! I am working on the next book in the series The Dragons of Laton, so please watch for it in the future! Until then, I hope you enjoyed this book and that you will leave a rating on Amazon/Kindle.

Sincerely
James Stevens

Made in the USA
Middletown, DE
29 November 2019